Maria Louise Pool

Mrs. Gerald

A novel

Maria Louise Pool

Mrs. Gerald
A novel

ISBN/EAN: 9783337000202

Printed in Europe, USA, Canada, Australia, Japan

Cover: Foto ©Andreas Hilbeck / pixelio.de

More available books at **www.hansebooks.com**

[See page 73.]

"JUDITH HEARD THE WORDS THROUGH THE OPEN WINDOW"

MRS. GERALD

A Novel

BY

MARIA LOUISE POOL

ILLUSTRATED

BY W. A. ROGERS

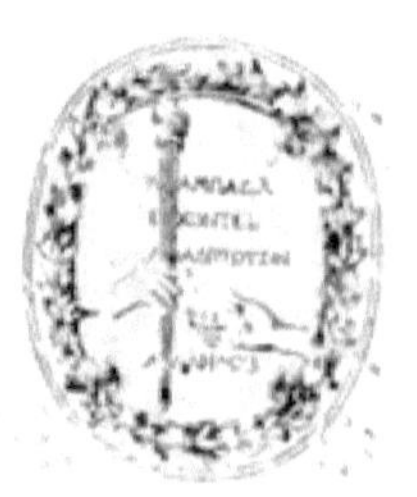

NEW YORK
HARPER & BROTHERS PUBLISHERS
1896

CONTENTS

ILLUSTRATIONS

Part I

MRS. GERALD

I

A BOTTLE OF BEANS

"I GUESS they're feelin' real poor in these days. I must say I'm sorry for the women folks there. I heard down to the store they were goin' to put up their seraphine."

"You don't mean Judith's seraphine?" asked Mrs. Macomber, looking up anxiously at her husband, who was standing by the cook-stove.

Mr. Macomber was slowly filling his pipe from some tobacco held in the palm of his hand. Occasionally he put his little finger into the bowl and pressed the loose stuff down more closely. He wore a green baize jacket which barely covered his hips, and which was buttoned up to the checked blue-and-white handkerchief tied firmly about his neck. This handkerchief was partly concealed by a white beard allowed to grow only below his chin.

You could not please Ellis Macomber in any way so much as to say to him, when you first met him, "Somehow, Mr. Macomber, you seem as if you'd been a seafaring man."

Then the rough old face would light up, and the man would reply, "You're right there, sir. Twenty-five years, lackin' three days, I passed on the briny. I was first mate of the best three-master that ever stepped over blue water. Then I broke my arm, 'n' I had phthisic, 'n' I ain't be'n nothin' since."

Mr. Macomber was so very long before answering now that his wife said again, "You don't mean Judith's seraphine?"

"Of course I do mean hern. You don't expect they've got two of um over to Grover's, do ye?" was the reply.

"You needn't snap me up so, 's I know of," said the woman. "But that was Judith's grandmother's seraphine, and they never did seem to mind how it squeaked 'n' wheezed 'n' carried on when they played it. They used to pour in oil somewhere, but it would squeak jest the same."

"Wall, they're goin' to put it up."

Mr. Macomber now reached over and took a match from the shelf above the stove. He drew it across his trouser-leg and sucked hard at his pipe.

"I d' know 's I know what you mean by puttin' it up," now remarked Mrs. Macomber.

Her husband looked at her pityingly. He always maintained that he didn't think women was called upon to know very much, not so long as men was round to tell um." For the last ten years he had been constantly round to instruct his wife on every possible occasion; but still there were many times when even he would have been gratified if Lucindy had manifested a somewhat stronger intelligence. Mr. Macomber eyed the smoke rising from his pipe before he replied.

"It means they're goin' to have kind of a raffle for that seraphine," he said; "anyway, that's what I call it. Folks may call it what they please, but I call it kind of a raffle."

"What! Like a Thanksgiving turkey? 'N' the Grovers are church-members!"

"Lucindy, can't you wait a minute? I ain't said nothin' 'bout a Thanksgiving turkey."

Lucindy waited. She took off her spectacles and patiently rubbed the glasses with an old silk handkerchief. She was saying to herself that she "s'posed Ellis 'd be jest so tryin' the longest day he lived." She looked at him as he stood there smoking on the other side of the cook-stove. His entire employment was strolling about the village, sitting on the wharf, or in the store, and hearing every bit of gossip there was. He never let any news escape him, and nothing was too trivial. He followed up a scent as a fox-hound follows a fox—not as rapidly, but as persistently. Then he went home and told Lucindy. And he usually ended his tale by remarking that it "would be jest like her, bein' a woman, to go 'n' spread that story all over the neighborhood."

"Yes," now began Mr. Macomber, after he had made his wife wait a sufficiently long time, "I call it a sort of raffle. They're goin' to fill a bottle full of beans, 'n' then anybody that wants to guess how many beans there is pays twenty-five cents a guess, 'n' the one that gits the nearest has the seraphine."

"I declare!" Mrs. Macomber pulled off her spectacles again and hurriedly renewed the wiping of them. "How long's the bottle of beans goin' round?" she asked.

"Jest long 's anybody wants to guess," was the answer.

"I s'pose everybody 'll take a chance, won't they?"

"I expect so. I met Mr. Eldridge comin' up from the wharf. He said he was goin' to guess ten times, 'n' if he got the old machine he sh'd fling it off Gun Rock."

"But his girls is real musical," said Mrs. Macomber, shocked at such vandalism. To her the Grover seraphine was a fine instrument in spite of its wheezing. She wished she might be so lucky as to get it. She had decided in her own mind to have one guess out of her own savings, and she hoped Ellis would take another. That would give them two chances.

"The Eldridge girls have got a pianner," said Mr. Macomber. "But I guess Mr. Eldridge pities the Grovers. He said he'd do a good deal to help the Grover girl, but he s'posed everything 'd go right into Hanford's pocket. He said he never knew such a darn convenient liver complaint as Hanford Grover had. He said he'd be one of ten to ride Grover out of town on a rail any time. He didn't say darn ; he said damn." Mr. Macomber set his teeth hard on his pipe and chuckled. He was now in the full tide of narration, and his wife leaned back to listen. "Curious how everybody feels 'bout them Grovers, ain't it? I stopped into Mis' Guild's, 'n' I arst her if she'd heard 'bout the seraphine's bein' put up, 'n' she hadn't heard a word. She said she couldn't really afford to take a single guess, but she should make out to take two, anyway, not that she wanted to do anything for Hanford, but she did pity his women folks. Near 's I can find out, everybody thinks that way, 'n' I'll bet there'll be lots of quarters paid out for guesses. I should like to have the seraphine myself. 'Twould be kind of pleasant winter evenin's to see it settin' there between the winders."

"So 't would," said Mrs. Macomber. She looked at the place her husband had mentioned. This space was now occupied by a table with a red cloth on it. "I always did wish we could afford a piece of music," she said. "I know we can't either of us play, but it would be a satisfaction to know there was a piece of music in the house."

"That's a fact. I kinder hanker after that seraphine. I d' know but I sh'll make a raise 'n' take two chances. If you have one, Lucindy, we shall have three between us. 'N' you know it's helpin' a neighbor. It makes us feel kind of different 'bout spendin' the money, seein' it's helpin' a neighbor."

"So it does. 'N' then there's somethin' excitin' 'bout guessin' in that way," said Mrs. Macomber, with some eagerness, "'n' not knowin' whether you're goin' to git anything or not." She fixed her eyes on the table that stood where the seraphine would stand if they got it. "Yes," she said, "'twould look real well there ; 'n' I always did wish I could have a piece of music in the house." She rose and moved the table away, then gazed at the empty space. There was a slight flush on her wrinkled face as she turned to her husband and asked, "Do you really think, Ellis, that there's any likelihood of our gittin' it?"

"Jest as much as there is of anybody's havin' it. I shall bring the bottle over here, 'n' we can look at it's long 's we want to 'fore we give our guesses."

"I shouldn't care much if 'twas so wheezy," responded Mrs. Macomber, evidently referring to the seraphine and not to the bottle. "'Twouldn't make much difference to us, Ellis, you know, as we ain't neither of us musical."

The next day Mrs. Macomber moved the table two or three times from its position, and contemplated the space thus left between the windows. Her husband had started forth on his daily rounds. He would not be likely to be back much before noon. He had not known any particulars as to when the bottle would be ready for guesses, but he hoped to find out that day.

It was half after eleven, and Mrs. Macomber had put the potatoes on to boil. She was looking over the money she had taken for eggs within the last month, and wishing she could justify herself in having two guesses, when she heard some one coming up the walk from the road. She knew it was not her husband's step. The door was open, and the June sunshine poured across the kitchen floor.

"I don't s'pose there's no need of knockin' now no more'n there ever was," said a fat, jovial voice, "so I guess I'll walk right in with my bottle." A thick-set woman climbed heavily up the step and sat down in the nearest chair. She coughed, and then laughed. "I tell um," she said, "that I need a bottle of beans passed round for me 'bout 's much 's anybody. Only I ain't Hanford Grover, 'n' I ain't got the liver complaint." Here she laughed again. "I declare," she went on, "if Hanford ain't got the most accommydation' kind of a complaint that ever I heard of. He can sleep well with it, 'n' eat hearty, 'n' be reg'lar to meetin' 'n' all the neck-tie parties, 'n' strawberry festivals, 'n' everything else where there's a chance of a meal. D'you ever see him eat cake to one of our sociables?"

"Yes, I've seen him."

"Then you know 'thout no description from me. You

see, he's got a kind of a liver that lets him do everything but work. And it comes mighty hard on his women folks. Of course, Ellis has told you 'bout these beans. Here they be." The speaker reached forward and set down a quart bottle filled with black beans on the table. " You c'n give as many guesses as you c'n spare quarters. I've guessed three times, 'n' I couldn't afford it no more'n I c'n fly. But I'm willin' to help Hanford Grover's women folks all I'm able."

Mrs. Macomber took the bottle in her hand and looked at it. She had expected to see white beans, and she told her companion that somehow white beans would have seemed more "sootable."

" It don't make no difference, as I can see," was the response.

" Mebby it don't. Must I guess right away?"

"Oh no ; keep the bottle till towards night ; then p'raps you c'n bring it back to me. I told um I'd try to git it round in this neighborhood. You c'n set down your guesses there," she put a sheet of foolscap beside the bottle, " and you can bring me the money when you fetch the bottle. It's gittin' to be real summer weather, ain't it ? Most hayin' time, too. I always dread to have the grass cut, 'cause then summer seems most gone. There ain't no summer to speak of after the grass is cut."

Mrs. Macomber had put down the bottle of beans, and now she took it up again.

" It seems almost kinder like gamblin', don't it ?" she asked, with a hint of fearsome delight in her somewhat flat face. " But, then, it's to help a neighbor, 'n' I shall spare all the money I can. I've decided to take two guesses, 'n' Ellis he'll take two, though it's more'n we really ought to do. Then, you see, if we don't git the seraphine, after all, why we don't git nothin'."

" But it's for a neighbor," said Mrs. Guild, repeating her companion's words, " so we needn't begretch our money."

" I s'pose somebody 'll git it that don't care nothin' for

it," now remarked Mrs. Macomber. "I was tellin' of Ellis that 'twould set first-rate between them two winders."

Mrs. Guild glanced at the place mentioned, but she did not seem much interested in this phase of the subject. She leaned back in her rocker instead of going. The rocker was comfortable, and the sun was hot.

"I can't help thinking about Judith, 'n' wondering what she'll say 'bout this bean business." She shook the bottle reflectively as she spoke.

"Judith!" exclaimed Mrs. Macomber; "why, I thought she was the one that started the whole thing."

"No she ain't, either. She don't know a word about it. She ain't been to home for two weeks. 'Twas Mis' Grover that got it up. She mentioned to Mis' East that she wished she could raise money on something. Grover he ain't worked a stroke for more'n six months, 'n' they owe everybody, 'cause Judith couldn't keep on at the factory on account of their shuttin' down, you know."

"But where is Judith?"

"She's up to the North Village. She's doin' the house-work for her cousin Joyce, the Joyce children being all down with the measles."

"I want to know! I thought she was to home."

"No. 'N' I'm thinkin' that if we want to take chances in that seraphine, 'n' help um along, the sooner we do it the better. When it's done it'll be done, and there's no tellin' how Judith 'll look at it."

"Judith's a real good girl."

"I know she is. But there's no tellin' how she'll look at it."

Here Mrs. Guild rose from her chair. She said she dreaded going out into the hot sun, but she s'posed she might 's well start. She came back to the door to say that she guessed Mr. Macomber 'd like to take that bottle round, and he was welcome to do it if the heat kept on.

When that gentleman came home to dinner a few minutes later the first thing his wife said was, "What do you

think, Ellis? Judith don't know 'bout this bottle of
beans."

But in spite of his wife's assurance to the contrary, Mr.
Macomber professed to believe that Judith did know. He
said "'twa'n't reasonable to think they'd do such a thing 'n'
she not know it."

As the days passed on the bottle circulated in the
vicinity. People volunteered to carry it in this direction
and that, and the list of guesses on the foolscap grew
longer and longer, and the quarter-dollars accumulated.

II

THE DAUGHTER

Mrs. Guild held the funds. Mr. Hanford Grover called on her with a view towards getting an advance. But he did not succeed. Mrs. Guild had been sitting at her back door shelling early pease. She heard a shuffling footstep coming along the road, and she saw a tall figure slowly turning in at the gate. This figure wore a long linen duster, brown linen pantaloons apparently just washed and ironed, and a tall, black silk hat with a very narrow rim. If there is anything that can make a man look desolate it is a silk hat which has been out of style for several years.

Mr Grover carried a cane, and when he did not forget to do so he leaned on this cane as if he needed its support. He had a thin face, shaven—all save a small tuft below his underlip, a tuft which on a gayer face might be called an "imperial." He had a heavy mouth so filled with glistening artificial teeth that it was with difficulty he could bring his lips together over them. His pale, greedy-looking eyes wandered over the snug, green-blinded house, at the door of which Mrs. Guild sat. He came up and placed himself on the door-step. He took off his hat and wiped his bald head.

"I was thinkin' as I come along," he said, "how mighty lucky you 'n' your husband 'd always been, Mis' Guild—no sickness; no money goin' out for medicine. If I'd had my health I could have had jest as good a place as this. 'N' here I be—nothin' laid up; 'n' house moggidged; 'n' I need some kind of sarsap'rilla this minute. I ain't been able to git much sarsap'rilla this spring; 'n' here 'tis June, 'n' most July."

"I sh'd think you might dig it," said Mrs. Guild, shortly, her mouth snapping together something like a spring after she had spoken.

"I ain't able. But I needed tonin' up so that Priscilla she went over to the Williams wood-lot 'n' dug a few roots. But she had to take the little girl with her, 'n' she couldn't go round quite so fur 's if she hadn't had the child. Sarsap'rilla 's ruther skerce. 'N' somehow 'tain't quite so effectual 's when you buy it with a little liquor in it. I s'pose the liquor stimulates some. 'N' Priscilla she says what I need is stimulatin' "

Mrs. Guild kept her mouth shut tightly. She flung some pea-pods down with such violence in the pan that they bounded over on to the door-stone, where Mr. Grover gathered them up, remarking that he wished he had a mess of early pease, and that he should have planted some if he'd been able.

"You had a garden last year," said Mrs. Guild.

"Yes; Judith she made the garden last year. It was good for her to have the fresh air night 'n' mornin' when she was out of the shop. It's surprisin' how tough 'n' well Judith is. Health is a great blessin'. I hope Judith appreciates it."

"So Judith worked in the shop 'n' took care the garden?"

"Yes. It's a mercy she's so tough. I d' know where she gits her constitution from, I'm sure. I s'pose she takes back somewhere."

"Yes," said Mrs. Guild, "I guess she does take back in more ways than one." She rose as she spoke. "You'll have to excuse me, Mr. Grover, unless you c'n come in 'n set a spell. I must git these pease on."

Mr. Grover rose also. He replied that he thought he would set a while. And when he was comfortably established in the best chair he remarked that he "s'posed he hadn't ought to have come out till after he'd had his luncheon, for it didn't do for him to git faint. He thought that when he over-et himself it didn't hurt him so much as it did to git faint." These words were received in absolute silence. But Mr. Grover was comfortable, and the manner of his hostess did not affect him in the least. Presently he asked how the guesses on the beans were coming on.

"Tollerble well," was the reply.

Mr. Grover took his handkerchief from his hat, which stood on the floor by him. He wiped his bald head once more. He said he understood that his hostess held the money for these guesses. Yes, she did. Here Mrs. Guild's mouth snapped up again so very much like a steel trap that it almost seemed as if Mr. Grover were caught in that trap. But Mr. Grover did not appear to think himself caught. He put his handkerchief back in his hat, and said that he s'posed it was time for him to have a little advance from that fund. The bean bottle had been going some time now, and—

"I can't let you have any advance," here interrupted Mrs. Guild. "I ain't goin' to touch that money till the bottle has gone back to your wife, 'n' the beans been counted ; and then I sha'n't give the money to you, Mr. Grover."

The man brought his heavy lips forward over his teeth and held them shut an instant, thus making his face extremely ugly to look at.

"I expect," he said, at last, "that I'm the head of my family, ain't I?"

"It don't make no difference to me whether you be or not, 's I can see," was the answer. "I sha'n't give you none of that money."

Mr. Grover rose. His eyes looked whiter than ever, but he was smiling—that is, his mouth was drawn away from his teeth. It was while he was standing thus, with his hat in one hand and handkerchief in the other, that a loud rumble of wheels was heard.

"That's the noon stage," said Mrs. Guild, briskly. "It's consid'able early to-day, seems to me. Why, it ain't stoppin', is it?"

Yes, it was stopping. She went to the door as the stage, which had really degenerated to a roomy covered wagon drawn by two horses, came to a stand-still. A girl with a large satchel in her hand stepped out. She glanced up at the door and smiled as she paused to pay the driver.

"Why, if that ain't Judith herself!" cried Mrs. Guild. She hurried down the yard, her big face shining with delight. She took the bag from the girl's hand, flung an arm over her neck, and kissed her loudly. "Well, I am surprised!" she exclaimed. "Come right in. When Nathan gits back he'll harness up 'n' take you home—that is, if you must go."

"Yes; I guess I must go," was the answer. "Do you know how the folks are?"

"'Bout the same." Mrs. Guild rather delayed the girl as she walked up the path. "How'd you leave the measles?" she asked.

"I didn't leave any measles," with a laugh; "they're gone. That's why I could come home."

Mrs. Guild followed the girl. In a moment Judith stopped in the doorway.

"Why, father!" she said. Then she walked forward and her father kissed her cheek, and said it was a wonder how tough she was looking.

Mr. Grover was thinking that, now his daughter had come and would be invited to dinner, he would have to be included in the invitation. And he would be taken home in Mr. Guild's carriage with Judith.

Mrs. Guild was thinking the same thing, and wondering how she could prevent this man from having his dinner with them. And she knew that she would have to submit.

"Take your hat right off," she said to Judith. "Go in my bedroom and wash your face if you want to. It's dretful dusty, ain't it?"

The girl did not immediately wash her hands. She had poured some water into the bowl, and was standing before it, her eyes drooped, her face showing both weariness and resolution.

It was a curious fact that when you saw Judith Grover for the first time you had an indefinite feeling that you had known her, or that you had been wishing to know her. But gradually that feeling wore away, or it left only the phase that you wished to know her. She was so dark that you expected her to seem languid, as if with a Southern languor. Perhaps she could seem thus; it indeed appeared as if that manner must be her natural manner, only that, being a New England girl and the mainstay of her family, she had no opportunity for anything but work and planning for herself and others. And another first impression of a discerning observer was sure to be that she only lived now a stinted life, but that she did not know it was a stinted life, never having been acquainted with any other. The hands that she at last put in the water before her were hardened with labor that had been wellnigh incessant since she had begun to grow up. It is a piteous sight to see young hands hard, and to know that they will but grow harder and harder with more and more work.

But Judith had never thought of pitying herself. She had no time to think of anything but that she must earn all she could, and plan to make her money go as far as possible. And yet there seemed to be dreams in the brown eyes, and a tenderness in the mouth which suited well with its contour and its color. She was dressed in a dark gingham and a thin black sack, garments without the least "style" to them, and which were respectable, and no more. She was always glad when the warm weather came, for she had never yet had anything to wear in the winter that was a sufficient protection from the cold.

Sometimes two or three families in the town who had plenty of everything had sent over cast-off cloaks and shawls to the Grovers. But no one had ever seen Judith wearing any of these clothes. Once there had been a jacket from the Eldridges which had just fitted Judith. Mrs. Grover had taken it out of the box and insisted that the girl should try it on. Judith had stood stiff and still during the process, and had refused to look at herself in the glass when her mother had buttoned it up and was gazing at her daughter in admiration.

"I declare, it fits grand!" exclaimed Mrs. Grover. "I didn't know you were so good-looking, Judith. But you don't have any chance—poor folks don't have any chance. You've got to wear this jacket, anyway. You never do take anything that's sent here to us."

Judith glanced down at the sleeves, holding her arms out as she did so. "I sha'n't wear it," she said. "You can make it smaller for one of the children. I don't believe father *can* wear this, anyway." The girl's lip curled as she said the last sentence. Then she added: "Perhaps he can change it for some kind of medicine. What kind is he taking now?"

"Yellow-dock."

Judith gave a short laugh. She began to pull off the jacket.

"Won't you keep it for yourself?" her mother pleaded, going closer, and taking hold of the girl's arm.

"No."

"Please! You look so well in it."

"No. You and father may do what you please, but I'm not going to live on charity, and I shall work as hard as I can for you all." She flung the jacket down in a chair as she spoke.

"Oh, Judith!"

Her mother's voice irritated her, but she did not reply until she could say, without showing that irritation: "You know I never have taken such things from the neighbors, and I ain't going to, either."

Then Mrs. Grover had sat down and begun to cry. She said she didn't know what was going to become of them, she was sure; and sometimes she didn't know as she cared. Having said this, something boiled over on the kitchen stove, and she sprang up exclaiming that it was the yeller-dock, and that she knew that kittle wouldn't hold so much; but it had got to be three quarts boiled down to one quart, and that was the only kittle they had. Judith stepped quickly forward and swung off the vessel, placing it in the sink, while a strong, bitter smell pervaded the room. Mrs. Grover began to mop up that portion of the liquid that had run over on to the floor.

"I should think your father's stomach would be in a dreadful condition with all the stuff he puts into it," she said, as she was on her knees by the stove.

"I'm sure I don't know which would be worse," responded the girl: "to have a man drink, or be given over to dosing himself all the time."

Mrs. Grover had now risen, and was rinsing out her mop. She was a little, bent, round-shouldered woman, who was really only fifty, though she looked seventy. She had no teeth, and her voice had a hollow, lisping sound. She seemed always to have on the same calico gown, and the same apron, made of men's shirting, girded about her. Her shoes were never drawn up at the heel, but were trodden down there so that her heels were never shod, and her shoes flapped with every step she took on the bare floor. People who had known her before her marriage were fond of saying that they should never know her now. Twenty-five years of life with Hanford Grover were stamped upon her aspect.

When Priscilla Stetson had married Mr. Grover she had been the teacher of the school in the Clapp neighborhood. She had been what the people there called "a real dressy girl," and she had painted a little. Three of these "oil scenes" were hung in the best room now, but Mrs. Grover always tried not to look at them. The memories and the dead hopes that hung about those pathetic pictures were like blows on sensitive flesh. She had been a "high-strung girl," and she had thought that Mr. Grover loved her. She was not quite so sure that she loved him, but she was positive that she respected him, and she did not believe much in being in love.

In those days Hanford Grover had not begun to take medicine and to watch for symptoms, and he had just inherited a good farm, and was apparently altogether eligible; and he did not then have those shining white teeth from the dentist's. So Miss Stetson married him, and children began to come, and Mr. Grover immediately began to manifest a disinclination for work, and an inclination for patent medicine and stewed herbs. And the dressy school-teacher ceased to be dressy, and almost stopped caring whether she used her nouns and verbs right or not. But she tried not to give up her habit of speaking correctly for the sake of her children. Some of them acquired her way of speaking, and some of them lapsed into their father's way.

As the years went on Judith, the eldest, became the mainstay. She took up the burden without whining, but she grew to hate her father. She tried to conceal this feeling; she never spoke of him when she could help it. Sometimes he caught her glance fixed on him in such a way that he felt like writhing. Then he would take the first opportunity to speak of the respect that children owed their parents.

Now as Mr. Grover sat in Mrs. Guild's kitchen he told himself that Judith must have brought home some money from the Joyces—not much, but some. He wondered how he could manage to get hold of a portion of it.

Since she was eighteen Judith had not handed her earnings to him, and she had only given a part of them to her mother, for she was never quite sure that her father would not get the money from his wife. She had paid debts with her money, and spent everything on the family. There was no other way that she could see, and no other way in all the years to come but just to keep right on as she had been doing. In spite of the measles, she had really rested at her cousin's. And now, the moment she had returned, even before she reached home, here was her father; and he would stay the two hours she had planned to be with Mrs. Guild, and then he would ride home with her.

Judith lingered a moment at the small looking-glass in the bedroom. She was mechanically brushing back her hair, and thinking—she seemed to herself to be thinking a thousand things in a vivid way that appeared strange to her. She put down the brush at last. She went to the window and glanced out, then gazed intently up into the clear blue of the June sky. A thrill of delight went through her as she gazed. "Somehow I don't have any time to enjoy anything," she thought, as she turned away from the window.

Mrs. Guild opened the door and came in. "I guess you better come right out to dinner," she said. "Mr. Guild's got home. He's puttin' his horse out. Why, Judith, what's the matter?"

There were tears in the girl's eyes, but they did not fall. She passed her hand quickly over her face.

III

OLD PLAYMATES

"I s'pose you're dretful tired," said Mrs. Guild, sympathetically. "Mebby the Joyce measles didn't come out good, and that worried you."

The girl laughed resolutely. "Yes, they did come out in the best kind of way. Is father going to stay to dinner?"

"Yes."

Mrs. Guild refrained from saying "of course he is," and the restraint this refraining involved made her grow red in the face.

When Mr. Guild entered he nodded shortly at Mr. Grover, shook hands with Judith, and, being a jocose man, he asked, "Well, how's beans, Judith?"

Mrs. Guild coughed warningly, but her cough was entirely unheeded, for when they had all drawn up to the table, Mr. Guild, stirring his coffee with a swift, rotary movement, remarked that he didn't s'pose Judith knew what a business woman her mother was gittin' to be.

" Nathan !" said his wife, warningly.

"Oh, I'm all right," responded the man, who had never been known to understand anything without a full explanation, "only I wanted to ask Judith if she didn't think that bean-bottle idea a good one. I've been thinkin' I should take another guess."

" Mr. Guild, will you pass the p'taters to Mr. Grover?" asked Mrs. Guild, with some ferocity in her manner.

" I don't know what you mean," said Judith. She thought her father's face had something peculiar upon it. She began to grow indignant

"Oh, I thought you knew all about it; I thought it was your notion," said Mr. Guild. "Mary, what are you looking at me so for? I ain't doin' nothing. Didn't you get up the bean-bottle?" turning to the girl, who felt her hands growing cold, she hardly knew why. But of course there was some new humiliation for the Grovers. Her eyes flashed over at her father, but he did not look up. He was eating greedily.

"Judith," now began Mrs. Guild, "I never did see such a stupid thing as Nathan is. You see, we didn't mean to tell you till the thing was done and we'd got all the money we could."

Judith pushed her chair from the table. "Do you mean that you've been taking up a collection for us?" she asked; her voice rang in the low room.

"Daughter," said Mr. Grover, "I hope you'll show a proper spirit of gratitude."

"Father, please don't speak to me now," she replied. Then to her hostess, "I want you to tell me what's been done. I don't want the neighbors to give us anything. I can take care of the family. I—"

"Judith's so tough and well," here interrupted Mr. Grover. "Folks in health don't appreciate what a blessing health is. Mr. Guild, I'd be obleeged for some more of that cabbage."

"I can take care of the family," repeated the girl.

"You needn't flare up," now said Mrs. Guild, "but I was afraid you'd do jes' so, so I didn't mean you should know anything about it till the money was handed over to your mother. But I don't see what you can do, as 'tis now. You see, your mother said that—that Mr. Grover was never so in debt 's he is this minute, 'n' something 'd got to be done, 'n' you can't do everything. So she's put some beans in a bottle, and we're goin' to guess at twenty-five cents a guess, 'n' the one that hits it 'll have your seraphine."

"But the seraphine isn't worth a cent!" sharply.

"Daughter," said Mr. Grover, as soon as he could artic-

ulate on account of cabbage, "you shouldn't speak in that
way. 'Tain't becomin' in a young person."

"Nobody can possibly want that seraphine," went on Judith. "I don't see what made mother do such a thing."

Having said so much, the girl tried to control herself
and to go on with her dinner. But all her hunger was gone.
The corned-beef lay on her plate untouched. She swallowed some coffee. She was inwardly angry at sight of her
father eating swiftly, and with an air as if he could keep up
the process indefinitely. She wondered what her mother
and the children were having for dinner. Very likely it was
nothing better than hasty-pudding. As soon as she could
she rose from the table. She said she thought she would
be starting for home. Her father gave her a look. He
was drinking his third cup of coffee, and he knew that he
would be expected to go with her.

"You sha'n't stir a step yet!" exclaimed Mrs. Guild,
briskly. "Nathan 'll take you over bime-by; won't you,
Nathan?"

Mr. Guild nodded. He said he didn't ask nothin' better than to wait on pretty girls.

Judith went to the door of the bedroom where her hat
was. She turned, and glanced beseechingly at her hostess,
who rose and joined her. When the two were in the little
room Judith seized the woman's arm. "Don't tease me to
stay!" she pleaded. "I'd rather walk than to ride with
father. It's dreadful to say it, but I know you won't tell I
said so. I want to be alone until I can think this over.
And I shall have time enough in the three miles from here
home. I should be glad if Mr. Guild would bring my satchel
over some time when he's going that way."

"Oh, Judith," responded Mrs. Guild, "it don't seem to
me you're right when you hate to have friends help you
any!"

Judith was hurriedly pinning on her hat before the glass.
Her young face was so troubled that Mrs. Guild was more
sorry than ever for her. "You don't know how 'tis," re-

turned the girl; "I can't tell you, either. Now, good-bye. I shall come over and see you as soon as I can. I'll go right out this porch door." She hastened across the yard. She turned back to see Mrs. Guild still looking at her. She retraced her steps. "I do hope," she said, in an unsteady voice, "that you won't think I don't know how kind you are to me." This time she almost ran out of the yard. When she reached the road she slackened her pace to a steady, swift walk.

In half a mile the highway turned and ran by solitary pastures, where cows were feeding and over which crows sailed. Here, in the June days, the song-sparrows and blackbirds and robins and their kin held festival, and snuffy brown chipmunks darted across the sweet-ferny spaces. There were frequent clumps of white birches by the roadside—outposts, apparently, from the pastures.

As Judith approached one of the birch-clumps a young man who was peeling off a wide strip of bark turned and saw her. At the same moment she saw him, but she was walking on without giving him a second look. He was a stranger to her, and her mind was preoccupied. The man's hat had fallen off, and lay on the ground near him. He had one arm around the tree trunk, and the other hand had been carefully pulling back the bark. It was not probable that Judith noticed that he was in appearance rather different from the ordinary youth of the town. He was fair, with girlish-looking hair worn rather long; a meagre yellow beard pointed down from his chin, and a thin mustache was twisted upward, revealing a large, irregular mouth that had an appearance, not unpleasant, however, as if its owner were fond of the good things of this life. He was clothed in gray corduroy coat and knickerbockers. It was doubtful if this town had ever seen such a costume before. Had not Judith been so absorbed she would have noticed this dress.

She was hurrying by, having barely seen him, when the man stepped forward into the road behind her, standing and

watching her for the space of half a minute.   Then he darted back, snatched up his hat, and ran after her.   As he
reached her side, still with his hat in his hand, he exclaimed,
"Well, Judith Grover, you are a cool one, upon my word!"

She stopped and looked at him, her face flushing somewhat as she did so.

"Now don't you dare to say you don't know me," he began again, with some eagerness.   "Because if you do, I shall
think it is only airs. and I can't believe you would put on
airs, little Judith Grover."

"Little!" echoed Judith, laughing ; "I am as tall as you
are, every bit, Lucian Eldridge."

She held out her hand, which he took closely.   He came
somewhat nearer.

"After ten years one might think you would let me kiss
you," he said, with an air of being only half in earnest.

"I don't know why we should begin kissing now," she responded.

They were still holding each other's hands and gazing delightedly at each other.

"I didn't know but gratitude might suggest to you to give
me a good hug," he answered.

"Gratitude?"

"Yes; for all the times I used to drag you on my sled
and make the other girls envious.   You know, if I wasn't the
handsomest boy, I certainly had the best sled."

"I remember," went on Judith ; "your sled was carpeted
with a bit of red carpet, and it was painted blue with a pink
lion on each side.   Yes, it certainly was the best sled."

"Didn't we use to whiz down the Fassett hill, though?"
asked the young man.

He still kept the girl's hand.   He was thinking that he
had not had the least idea that he should be so glad to
see Judith Grover, and he was surprised to find it such a
distinct pleasure to look in her face.

"Yes," said Judith, "we had good times."   Then suddenly
her face grew less bright, and without intending to speak in

that way, she yet said, "Good times are about over for me, I think." As soon as she had spoken thus she was ashamed of having done so, and hastened to say, "But you'll think I'm blue, and I am, just a little. Still, I know how foolish I am just as well as if you told me. I must be going."

"All right. I'll go with you."

Young Eldridge immediately fell into step and walked beside her. She glanced over him again and then laughed.

"Are you laughing at me?"

"Yes."

Eldridge smiled delightedly. "Anything to make you cheerful. But what amuses you?"

"Your clothes. Is that the way the men dress where you've been?"

"Sometimes. Don't you think this suit is becoming? 'Becoming' is what you girls say, isn't it?"

"Yes, that's what we say."

The young man's smiling and intent gaze was on his companion. He was wondering about her. He had hardly thought of her in the ten years since he had seen her. He had been at home frequently in that time, but it had not happened that he had met Judith. How shabbily she was dressed! What true eyes she had! How lovely it was to have her look straight at you!

IV

MR. GROVER COLLECTS A SMALL SUM

"Have the folks in the village seen you in that rig?" asked Judith.

"Yes; this morning. I only came late last night. Right after breakfast I went to the store — I hoped I should meet old Ellis Macomber. I wanted to see his green baize jacket. I couldn't feel really at home until I had seen that jacket. I suppose it's the same one he used to wear when you were my best girl, Judith?"

"The very same one. But I was not your—"

"Don't, please, go and wound me by saying you were not my best girl!"

As he said this Eldridge faced round into the path in front of his companion and made her stop in her walk. He was laughing, but there was a suspicion of earnestness in his manner. He was going to say that he had always thought of her in that light, but he knew that he had hardly thought of her at all, and there was something so truthful and sincere in what he called this girl's "atmosphere" that he could not quite tell an untruth to her.

Judith hesitated an instant. "You were awfully kind to me with—with that sled — and skating — and when we went huckleberrying. Don't you know how you used to pick into my basket because I had to get all I could to sell, and you were not obliged to go for berries anyway?" Now she lifted her eyes to his face. She spoke more lightly as she went on: "You were certainly what Mr. Macomber would call a 'fust-rate little chap.'"

Eldridge put his hand on his heart and bowed deeply.

"And if you will kindly allow me to see you, now I've come home, you'll find I've grown into a 'fust-rate' young man. Must you hurry?"

"Oh yes. Mother 'll want me. I've been away for a couple of weeks. My Joyce cousins have had the measles, and I've been helping them."

"Helping them have the measles?"

"Put it anyway you please. But I must go."

She began to walk fast now. But the young man kept beside her. He was silent for a few moments. He was recalling all he used, as a boy, to hear said about the Grovers. And he was trying to understand how he could so completely have forgotten them, or how he could now remember them so vividly.

"I hope you have prospered in all these years," he said, finally. And as soon as he had spoken thus he knew it was an awkward thing for him to have said, for no girl who was prosperous in the usual meaning of that word would look so shabby as Judith looked.

"Thank you," she answered. She held her head a little more erect as she continued, "We get along as well as most folks who work for a living. Of course, we've got to work ; but we expect that."

"Is your father's health any better?" Eldridge supposed that he must put that question.

"Father is about the same," was the stiff answer.

"Proud little girl!" he murmured, his face softening wonderfully as he spoke. He put out his hand and took hers quickly again, thus detaining her in her rapid walk, for he stood still. "We used to be friends when we were children," he said, "and there's no reason why we shouldn't be friends now we are grown up. I won't go any farther this time with you; but I'm coming over to see you all. And I'm going to have my pay for letting you slide on my sled and for putting huckleberries in your basket. And there's a lot of interest due, and you'll find me an exacting usurer. Good-bye now, Judith."

Eldridge stooped and kissed her hand. Then he stepped back and lifted his hat. Judith smiled swiftly and involuntarily at her companion. Then she went on alone down the road.

Young Eldridge remained where he was for a few moments. He looked about him for a convenient resting-place, and saw nothing better than the wall. So he established himself upon that under a pine-tree, and began gazing up into the thick branches above him.

"That pine knows it is June," he presently said, aloud. Then in an apparently irrelevant manner, "How hard her hands were! I suppose she works so that she has no time to know whether it's June or not."

He thrust his hands into his pockets. He was still looking into the pine-tree, but his eyes were now half closed. He was thinking of the expression in Judith's face, and a thrill went through his heart as he thought. How did she happen to grow up into such a woman? Why, it was delicious to talk to her, and to see her face lighten and darken as he talked. And she had no idea about making eyes, and using those silly flirting ways that other girls used. It was too bad that she had to work and spoil her hands. What a thundering old brute her father must be! Was Hanford Grover going on in the same old way?

Eldridge recalled one thing after another. He remembered now that people used to say how sorry they were for Grover's family. And now he came to think of it, Judith never had any warm clothes when she was a child and came to school. He used to be sorry for her then, but she had a way with her that kept him from telling her he was sorry. She had that way now. And he liked it; only it somehow prevented his approach. But he was glad he had kissed her hand; though, now he thought of it, it must have seemed to her a very strange thing for him to do.

"Poor little thing!" he said, aloud. "Why don't some of those patent medicines carry off old Grover? I suppose he takes them now just the same. Odd I should have forgotten."

While the young man sat there rather absently watching the birds and the squirrels, and finding his thoughts growing more and more vague in the happy reverie that youth and a June day may induce, there came the sound of slow, dragging steps from the direction in which he and Judith had come an hour before. Eldridge turned his head and saw a man in a tall silk hat and a long linen duster walking towards him.

When it became known to Nathan Guild that Judith had started to walk home he decided that he should not harness his horse that he might convey Mr. Grover to his residence. He informed that gentleman that he guessed 'twould do his liver good if he took the exercise; and so Mr. Grover was obliged to go home as he had come. But though his system was now fortified by what he called a "biled dish," he was in a bad frame of mind because he had not succeeded in getting Mrs. Guild to advance some of the money which she held for guesses on the number of beans. His teeth glittered viciously in the June sunshine, and he struck out cruelly with his cane at the lavish clumps of daises by the road-side as he came along.

After a moment's steady gaze Eldridge announced to himself, "Why, it's the miserable old wretch himself! But I've never seen those teeth before." He got down from the wall and sauntered along towards the approaching figure.

Mr. Grover looked sourly at the young man. It always made him feel sour to see a prosperous human being; and this youth with the well-fitting clothes, the easy manner, and the somewhat saucy smile was the picture of prosperity.

As the elder man came nearer he began to be more curious. Of course this was not a townsman, and there was no such thing as a summer visitor known in this part of the world.

"I cannot be mistaken," said Eldridge, moving forward and speaking with great seriousness, "I must be addressing Mr. Hanford Grover."

"That's my name. But you have the advantage of me,

young sir." Mr. Grover felt that he could be as polite as any one. He immediately thought of the bottle of beans, and wondered if this stranger could not be induced to take a few guesses. When the money for those guesses was paid he meant to get the most of it into his hands. It should not go to pay debts when his system stood in such need of a toning-up medicine.

" Don't you remember Lucian Eldridge, Mr. Grover?"

By this time the young man was disgusted with himself because he had spoken ; and he had a morbid and increasing desire to strike out from the shoulder at those teeth and knock them down the old fellow's throat.

Mr. Grover's smile increased in width and brilliance. He held out his hand and exclaimed, effusively, " Bless me! Now I see the Eldridge look. Have you been to home long?"

" About twenty-four hours." The young man was already trying to go away, but his companion held on to him.

" Then you ain't heard nothing about that little plan of the bean-bottle?" Mr. Grover was so afraid that Eldridge would escape him that he could hardly enunciate.

" The bean-bottle? Of course I haven't."

Eldridge looked at his watch. He was thinking how sickening this man was, and wondering why he had been such a fool as to speak to him. But he knew very well why he had done so.

" You see, I enjoy dretful poor health," began Mr. Grover, hurriedly, " 'n' I ain't be'n able to work for some years. Judith she's real tough 'n' can earn, but a woman's earnin' ain't like a man's, you know. My liver's most always too toppid, or else it ain't toppid enough. So you see there 'tis —'n' I need some kind of medicine constant. There's a new elixir out now ; it's said to be mighty good for bile ; if you've got too much bile it reduces it ; 'n' if you ain't got enough it increases it. I ought to have some of that elixir— I'm always trying to git my health so I c'n work for my family."

Eldridge made an inarticulate murmur of assent. He put his hand in his pocket. Was the man begging?

"You c'n have a guess on them beans for twenty-five cents," went on Mr. Grover, "and if you guess right you'll have our seraphine. Everybody thought 'twas a real good plan to sell the seraphine in that way. If you feel like taking a few chances you c'n give me the money now, and then go to Mrs. Guild's and see the bottle of beans and put down your guesses."

"All right. I'll take twenty guesses."

Hanford Grover almost jumped at the success attending this effort. His long face grew red with the sudden triumph. He took the bill that Eldridge extended to him and crumpled it quickly into his waistcoat-pocket. It was a moment before he noticed that the young man had left him. Then he turned and looked at the figure striding along the road.

"Lucian Eldridge," he shouted, "be sure 'n' go 'n' guess on the beans at Nathan Guild's! We ain't objects of charity."

Lucian whirled round and nodded. Mr. Hanford Grover turned at a corner that led towards the village. He was saying to himself that he would try two bottles of that elixir. According to the advertisements it was a sure cure, and he would still have some money left to get something for that pain he thought he sometimes felt on the left side of his head, and which he rather hoped was a touch of "nooraligy." He had never had nooraligy yet, and this omission seemed almost like a slight put upon him by Providence.

JUDITH AND HER MOTHER

ELDRIDGE went straight to Nathan Guild's house. When he was a boy he had liked the Guilds. He now found a keen pleasure in renewing his old associations. Mrs. Guild had had a jolly, shrewd face. It was the same face that appeared now at the door in answer to his knock—no older, he thought. He stepped forward, put an arm around the woman's neck, and kissed her cheek.

"I want a cooky with sugared caraway-seeds on top of it!" he exclaimed, with that intimate, good-natured laugh of his which went so far towards making people like him. Mrs. Guild pulled him into the house and pushed a chair towards him.

"I ain't forgot how you used to like them cookies," she said. Then she looked him over from head to foot. "Be them men's clo'es that you've got on?" she asked.

"Certainly, since I wear them," with an assumption of dignity. "But what is the bean-bottle, Mrs. Guild? Bring it forward. I invest in it. I didn't expect to come home to be tempted by a lottery immediately."

When the young man had put his name down Mrs. Guild waited for him to give her the money. She looked over his shoulder and saw the munificence of the sum, and she said that the Eldridges always was generous, and they could afford to be; but them that could afford to be wa'n't always so. Then she told him that he must give her the five dollars, for she held the amount until the guessing was all through, and she added that she did hope that Judith would be kind of reasonable; but that girl was so proud that you couldn't help her any, and she would probably end by killing herself with work trying to support um all.

Eldridge hesitated a minute, much to Mrs. Guild's surprise, before he handed her his second five dollars for the Grovers that day. But he said nothing. He listened while Mrs. Guild talked profusely about the whole Grover family and the origin of the seraphine plan. She ended by asking if he had seen Judith since he came home. He answered carelessly that he had met her on the west road that morning.

"I always did like Judith," said Mrs. Guild, heartily. "But I do think she's got kind of stiff notions about some things. When she marries I d' know, I'm sure, what 'll become of the rest of um."

"Is there a prospect of her marrying?"

"I ain't sure. She don't say nothing about it. Mebby there ain't anything in it. But I've heard that one of the Rylances in the north part of the town has been thinkin' about Judith for some time. I s'pose she's seen him now while she's been over to the Joyces."

Eldridge sat a few minutes longer. He ate one of the caraway cookies. He affirmed that it was just as good as when he had stopped on his way home from school and Mrs. Guild had given him the same refreshment. But, in truth, he did not know what he was eating. He was thinking of the Rylances. And when he had left Mrs. Guild's and was strolling towards home he was still thinking of them, and wondering which one it was. There had been three Rylance boys, and they used to walk over to the school. They had always, in the winter, had their caps tied down by red wool "comforters." In sledding-time they never had sleds, but "jumpers," which they made themselves.

Lucian Eldridge was not aware that this mention of a Rylance as a probable lover of Judith Grover's went a great ways towards deepening and confirming the interest he had suddenly felt in the girl. That afternoon he rode over to the " north part " solely to see the Rylance house and farm, though he told himself when he mounted his horse that he didn't know which way he should go.

When young Eldridge went to bed that night he was quite sure, after all, that he shouldn't be bored now that he had come home to stay until he could think what he really wanted to do in the world. He had been rather afraid that he should be bored. But he found things much more interesting than he had expected they would be. And how long before it would be proper for him to call on the Grovers? He might happen around there the next day. He would take some of those Maréchal Neil roses that were growing in the garden to Mrs. Grover. And perhaps Judith's eyes would have that lovely look in them—the look that had been there when she had spoken of his having put berries in her basket. Really, it was very lucky that it didn't seem likely that he should be bored. It was a fine thing to be home again. And the Rylance house and farm looked as if the owners had rather a hard time to get along. At this point in his thoughts Eldridge fell asleep.

Judith, when she had parted from her old playfellow, had not felt that she had time to linger out-of-doors in the beautiful June weather. She must always hurry by beautiful things. She had done so all her life, and she gave little time to repining ; she had no time for repining, either. When she came within sight of the house her mother was in the field at the south spreading some newly washed clothes on the grass.

At sight of the bent figure in the old gown and the everlasting shirting apron, the girl's face changed and melted into a look of loving protection. She ran forward and crept under the one bar that was left in the two posts near the road.

Mrs. Grover, hearing steps, tried to straighten herself. She looked up right into the sunshine and blinked blindly. Then she put her hand above her eyes, uttered a joyful cry, and hastened forward.

"Oh, Judith! I *am* glad to see you!" she exclaimed. She kissed the girl on both cheeks. "There ain't anything worth while when you're gone, Judith. But I didn't dare to expect you 'fore next week. How did you get away?"

The quick tears had sprung to the girl's eyes at her mother's greeting, but she would not let them fall. She had no time for emotion of any kind. She walked to the basket of wet clothes and began taking them out and spreading them.

"The measles were so considerate as to be very light," she answered. "I suppose if our children have them, or it —somehow the measles always seem a multitude—they will go the hardest kind of way."

"But I don't mean the children shall stand any chance," was the anxious reply. "You don't think they've stood any chance, do you, Judith?"

For answer the girl turned quickly away. The high, somewhat querulous voice struck her as it had never done before, and it seemed to her for an instant that she could not bear it. She was surprised at herself that so short an absence should have dulled her memory in the least as to how things were at home.

The Joyces were thrifty people. They had been able to pay her two dollars a week, though she hated to be obliged to take anything. She had not spent a cent of that sum, save for her stage-fare, and the money for the four weeks was now in her pocket. She had felt a keen sense of gratitude for that money all the time she had been riding towards home, but now there was a sudden bitterness diffused through everything. She kept her face averted as she spread sheets and towels on the ground. A strange, furious rebellion was in her heart, she did not know why.

"You don't think they've stood any chance, do you?" repeated her mother, who had ceased her work, and who was gazing in a kind of beseeching way at her daughter.

"I haven't been here, you know," answered the girl. Then she made a great effort to speak cheerfully. She assured her mother that they could get along, even if the children did have the measles, and she had brought home almost eight dollars. She took her purse from her pocket as she spoke. She was going to give it to her mother; then she hesitated. "I guess I'd better keep it myself," she said. "Ill go round to the grocery store to-morrow and pay something towards what we owe."

"Oh, Judith," exclaimed Mrs. Grover, "I don't know what we should do without you! Yes, I do, too—we should all go to the poor-house. Sometimes I think we might as well as to be a-dragging you down all the time."

Judith wished to say something comforting, but she could not think of anything. She turned now and glanced at her mother again. The sight of the forlorn figure made her sob in spite of herself.

"Why, Judith!" Mrs. Grover came close to her daughter. The worn heart of the elder woman gave a beat of alarm.

"I don't know what makes me so foolish," said Judith, with some savageness, "but somehow this lovely day, and you looking so poor and wretched, and seeing father gobbling corned-beef up at Mrs. Guild's, and—and—I declare I didn't know I was so silly!"

"Mebby you're coming down with the measles," was the anxious response.

Judith threw her head back. She laughed. She hurriedly passed her handkerchief over her face. "I don't know when I've done such a thing," she said, firmly, "and I'm not going to do it any more."

"Did you see Tom Rylance when you was at the Joyces'?"

Mrs. Grover rather ostentatiously turned away, took a pillow-case from the basket, and began to shake it out. Therefore she did not see the color that rose slowly over the girl's face, or the sudden change of the curve of the mouth.

"Yes," she answered.

"I declare I d' know what 'll become of us if you get

married. We sh'll just go to the poor-house," with monotonous repetition.

"Mother!" said Judith, remonstrantly. The two went on spreading clothes in silence for a few moments. The girl was thinking what she had thought many times. She was saying the words to herself that she had begun to say almost as soon as she had entered her teens: "It isn't any use for me to think of any life of my own."

That evening, after the children were in bed, and while Mr. Grover was peacefully slumbering on the lounge, after having grumbled a good deal because he had no meat for supper, Judith asked her mother to come out into the yard. It was too pleasant to stay in the house, she said, and she wanted to talk, and she could never be sure that her father was not shamming sleep and listening. The two women leaned on the fence under the big clump of lilacs, whose faded blooms still lingered on their stems. A soft west wind blew over the fields and woods. The insects piped merrily. A smell of growing green things was in the air. There seemed a sense of hope and promise everywhere in the world.

Judith, being young, could not help feeling this hope and promise in a vague, delicious way. She had asked her mother to come out that she might talk about the bean-bottle that was circulating through the village. She could not prevent a certain incisiveness from coming to her voice as she announced that she should start out the next morning, get the list of those who had taken chances and the money from Mrs. Guild, and pay back the money where it belonged.

Mrs. Grover leaned heavily on the fence. She did not speak for some time after her daughter had declared her intention. She was conscious of a feeling of rebellion against the girl's power, and she reproved herself for that feeling. Then she almost wished that Judith had not come home until that money had been paid and spent.

"I was going to pay some of Hanford's debts," she said,

at last. "We've got to live. And you know how the shoe-shops have shut down so you ain't earned so much. And I thought—"

"Mother," interrupted the girl, "I know all about that. I mean to pay those debts. We shall have to live awfully close. I shall work—you know how I shall work—"

"Poor Judith!" whispered the mother, all her indignation gone. Then she said, pleadingly, "But there ain't any harm in that bean-bottle. The minister told Hanford that, under the circumstances, he didn't see any harm in it."

"Don't you know," began Judith, with the intolerant fierceness of youth, "that the seraphine isn't worth anything —not anything? If it were valuable—"

VI

TURNED OUT

So the girl talked. The mother cried a little at seeing this hope taken from her, but she was obliged to submit. She said that she didn't care for herself; she was past wanting anything. But the children—

"And sometimes, Judith, I don't know but I'm too hard on your father. Mebby he does need some of that elixir he's been talking about."

But the girl laughed scornfully. She was often frightened at the intensity of the bitterness with which she thought of her father. She held to her intention. Early the next morning she started forth. She secured the paper. She went to Mrs. Guild and made her give up the money. Nothing Mrs. Guild could say moved her from her determination. She only replied that it was an imposition to call that seraphine worth anything, and that she was not willing to accept charity.

"All I've got to say, then, Judith Grover," said Mrs. Guild, impressively, "is that you've no business to be so set as this about this matter. You're jest as liable to be wrong as anybody."

Judith toiled along the different roads all day, returning to their owners the money they had paid. She did not explain in many words. She repeated her statement about the worthlessness of the seraphine, and she added that it had been thought best not to carry out that plan. She would not stay to hear the remarks of the people.

"There's something wrong about that Grover girl," some

of them said. "She ain't got no right to carry things with such a high hand. We wanted to help um."

When she went home that night, weary in soul and body, Judith found her father sitting in a rocker placed outside of the door in the shade. He saw her coming, and leaned forward on his stick, watching her. His pale eyes had sparks of fire in them; his lips were drawn across his two rows of white teeth until the lips were almost colorless.

Hanford Grover had an evil temper, and it seemed to him that he had never been so angry in his life. Judith walked into the yard, and was going by her father when he said, "Stop!" She paused in front of him. She was so tired that there was a white circle about her mouth and an unusual languor in her eyes. Her whole face had that look which would excite a special tenderness in one who loved her. But Mr. Grover did not notice this. He had made his wife tell him where Judith had gone and what was her errand, and he had placed himself here an hour ago that he might see his daughter as soon as she came. "I hear you've been meddlin' in what wa'n't none of your business," he said. It was with some difficulty that he articulated distinctly, his rage and sense of having been baffled were so great. There was no answer to this statement, and this silence but added to his fury. "Ain't you got nothin' to say for yourself?" he asked.

Judith gazed at him. The gaze was like a scorching flame to the man. He felt that his child did not respect him. He knew that there was no reason why she should respect him, and this very knowledge but made him more furious. He opened and shut his mouth twice before he was able to say, "You jest answer me, you little viper you!" He lifted his stick and shook it at her, almost hitting her face. She did not blench, but stood perfectly still. "What you meddlin' for?"

"I'm not meddling."

"You be! You be!"

Mr. Grover made a great effort to control himself. There

were some things he wished to say. He wished that this girl was ten years younger; then he would give her a whipping. If he could do that now he thought it would be the only relief to his feelings, and he was certain that he must have relief in some manner.

"Have you be'n 'n' paid back that money?" he asked.

"Most of it. I didn't think it was fair to take money that way."

"You didn't think! Fair! You!" He stopped again.

"I'm willing to work every minute for the family," said Judith, her voice sounding weary and cold, "but—"

"You ain't the judge!" cried Mr. Grover. "I'm the one to tell. I'm the head of the family. I'm your father. Ain't you be'n taught in Sabba'-school to honor thy father? Ain't you? I say, where's the rest of the money? Where's what you ain't paid back? You tell me that!"

"In my pocket."

Judith made a movement as if she would go on into the house. She wondered where her mother and the children were. She did not know that Mrs. Grover, seeing how angry her husband was, had taken the three children into the pasture, ostensibly to look for June-berries.

"You sha'n't go in there yet. If I've got a child that won't honor thy father, I'll see about it."

Judith paused. She was looking at the man before her, and wondering if her mother had ever been in love with him. Then a faint red came over her face. She tried to behave respectfully. He was her father. She had been to Sabbath-school all her life until a few years ago, and the lessons she had learned there in regard to her parents still clung to her. She told herself that she must try to find the good in every one. Where was the good in her father? She knew that he was very scrupulous about going to meeting every Sunday and to the evening prayer-meetings. He usually prayed and exhorted at these latter gatherings, and he always seemed very much in earnest. She had often reproved herself for her inability to feel impressed at such times. Perhaps it was all because she could not understand him. The girl's face changed somewhat from its scornful expression, but she could not bring herself to speak any conciliatory words.

"That bean-bottle was goin' to bring a lot of money," now began Mr. Grover, his voice trembling with the intensity of his emotion, "'n' you've be'n 'n' put your finger in it, 'n' spoilt everything. 'N' I with the liver I've got, 'n' with symptoms of nooraligy! You're a thankless child, you be."

Judith's face began to harden again. Mr. Grover's tones grew louder. He rose to his feet. The more he thought of the matter the more infuriated he grew. He had been planning to have "butchers' meat" in abundance while that money lasted, and to experiment in several kinds of medicine. He was fond of saying that a person with his liver needed nourishing food. And here was this girl— The man's face grew livid. Several times since Judith was grown he had clashed against her will, and had always been defeated. He used to tell his wife that Judith would come to some bad end, for she hadn't never had her will broke.

"Why don't you speak?" He shouted out the words.

"I haven't got anything to say."

"Don't you ever think that mebby you c'n be mistaken?"

Judith made no reply. But the words seemed to penetrate some crevice in her armor.

"I tell you what 'tis," began Mr. Grover, lashing himself onward, "I ain't going to have no disobedient child under my roof. No, I ain't. One as disobeys and goes contr'y to her father every time she can, and that despises him— him as is constant to meet'n', 'n'—'n'—"

His voice went on incoherently. He was beside himself with rage and disappointment. He had been secretly nursing the plan about the seraphine for months, and he had put his wife forward to act upon it the moment that Judith was out of the way. And she had come home and ruined everything. The secret anger against his daughter, the antagonism towards her, blazed out now unhindered. The man did not care what he did.

"D'you hear me?" he cried, at the end of half a dozen furious sentences.

"Yes, I hear you."

"Then why don't you take your duds 'n' clear out, I say? I tell you I ain't goin' to have a disobedient child under my roof a-settin' an example to the other children. You may jest march!"

Judith was now so white that she looked ready to faint. But there was a strength in her face that showed that she would not faint. She walked by her father towards the open door of the house behind him. She pressed one hand heavily upon the door-casing as she turned her head towards the figure standing by the chair. "Do you mean that?" she asked.

"Yes, I do! Ain't you always goin' ag'inst me? And don't I know 't you ain't got no belief in my liver? 'N' now you've be'n takin' the bread outer your mother's mouth, 'n'—'n'—" Again he stuttered on to a silence.

Judith went into the house. She walked quickly through the rooms. The brilliance of the setting sun was in that part of the dwelling that was towards the west. She saw the robins flying about among the apple-trees as she looked out of an open window. A ray of sunshine fell full upon the red breast of one of the robins as he sat on a stone preening himself. The bird's bright eyes seemed to look directly at her. It was a curious thing that she should have a fancy that the bird knew that she was turned out of her home, and she had a tenacious love for the old house where she was born. She had hoped some time to be able to earn money enough to pay the mortgage which her father had put on the place. But as yet she had only kept the interest paid. She must keep up that interest even if other debts remained unpaid. She was thinking of this in the midst of her keen wish to find her mother. She went through every room. She noticed that the straw hats of the three little girls were gone, as well as her mother's old sun-bonnet. Did her mother know—was it possible that she knew that her husband was going to turn his daughter away from her home? At this thought Judith's heart seemed " to turn over," as the old expressive phrase is, and a chill as of age and hopelessness came to the girl. She had worked so hard. She had always denied herself everything. And now they did not care for her. Her mother had forsaken her. They had planned this.

Judith went up-stairs to her own room. She looked at the two or three cheap, worn gowns that belonged to her. She would not take them. Perhaps they might be good enough to make over for one of her sisters. Her scanty and shabby belongings in the old bureau—no, she would take nothing. She felt as if she were going to die, and should never need anything more. She took a scrap of paper from the cheap portfolio that a cousin had once given her. She stood a moment, with that and a pencil in her hand, gazing about her room. This room had a slanting roof and one window. If she should live a thousand years she would never forget the scene from that window. In heaven there could not be anything so dear as the sight of the stretch of low hills with birches on them, birches which had been cut off several times since she could remember, but which grew so fast that she hardly missed them before they were tall shrubs again, with bits of song-sparrows singing in them. She looked a moment intently through this window. Then she wrote on the paper :

"DEAR MOTHER,—Father has told me to go. Perhaps you want me to go. I shall leave the money that I earned at the Joyces in the right-hand corner of the lower bureau-drawer."

Having written thus, she hesitated a moment before adding :

" I thought I was right about giving back the money for the seraphine. I couldn't seem to bear it that we should get money in that way. Good-bye. I love you just the same."

Here she hesitated again. Then she wrote, her pencil bearing down blackly and heavily :

" Oh, mother, I love you just the same!"

VII

UNDER ANOTHER ROOF

Judith carefully placed this paper on the bureau. She put the money in the drawer she had mentioned. Then she suddenly pressed her hands over her face, standing still in the middle of the room. Then she hurried down the stairs and left the house by a door which would not lead her near where she had seen her father. She ran across that place where she had worked in her vegetable garden the summer before, and so out into the road. She went on towards the village. She had not yet begun to think where she should go. Any of the neighbors would take her in for a few days; she was sure of that. She thought of Mrs. Guild. But Mrs. Guild had plainly believed she had been taking too much upon herself when she had interfered in the plan concerning the seraphine. She hastened on somewhat blindly. Perhaps a plan would come to her. She must get work as soon as possible. There were rumors that the shoe business was going to "start up." Some of the factories would soon be running again.

The Eldridge factory was the largest ; it was there where she had worked as a stitcher, and she had earned very good wages, too, or she could not have done even as much as she had done for her family. She would go there now and make inquiries. She would have to take a room somewhere. She was walking so fast that she was nearly running. A film, not of tears, but it seemed of sheer suffering, was over her eyes. She could only see vaguely the way before her, and that it was filled with the red sunlight from the west. A glossy Irish setter strolled across the road in front of her, and the girl almost fell over him.

"Here, Random; come here, sir!" called a man's voice from the field. "What do you mean by tripping people up in that way?"

The dog ran into the field, and young Eldridge jumped over the wall and came towards the girl. He had a handful of roses in his hand, and he was looking eager and delighted.

"I was coming over to call in state," he began, "and to present these flowers to your mother. I— Why, Judith, what has happened to you?" He held out his hand, and she put hers in it. "Are they all well?" quickly.

"Yes, thank you, as usual."

Judith could not look at him. She was very sorry she had met him. She glanced down the road, as if she were thinking of running away.

"Then what is it? But don't you want to tell me?"

"I think I'd rather not tell now," avoiding his eyes.

"But perhaps I may help you. Judith, don't you know how I would like to help you?"

"But you can't—you can't."

"Don't be so sure."

"Oh, I know you can't. Now I must go. I'm in a hurry." She started on; but she turned back to say, "I know you are kind. But you mustn't be kind. I can't bear it. I shall break down, and I mustn't break down." She hastened on.

The young man stood where she had left him for a moment. But the dog galloped towards the girl for a few rods, then returned a little as if to invite his master to follow him; and Eldridge did follow. In a moment he was again by Judith's side. His face was red, and his eyes shone with his earnestness. "It's no use, Judith Grover, for you to try to run away from me like this when you are in trouble. I won't have it. I will help you, whether you'll let me or not."

Judith would not pause, and she could not weigh her

words. "I tell you you can't. No one can. I—I— Oh, Lucian Eldridge, I wish I hadn't met you now!" Her voice broke a little. "Won't you go away?" She turned her face towards him, but she did not lift her eyes. "Please go away."

He could not mistake her tone. But he was almost ready to run the risk of incurring her displeasure. He hurried on beside her for a few yards. Suddenly she paused. She put out her hand and rested it on his arm. She was conscious of the perfume of the flowers in the young man's hand, and it was strange to her that she could be conscious of such a thing in her suffering.

"You're as good as you can be," began the girl, in a halting voice, "but you know there are some things that we have to bear alone. I'm just as grateful— Oh, won't you go now?"

Eldridge suddenly thrust his bunch of roses at his companion, compelling her to take them. Then the two separated, each hurrying, as if flying from the other. It was a long walk to the village, and Judith believed that she would surely have time to make some plan, if only of the most temporary kind, before she reached there. But she found that she could not think. Thought was drowned in a strange, astonished suffering. When she came to the main street she paused an instant, trying to decide whether to go to the Eldridge factory or right on towards Mr. Guild's. Then she remembered that the factory would be closed, for it was after sunset now, and the long June twilight was beginning. She turned towards the right. She began to meet people who nodded to her and said "'twas a pleasant evening." They looked at her roses in surprise. She was so afraid they would ask her some question that she barely replied to their salutations, not pausing a moment. It was the time of day when everybody who could do so strolled out-of-doors.

There was Mr. Macomber coming along, with his exaggerated, rolling gait. Judith knew that she could not es-

"OH, WON'T YOU GO NOW?"

cape his questions if she met him. She glanced at her right and left—no, there was no escape. She went swiftly on, but he stood directly before her. "You're in a dretful hurry, ain't ye, Judith?" he asked. "I wanted to see ye. I wanted to ask what makes ye take such a stand 'bout that seraphine. Lucindy, she was in hopes we sh'd git it."

"How is Mrs. Macomber?" asked Judith, quickly.

"She ain't very well. Her asthmy's come on. I was goin' to the store, 'n' I thought I'd stop in 'n' ask Mis' Jessop if she wouldn't set with her for a spell. But I want to ask you why—"

"I'll go and stay with your wife," here broke in the girl. "So you needn't speak to Mrs. Jessop."

She did not wait for the man to make any reply. She sprang on as if she had found a momentary relief. She turned in at the gate of the little Macomber house, and walked through the kitchen into the sitting-room, where she found the mistress of the place sitting in a large chair, with pillows behind her and a footstool at her feet.

The old, patient face turned towards the new-comer. "Why, Judith," she wheezed, "I'm real glad to see ye! Set right down. I'm havin' one of my spells."

The girl sat down. She pushed her hat back. She felt like pressing her hand to her heavily beating heart, but she was afraid that would be too dramatic. Her hostess would "think strange."

Mrs. Macomber gazed at her, her tired eyes at last taking in something out of the ordinary in Judith's appearance. "There ain't nothin' happened, has there?" she inquired. And then, without waiting for an answer, she went on, pausing every now and then for breath: "I was real sorry when Ellis brought back the money for our guesses that you give him. I was in hopes we should have got the seraphine. I always did want a piece of music, though we can't play, either of us."

Judith did not reply. Mrs. Macomber was so mild and

weak in character that the girl could not feel angry, and
a definite wish had suddenly formed itself in her mind.

"Is any one using your front chamber?" she asked.

The woman's short breath grew shorter in her astonishment.

"No," she answered.

"Will you let it to me?"

No answer for a moment, during which time Mrs. Macomber stared absorbedly.

"Yes," she said at last, "I'll let it if Ellis don't object,
'n' I guess he won't."

"I'll take it, then," promptly responded the girl. "I'll
take it to-night. I hope the rent won't be much?"

She looked inquiringly at her companion.

"I guess twenty-five cents a week will do," was the answer. "Goodness gracious!"

Having uttered this exclamation, Mrs. Macomber's strain-
ing breath entirely prevented her from speaking for a while.
When she was a little easier Judith said:

"I wish you wouldn't ask me any questions — I can't
talk about it. I shall stay here, if I can. Father"—here
the speaker's voice entirely failed her — "father and I
have had a misunderstanding. No, I mean "—with intense
bitterness —"I mean that I understand him now better
than I ever did. He doesn't want me to live at home. I
should go farther away, only I must be where I can take
care of mother and the children—I must see to them. I
thought if you'd let me get my meals by your stove, and
have your chamber—and I'm pretty sure of a job at stitching when business starts up—"

"Goodness gracious!" cried Mrs. Macomber again.

"Please don't!" pleaded the girl.

"There! there!" gasped the woman, "I won't bother you
now, you poor thing! You jest set still, 'n' we won't try
to talk now. I guess things 'll come out right bime-by."

"I've got to bear things, whether they come out right or
not," was the answer.

So the two sat there in silence while the June day deepened into night. They heard the voices of a few people as they passed by the house. Once a cat set up a distressed mewing in the cellar and Judith let her in, and, under her companion's directions, gave her a saucer of milk. At last, just as the clock was striking nine, Mr. Macomber's unmistakable step was heard in the road.

Judith started. "I'll go up-stairs," she said, quickly. "Don't let him question me, please, Mrs. Macomber!"

In her haste she did not take a lamp, but she found her way. She would not go back for a light lest she might be asked something, and every word on the subject of her leaving home was like a pressure on a wound. She groped and fumbled until she was in the bit of a room under the roof. She found the bed, and laid herself down upon it. She laid upon her back and clasped her hands over her breast, lying motionless, while her brain seethed and throbbed.

VIII

THE HEAD OF THE HOUSE

JUDITH had a kind of terrible comfort in her position upon the couch. It was as if she were dead. All the dead people she had seen had been lying in this way. But they did not have thoughts of fire that made life intolerable. Their brains were cool.

The girl felt keenly the disgrace of being turned out of her home. It was a disgrace; it must be, even though it was a man like her father who had done it. Some people, of course, would always believe she had in some way deserved such a thing. And her mother and the children? Over and over, as if it were some mechanism that started the repetition, went the words: "Was mother willing to have me turned out? Was mother willing to have me turned out?" Even when she was trying to make plans for the future these words would not stop. "I've got to help them just the same. Father won't take care of them. I shall do it. Poor mother! Dear mother! Oh, was she willing to have me turned out?"

Thus the girl lay there. She would not change her position. To her morbid state there was an unwholesome comfort in that attitude. And at last she fell asleep. When she awoke she was shivering with cold. She rose and crept into the bed, only taking off her shoes, and huddling down desolately among the feathers, which rose up warmly about her. The kitchen clock and then the town clock struck three. It was already growing light. The long June day was beginning. She would not go to sleep again. She was brushing her hair at five o'clock, hearing the incessant, gruff hum of Mr. Macomber's voice below. She knew that he would soon start out and go through the village with his news. And she wondered if she could stay in the town. But she must stay. She could get work here, and she must be near her mother and the children. They would need her. If it were not for them she would go that morning, she did not care where.

Presently she heard the voice of her hostess at the foot of the stairs. The asthma fit was over, and she was calling Judith to come down to breakfast. The girl finally yielded to the kind insistence. She sat down at the table with the two. Evidently Mr. Macomber had been instructed by his wife, for though he looked as if ready to explode he did not ask a question. Indeed, he did not speak save to say "Butter?" interrogatively, when he passed that article to his guest.

At seven Judith went to the factory. Mr. Macomber, sitting with his wife in the kitchen, looked at her and then said "I swow!" with so much force that the very house appeared to vibrate in response.

"I ain't goin' to say nothin' more 'bout the Grovers," remarked Mrs. Macomber. "I've told you every word I know, over 'n' over."

Whereupon Mr. Macomber lighted his pipe, put on his hat, and started out. He felt that there were some delightful hours before him.

Judith thought she was in luck. Work was starting up. She could begin the next day. She could hardly wait to be at her place in the buzzing stitching-room. She would be obliged to put her mind on her work. That would be something. She felt as if the day would never end. She spent nearly all of it in her room. She could not bear to go out, for she did not wish to meet any one. She sat at the window and looked along the road over which she had come the night before. All day she watched, hoping to see a thin, bent, woman's figure walking on the highway, and coming towards her.

Her mother would read the note she had left, and she would come to see her. Surely her mother would come to see her. But the day passed, and no one came. She reasoned that her mother would start, and that any one could tell her where Judith Grover was staying, for Mr. Macomber had been through the village with his news.

At seven o'clock the following morning Judith was at her stitching-machine, and the hum of the machinery was in her ears. Her heart had grown very bitter within the last twenty-four hours. She was continually telling herself, " I thought mother loved me." And then she would add, " I must save all my money for them just the same. Father won't support them. He's got his liver to take care of." Her lip curled. A hard gleam came into her eyes.

When she went back to her room that night she paused with something like tenderness before the bowl which Mrs. Macomber had loaned her for the flowers. She bent over them ; the fragrance had changed from freshness to that scent which belongs to fading roses. Their heads were hanging over. All their brilliance was gone. The girl hesitated an instant, then she lifted the whole cluster and pressed her face down among the petals. But she put back the flowers hastily, and with a movement of great decision. She straightened herself and walked to the window. Her dark, richly colored face had an austere look upon it as she stood there.

After a few moments she went down-stairs, borrowed a pail, and started to Mrs. Jessop's for some milk. She had brought some crackers with her when she came from the shop. She made her supper of crackers and milk. She could not buy the two or three things she needed to cook with until she had earned some money.

Judith had decided what she would say to any one who questioned her—" Father and I have had a misunderstanding "—and she would say no more. This she told Mrs. Jessop. Every time she spoke that sentence she felt that her anger against her father grew stronger.

After her supper that evening she left the house and called at the few places where she had not returned the money for the guesses. The last house was the Eldridge home. She dreaded going there. It seemed to her that she could not go. But she kept straight on to the large house, the only mansion in the village. She rang the bell. Even then she wished to turn and run down the path that led between the tall syringas. But she stood still, her girlish figure half hidden by the vine that climbed over the lattice. By the time she heard footsteps in the hall she believed herself quite composed.

The door was opened by the younger Eldridge daughter, who exclaimed, "Oh, how do you do, Miss Grover? Come in."

The girl in the doorway, dressed in some light, flowing morning-gown, smiled with something like her brother's ease; and her smile resembled his.

"No, I thank you," was the prompt reply, spoken in a monotonous voice, for Judith had composed her speech and adhered strictly to it. "I called to hand back this money which Mr. Eldridge and Mr. Lucian paid for guesses. We have decided not to carry out that plan."

Miss Eldridge took the money in silence. She was looking at the girl before her in a bewildered way. There was a cold, decisive air, a sort of high, reserved expression that she did not in the least understand, but that made Judith Grover in her eyes something different.

Judith did not linger. She hurried down the syringa walk, breathing the heavy evening perfume of those flowers as if it were a wine of relief to her. She should get out of the grounds without seeing Lucian. She was sure if she should see him now, and he should be kind to her as he had been—

"Judith! Judith, I say! Why do you rush on like that?"

The young man came hastily forward, his straw hat in his hand, the warm smile in his eyes which Judith was frightened to think seemed to be a smile that belonged to her alone.

"I rush on because I'm in a hurry," she answered, hardly pausing in her walk as she spoke.

"I can take a sprint myself," he responded, placing himself beside her, and falling into step as if he had been waiting all day for this moment.

The two walked on without speaking until they were on the road. Eldridge's face had grown more and more grave until it was nearly as serious as that of his companion.

Finally he turned towards the girl and exclaimed, abruptly, "Judith, are you in trouble? Won't you let me comfort you? I want to help you. You must let me be a friend to you."

The girl wondered if he knew how gentle his voice was. She kept an unyielding control of her face. She thanked him in the most proper manner. She said he was very kind, but she thought she could take care of herself. And she did not particularly need any comfort. She should keep very busy.

For answer, Eldridge suddenly moved forward and placed himself in front of her. She stopped, perforce, and looked up at him. Their eyes met, and for an instant the woman's eyes held the man's gaze.

Eldridge mistily and deliciously asked himself how eyes could be so uttterly what he had been longing for all his life. And he had found them here, in his old home, and little Judith Grover was the owner of them. How strange it all was! And how intensely delightful!

But his old playfellow was not little any longer. She was tall, she was lovely of figure, she was— Why, how was it possible that there should be a certain opulent magnificence in this girl's presence? She was shabby; she certainly was not in the least stylish. What was it, then? With a quick movement Judith turned away.

"Good-bye, Lucian," she said. "I'm going in here." She hurried towards the next house.

The young man knew that he must not wait for her; there had been a decided dismissal in her manner. He went back into the grounds of his own home. He strolled there in the gathering dusk, the odors of the warm twilight deepening the mood that was upon him. When he heard the voices of his sisters as they came towards him he walked quickly away in an opposite direction.

As for Judith, she scrupulously kept on with her self-appointed task, and before it was really dark she had finished the returning of the money.

When she entered the Macomber house she lingered with the two occupants a few moments, hoping they would tell her that her mother had been there. But no. She went up the steep stairs, her heart aching, and at the same time growing hard. She sat down by the table where the fading roses stood. She leaned forward in her chair until her forehead rested on the Bible which was near the roses.

"I thought mother loved me," she said, in a whisper. Then, with a sort of triumphant tenderness, "She'll have to let me help her, anyway. I shall always love to help her." After a while she rose, took the flowers from the bowl, went to the open window and flung them out. "They're withered," she said.

At the same time, three miles away, on the Grover farm, the children had been put to bed. They had confided to each other that "Ma was so odd they didn't know what to make of her. 'N' 'twas so lonesome they didn't care what became of them." Then they had gone to sleep.

Mr. Grover was sitting in his favorite place just outside of the "end door." He had the best chair placed on the grass there, and he was leaning comfortably back in it with his feet on a small wooden "cricket." He had eaten a copious supper of ham and potatoes. There would be some rump-steak for breakfast. He had bought three bottles of the elixir, the ham, and the steak, and he still had a dollar and a half of the five dollars which young Eldridge had "advanced"; for he called the money advanced to him. He liked that phrase.

He had just told his wife that he thought the elixir "Stimerlated his liver in about the right degree. A person always had to be careful and not stimerlate too much. The man who made the elixir knew what he was up to; there was no mistake about that."

To these remarks Mrs. Grover had only replied by something inarticulate. She was sitting in a hard chair just within the door, and was leaning her head against the casing, gazing out beyond her husband into the semi-darkness. She was thinking of Judith, but she did not speak of her. She had not spoken of her after that night when the girl had left.

Mr. Grover seemed in much better spirits when his eldest daughter was absent, and in particularly good spirits now. He did not worry. He believed that he should be taken care of. In his own words, he was confident that "the Lord would provide." The presence of Judith, who worked hard and spent her money for him and his family, and who did not approve of him, was not agreeable.

When he had told the girl to go that night he had not done so from premeditation, but the words had come as a sudden and natural sequence to his anger against her. He had not regretted them to any degree. He had sat still and seen her walk away from the house by the back door. Of course he thought she would soon come back, say, in a week or two, and he still thought so. He had heard her go up the stairs to her own room, but he noticed that she did not take any bundle with her. Of course she was coming back "before long."

After a few moments he began to be curious as to what she had done in her room. He hesitated a little; then he rose and looked towards the pasture. His wife was not coming. He hurried up the stairs. The chamber was towards the west, and it was still light. He scanned the room. He saw the scrap of paper on the bureau, and he made haste to read it. Of course he would read it. Wasn't this his own house?—though Judith always paid the interest on the mortgage—and wasn't it his own daughter who had written the note? True, it happened to be written to his wife, but he was the head of the family. Having read the few words Judith had pencilled, he immediately opened the bureau-drawer and took the money she had mentioned. This also was his, for the husband was the head of the house.

IX

A NEW-COMER

It had always been very trying to Mr. Grover that Judith had chosen to give the money she earned to her mother. It was true that he had usually taken a great deal of it away from his wife. Of late the girl had kept more of her money in her own possession and supplied the wants of the family from it. This also was very trying. Now, having read this note and taken this money, of course he could not inform his wife of the fact. But he was not going to lie. He never did lie.

When Mrs. Grover came down from the pasture she hoped the storm had blown over. She asked where Judith was. Mr. Grover said he didn't know.

Was she coming back that night?

Mr. Grover didn't know, but he rather guessed not. They had had some words, he said. The girl was not as respectful as she ought to be to her "pirent." Didn't the Bible say "Honor thy father"?

Mr. Grover did not seem as angry as his wife had thought he would be, in view of his state of mind when she left him. In fact, that gentleman was quite soothed, not to say exultant, thinking of the money he had in his pocket. It was a good while since he had had so much money. If the time came when it should be known how he had obtained these funds, and some particulars of this evening should be disclosed, he would revert, as usual, to his position as head of the house.

It must be acknowledged, however, that when he saw his wife's face that night after the lamp was lighted he was sorry for her. Not sorry enough to explain anything to her, but enough to feel himself quite a virtuous and tender-hearted man. And the next day he was still sorry. He went down to the village, being curious and interested himself. He came back and informed his wife that Judith was stopping with the Macombers; he supposed when she got ready she would come home. Indeed, Mr. Grover wondered how much in earnest he had been when he turned the girl out of the house, and how high a stand he ought to take on the subject. He had learned that Judith had said that she and her father had had a misunderstanding. In view of this remark of hers it seemed as if he could give almost any explanation.

Mrs. Grover heard him in silence on his return. She was sitting with the youngest child, a girl of three years, on her lap. The child was leaning her head on her mother's shoulder. The head was hot and the eyes dull. After a while the mother laid her burden down on the lounge. She tried to go about some household duties, but everything went wrong.

As she passed back and forth in the room she saw through the window her husband's figure sitting in the pleasant shade of the lilacs while she worked. Gradually her lips became compressed, and a red spot came upon each cheek. It seemed to her that the sufferings of years were all rising before her and making themselves felt again. She recalled herself as she had been when she taught school and was considered " dressy."

She glanced down at her checked shirting apron. Then she looked again through the window at her husband. Something, she did not know what, was beating in her pulses and making her blood hot. She felt as if she had not seen Judith for months. Judith's father must have said something very bad to make her stay away like this. She must see Judith. Suddenly she put down the broom with which she had been sweeping and walked out-of-doors to where Mr. Grover was sitting.

He wondered why she was coming with such an air of
resolution. He did not wish to be disturbed just then.
The process of digestion, aided by the elixir, was going on
in a very comfortable manner. His wife came and stood
directly in front of him. He hitched his chair a little and
frowned.

"Hanford," said the woman, "I want to know what you
said to Judith. You've got to tell me. 'Tain't like her to
stay away so."

"I told her," answered Grover, emphatically, "that she
wa'n't honorin' thy father. I told her to remember what
her Bible said. She got some mad. I ain't above confess-
in' that I lost my temper a little. I'm a human bein', 'n' I
lost my temper."

"Was that all you said?"

Mrs. Grover had folded her arms and was standing straight-
er than was usual with her. The sight of her thus erect was
extremely irritating to her husband.

"That was about the heft of it," he answered.

Then he tried to absorb himself in the contemplation of a
distant point in the landscape.

"I don't see how that could be all," she responded.
"'Tain't like Judith to go off 'n' stay, 'n' not send any word
to me. You're sure she didn't send any word to me?"

The wistful and yet desolate tone in which this question
was put did not affect Mr. Grover otherwise than to make
him more impatient.

"No, she didn't," he snapped.

Mrs. Grover stood a moment longer. Her eyes were
smarting and her breath was coming quickly.

"I s'pose you know," she said at last, trying to appeal to
the man in a vulnerable place, "that Judith's all the support
we've got."

"Mebby she is. But if she is, she'd better remember
what the Bible says 'bout honorin' pirents. Besides, I guess
the Lord will provide. Ain't we taught that the Lord will
provide, Mis' Grover?" When he wished to be particu-

larly impressive Hanford always called his wife "Mis' Grover."

There was no answer to this question. Mr. Grover crossed
and uncrossed his legs, and again tried to find a point in
the landscape which would really absorb his mind. After a
moment Mrs. Grover went back into the house. She worked
so hard that day, and the next, and the next, that the moment she laid herself down on the bed she fell asleep from
sheer exhaustion.

One afternoon when Judith had been away nearly a week
one of the little girls came home from school and said she
had seen Judith, that the elder sister had been waiting for
her at the corner, had hugged her and most cried, and had
given her this, and told her to be sure and not lose it, but
to give it to mother. "This" was a silver dollar, warm and
moist from lying tightly clutched in the child's palm.

Upon receiving the money Mrs. Grover had burst into
tears. She said "it wa'n't no use; she was going to see
Judith that very night." She rose from the supper-table,
pushing back her chair with a rebellious movement. Mr.
Grover stamped his foot heavily.

"Priscilla!" he cried, "don't you stir one step!"

The woman paused. She glanced at her husband. There
was that hard, domineering look in his eyes which had always made her afraid, always controlled her.

"She's a disrespectful child," he went on. "Let her be!
Let her be, I say. If she wants to come 'n' ask my forgive-
ness, why, let her come."

This thought came to the man, and he immediately decided that this would be a good stand to take. He repeated his last sentence, and he added that he hoped his wife
understood what he meant. "There wa'n't goin' to be no
runnin' after that girl. The husband was the head of the
house. The wife's place was to obey."

Mrs. Grover turned away. She went blindly out of the
room. She wanted to be alone, but she had no place
where she would not be disturbed. She snatched her sun-

bonnet from its nail in the kitchen and went out of the house. She did not care where she went. Her whole heart longed for her daughter. She hurried across the road and into a field that sloped upward until it was merged into a pine wood.

After a few moments she paused, and from this height she gazed along the road that led to the village. There was no one visible. Yes, far away was a horse and wagon, but she hardly noticed it. She was longing for the sight of a girlish figure. She could almost think that this very longing for Judith would bring her child to her. It was late in the afternoon, but the sun was still fully an hour high. By this time Judith was out of the shop. Perhaps she was sitting in that chamber at the Macombers'. How strange for Judith to be there!

Mrs. Grover wished that she had not spoken of going to see her daughter. Then she would not have been forbidden. As she recalled her husband's face of a moment ago she felt that she hated him almost as much as she feared him. She knew that she should not dare to disobey him. But Judith had never been afraid of him. And Judith had generally been able to keep up an appearance of respect.

She looked down towards the house. She saw her husband walking about in the yard. He had on his long linen duster and his tall hat. At sight of him a wild fury rose in the woman's heart.

But it was a useless, objectless fury; she knew that very well. She would always remain with him; always sacrifice herself for him. She had begun by effacing herself early in her married life, and she could never assert herself again, not even for Judith; no, not even for Judith.

This knowledge made the woman still more furious. The knowledge of her own weakness, which she could not overcome, seemed as if it would drive her mad. Perhaps she would never see Judith again, and there she was, only at the village.

Mrs. Grover's eyes were fixed dully on the horse and

wagon which, from ill-defined objects, had grown plainer and plainer. There was one person, a man, in the wagon, and Mrs. Grover saw that he bowed to her. She tried to put her mind on him. Did she know him? He had stopped his horse and was hitching him to the fence. He sprang over the fence and came striding up the hill.

"I thought 'twas you," he said, holding out his hand. "Is Judith to home?"

He looked eagerly down to the house as he spoke.

"Why, Tom Rylance!" was all that Mrs. Grover said.

X

LITTLE EM

Mrs. Grover shook the young man's hand, and then dropped it. He withdrew his gaze from the house and looked at his companion, showing long, well-opened gray eyes that were apparently somewhat out of place in his thick-set face, with its heavy jaw and heavy mouth. He was dressed evidently in his best—a ready-made suit that did not fit him, and which would have made even Lucian Eldridge look awkward; his checked red-and-blue necktie was arranged with great care, and had evidently been selected as appropriate to a state of being dressed in one's best.

"Is Judith to home?" he repeated, after a moment.

"No, she ain't."

"Are you expectin' her?"

"No."

"She must be out of the shop by this time." Rylance turned and looked down the road.

Mrs. Grover was trying to command her voice so that she might reply. "She ain't livin' to home now," she answered. There was even more in her tone than in her words.

"What's the trouble?" quickly inquired the young man.

"She 'n' her father have had some misunderstandin'."

"What? You don't go 'n' take sides ag'inst her, do you, Mis' Grover?" Rylance's face grew red.

"No, I don't. But, then, he's my husband, you know."

Rylance made no response. He presently asked, "Where is she?"

"They say she's stoppin' at the Macombers'. You see, she interfered— Oh, I don't know what I shall do!"

"Don't cry, Mis' Grover!" said the young man, helplessly. He wanted to hurry away.

"Are you going to see her?"

"Yes."

"Give her my love; oh, Tom, do give her my love! Tell her her father don't think it's best for me to go 'n' see her now. Stop a minute. Be you goin' right 'long?"

"Yes."

The woman caught hold of Rylance's arm. She clung to it regardless of the fact that her husband, walking about in the yard, could see her. "Tom," she said, "you make her know that I love her, won't you? You be sure 'n' make her know that. Tell her I wanted to come 'n' see her, but Mr. Grover he didn't think 'twas best. A woman's got to obey her husband, you know."

"I'll tell her; I'll be sure 'n' tell her," replied Rylance. Then he hesitated, but resolved to give up the hope of seeing Judith alone if her mother would go with him. "Come," he said, with energy, "you ride right over with me 'n' see Judith, 'n' I'll bring you back. Of course, Mr. Grover won't care. I'll go 'n' tell him."

"No, I can't go. You don't know how 'tis, Tom. 'Tain't best for me to go. I d' know how it's comin' out, I'm sure. I s'pose it's a woman's place to submit."

Rylance hastened down to his horse. In a moment he was driving away.

Mr. Grover beckoned to his wife. Slowly she retraced her steps until she had entered the yard. "What's Tom Rylance round here for?" he asked, sharply.

"He came to see Judith." Mrs. Grover did not look at her husband as she answered him.

"Is he courtin' her?"

"I don't know," dully.

"Women don't know anything!" burst out Mr. Grover. "I hope she won't encourage that Rylance. The Rylances are poor as poverty. I tell you what 'tis: I've made up my mind that young Eldridge 's got his eye on Judith."

But even this information did not rouse Mrs. Grover; it might have done so if she had believed it. She stood looking at her husband in silence.

Mr. Grover was walking about, his hands thrust into the pockets of his duster, which flew back as he moved. "Them Rylances!" he exclaimed; then he glanced at his wife and concluded to say no more. You couldn't expect to make women understand things.

It was that evening, while Mrs. Grover sat holding her youngest child, who still seemed ailing, that Lucian Eldridge carried out his intention of calling on Judith's mother. Mr. Grover was smoking at the door. He sometimes smoked, for he said it was good for digestion.

A horseman came galloping from the direction of the village. He galloped in at the yard and dismounted. Young Eldridge came gayly forward. He had another bunch of roses which he had brought for Mrs. Grover. He insisted upon going by the man in the doorway. He found Mrs. Grover, and put the roses in the lap of the child she was holding.

Hanford followed him. He was very sweet to the young man, and when the visitor had gone he exclaimed, "There! What d' I tell you, Priscilla? That feller didn't come here jest for your sake. If Judith only works her cards right—"

But the woman said nothing. She felt sick, and a cloud of depression settled down upon her. She had given up hoping that Judith would come back; and again came the thought that she might never see her again. The child she was holding became more feverish and fretful. If Judith were only there the burden of work and responsibility would be shifted to her young shoulders. As the evening deepened into night the woman still sat holding the little girl who moaned and cried out when the mother tried to put her on the bed.

Mr. Grover retired at his usual time. Before going he

suggested that Priscilla have one of the other children steep some catnip tea for the sick child. Then he sought his couch and slept soundly until he was roused by having his arm pulled by some one. He resented this; he said it was injurious to be roused from a sleep.

"You've got to go for the doctor, Hanford," said his wife. "You've got to go right off. Em's got a sore throat. She's sick."

Mr. Grover rose. He said it was a pity that a man couldn't rest in his bed nights. He grumbled all the time he was dressing, but he started out on his errand. When he had reached the gate his wife called to him. "Don't you think we'd better have Judith come home?" she asked. "I d' know what we shall do without her."

"If Judith's sorry for what she's done—" answered Mr. Grover. Then he hurried on. He did not stop at the Macomber house, though he went by it on his way to the doctor's.

At a corner a horse came trotting briskly round. It was young Eldridge in the saddle. He was just returning from a long ride. He saw the linen duster and the tall hat, and recognized them. He pulled in his horse.

Mr. Grover's first thought was to make a person useful to him. It was more than half a mile to the doctor's. He explained his errand to Eldridge and asked him to go. It was for this reason that this young man was able to tell Judith, when he met her the next noon coming from the factory, that the little one at her home was ill.

Judith's dark face turned pale. "What! little Em?" she cried. She clasped her hands.

Yes, it was the youngest; the one to whom Judith felt like a mother. Had she not always had the care of the child?

The girl's first impulse was to turn and run towards her home. Then she remembered that she had been "turned out." And now her face grew red. Her eyes flashed fire. She felt the sympathetic gaze of her companion, and it somehow made things more tolerable, at the same time that it seemed to take her strength away from her.

"I'll get my horse and buggy, and take you right over," said Eldridge. "You're too tired to walk."

"No, I can't go," she answered, coldly. She drew herself together. But she was longing to tell her companion that she was turned out. Instead, she exclaimed, in a low voice, "It's dreadful to have such a father as I have!" She clinched her hands. She thought of how he was keeping her now from little Em. "I think I know how murderers feel," she said.

Eldridge was shocked at the violence of her words.

She would not linger longer. She went back to the factory. She remained there all the afternoon, and she sat in her room until it was dark in the evening. Then she left the house. She told Mrs. Macomber she would take the front door-key, as she might be out until ten.

Once in the road she sped along towards her home. She supposed it was because Em was sick that she felt so strange—so bowed down with a strong fear.

XI

"I WANT MY JUDE!"

ONCE out in the beauty of the evening Judith for a few moments felt more calm. The soft sweetness of the air unconsciously soothed her. She did not hurry, as she had intended doing. She was able to think now that no one had told her that her baby sister was dangerously ill. She could not believe that her mother would fail to send her word if Emmeline were very bad.

She went by Mrs. Guild's house. That lady was in the yard trying to fasten a blind in place. "That you, Judith?" she said, in some surprise. "Ain't you out ruther late for you? I was jest goin' to bed, 'n' then I knew I shouldn't sleep a wink if this blind kep' up a clatterin'."

Judith leaned on the fence as she answered. "And I knew I couldn't sleep if I didn't know how my little Em is to-night. I thought, perhaps, I could catch a glimpse of mother and ask her about the baby. I've heard they had diphtheria up to the other village."

Mrs. Guild came to the fence and leaned on it beside the girl. She looked at Judith sharply in the dusk. "Ketch a glimpse of your mother?" she said. "What do you mean? Ain't you goin' in over there?"

Mrs. Guild saw Judith's hands suddenly shut tightly as they rested on the fence. That impulse which we all feel to try to share our sufferings made Judith suddenly exclaim, passionately, "I can't go in there! Father's turned me out! Oh, I hate him! Mrs. Guild, I'm frightened at myself. I must be so wicked."

The woman did not speak for a moment. She was more

startled than she would confess. She had never seen Judith just like this before. She put her hand on the girl's shoulder. "Now, don't you worry," she said, gently, but with a feeling that she was very ineffective. "Things 'll come out right somehow. We all know what your father is. I s'pose he was mad 'cause you would pay back the money for the guesses?"

"Yes."

"Well, well. You know, Judith"—hesitating—"you do carry ruther a high hand sometimes."

The girl said nothing. Mrs. Guild could only repeat that she guessed things would come out all right.

"Yes," said Judith, "they may be right, but they may break our hearts, all the same." She turned to go away. She began to hurry now. She heard Mrs. Guild call after her, cheerily, "Don't be discouraged, Judith!" and she turned and waved her hand.

All at once the sense of haste grew upon her. She did not know how she had been able to linger talking with Mrs. Guild. She was near the entrance to a cart-path which led across a rocky pasture bordering on the ocean. If she took this path she would save nearly half a mile of the distance. She did not hesitate, but turned in and walked quickly, stumbling somewhat over the rough way.

It was not long before she met a young man who worked in the stitching-room at the factory with her. He glanced at her, and then glanced again as he said good-evening. He turned and asked if he shouldn't go with her. Was she going by the Great Rocks? Yes, she was. "That way is so lonesome, you ought to have company, Judith," he said.

"Oh no," answered the girl, "I'm not afraid. And I know the way so well that it doesn't seem lonesome to me."

She thought it was strange that she should meet still another acquaintance a short distance farther along. This also was a shop-mate, a girl who was almost running, and who paused long enough to say that "you never 'd ketch her in that path again in the evening." But Judith laughed at her.

As she went on she came nearer and nearer the shore, and the sound of the water grew more distinct. It was flood-tide, and with a wind off the land, so that the ocean made very little noise—only a sort of long sobbing among the pebbles of the beach.

Judith came out from among the scattering birches and pines, where it had been very dark, to the open, high pasture whence she could see the wide stretch of water lying blackly under the heavens, with now and then the glitter of a star upon it.

As she walked Judith's eyes were fixed on the ocean. She knew it as one knows an old friend whom one loves. The sight of it, dark, with the slow under-heave of its bosom, was like a restorative to the feverish mood of the girl. There was the faint gray glimmer of a small sail in an inlet that came pushing a short distance up into some marsh-land below. The sail was flapping idly, and the sound of the oars dipping in the water came plainly in the still, sweet air. Judith knew well the long, shallow beach where the boat would land.

It was scarcely nine o'clock, and the June day was not long since ended. Again Judith was conscious of that longing to have time to enjoy something. There was always upon her that stern, unrelenting grip of necessity. She was now very near her home. If it were lighter she would be able to see it off to her left, down from the cliffs. She looked wistfully towards it; she could see the shining of one light. That must be in the little bedroom where Emmeline was lying ill.

Judith was about turning to go down from the cliff when she saw some one hastening up. This person was a man, and the next moment she recognized her father. He had on his tall silk hat, but he had replaced his duster by a wool coat. She nodded to him, and was walking on. He stared at her in surprise. Then he said, "It's you, ain't it, Judith?"

"Yes. How's Em?"

Instead of replying, the man asked, "Was you comin' to tell me you was sorry for what you'd done?"

"No."

"I was tellin' of your mother that you'd got to say you was sorry for what you'd taken on yourself to do," said Mr. Grover, in a strident, domineering way. "You hadn't no right to do it. 'N' now your sister's sick we can't git her things nor pay the doctor 's we could if you hadn't meddled. You always pretended to think a lot of Em."

"Won't you tell me how Em is?" The girl's voice was hardly above a whisper, but it thrilled in strange contrast to that of the man.

"She's real sick."

Judith looked away. She could hardly tell whether her father was exaggerating or telling the simple truth. She turned back and forced herself to ask a favor of him, although the doing of it hurt her physically. "Will you let me go in and see my little Em? I'll help take care of her."

Judith's very heart was in her request. But Mr. Grover could not know that; he did not feel things in that way. And he thought it was an excellent time to show his authority and to discipline his daughter. "You jest tell me you're sorry you meddled in that seraphine business," he said, with a good deal of impressiveness.

Judith turned herself again towards the old house where the lamp burned. "No," she answered, "I can't tell you that, because I thought I did right. It wasn't fair to try to raise money in that way."

Mr. Grover began to say something violent. Then he bethought himself of his belief that young Eldridge had taken a fancy to Judith. If he had really done so, then it would be better for Mr. Grover if he should keep "on the right side" of his daughter. But he wanted to maintain his authority. He tried to infuse a little mild dignity into his manner. "Be you and Lucian Eldridge goin' to set up courtin'?" he asked.

Judith shrank back, sickened by the question. "No," she said, forcibly.

Mr. Grover's face grew black. He had had a feeling that it would be quite easy to get money from young Eldridge. If he and Judith were to "set up courtin'," why, it would be worth while for him, Hanford Grover, to reconsider his order to Judith to stay away from her home. And he did not know girls well enough to guess that a denial in such a case might mean absolutely nothing. "You're a disobedient, bad child," he cried out now, in a loud voice, "and don't you step your foot inside my house! Do you hear?"

"Yes, I hear." The girl's face was so pale that it looked almost luminous in the darkness.

Mr. Grover put his stick down sharply on the ground. He made such a quick movement to go on that he almost fell over the cliff. Judith started forward and caught his arm. He shook her off and straightened himself. "You're an ungrateful girl!" he shouted. He walked on farther away from his home.

Judith stood there alone a moment. She had both hands pressed to her bosom. Her face was turned towards the house, dimly seen below. She began to run down the steep path towards that house. Presently she was looking in at the window of the room where the light was. She saw Em lying propped up with pillows and her mother sitting close to the bed, holding the little hand and bending over the child. Em's face was drawn, and she was breathing heavily — that dear little face, which always brightened so at sight of Judith. The elder sister's eyes were fastened to that form on the bed. Em threw up her other hand. "Take me, mummer, take me!" she said. Judith heard the words through the open window.

Mrs. Grover bent over to lift the child. But the little one turned capriciously away, saying, hoarsely, "No; you don't carry me good. I want my old Jude! I want my Jude!" She began crying piteously, gasping and coughing as she did so. "Ain't Jude comin'?" she asked. "I don't want you. You ain't strong. Oh! Oh! I want my Jude!"

The plaintive voice, thickened by the throat disease, ended in a long wail. The girl watching outside saw the tears fall from her mother's face as it was bent over the child.

XII

SHE CLUNG TO IT AS SHE PRAYED

JUDITH shut her lips closely. She walked round to the back door. But here she paused a moment. In spite of what Mr. Grover so frequently asserted in regard to his daughter's not honoring her parents, she had grown up with the instinct and the desire to honor and obey them. That instinct of obedience was alive in her now, and it hurt her to do violence to it. She did not reason about it; she only felt wicked and sacrilegious in the act of disobeying. But she stepped over the threshold and hastened to the bedroom. The child's dull, half-closed eyes suddenly opened widely in a flash of happy recognition. She stretched out her arms, crying, " Here's Jude ! Jude, take me !"

In an instant the girl was beside the bed. She lifted the little form so dear to her, carefully wrapping a blanket about it. Her heart gave a great bound when she felt the childish arms go close round her neck. She began to walk about the room with her burden, singing softly under her breath.

Mrs. Grover sank back in her chair, her first emotion being one of relief and relaxation. She breathed a long breath. Judith had come. Things would all be right now. Em was " dreadful sick," but Judith would know how to take care of her. Then she suddenly remembered. " Oh, what will your father say ?" she exclaimed.

The daughter's strong glance met the appealing eyes of her mother. " Don't let's think of that now," she responded. " You see, I had to come when I heard Em was sick. Don't worry. I won't stay after she's better."

The little arms began to cling still more closely, and Em sent up a wail as she heard these words, half understanding them: "Oh, don't go, Jude! Stay with your baby!"

Mrs. Grover, worn out by the keen anxiety of the last few hours, covered her face with her hands and groaned. She could not put entirely away the thought of her husband and his displeasure. She had lived too many years under his control. His will had grown to be to her like some mighty thing overshadowing all her life, something which could no more be disputed than the will of God. And yet this woman had a larger mind, a larger nature in every way than belonged to the man who ruled her. But the gaze of that cold, selfish blue eye could quell her.

In a short time the sick child began to seem more comfortable. She rested in her sister's embrace, and drew strength from her. Judith continued to carry her about. Mrs. Grover, every few moments, would say, anxiously. "I wonder where your father is. You ain't heard him come in, have you?" And Judith would shake her head.

"I never saw him more set nor more tried in my life," said his wife. "You couldn't have done anything to make him madder."

To this the girl said nothing. She glanced wonderingly at the speaker. She was asking herself if all wives felt like this about their husbands when they really came to live with them. Should she feel thus if— Here she forcibly detached her thoughts from that subject and bent her flushed face over the little head on her shoulder. "When is the doctor coming again?" she asked.

"Early in the morning. He said Em was having a touch of diphtheria, but he hoped he could subdue it. He said it was going light up to the other village."

Judith could not at first speak for the dread in her heart. She had never seen any one ill with this disease, but it seemed to her that Em was very sick.

"Hanford was sorry he hadn't known what was the matter before," went on Mrs. Grover, as if stating an ordinary fact, "for he was afraid he'd been exposed already. He said he shouldn't come near the child again, for it wouldn't do for any one with such a liver as he has to be careless. He said 'twas a man's duty to take every care of himself. He's been out-doors a good deal since. I told him if he kept out-doors he'd stand the best chance not to have it."

Judith was silent. She sat down on the bedside with Em in her arms. Her mother looked at the clock and gave the child a spoonful of medicine. Em cried and sobbed and coughed, but finally swallowed the liquid. Then she fell asleep in her sister's arms, often starting up wildly and crying out that " Jude mustn't go."

Judith grew cold and stiff and aching, but she resolutely maintained her position. Sometimes she would listen for the sound of her father's footsteps, for she saw that her mother was listening.

It grew on to midnight, and Mr. Grover had not returned. Once Mrs. Grover lighted the lantern and went to the barn, thinking her husband might have come back and gone there for fear of infection.

A gentle south rain was beginning to fall, and the drops stood upon Mrs. Grover's gray hair when she came in from the yard with her light.

" Mother !" cried Judith, sharply.

The woman dropped her lantern with a crash. She ran forward. Em had suddenly flung up her arms. Her face grew purple. But her eyes had love in them as they turned to her sister. Judith was still holding her. She had sprung to her feet. That strain of agonized longing to help was upon her.

" My Jude !" said the child, hoarsely. She leaned towards her sister. She gasped. She stopped breathing.

The girl laid her burden down upon the bed. She straightened the little limbs that had always run to meet her. Her hands were cold and stiff, but they obeyed her will. When she raised herself from performing this duty she turned towards her mother.

The woman's poor, round-shouldered figure was lying on the floor near the door which she had reached when she had seen that never-to-be-mistaken look on the face of her baby. The sight had been too terrible for the tired, overworked mother, and she had fainted dead away.

As Judith knelt down by her she almost felt that it would be a pity to rouse her. For these few moments her mother was not suffering. The girl wondered at herself that she felt so calm. It seemed to her that she could do anything; she was conscious of what appeared a miraculous access of strength. She forgot all about her father. She only knew that she must take care of her mother. Little Em would never need her care again. She found the camphor in its place in the cupboard. She rubbed her mother's face and hands. She lifted her to the old lounge when she revived. She made her drink some currant-wine which she herself had bottled the previous summer.

When she recovered consciousness Mrs. Grover immediately girded herself. She must not give way again. She went and stood by the bed where the child lay. Judith came to her side and put her arm about her. The two looked down at the small, quiet, lovely face on the pillow.

Suddenly, notwithstanding all her efforts, Judith began to sob furiously with all the abandon of youthful sorrow. But her mother did not sob. She turned to her daughter and stroked her face. " You're my dear Judith," she whispered. " Cry—cry. I wish I could. But I'm too old. I ought to be where Em is gone."

" Oh, mother! mother!" Judith said no more. She resolutely put down the manifestation of emotion.

Very soon the two women were obliged to begin to discuss what should be done. Mrs. Grover had not allowed the other children to come near Em, and now they must be kept away. Judith would change her clothes, and take her sisters over to Mrs. Guild's. She was sure Mrs. Guild would let them stay awhile with her. There would be disinfecting to be done, and Em must be laid away. There could be no funeral. Everything must be arranged so that the disease need not spread.

Once Mrs. Grover exclaimed, "Where can your father be?"

Judith went to her room and prepared to go away with the children, and soon the three started out, the two younger so dazed that they could hardly ask questions.

Mrs. Grover stood at the door with the lamp in her hand. The mild rain was still falling. She saw the drops glitter on the umbrella which Judith tried to hold over her charges. They did not look back. They hurried on out of sight.

The woman was left alone with that form of Em which was lying on the bed. She went and stood beside it. The heart of the wife and mother turned involuntarily, but with a terrible sense of hopelessness, towards the husband and father. He was little Em's father. Surely, surely it was but natural that she should think of him. But if he were here he would be fearing that he might take the malady. But he would mourn—yes, he would mourn.

Then, dimly at first, but more and more brightly, the woman's mind grasped the sense of the presence of a greater Comforter—a Father whose love was sweet and strong and ever present. She believed in religion; she was a member of the church, and always went to meeting when she could. Still she could not but realize that she had never in her life so felt the sustaining of a Father's love. She knelt down by the bed. She took Em's hand. It had not yet grown cold. She clung to it as she prayed.

XIII

"YOU SEEN HIM LAST"

ALL the time she wished that her husband might be there to pray with her. She tried piteously to forget his absorption in himself, or to excuse it. When she rose she lighted the lantern and again went to the barn. She was anxious, but her anxiety was dulled by grief. Mr. Grover was not in the barn. Where could he be?

After she reached the house she held the lantern up to the clock. She saw that it was twenty minutes after one. Yes, if there were room in her mind she would be still more anxious. But one's emotional powers, whether for grief or joy, have their limitations.

The cat had come in with her and was rubbing against her ankles, purring loudly. Mrs. Grover felt that she could not endure that sound of comfort. She took up the cat and thrust her out into the rain. Then she immediately repented of what she had done. Em had been fond of her kitty. She opened the door, and the animal stepped in and began to purr again. Mrs. Grover looked down at it, saying aloud, "I guess I can bear a little thing like that."

She began to look forward to Judith's return. Over and over she said to herself that she didn't know what she should do without Judith. And when Hanford came back, would he recall his words and say that their daughter might come home?

But where was Hanford? How strange it all was tonight! Sometimes it seemed to the woman that everything was unreal, and presently she should find that her husband was there and that Em was not dead. Two or three times more she took her lantern, and, followed by the cat, she explored in every direction about the house. Once she went forward a short distance along the path towards the cliff.

The tide had turned to go out now; she knew by the change in the sound of the water against the Great Rocks. With a feeble iteration her mind dwelt upon the calculation as to how long it would take Judith to go the three miles to Mrs. Guild's with the children and to return. It seemed to the mother that she could not wait for her daughter to get back. That feeling of impatience for the girl's return gradually overrode all other emotion, growing more poignant with every moment.

As for Judith, every step that she took away from her mother was a pain to her. When she had reached Mrs. Guild's and roused her friend, told her story and seen the little girls taken into the house, she turned and began to run homeward. She was running against the rain now. The wind, still southerly, had risen somewhat.

Judith did not try to hold her umbrella open. She let the water fall on her face as she splashed through the puddles which were now forming in the road. She wished that it might rain still harder; she wanted to feel the rush of it on her cheeks, which burned hotly. At last, panting, she turned into the yard. There was the light just as it had been a few hours before. And now Em was gone.

Neither of the two women could ever think calmly of that night. And years after a warm south rain would always bring to Judith a keen memory of those hours and that same sickening throb of her pulses. At last the morning came—nay, it came soon these June days.

It was Judith who attended to everything. She went to a neighbor and had him dig the grave at the end of the garden. It was she who helped him put what was left of little Em down in the earth when the cheap coffin was brought. She was willing to help, and it was well that she felt so, for people were afraid to come near.

The rain spattered down on the coffin. With a morbid persistence Judith tried to think where she had seen the lines :

> " Blessed is the bride that the sun shines on ;
> Blessed is the corpse that the rain rains on."

Anyway, little Em was blessed. God had blessed her. He had taken her. That was well.

By the close of that day Judith was sitting alone with her mother in the kitchen. It was almost sunset. The rain was over. The clouds had formed themselves into long, parallel lines, and below them, on the very horizon, was a wide bar of bright amber light. It was fair, and it was going to be cooler. The robins were giving out short, clear calls among the old apple-trees.

Judith was sitting with her face shaded by her hand. She was wondering if Em could hear the robins. Was she where she could hear them and love them as she had heard and loved them the day before ?

"Judith," said her mother, suddenly, "you don't say anything about your father."

The girl roused herself. " No," she answered, " I don't know what to say, and I've been so bewildered. Things have happened so fast."

Mrs. Grover rose. She moved restlessly about the room. " I'm just as worried as I can be. We've got to do something, Judith."

The girl also rose now. " What shall we do ?" she asked. Then she added, hesitatingly, " Somehow it always seems as if nothing would happen to father. He'd be sure to take care of himself." She could not prevent the bitterness from coming into her voice.

" I guess we c'n go up on the cliffs 'fore it's dark, don't you ?" asked Mrs. Grover.

Judith walked to the back entry, where her hat hung. She took a small shawl and put it over her mother's shoulders. The two were just stepping out at the door when a man entered the yard and came quickly towards them. It was Mr. Guild.

"Walk right in," said Mrs. Grover, with mechanical hospitality. She set a chair for her guest. He took hold of the back of it instead of sitting down in it. He seemed to be trying not to glance at Judith.

"I hope there's nothing the matter with the children," said Mrs. Grover, hastily.

"No, oh no; there ain't nothin' the matter of them."

"The doctor said he thought we could get through the disinfecting so it would be safe for them to come home in a few days," said Judith. And she added, with a tremor in her voice, "It was so good of you and Mrs. Guild to take them. We sha'n't forget it."

"We ought to be neighborly, you know," responded the man. He kept looking furtively at Judith until at last she noticed the gaze. With an effort he withdrew his eyes. "I s'pose Mr. Grover's got home 'fore this, ain't he, Mis' Grover?" he asked.

"No, he ain't," was the answer. "Judith 'n' I were just going up to the cliffs. I'm most worried to death about him."

"Then you ain't heard?"

"Heard what?"

Mrs. Grover stepped forward and caught hold of Mr. Guild's arm. But Judith did not stir. When the man went home he told his wife that Judith never moved or spoke, and that he didn't know what to think of it.

"I don't b'lieve in bein' alarmed 'fore there's any occasion," now remarked Mr. Guild, in a voice that he tried to make judicial, "but—wall—some folks think mebby Mr. Grover's fell off the cliffs."

Here, in spite of a strong resolution to the contrary, the speaker turned and gazed with a strangely penetrating look at Judith. She returned the look with dilated, fearful eyes.

"It wouldn't be like him—" she began. Then something, she knew not what, in the man's face made her pause. A vague horror began to come over her.

"You seen him last, didn't you, Judith?" suddenly inquired Mr. Guild.

"I don't know whether I saw him last," she answered. "It was about nine o'clock when I met him on the cliffs, not far from the Great Rocks."

"I guess he ain't be'n seen sence," responded the man.

Mrs. Grover started towards the door. "Come, Judith," she said, "we can find him. P'raps he's fallen and broke his bones. I'd have gone for him before only I was expectin' him every minute, and—and you know how it's been."

"You needn't go," said Mr. Guild, in a voice that made Mrs. Grover grow whiter than ever. "There's five or six of us men be'n lookin'. 'Tain't no mercy to keep things back no longer. Se' down, Mis' Grover. 'Tain't no good to stand." He gently pushed the woman into her chair. She sat staring up at him as he went on. "You see, Ellis Macomber was comin' over the cliff-path this mornin'. He's always peekin' round to see what he c'n see. He was lookin' over the cliffs, 'n' he seen a hat lyin' up on the pebbles there. It looked kinder natural to him, bein' a tall silk hat. So he climbed down, 'n' he brought the hat back to the village. It didn't take him long to spread the story. A lot of us went down. We found Mr. Grover's cane wedged in among some stones jest as if it had be'n washed up 'n' lodged. There ain't no mistake 'bout the cane 'n' hat bein' Grover's. We've be'n lookin' most all day. We've telegraphed to the towns up 'n' down the coast here. Thought we would, though didn't think 'twas much use; 'n' 'twa'n't."

Mrs. Grover was twisting her hands together, her eyes on the speaker's face.

Judith was quiet. There was some blackness in this story which she had not yet fathomed. She was still wondering, in the midst of the shock she felt, as to what else was coming.

There was silence for a few moments. It was broken by Mr. Guild's turning to the girl and repeating, suddenly, his words, "You seen him last, I guess, Judith."

There was that in the tone with which these words were spoken that made Judith lift her head with a quick, curious feeling of self-defence. "I don't know whether I saw him last or not. I told you when I did see him, Mr. Guild."

At this the man gazed yet more intently at the girl. Then he suddenly set the chair which he had been holding forward with a crash on the floor. "I declare," he cried out, "I don't care a damn what folks are a mine ter say! I know what I think. What if you was on the cliffs with him? What if you 'n' he had said things? No; I tell ye I don't care one damn!"

A deep red rose to Judith's face, remained an instant, then subsided, leaving her white. But she still stood upright, gazing at Mr. Guild, who now, having relieved his mind, began to appear more like himself.

Mrs. Grover was still bewildered. She did not in the least know what the man's words had signified.

"Do they think my father is drowned?" Judith asked, at length. Mr. Guild nodded. "And do people think that I—"

Judith paused. The words she was about to say seemed impossible of utterance. But she was going to speak them.

Judith began again: "Do people think that I would do anything to hurt my father?"

Mr. Guild shuffled his feet about. "I don't b'lieve it's worth while to follow that up."

"Yes, I want to follow it up." she said.

"I guess that's about it," he replied, hesitatingly. "You see, everybody knows that you 'n' he have had a fallin' out. 'N' folks didn't blame you 'bout it. 'N' some folks think mebby you 'n' he got to quarrilin', 'n' you got excited, you know; 'n' you might have given him a little push, not mean-in' much; 'n' he, bein' on the edge there, jest toppled right over. That's the way some folks talk. 'N', you know, some things you said 'bout him yisterday, 'n' how you felt. 'N' there was William Mackay was goin' 'long the cliff last night, 'n' he heard your voices: 'n' he heard your father call you a disobedient, bad child, and tell you not to set foot in his house agin. 'N'—"

Here he paused, unable to go on, seeing the horror grow-ing in the girl's face. He turned and walked to the window. He saw the wide band of pale yellow sky beyond the line of pines.

"I guess it's goin' to be pleasant to-morrer," he said, in an indistinct voice.

He heard footsteps coming across the floor towards him, but he would not move. He did not stir when Judith's voice said, insistently, "What else were you going to say, Mr. Guild? You must tell all."

There was no response for a moment. Then Mr. Guild

suddenly dashed his right fist down on the palm of his left hand, exclaiming, "I vow you've always had a thunderin' hard time, Judith! I vow you have!"

It was a perceptible space before Judith spoke again. Then she said, "What else did William Mackay tell?"

Mr. Guild looked at her pleadingly. It was as if their places were reversed for the moment. His rugged, weather-beaten face worked. "Can't you jest let that go?" he asked.

"No, I can't let it go."

"Wall, Mackay said that he though he saw you put out your hand towards your father's if you was goin' to push him over."

"Did he see him go over?" Judith's voice sounded high and harsh.

"No, he didn't; 'twas dark; but he s'posed mebby you might have pushed him over, bein' mad 'n' excited, 'n' he so provokin', you know. He wa'n't certain you did put your hand out."

During this talk Mrs. Grover was sitting leaning far forward in her chair, her eyes on the two. Her lips were parted, and there seemed to be a veil of horror over her face.

"I did put my hand out," said Judith, still in the same harsh voice, "but it was not to push him. He stumbled, and I caught hold of him. But nobody will believe that. Since we were saying unpleasant things, and he is missing, people will want to think I killed my father. Mother"— the girl took a step towards the woman sitting there —"mother," sharply, "do you hear that? They think I pushed father off the cliff!"

Mrs. Grover rose. Her bent form straightened. Her face cleared from the veil that had been over it. She walked to her daughter's side. She put her arm about the girl and held her closely. Her head reared itself. Her faded eyes flashed. "I don't care what they say!" she said, loudly. "They're a set of fools! Let them talk! Judith, my Judith! Let them talk!" The fire faded from her aspect as suddenly as it had come. She flung herself on her daughter's neck and clung there.

Judith stood, tall and strong, holding her mother close to her, not glancing down at her, but looking over the bent gray head at the man before her.

"Oh, by George!" cried Mr. Guild, in a thick voice, "I can't stand this! Damn Bill Mackay! Damn um all! What d'you make me tell you for, I should like to know?" He drew an immense handkerchief from his pocket and openly began to cry into it.

Judith led her mother to a chair and put her into it. Then, overcome by a sudden physical weakness, she sat down near her and covered her face with her hands. But she did not sob. She was perfectly still.

In a moment Mr. Guild lifted his head, looking rather ashamed. He passed his handkerchief vigorously over his countenance. He walked to the door and stopped, with his hand on the latch. He began to speak, with his back to the two women: "I come over here 'cause my wife made me. She said I'd got to come 'n' tell you what folks was sayin'. She said you might find it out some way 'twould make you feel even worse 'n to have me tell it. 'N' she said to be sure 'n' say that after folks 'd had their talk out 'twould all blow over. 'N' 'twill, of course. It's got to blow over. 'N' she was partickerler 'bout my makin' you know 't we didn't believe a word of it—not one devilish word of it." Having spoken thus, Mr. Guild opened the door and shut it quickly behind him.

Judith heard his feet stumbling rapidly along the yard; she heard the sound with a strange keenness. And she heard and discriminated between the different notes of the crickets that were playing vociferously all about the house.

The dusk was deepening now. The odors of the June evening were becoming more heavy; they floated in through the open windows. A sudden, imperative longing to be alone took possession of Judith. She must be alone if only for a brief time. She rose. She hesitated, her face towards her mother. "If you don't mind, I'll go out a minute," she said, speaking scarcely above a whisper.

Mrs. Grover nodded. She watched the girl go out. Then she herself left the house. But she did not see Judith. She went to the lower end of the garden to the fresh mound there. She thought it would be a comfort to pray by Em's grave. There must be comfort somewhere. There was nothing left for her but to pray.

Judith, as soon as she had stepped without the door, began to walk fast—she did not at first notice in what direction. Presently she became aware that she was going towards the cliffs. She paused. The sweetness of the sea-salt air swept across her face. In this sweetness was mingled the odor of wild roses.

All the girl's senses were painfully awake. A terrible and passionate consciousness of the possibilities of happiness was mingled with her present misery. She was partially aware that she was never so capable of knowing rapture as in this time of wretchedness.

Naturally her thoughts and her feelings were magnified and exaggerated. She thought of her father with a violent questioning. She could believe for the moment that she had power to wrest from God the secret of his fate.

Then suddenly there came upon her an unspeakable horror of those cliffs. Was it only last night that she had walked there and begged her father to let her go and see little Em? She had disobeyed him. She had held Em in her arms. Surely it had not been wrong to disobey him? And she had comforted Em.

She was hurrying away from the vicinity of the cliffs. She walked out upon the highway and sat down under a low, thickly growing pine-tree.

The Grover home was in so retired a spot that there was little likelihood that any one would come along the road. Sitting there alone in the warm and fragrant dusk Judith was beginning to think it possible for her to have coherent thoughts once more. She was just telling herself that there was nothing for her to do but to go on living right there ; to go on taking care of her mother and the children. She had no money to go anywhere else. And wherever she went that story, her story, would be sure to follow her, and be worse for her in a strange place. " I must think this over exactly as if it were about some one else," she said, aloud.

Was that the sound of horse's feet and of wheels? Well, she could stay where she was. The pine-tree would hide her. She shrank farther in among its branches.

The horse came on quickly. The animal was drawing an old, shabby wagon. In the wagon sat a young man whose eyes keenly took in every object in the dusk. He pulled up the horse.

" Is that you, Judith ?"

The girl rose and came forward. Tom Rylance sprang out of the wagon.

" I want to see you—I want to see you alone," he said, quickly. " Will you get into the carriage, or shall I go home with you ?"

XV

"NO"

"You may go home with me," answered Judith. "But mother is there."

"I tell you I want to see you alone," repeated Rylance.

"I'll get in, then, and drive with you to The Corners. I mustn't leave mother alone for long." As Judith said this she came forward still farther. Then she paused, and said, "I ought to tell you that we've had diphtheria here. Em died."

"Oh, Judith," exclaimed the young man, "how you must have suffered! I ain't afraid of ketchin' anything. Come—come."

He helped her up to the seat and then sprang in beside her. He turned the horse round and hushed him down to a walk. Then he slipped his left arm through the lines and turned towards his companion.

It was not so dark but that she could see that Rylance was very pale in spite of the tan, and that his heavy jaw looked more resolute than ever.

"You see, Judith, I couldn't help comin' right over. I couldn't, noways, have got through the night without seeing you."

There was no reply to this.

"Of course," he went on, "when I knew you was in trouble I had to come. Ellis Macomber was up to the north part this afternoon, 'n' he told our next neighbors, 'n' they told mar, 'n' when I got in from plantin' mar told me. I wanted to harness right up then 'n' come down here 'n' see you; but I had to wait till after supper."

As he finished speaking Rylance put his arm over the back of the seat, but the arm did not touch the girl.

"What did you hear?" asked Judith.

"Why, 'bout you 'n' your father, you know. 'N' I wanted to tell um that I didn't blame you none if you did push him off. But I wouldn't say nothin'—I jest kep' my mouth shut. I thought 'twas the best way."

"You wouldn't blame me, then?"

The girl's eyes fixed themselves on the face beside her. Her heart was beating fast.

"No, indeed, I wouldn't. I know how tryin' he's always been, 'n' then turnin' you out, as he did. If I knew you pushed him over I should love you just the same. Oh, Judith, I've got to love you, no matter what you do!"

Judith shivered. She kept her eyes on Rylance's face. "But I didn't do that!" she exclaimed. "Oh no, I didn't do that!"

The young man turned yet more towards her. "Didn't you?" he asked.

"Could you think it for one instant?"

There was something in her voice that made Rylance cold. He hesitated. "I didn't really think it," he answered. "When I remembered how your father 'd been to you, and how one's temper rises up all of a sudden like a—like a whirlwind—I—but— Oh, Judith, why do you look at me like that?"

Rylance stopped his horse. He seized Judith's hand and held it painfully close. "But I didn't care what you'd done!" he exclaimed. "It don't make no difference to me, I love you so. And I come over to-night to ask you to marry me right off. Then I c'n stan' between you 'n' everybody. I tell you they'll have to deal with me then. When you belong to me 'fore all the world I shouldn't think of anything but how happy I was. Let um talk. We sha'n't care. I tell you, Judith, I could almost wish you had done some dreadful thing so 't I could show you how I love you. There never was no man in this world that ever loved a woman 's I love you."

Rylance bent forward as if to kiss the girl, but she shrank away, and murmured, " Don't, Tom, don't!"

"Why not?" he asked, savagely. "What makes you like that always? You never would hardly let me kiss you. I don't understand it."

Judith was leaning as far away as possible from her companion. There was something like fright in her aspect—fright, and a deep perplexity. "You must foregive me, Tom," she said, gently.

His look changed instantly. "No, no," he said, penitently, "it ain't me that's got to forgive. It's you. I d' know what makes me say things to hurt you, 'n' you in such trouble, too. But I do wish you'd say you'd marry me right away. Won't you, Judith? You know we've been 's good 's engaged a long time now." He moved and gathered up the lines in both hands. But he could not keep his eyes from Judith's face.

The girl was motionless. She seemed to be holding herself thus by a great effort. Finally she turned. "Tom," she said, softly, "you know I never would really be engaged to you. You must remember that. Don't you remember?"

"You know it amounts to jest the same thing as an engagement."

He was resolved to be gentle—that is, if he could possibly keep himself in hand. What was she coming at? he questioned, inwardly.

"Not just the same."

"It does. Ask anybody."

His voice began to grate. He could not understand. He didn't believe many men would come forward as he had done. Not but that it was a privilege and a happiness to do it. He told the truth when he said that he did not care what Judith had done; or if he cared, that feeling made no difference in his love.

"You know I always told you, Tom, that I didn't see how we could ever marry: that I'd got to take care of my family; that I wouldn't bring them as a burden to anybody, and—and— Oh, Tom, you know what I said! You know I didn't promise!"

Judith's eyes, large with pain, were fixed on the man's face. He met the look, his blood leaping as he did so. She had never been so lovely in his sight. But he could not quite control the barbarian in him. He had been used to having his own way. He had dominated everybody at home.

" I know what you said," he responded. " And I know what I said—that I was engaged to you, whether you was to me or not ; and I'd take your whole family, father 'n' all, 'n' slave for um all my life if you'd marry me. And I will, Judith. We c'n manage some way. Let's go over to the minister's to-morrer 'n' be married. It 'll be the best thing all round. Do say yes! Jest think how I've waited! Ain't I been patient? I tell you, I've about got through bein' patient. Say yes, Judith !"

The girl's hands were clasped in her lap—clasped tightly, as if to help her bear the strain upon her. There was nothing in her, she thought, that did not say " no " to his urging. She was going to say no ; but, womanlike, she hesitated. She knew that she was in a wrong position. She knew that she ought never to have allowed such an arrangement, and she could not understand why she had allowed it. Looking back now it was as if it had been some other identity than her own that had permitted a sort of half-engagement with Tom Rylance. But she did not promise, she remembered.

Can we not all recall deeds like that—actions in which we have taken part, and which, in the retrospect, seem to have been performed by some other person? But some part of ourselves did this thing or permitted it to be done, and now we abide by it, or suffer for it, or are happy in consequence of it.

She remembered the time, nearly two years ago, when she had entered into this one - sided bargain — only bargains are never really one-sided, no matter how much we may try to believe them to be so. She liked Tom Rylance warmly

—she liked him now. But— Her mind struggled to make things plain to itself. She turned and gazed appealingly at her companion. "I can't," she said—"I can't do it."

Tom's mouth compressed itself. His jaw became more than ever like that of a bull-dog. "Let's have it out now," he said. "I'm goin' to understand this business. You mean you don't care for me?"

She broke in, eagerly, "I care for you so much, Tom."

"Then let's be married."

"I can't do it," she said, once more.

"Why not?" the primeval savage springing up again.

It was unlike herself that she did not go right to the foundation truth. "It wouldn't be right," she began, "for me to marry you. I'm under a cloud. People will always wonder if I really pushed father off the cliff—" She stopped a moment to gain control of her voice. Then she went on, "And some folks will believe I did do it. And mother and the children — No, no, I won't have you take care of them. We must give it all up. But you needn't think of me as being happy, Tom. I don't think I shall ever be happy. I suppose I shall get used to things. I mean to work real hard. And I sha'n't ever marry. It's not in the least likely."

Tom waited before he spoke. Then he said, "I want to ask you just one question."

She averted her face, and he noticed that she did so. The action made him furious, but he tried bravely to compose himself.

"I want to ask if you love me, Judith, and you've got to answer me. It's fair that you do answer me that, now, ain't it?"

"Yes, it's fair."

"Then tell me." The young man sharply made the horse stop in its walk.

"I do love you— in a way."

She turned towards him fully now, and looked up at him.

She put her hand on his arm. He could see her eyes glowing through the dusk. A tremor of hope and longing went over him. But in the bottom of his heart he knew there was no hope.

"In what way? Don't you keep nothing back, now."

"No, no; I won't. I love you dearly as a friend, a brother, Tom; in all the way that I must ever love any man. Don't you see that even if I did love you in the way you want me to I couldn't possibly marry you? Tom! Tom! do be kind to me now!"

She pressed her hand down on his arm. He was dear to her. He was part of her old life when she had been young, and before the burdens had begun to bear so heavily upon her. Well, she would never be young again, and she must square her shoulders for their load. She supposed that some women were free to be happy. And again, like a flash of light in darkness, there came to the girl the knowledge of the possibilities of happiness in her own nature. How strange it would be to be able to allow those possibilities to become realities! But Judith knew better than to let such thoughts live. She strangled them mercilessly, as she had always done.

Rylance fought visibly with himself. The girl's touch on his arm was tenderness itself. It seemed to subdue in some degree the fierce selfishness of his passion for her. "I'm goin' to be good to you," he said, finally, in an unsteady voice. "But I guess you better get out of the wagon. I don't want to see you any more now. I can't bear it. I might say something I should wish I hadn't said."

Judith jumped quickly down to the ground. But she turned instantly. "Wait one minute, dear Tom!" she exclaimed. "You know if I loved you—loved you every way, I mean—I wouldn't marry you just because I did love you: I should spare you that. I've got my work. And you know what folks think I've done. Good-bye, Tom."

He opened his lips to speak, but he said nothing: his voice did not come. He was gazing down at the girl's face,

and he was inwardly cursing the darkness, which kept him
from seeing that face more plainly. He leaned forward and
struck the horse with the lines.

Judith had hardly time to start back from the wheels as
they rolled forward. She waited a little before going to
the house. She knew that she had folded down one leaf
of her life. This episode was over. Rylance would never
willingly see her again. And so it proved. She came to
think of her acquaintance with Tom as something that had
been the experience of some one else. Only it was upon
her own individuality that such experience was indelibly
stamped, whether she recognized this fact or not. Soon
she hurried back to her mother, reproving herself that she
had been so long away from her.

The next few days passed with that strange and solemn
swiftness with which time goes after a great grief and
change. Mother and daughter remained at home. They
went about their duties with mechanical precision. They
obeyed scrupulously the doctor's orders in regard to disin-
fection.

At the end of the week the two children were brought
back from Mrs. Guild's. At the beginning of the next
week Judith went again to the factory. She must lose no
more time, for time was money. She knew that her shop-
mates looked at her curiously, and she felt herself harden-
ing beneath their gaze. She went the first noon and gave
up her room at Mrs. Macomber's.

Mr. Macomber was just coming from his daily journey to
the wharf and the stores. Judith saw his green jacket in
the distance, and she knew she could not avoid him. He
waved his hand at her; he almost ran in his eagerness.
"Wall," he said, "so you've got to work agin?"

"Yes."

The man stared at her unrelentingly. He appeared to
think that he should discover some astonishing change in
her, like the loss of an eye or a tooth, if he could only look
long enough.

“ I s’pose there ain’t nothin’ been heard of your father ?”

“ No.”

“ I s’posed not. I guess you won’t hear nothin’. Hev they carried over his cane ’n’ hat ?”

“ Yes.”

“ There wa’n’t no doubt ’bout their bein’ his’n, was there ?”

“ They were his.”

“ I could hev taken my oath to um in any court. You don’t s’pose there’ll be no court, do you ?”

Judith restrained the manifestation of her terror. It had not occurred to her that there could be what Macomber called “ a court.”

“ I don’t know,” she answered.

The man was saying to himself that Judith “ didn’t have much feelin’, ’n’ ’twas well she didn’t.”

“ No, I guess there won’t. Mr. Eldridge—the old man, I mean—said there wa’n’t much to have a court about. He said he guessed they wouldn’t arrest you ’cause you happened to see your father on the cliffs. ’N’ he said there wa’n’t no body, ’n’ a court couldn’t bring much of a charge ’thout no body. Ye see, you’ve got to hev a body to make much of a charge. Of course, your par’s drownded—I guess there ain’t much doubt ’bout that; but you can’t prove nothin’ ’thout no body. How’s your mar gittin’ along ?”

“ She isn’t well.”

“ Ain’t ? I s’pose not. You couldn’t really expect her to be real well. Does she hev no expectation of findin’ the body now ?”

“ No.”

“ I shouldn’t myself. It may hev be’n carried out by the tide, ’n’ it may be thrown up on the shore hundreds of miles away. You can’t tell nothin’ ’bout them things. ’N’ mebby there won’t no body ever be found. Was you comin’ in, Judith ?”

“ Yes ; I wanted to see Mrs. Macomber.”

The man removed himself from the gate and allowed the girl to pass. She had resisted the inclination to go, and return when Mr. Macomber was gone. She rarely turned back. And now, though her very lips were white with the strain upon her, she walked up the path and into the house.

XVI

UNCLE DICK

The Eldridge family were at breakfast. There were the father and mother, the two girls, and the son, Lucian. But there was a plate and a still unfilled chair at the right of the hostess who, as she poured coffee, frequently glanced in the direction of the door.

"I suppose you are thinking of Dick," remarked Squire Eldridge. "There's no knowing when he'll come down. Sometimes he is waiting for his breakfast at seven, and then he is in his room till near noon. It's out of the question to wait for anybody like that."

The speaker set down his coffee-cup with more emphasis than was necessary. His wife looked at him deprecatingly.

"You never did have any patience with Dick," she said. "You know he insists on our not making any difference in our meals. He says he'll take his chance."

"Oh, well," was the response, the squire trying to be good-humored, "if you can stand it, I'm sure I can. And it ought to be easy to put up with the whims of a man who has as much money as Dick Gerald has."

Here Mr. Eldridge laughed, and took his book again, for he had the unsocial habit of reading at his meals.

Lucian was silent. He had come home from a short absence late the night before, and he had that aggrieved feeling which one is apt to experience who has not slept sufficiently.

"I wonder how the Grovers are," remarked the younger daughter. "I'm just as interested as I can be in that family. They do seem to have things what you might call real tough."

"Can't you find a more lady-like phrase than real tough?" plaintively inquired the mother.

"No, I can't. Real tough is what I mean."

Mrs. Eldridge shuddered a little, but she said nothing more.

Lucian looked up. "What's the matter with the Grovers?" he asked. "Isn't the old man well supplied with patent medicines?"

Before the girl could reply the door opened and a man of about fifty sauntered in, and took the seat by Mrs. Eldridge, who was his sister. This man was tall and spare. He was dressed in light trousers and a Prince Albert coat of irreproachable cut. His linen was immaculate; his narrow black tie looked fresher and more elegant than any narrow black tie ever looked before. His forehead was high and retreating, and a wisp of gray hair was brushed up on each side, meeting in a double curl at the top. His eyes were gray and deep set. His mustache was very long and thick. His cheeks and chin always had the appearance of having been shaved the moment before. He had a very probing way with his eyes, and a sort of unbelieving, sceptical look on his whole face. He wore a large ring with a carved black stone in it on his left hand. His hands were long and white, and his nephew Lucian had always had the idea that these hands betrayed, even more than the face of their owner, the keen, curious, mocking mind.

The whole outward appearance of "Uncle Dick" was as if arrayed for an afternoon call. He always dressed in this way for morning, and for any evening function whatever. He said he meant to be well-dressed, but he "would never be such an idiot as to wear a swallow-tail." He did not explain why it was idiotic to wear the conventional dress-coat. When his nephew had once put that question to him the elder man had smiled whimsically, gazed an instant at his interlocutor, and then said, " So many fools have worn that kind of a garment that now the garment takes its revenge and makes a fool of a man who puts it on."

Richard Gerald, no matter how absurd was his statement, invariably uttered it in such a way that you almost believed it at first. Now he glanced about the table, spoke a comprehensive "good-morning" in a remarkably agreeable voice, took his coffee, returned it and said that it appeared to be a blend of two coffees, and he could never endure a blend, anyway. Would his sister please have some plain hot water brought in? Plain hot water was precisely what he needed this morning.

Mrs. Eldridge volubly offered tea, chocolate, coffee of pure Mocha or Java ; but her brother answered decisively, " Plain hot water, Caroline."

When the servant had brought this beverage, and the receiver of it was sipping from the cup with an air of great luxury, Lucian turned to his younger sister and asked again : " What's happened to the Grovers, Belle?"

"Quite some, I should say," was the brisk reply. " The youngest has died of diphtheria, and they say Judith has pushed her father off into the ocean near the Great Rocks. And how can one blame her much?"

" Belle !" said her mother, reproachfully.

" Really," said Belle, who invariably repeated an offence when her mother reproved her for it, " if my father were like Hanford Grover I should have pushed him into the sea long ago."

Here the girl looked affectionately at her father, who had put down his book permanently when Mr. Gerald had come in. Mr. Eldridge smiled back warmly in response.

Lucian had involuntarily pushed his plate from him at his sister's reply. A change like a sudden blackness came to his face, and the effort with which he banished this look was visible to his uncle, whose absorption and delight in his hot water did not prevent him from noticing everything.

"I suppose you're joking, Belle," said the young man; "but it's poor taste to joke in that way."

"I'm not joking at all," was the response, in the same brisk manner. "I'm in solemn earnest."

"Then I must say you're very disagreeably flippant," returned Lucian, with fraternal frankness.

"And you're quite delightfully outspoken, Lucian, dear," Belle said, flashing her eyes over at her brother.

"I always did say," now remarked Mr. Gerald, suavely, "that family life was the most blissful of any conceivable existence."

"A bit of sparring does no harm," said the squire. He was always secretly wincing at his brother-in-law's remarks, but he had thus far been able to conceal this fact.

Mr. Gerald prepared to eat an egg in the shell. In this operation his hands seemed longer and whiter than ever. Lucian tried not to watch them. The young man was thinking of Judith, and of her grief at the loss of her little sister. He would not consider the other statement made by Belle, for it was, of course, merely an invention of that young lady's. He had decided not to ask any more questions of any member of his family. After breakfast he would drop in at Mrs. Guild's and learn what there was to know.

But Mr. Gerald had made up his mind to interrogate. He liked to make Belle talk, and thus indirectly shock Belle's mother. As for the people of whom she had been speaking, he knew nothing and cared nothing about them.

"Let us go on with this village history," he said, as he put his egg-spoon into his egg. "There seem to be vicissitudes here in this corner of the world, of course, for there's no difference in parts of the world, anyway. Belle, who has died of diphtheria?"

"A child — one of the Grovers. They live out of the village a bit. The father won't work; he would rather take patent medicines and enjoy a bad liver. So they're just rotten poor—"

" Belle!" from her mother.

" Yes, they are rotten poor.   Judith is different—"

" Not rotten poor?" interrupted Mr. Gerald, lifting his eyebrows somewhat.

"Oh yes," with a slight laugh, "she's just as poor, of course; she works like a slave and takes care of the whole of them. When she was away they tried to raise money with a bean-bottle on an old seraphine. I'll tell you all about it some time, uncle."

" I shall insist that you do so," from Mr. Gerald.   "A bean-bottle on an old seraphine! Yes, you must tell me about that."

" Yes, and father and Lucian took a lot of chances, so as to help, you know; and when Judith came back she just stepped on the whole thing. She said it wasn't fair, and the seraphine wasn't worth anything, which was the truth; and she went round and paid back all the money that had been given for guesses. She came here. I went to the door to her. I declare I just wanted to hug her, she looked so proud, and so—so—well, so splendid, somehow."

" I never could find out," said Mr. Gerald, "what one girl means when she calls another girl 'splendid.'"

"Why, she means splendid," answered Belle.

" Thank you; please go right on."

"Well, Judith paid this money back, and that made her father so terrifically angry that he turned her out of the house."

"What!" exclaimed Lucian, quite taken by surprise.   He said nothing more; but he felt his uncle's eyes sweep over him.   It was too late to be sorry he had spoken.

" Dramatic scene, undoubtedly," said Mr. Gerald.

" Yes, Mr. Grover turned her out, though she has supported him and the rest of them since she was big enough to learn to stitch in our factory. And then the youngest child was sick, and Judith wanted to see her, and her father wouldn't let her. She had met him on the cliff by the Great Rocks and asked him to let her go home, so they say; and she pushed him off, and he fell over and can't be found, and is drowned, of course; and a good thing, too."

"Belle!" The mother's voice sounded like a small, reiterative note on some instrument.

"Yes," repeated Belle, "an awfully good thing, too, I say."

Lucian, during this story, had exerted himself to the utmost not to reveal the emotion it caused, and in consequence he showed no emotion at all—not even a natural surprise and interest.

Mr. Gerald did not look at him again save in the most casual way. He was saying to himself, "My nephew knows more about this Judith Grover than anybody here. Let us inquire into this. Lucian is a ridiculously good fellow. Let us protect him."

He looked over at his brother-in-law. "Is it going to be an affair of the courts, Alfred?" he asked.

"Oh no, I'm sure not. Of course, she didn't do it. There's no real testimony. Because they were not on good terms hardly constitutes evidence."

"Circumstantial, entirely?"

"Certainly; and slight at that. And the body hasn't been found. You can't say a person's been killed until somebody has seen him dead, you know. Terrible thing for the girl, though—terrible. There never was a better girl in the world." Mr. Eldridge spoke more and more earnestly.

Lucian did not know how gratefully he was looking at his father, and no one, save his uncle, noticed his face.

"Upright, honorable to the last drop of blood in her," went on the squire. "I've known her ever since she was born. I never in my life knew any one who so valued truth, who would so honor her word. Why, Dick, you may think me silly enough, but if there was overwhelming evidence that she pushed her father off the cliff and she told me she did not do it I should believe her."

"Bravo, father, bravo!" cried the elder daughter, "so should I."

"I'm sure I'm glad you've kept such faith in human nature," said Mr. Gerald. "For my part, I haven't been so lucky. I think any one would break a promise if the right thing were brought to bear. It all depends upon the right thing, you see. Particularly do I think women don't know or care what a promise means. They seem to be lacking in a certain moral fibre which makes a person value a passed word. I hope you ladies will pardon me," making a comprehensive bow. "But you make me quite interested in this girl. Robust, plain sort of a person, I suppose?"

"I think she has good health," replied the squire, rather coldly, "but I don't call her plain; neither do I think she is beautiful."

"Oh no, not beautiful in the least," said Mrs. Eldridge, positively; "but she has always been a very worthy person," in that tone which some women invariably use in speaking of other women who are not in their set.

The squire frowned a little, but he made no other sign that his wife's words irritated him. He rose, saying that he must go if he was to catch the train in the next town. Then he paused to add that the fellow who said he saw Judith and her father on the cliff, heard them quarrelling, and so on, was a fellow whose word would not be taken even against a thief.

XVII

AN INTRODUCTION

As soon as Lucian had left the breakfast-room he went into the hall and took his hat. Going out towards the road his uncle met him, cigar between his lips, and having the appearance of starting for a stroll.

"I'm always in luck," said the elder man, affably. "I was going to walk, and I meet you who are also going to walk. You'll let me accompany you?"

Lucian put great constraint upon himself. He answered that he should be glad to have his uncle's company, thus telling a downright lie, and then despising himself for so doing. Mr. Gerald's eyes twinkled.

The two men walked down towards the village street. Lucian's hands were thrust into the pockets of his sack-coat, and he indulged himself in clinching them there, while he was swearing inwardly. He had been brought up by his mother in something like awe of his uncle Dick. His uncle Dick was enormously rich, and it was but natural that he should leave his money to his nephew—that is, if Dick would only have the sense to remain unmarried; and thus far he had had that sense. But it must be owned that Richard Gerald was a man who would have had great influence even without money; with it he was very powerful if he chose to be. But one never knew when Gerald would choose to do anything, or what he would choose to leave undone. In his life of fifty years he had committed some very eccentric deeds.

As for Lucian, his uncle had from boyhood possessed a curious attraction for him, partly the attraction which a clever man of the world has for a younger man, and partly that subtle something which a cynical, able mind so often wields over other minds. There is a force in mere cynicism that is a factor in life, and that acts like a kind of rust.

Gerald talked desultorily as he walked with his nephew. He had never quite made out Lucian; he had not been able to classify him permanently. And one of the first things that Gerald did in regard to other human beings whom he met was to label them and, as it were, hang them up in some chamber of his brain.

"Lucian is clever," he used to say to himself, "but he has a sort of volatile look. The deuce is in it that I can't yet tell whether or not he is really volatile. He's just the man to make love to women and for women to adore. But here he is nearly twenty-seven years old, and I can't find out as he has even been in love. He is the frankest and the most secret human being I ever met."

When the two men came on to the road where the "thick settled" part of the town lay, Gerald suddenly turned to his companion, and, keeping his eyes on Lucian's face, he said, in a careless tone, "I suppose you know every soul in this place. There's a girl coming across the pasture there. Who is she?"

In spite of the careless tone the young man was on guard immediately. He did not know how he knew, but he did know instantly, before he looked, that the girl was Judith Grover. He glanced in the direction mentioned.

Yes, there was Judith. She was coming swiftly, walking with the free step of youth and strength and unconventionality. Her hat was pushed back somewhat, and there were two or three dark locks lying close and damp upon her forehead. She was thin and pale and tired-looking, but at the same time there was an appearance of invincible strength and vigor about her—a something which Gerald directly called by the contradictory term of feminine virility.

Lucian's hat came off, and then Gerald doffed his. He

was delighted with the unaffected smile which returned Lucian's greeting.

"Who is it?" he asked again, now in a swift whisper.

"It's Miss Grover"

"The one they were talking about?"

"Yes."

"Present me, then. I insist upon it."

By this time Judith had reached the fence which separated the field from the road. She stooped to let down the bars, and Mr. Gerald darted forward and made the rails clatter to the ground. He offered his hand to help her over, but she stepped lightly across without seeming to see the hand. She was going on quickly, and Lucian wished to let her go on. He knew, however, that he must obey the warning touch of his uncle's hand on his shoulder.

"Surely you and she are old friends enough," whispered Gerald.

The life-long habit of yielding in everything to his companion made young Eldridge call, "Miss Grover!"

Judith stopped. She half turned, waiting their approach. Gerald noted how extremely shabby her clothes were, and, notwithstanding that fact, he also perceived a certain nobleness in her figure and pose. To his great surprise his interest grew with every moment. He had not expected to see any one in the least like this. He had pictured to himself, perhaps, a girl of a rustic prettiness who blushed when spoken to, and who, if she had been in the same station in England, would have courtesied when she met him.

"Miss Grover," said Eldridge, with considerable ceremony, "my uncle wishes to be presented to you. Will you let me introduce him?"

He could not have spoken with more deference; and he could not know that his manner was like a sudden, lovely balm to the girl's wounded spirit.

Nevertheless, Judith was obliged to force herself to acknowledge politely Mr. Gerald's greeting. She shrank from seeing any one. She had been wishing as she walked across the field that she might bolt and bar herself in the old house with her mother and the children, and never see another face save theirs from year's end to year's end. She was wishing this so strongly that she was already planning how she might make such an arrangement.

Perhaps the foreman at the factory would send shoes home to her. She might put on the buttons. But she would not earn nearly as much. They would starve, literally. She wished it were not too late to make a garden this year. There was so much "living to be had from garden-sauce." Beans and corn went a great ways, and as for butcher's-meat, of course they couldn't expect that. Debts must be paid; and if it could only be that no more debts need be incurred!

Resolutely the girl, as she came over the pasture, was facing a life as bare and arid as life could well be: resolutely, though the young and healthy blood coursed richly through her vigorous body and demanded happiness. She would not flinch as she looked into the future. That future meant for her the most unremitting work and a starved existence. Underneath all that work was the continued consciousness that people would always, when they looked at her, ask themselves whether she really did push her father over the cliff. She thought of the time when her sisters would be grown, and she and her mother would be alone in the old house, for she supposed her sisters would marry and move away. Life was not barred for them.

Yes, she was very sorry it was too late to make a garden. Perhaps she could spade up a small space and plant some late beans. She could do this, and hoe them in early mornings before the shop was open. And she would not forget to try to arrange that she might have work at home, and so gradually cease to see people.

She longed for time to mourn for little Em. She had no leisure even for that; she could only know that there was a leaden heaviness upon her besides the trial about her father. And nights when, weary and, as it were, sodden with overwork, she laid herself on the bed she hardly had a chance to cry a little for Em before heavy sleep came on.

All these thoughts and feelings were in her consciousness as she walked towards the shop that morning and saw the two well-dressed, prosperous looking men sauntering along the highway.

She had been kept from the factory until now, in the middle of the forenoon, and she would be "docked" for these lost hours. An hour that was not filled with hard labor was "lost." She had learned to know that among the very first things she could remember.

Mr. Gerald's salutation was of that kind which some men of the world are able to employ; it was something that held in it a suggestion of homage, also a hint of respectful sense of attraction that could not be unheeded by the dullest woman on the face of the earth. And it had in it a sufficient element of sincerity. It was plain that Judith did not wish to linger. She seemed poised, ready for immediate flight. And in a moment she hastened on.

"I was on the verge of asking her to let us walk with her," said Mr. Gerald, "but, you see, I couldn't do it. Odd what men and women will grow up in an outlying place like this! That girl will never have an opportunity, of course. Splendid animal, as well as splendid human being! But she will never develop into anything." Here the speaker suddenly faced round upon his companion. "You're a blind bat, Lucian! Well," with a foreign shrug, much in use with Gerald, "lucky for you that you are blind. Now I—"

Gerald swung his stick round and gave a short laugh, covertly watching his nephew as he did so. As for Lucian, he was surprised at himself that he could come so near hating his uncle.

XVIII

ON THE CLIFF-WALK

WITHIN the next quarter of a mile the two men saw coming towards them a man in a green baize jacket. He was stumping along quickly, and he drew up directly in front, nodding in an off-hand way, and asking, eagerly:

"Heard the news, Lucian? You've be'n away this some time, ain't ye? Stirrin' kind of a spell round here. I jest seen Judith Grover go 'long. Guess you ain't had a chance to hear the partick'lars, hev ye?"

Mr. Gerald smiled encouragingly at Ellis Macomber. He wanted to hear what he had to say. But Lucian drew back with a quite unaccustomed haughtiness.

"I'm going on," he said, abruptly, and he strode forward, throwing back his shoulders and taking a deep breath as he found himself alone. He had not been alone a moment since he had heard that story about the Grovers. Now his face softened from its lines of restraint.

He hurried forward, hardly having yet determined where he should go. Anywhere, so that he might be sure of being alone. He gave up seeing Mrs. Guild at present. He suddenly found that he could not bear to see any one who would pronounce Judith's name. "Blind!" He spoke the word aloud in a rage as he traversed the pasture into which he had gone after a moment's walking on the road. In the pasture was solitude. "Blind!" Oh no, he was not so unseeing as his uncle chose to suppose. But of course the best thing for him to do was to go away and stay away. Could he do that? He knew himself well enough to believe that, if he remained, he would be continually trying to see Judith. He had been sure of that much about himself during his short absence from home. But now that she was in trouble the feeling was ungovernable. If she were in distress he must help her.

Coming out upon another road he stood still. Here was where he had first seen the girl after his return from abroad. There was the birch he had been peeling when she came along the road. The happening of a great misfortune seemed all at once to have broken all thought of reserve from the young man's consciousness. If that had not happened he might have gone on, he knew not how long, not thinking anything but that it was pleasant to meet Judith now and then.

Eldridge started forward again, going towards the Grover farm. He heard the sound of the incoming tide beating up against the Great Rocks. The sound made him pause and shudder. It was up yonder, on that cliff, that Judith had walked with her father. Did she grieve for him any? Of course the man was drowned.

Presently Eldridge began to ascend the slope which led to the cliff-walk. From here the ocean stretched away illimitably. The morning sun shone on it and dazzled him. Swift spears of light from the bright water smote his eyes. He went to the utmost verge of the cliff, where it went sheer down. He threw himself on the ground and thrust his head forward to look over.

It was nearly flood-tide, and the water was dashing up against the side of the hill. It had been nearly flood-tide that night when Grover had fallen down there. And it had not been a storm. Couldn't the man swim? The full tide prevented him from falling upon the ragged rocks.

What a ridiculous thing it was to think of the possibility of the man's being alive. If he were alive there was every reason in the world for his appearing, and not one reason for his refusing to come home.

Eldridge rose to his feet. He had felt an imperative desire to come here again, although he had known the place thoroughly as a boy. He sat down in the shadow of one of those stunted, east-wind-blown savin-trees that seem a part of the New England coast. The spicy odor of the rough foliage was drawn out by the sun.

He had not been seated long when he heard footsteps, and he started up, thinking of only one person who could come here. But it was not Judith, but Judith's mother who came toilsomely up the incline and stood nearly in front of Eldridge, who had not moved forward. The slight, round-shouldered figure was clad in its calico dress and long shirting apron, a sun-bonnet on its head.

Mrs. Grover stood perfectly still, gazing out towards the offing. It is the habit of the old-fashioned New-Englander to stand still under the blows of fate.

After a while the woman took off her head-covering. She dropped the bonnet on the ground. She put both hands up to her head and pushed her hair back as though it troubled her. But there was no impatience in her movement. For an instant she held her hands pressed to the sides of her head, thus framing her worn and wrinkled face in her worn and wrinkled hands.

Eldridge felt as if he were guilty of sacrilege in thus staying there unseen. He thought there could be nothing more pitiable than that solitary, bent figure, with the sun shining on its gray hair. He wished that he could do something for this woman. A poignant desire to be of use to her, to comfort her, took possession of him. But he knew his powerlessness. He moved a careful step away from her.

She started, gave a little cry, and turned towards him. "That you?" she exclaimed. And then, with a touching accent of apology, "I'm dreadful nervous. I git scared at everything."

The young man took Mrs. Grover's hand and held it. He had an impulse to put his arm about her and make her lean upon him. The sun was on his face now, and the woman, lifting her blurred eyes, saw there a wonderful gentleness and tenderness — at least, it seemed wonderful to her. She had shrunk determinedly from the few neighbors who had come to see her. She wanted to announce that she would see no one who could believe it possible that her girl, even in the wildest anger, could push her father off the cliff. But they would talk about it ; they were talking about it, she knew, and she could hate them for it.

There was Ellis Macomber had walked all the way out to the farm merely to see "how she took it." Mrs. Grover had been sure that was why he came, and she had stood in the door and thus prevented his entering ; she had not shut the door upon him simply because she had not had the courage. Even the kindest of those who came had been curious, and Mrs. Grover was so sore that she felt their curiosity more than their kindness. For the first time in her life she had a wish to bar out every one, since she could not know who were those who thought her Judith capable of such a thing. And they all talked. With unavailing, weak fury the mother felt that she could hate them for merely talking it over. But Lucian Eldridge—she did not know why his presence was such a comfort to her. Her soul seemed to be groping towards him now as she gazed at his young face, which was filled with sympathy.

All at once she remembered that she did not know whether he thought Judith had "done that" (this was the phrase by which she always referred to what had happened), or believed that she could by any possibility have been guilty of such a deed.

"Somebody told me you'd been away," she said. "Mebby you don't know how 'tis with us."

"Yes, I know. I was coming to see you."

"Was you?" Mrs. Grover drew in her breath. She compressed her lips before she opened them to ask, "Well?" She had meant to say more, but she found that she could not add another word.

"Of course, I know she couldn't do such a thing." Lucian spoke with energy. He pressed the hand he held.

Mrs. Grover suddenly pulled away that hand. She had

meant to cover her face, but she had a characteristic fear that such a movement would seem too much like what she would call " taking on," and she would not do that before any stranger. She turned her head away, and made a strenuous effort to keep her features steady. She walked to the savin as if she would lean against its trunk, but she did not lean. When she was with her daughter she allowed herself to give way, conscious of sustainment and strength from that stronger nature. But now she must bear her burden alone.

It was very hard, though. The tender sympathy of her companion seemed to fill the very air. The next moment the tired woman felt that she could not hold out against it. She suddenly flung her arm about the savin. A strong sob shook her.

" You see," she burst forth, " I've lost my husband 's well 's goin' through all the rest ! Folks don't seem to think nothing about that. They don't seem to remember 't I've lost him. Judith don't seem to think 'bout that. She's grievin' for little Em—'n' so 'm I—"

Here the words choked her. She pressed her forehead against the tree trunk. In a moment she began again, her sentences seeming to hurt her as they came, though they must be spoken :

" I know how folks thought about Mr. Grover," she said. " They didn't half of um believe he had no liver trouble, 'n' they thought he ought to work more. It wa'n't none of their business. He was a real good provider 's long 's his money lasted. He had beefsteak that very last day—"

Here another pause. Mrs. Grover left the tree and stood up straight.

" He 'n' Judith had some difficulty," she said ; " but there ain't many families where there ain't any difficulty, only things don't happen so to them. Judith's got a will that there can't anybody go against. She's the best girl in the world, but I ain't made up my mind yet whether she had any right to do 's she did about the bean-bottle. Her father said she had no right. He was real set on that.

And he needed the money. He really needed some kind of medicine for his liver. He was ha'sh, though; yes, he was ha'sh."

Mrs. Grover had not spoken so much since that dreadful night. Eldridge listened in amazement. He did not understand that inexplicable tendency which could prompt the widow to begin immediately to idealize her lost husband. And he could say nothing in response to such remarks.

Mrs. Grover blindly had a sense that something had come between her and the gentleness she had felt from Lucian, and she resented this fact.

"Folks didn't 'preciate Hanford," she said, in a harder voice.

There was no reply to this remark either. Eldridge was puzzled. He did not know what to say, and he did not wish to leave her. Suddenly Mrs. Grover started to go down the walk. Then the young man's pity for Judith's mother overcame everything else. He had never in his life seen anything so desolate as that bent figure of a woman. He went to her side and drew her hand through his arm.

"Let me go with you," he said, in a whisper.

She tried to walk more erectly. "I d' know why I've gone on so," she said, tremulously. "I never meant to say anything to anybody—only Judith. I'm all broke down. I ain't good for nothing. I wish we could just shut ourselves up here 'n' never see folks any more." She was openly weeping now. "I d' know how 'tis, but there's something or other 'bout you, Mr. Eldridge, that makes me don't care whether I keep up or not. And do you remember how you brought some roses and put um in little Em's lap when she was sick, 'n' I was holdin' her? She took lots of notice of them roses. I've got um saved up now in the middle bureau-drawer with Em's things. You're real gentle; there's a look in your eyes that makes me cry, and thankful to cry, too. I d' know how 'tis."

The two walked in silence down the path. The woman leaned heavily on Eldridge's arm.

XIX

"IT WAS LUCIAN"

WHEN they had reached the end of the high path they turned into an outlying pasture belonging to the Grover farm. Here Mrs. Grover paused and took her hand from the young man's arm.

"Let me go home with you," he begged.

She looked at him earnestly as well as she could for the tears which kept gathering and falling.

"I d' know how 'tis," she repeated. "You haven't said anything. I guess it's 'cause I've talked myself. Don't you s'pose it's that?" with a touching simplicity. She had given up trying to speak correctly.

"Yes," answered Eldridge, "it must be that. But I do wish I could do something for you—for you all."

She resumed her walk, and her companion kept beside her. "There ain't nothing to do."

After a while they came to the path that led up through what had once been the garden. Mrs. Grover stopped again. She had been carrying her sun-bonnet in her hand. She now put it on, and drew it forward over her face. Without looking at Eldridge, she said, "I'm going to little Em's grave. I go there and I go on the cliff every day—when Judith ain't here. Somehow I wish you'd come to the grave with me. She took so much notice of them roses."

Eldridge said "Yes." They went along over the unthrifty looking land. Everything all about was unthrifty looking—had a melancholy aspect, even beneath this summer sun.

Mrs. Grover led him to the fresh mound in the garden.

Close by it was a small cleared space—smoothed, and evidently planted.

"Judith put in some mignonette seed there," said Mrs. Grover, now speaking quite calmly. "She thought if she watered it and took real good care of it 'twould come up so 's to blossom 'fore frost. 'N' I guess 'twill. Em she was fond of mignonette. She used to say somehow it smelt like sunshine."

"So it does," said Lucian. He was looking down at the grave. He was thinking many things; foremost among them was the thought that he would have Judith Grover for his wife.

The picture of her as he had seen her an hour ago was vividly with him. To him she was as strong as she was beautiful. He fancied that she was the complement, the other part, of his nature. And what sincere lover does not fancy thus? In his mind he had already overridden every possible obstacle, and was imagining how he would make things easier for this family, which had had things so hard.

Mrs. Grover knelt down by the mound. She passed her hand softly over the gravel, carefully picking off some small stones and throwing them away. The reticent, broken-down woman seemed to feel it an exquisite relief not to be reticent in the presence of this young man who had said so little, but whose heart had mysteriously come so near her own heart.

"When it gets a little later we're goin' to sow some grass seed on the grave," she said, without looking up, and speaking from the depths of her sun-bonnet. "Judith's goin' to bring some loam in the wheelbarrow from the side of the road. We want it to be pleasant here."

There was very little more said. At last Mrs. Grover remembered that she ought to be "doin' something in the house."

When they had reached the door Lucian asked where he should find the wheelbarrow. He wanted to bring the loam.

Mrs. Grover did not try to prevent him. She went with him to the ruinous barn; she found some worn old tools for him to use.

An hour later and the young man had done his task. He was standing by the grave, which was carefully covered with rich earth. He had told Mrs. Grover that he would bring some grass seed.

"I can't tell you how much obliged I am," she replied. "You've done me a lot of good."

"Don't think of me as a stranger. Let me come sometimes," he answered.

When he walked home, carefully keeping in the pastures that he might avoid meeting any one, he had a feeling that there was a relation established between him and that desolate family. He was glad to think that he had set up a kind of sentimental right to be their friend and to see them. The young fellow's nature had so much of gentleness and sweetness in it that sometimes he did not have credit for all the strength he possessed. It was not a blustering strength, and it was not, perhaps, the kind that made such a leaven in Judith's character. It may be it was for that very reason that he was so strongly drawn to her.

"Curious," suddenly began Mr. Gerald at dinner that night, "how one never imagines correctly about a person one has never seen."

Here he glanced at Lucian, who returned his glance in such a veiled way that his uncle could make nothing of his face, and consequently admired his nephew more than he had ever done. But the young man knew very well who it was that was in the man's mind, and he chafed under that knowledge. He had a desire to rise and fling out of the room and out of the house. But he sat calmly quiet and put more sugar in his coffee.

"You were saying, Uncle Dick?" he remarked, gazing with unreadable eyes across the table into Mr. Gerald's face, as that gentleman paused in his talk.

"That things never turn out as you expect," somewhat

brusquely replied Mr. Gerald. "Now there's that girl, that Miss Grover, whom we met this morning—"

"Oh, Uncle Dick, you've seen her, then?" interrupted Belle from her end of the table. "Now tell me, do you think she pushed her father off the cliff?"

"That's entirely immaterial to me," answered Mr. Gerald, easily. "Now my habit of mind is not to care in the least who or what a woman is if she be interesting."

"Richard," expostulated his sister, "don't talk so before my girls."

"Oh, uncle, please go right on. Your words sound so improper," pleaded Belle.

"No, indeed," was the prompt response, "I'm not going to be charged with corrupting the minds of my nieces. Naturally, Caroline would never forgive me. But I suppose I may be permitted to quote that goodness is often uninteresting, while —"

"Richard!" again exclaimed Mrs. Eldridge.

Richard bowed with great suavity to his sister and remained silent. The two girls exchanged glances with each other and the younger one pouted.

When the meal was over it was still daylight, though the sun was near the horizon. Lucian had made up his mind he would call at the Grovers. It would be useless to try to meet Judith on her way from the factory. Besides, the young man was eager to demonstrate openly that he cared for her. He wished it to be known in the village that he was her friend, and that he believed in her. He would not lurk about anywhere hoping to see her in an apparently accidental way. His sister Belle followed him into the garden.

"I've been wishing you'd take me to call on Judith Grover," she said, abruptly. "You know her better than I do. Take me over there. I want her to know that I'm her friend, and I don't want to go alone. I can't help thinking how she looked that day she came here—so proud and so strong! I call her a heroine, and she's the first heroine I ever saw in my life. Now, Lucian?"

She looked at her brother eagerly. With a sudden, impetuous movement Lucian drew the girl to him and kissed her. Belle held him close with her arm about his neck while she whispered, "Why, Lucian, is it so bad as that?"

She did not lift her head, and she did not see the glow that came to her brother's eyes. He did not speak for a moment. Then he said, in a rallying tone, "What a sentimental little creature you are, Belle!"

She raised her head. Could it be possible that she had been mistaken? She flounced out of the arm that held her. "Who's a better right to be sentimental, I should like to know? But you needn't try to deceive me. I know a few things."

"So glad. I'll have old Blacky put into the phaeton. We'll drive over now. And we needn't advertise to the whole household where we are going."

When Belle came out ready for the drive she brought with her a bunch of pale roses, which she carefully held in her lap.

Mr. Gerald was strolling along the drive, taking his after-dinner smoke. He elaborately raised his hat as they passed, and he smiled under his mustache in a way that did not disturb the apparent repose of his face.

"It's a pity Uncle Dick wasn't born in France," somewhat viciously remarked Belle, when they were well on the road. "He's a regular Frenchman. Sometimes I like him and sometimes I hate him."

The girl chattered on with her usual freedom and frankness, but when the horse's head was turned into the rarely travelled road that led to the Grover farm she became markedly silent.

In the farm-house the family were at the supper-table. One of the children had whined a little because she wanted something besides bread and milk. She had been reproved so sharply by her mother that she was now choking over her bowl.

Judith ate what she could, but of late food had no flavor

for her. Every faculty of her being was absorbed in the effort to find out some honest way whereby she could earn more money. If she could start fairly out of debt it seemed to her that she could make her mother and the children comfortable. But she could not start so. And to her independent and honest spirit the thought of the debts was continually with her—hounding her, stabbing her. She must save something out of every day's wage, something to go towards the debts. This necessity kept down the sum that she felt she could spend on the wants of life to a fearfully small amount.

Sometimes she wished that she could do as some people did—go on contracting debts wherever they could, not caring whether they were ever paid or not. But it was simply impossible to do that. She chafed so in her attempt to perform the impossible, in her hourly struggle to put all feeling from her, that she became gaunt and old-looking. But there was still in her face, her figure, her air that something which marked her as different from her surroundings—that nobility and strength and inherent sweetness ; only the latter quality was kept submerged beneath the waves of adversity in which she was struggling.

Now, as she sat at the bare table and knew that her mother and the children ought to have more and better food, her soul seemed to be fighting against itself and against fate. She could not eat. She sat with a stern face looking at the others. She knew that this was wrong also ; she ought at least to try to seem cheerful. She thought of God. Since He permitted these thing they must be right. After a while she would get herself in hand. She was resolved not to make a sombre home for these dear ones. She should be able presently to do better

Now she rose from the table and went out-of-doors, going towards the garden She was continually, in the midst of everything, thinking of Em and her sweet, loving ways. Em could never have grown up into a sordid, care-corroded woman, such as she herself was becoming. Yes, she was growing sordid, and her whole being revolted from that quality. Beneath all this, that encompassed and overlaid her, Judith was always half aware of some strange tropical longings that seemed to have come to her from a life she had lived somewhere else. These longings were continually cropping into sudden and acute life, and were as suddenly and strongly put down.

She had never thought anything about a theory of a pre-existence, she had heard none of the talk so common in these days. She knew absolutely nothing of it. What she knew was that she must keep on fighting as long as she lived. She would not have shirked if she could.

She came to Em's grave. She had been thinking there might be time for her to bring one barrow-load of loam. When she saw the care, the apparently loving care, that had been bestowed upon the mound since morning a quick dimness came to her eyes and a trembling to her frame. Whoever had done this, it was a kind act. She weakened under it. She knelt down and covered her face with her hands, swaying back and forth in the violence of her weeping. She was still in that attitude when her mother came to her.

"Judith," whispered the elder woman, "wa'n't he real kind?"

The girl lifted her swollen face. "Who was it?"

"I thought you'd know right off. He brought them roses, you remember."

"Oh, it was Lucian," responded Judith, calling young Eldridge by the name familiar in childhood.

"Yes. He met me on the cliff-walk this morning, and he come home with me, and he did this. He says he's going to sow some grass seed if we'll let him. But you come in 'n' bathe your face quick 's you can. He 'n' his sister are here. They've just drove up. You must hurry."

XX

MR. GERALD'S CALL

When Judith followed her mother into the now darkening sitting-room the two visitors rose to greet her. She wondered how any woman could look so lightly care free, so in tune with all bright things, as did Belle Eldridge. She felt herself to be like a black cloud coming upon the horizon. But she smiled as she gave her hand.

Belle's blue eyes darkened a little as she clung to the hand; then she suddenly reached up, put her arm round the tall girl, and kissed her warmly. "You must be so unhappy!" she cried, in a whisper. "I wanted my brother to bring me. I wanted to let you know—"

Here Belle found that she was not quite sure how to end the sentence, so she did not try to end it.

Judith's firm red mouth quivered slightly, then was brought under control. She had just wept all her tears out there in the garden. Belle, gazing at her, thought that she had never before known the meaning of the word "dusky" as applied to a woman's face.

"It's so good of you," said Judith, simply. Then she turned and shook hands with Lucian.

She sat down. She detected the odor of roses in the room. She recalled the handful of roses which Lucian had thrust upon her on the road that day It was very hard to speak. She was thankful to her mother for beginning to talk, and to Belle for joining in and keeping the conversation going.

When the guests rose Belle was wishing she could say that her mother would come soon to call, but she knew that she could not truthfully make such an announcement. The girl was not aware that Judith knew nothing of the importance to be attached to Mrs. Eldridge's visit, and that their own call was of no official worth ; that it was only a sign of their individual feelings. And so Judith in her heart was perhaps unduly grateful for Belle's kindness. She was comforted by the visit more than she would have thought possible. She was almost pitiably thankful for a kindness that did not trench upon her pride of independence.

She slept that night as she had not slept since her father's disappearance and Em's death.

The next week passed more calmly. Judith worked at home and in the shop every waking moment. And sometimes she thought she made some progress in the art of seeming cheerful.

It was one night in the second week that Mr. Gerald came. He sauntered into the yard as if he had been used to coming into that yard every day for years.

Mrs. Grover was lying down. She was not as well as usual. She said she must have taken cold. But she resolutely asserted that she wanted nothing, only to rest.

Judith was sitting in the doorway mending stockings by the last gleams of daylight. She rose, looking with a slightly cool surprise at this new-comer.

Mr. Gerald was very much at his ease. He took off his hat as he begged permission to sit down a few moments on the step—after Miss Grover had resumed her seat. So Judith went on with her work. Mr. Gerald talked, not in the least cynically, but with a gentle humor that began to amuse the girl before she was aware of it.

The dusk deepened into darkness, and still the man lingered. Judith invited him into the house, but he said that he was not one of those idiots who stopped in-doors in the summer.

"You'll smile in derision at me when you know my errand, Miss Grover," he said, after a silence.

Her work had been laid aside. She sat with her hands

folded over the stockings, the profile of her face dimly visible to the man sitting below her.

He was very much at his ease, and the girl had ceased to wonder why he had come. She was really enjoying his call. As she made no reply, he asked if she had no curiosity.

Judith was wondering, not about his errand, but as to why she was not disturbed by his presence. She turned towards him as if waiting for him to go on.

Mr. Gerald leaned a little nearer. He was congratulating himself that a summer evening and the presence of a woman like this woman still had a remnant of power over his pulses ; and he was surprised as well as gratified. He had not come for any sentimental reason, but a mixture of sentiment would be highly agreeable.

"I came here to talk with you on the subject of marriage," he said, deliberately.

She smiled.

"I see you don't understand me," he went on ; "not marriage in general, but our marriage, Miss Grover."

Judith's smile faded. She involuntarily drew back. "Don't you think it is poor taste for you to talk like that?" she asked.

She had no thought that he was serious, and she was offended. Did he think she was of so little consequence that he could jest with her in that way? She drew herself up still more.

"I knew you would be unjust," Mr. Gerald said, in his usual tone of suavity, in which one was never quite sure that there was no cynicism. "But I'm going to make you listen to me. I always know what I want ; I know immediately. When I met you in the street the other day I was positive that you were the woman to be my wife."

Judith rose to her feet. Mr. Gerald rose also. She stood tall before him, with her head held high. The man's eyes gleamed with delight in her appearance.

"I don't think I need to listen to you any longer," she said, coldly.

"Why not? I suppose a man has a right to tell a woman when he wants her to be his wife?"

Judith did not reply. She had not divested her mind of the monstrous idea that he was acting a part for some reason—perhaps for pastime.

"I mean what I say."

The two stood looking at each other like two opponents.

"Yes," said Gerald, with a ring of determination, "you and I are going to be man and wife within six months."

Again Judith made no reply. She was beginning to be convinced of her companion's sincerity, and this conviction brought with it a bewilderment that was like a cloud over her brain.

"I tell you," he went on, after a pause, "I'm a man who has seen a great deal of life. I've had my furores of passion and know just what they are worth. I've been thinking for a few years that I would marry. I didn't want one of the women who dress and make eyes. I've had more than enough of them. I want you. You are a strong woman. It will be interesting to subjugate you; for I shall do that. It will be difficult; nevertheless, I shall accomplish it. You don't think I shall; and perhaps you think I am not wise to tell you of this in advance. I'm not making love, you know. We are arranging a bargain. Let us look the matter in the face. You are under a cloud. I don't care a farthing for that. I wouldn't care if you had killed your father. I can take care of you. You are so poor that you can't provide for your family. You would keep on with the struggle, but you can't succeed. I have figured the thing out exactly. I know all your debts, incurred, many of them, because of your father. I know precisely what you earn. And if any of you should be ill, if you yourself should be ill, what then? You know what then. But I'm not one of those brutes about whom novels are written, and who force penniless maidens to marry them. You will think this proposition over in all its phases, and you will see it as I do. Miss Grover, do you understand me? You will see it as I do."

"'I DON'T THINK I NEED TO LISTEN TO YOU ANY LONGER'"

A certain strain had come into the man's voice. Judith heard it without knowing what it was. It had the curious effect of rousing her combativeness at the same time that it made her wonder as to the power of her own will. She had never felt this wonder before.

"No," she said, at last, "I do not think that I shall see it as you do."

Mr. Gerald smiled, but in the dusk she did not know that.

"Do not trouble yourself to refuse me," he answered. "I know very well that that is what you are going to do. That is quite of course. I will now wish you good-evening."

He took off his hat with elaborate movement, bowed deeply, and then walked out of the yard.

Judith stood leaning against the door-casing. She put her hand up to her forehead and pressed it there. She was inclined to smile, only there was something strange and almost weird about the interview. In the morning she would find that she had dreamed it. She heard Mr. Gerald's footfall sounding on the still road. Yes, he had certainly been there. He had—

"Judith!" called her mother's voice.

The girl gathered up her mended stockings and carried them in. She found her mother sitting bolt-upright on the lounge. She seemed to be shivering. Judith wrapped a shawl about the frail form, saying, as she did so, "I thought you were asleep, mother."

"I was jest drowsin' when I heard a man's voice," was the answer. "I couldn't help hearin'. Doors and winders were open, you know."

The girl did not speak. It was very dark in the house. These people did not have a light unless it was absolutely needed.

Suddenly Mrs. Grover said, "I wish you'd kindle a lamp. I feel 's if I wanted a lamp." She spoke querulously.

In silent surprise the girl did as her mother wished.

"Set it right there," pointing to the table ; "I want it where I c'n see you, Judith."

The elder woman looked long at the girl. As the gaze continued, Judith's blood ran slower and slower in her veins. She would not break the silence.

"I heard all he said," Mrs. Grover finally began. "I heard every word. I was 'fraid I shouldn't hear, 'n' I got up still, 'n' went to the winder."

.Again Judith did not speak. Her mother's pleading eyes were stabbing into her heart.

"I never listened before," said Mrs. Grover. "'Taint my habit." She shivered, and drew her shawl closer over her shoulders. "I s'pose he's a rich man, ain't he?"

"I suppose so."

"I heard Mis' Guild tellin' that he was worth more 'n two million."

"Very likely."

"More 'n two million," repeated the woman. Then she shivered once more. She kept her eyes fixed on her daughter's face. After a moment she said that when she married Hanford she wasn't a grain in love with him. She didn't s'pose 'twas necessary. But she respected him, and it was better for a woman to be married. And women grew 'tached to their husbands. She knew Hanford 'd been unlucky, 'n' had liver complaint. But women grew 'tached to their husbands. She s'posed folks generally didn't expect to be much more 'n 'tached to their husbands. When she had repeated this phrase for the third time she stopped. But she continued to keep her eyes on the young and darkly pallid face the other side of the lamp.

XXI

A LOVER

"Mother," said Judith, at last, "what do you mean?"

"Oh," returned the woman, desolately, "I don't mean nothing. I guess I'll lay down agin. I shouldn't wonder if I was comin' on with a low fever."

Judith suggested that her mother go to bed. She helped her to undress, and then brewed some pennyroyal tea. She sat on the side of the bed while her mother sipped the hot drink.

When she had taken the cup from her Mrs. Grover said, with feeble emphasis, "There's one thing I do want to say, Judith, 'n' that is, don't you go to flyin' in the face of Providence. Don't you do it."

The next morning Judith came down as soon as it was light. With a sinking of the heart, which no one who has not felt it can understand, she saw that her mother was ill—not violently ill, but in a low, feverish state that would incapacitate her for work. But Mrs. Grover insisted that Judith should go to the factory; the two children would stay at home and wait upon her.

In the evening, when the girl sat beside her mother, who was lying on the lounge, a hard, thin hand was put impressively on Judith's arm.

"Have you be'n thinkin' 'bout what I said?" she asked, in a dry, eager voice.

Judith nodded. She was so sick at heart that it was difficult to speak.

"It's more 'n two million. I can't imagine so much money." The woman lay silent. Then she began again:

"Of course, I know well enough you ain't in love with any one. Now there's Tom Rylance—"

"Mother," began Judith, hurriedly, "I want to explain to you that love isn't for me. I wouldn't marry any man who thought he loved me, for he'd have to bear my burden too. Some folks think I've committed murder. You needn't look so. That's what they think. No, I never would marry any man who thought he loved me. I'm a marked woman. I'm not going to be happy. But I can bear it." Judith sat erect and threw back her shoulders.

Her mother kept her hold on her arm. "I married your father—" she began again; but Judith said "Please don't!" in such a way that she did not go on.

It was in this way that the following week passed. Mrs. Grover succumbed to a fever that held her helpless. The neighbors came, and brought jellies and blanc-mange. The children did as well as they could. But on Judith the burden was heavy. She slept very little, for she was often up to do something for the sick woman.

Every day her mother would gaze pathetically at her, and would then hope that Judith knew what she was doing. Once she said it really did seem providential, as Judith had made up her mind not to marry any one who loved her.

The girl did not ask what was providential. Her mind weakened and grew hazy under the strain. She wished that she might sleep for one long night. Perhaps that rest might clear the atmosphere. She became aware that she was not seeing things right. Every time she looked at her mother she felt guilty.

Two or three times Lucian called. He found Judith cold and strange. He could not understand her. He was aware that his uncle watched him closely. Sometimes the younger man would lift his head defiantly and return the gaze. Then the elder man would thoughtfully pull his mustache and smile. At such times Lucian was sure that it would be a great satisfaction to hit out from his shoulder hard at the

handsome, well-preserved face that seemed to wear an unreasonable expression of triumph.

Why should Gerald be triumphant? Lucian grew inwardly furious asking himself that question. And Judith
did not seem the same to him. Not that she had ever been
very cordial, but she had been different. What puzzled him
still more was the attitude Mrs. Grover now assumed towards him, for she had been far kinder than her daughter had
ever been. She was now constrained and unlike herself.
Was it because she was ill? Lucian carried her flowers and
dainties. Sometimes Belle went with him, and the two sat
with Mrs. Grover and waited upon her while Judith was at
the factory. She was not so ill that it seemed absolutely
necessary that the elder girl should stay at home, for the
poor must do as they can.

One day at dinner Mrs. Eldridge remarked that she understood that Lucian and Belle had taken a fancy to do a
little slumming. She spoke languidly, but there was a sting
in her voice. Her son's eyes caught fire instantly. Uncle
Dick ostentatiously did not look at him. Belle pressed her
foot on his under the table, and he smothered the disrespectful answer that had rushed to his lips to be spoken.

Belle responded, in as languid a voice as her mother had
used, that there was no place in town where they could slum,
but that she should like it above all things if there were,
doing good gave one such a comfortable feeling. It was to
the soul what a new seal-skin jacket in winter was to the body.

"Belle, you sound irreverent," said her mother, whereupon
the girl immediately repeated her remark, and then laughed
in a light, saucy manner.

At the first opportunity Belle frankly told her brother
that he came very near being a fool that day at dinner.
What was the use of his getting mamma up on her ear, she
should like to know?

Lucian began to be very wretched in those days, and he
was becoming more and more in love with Judith. Her distant and yet kind manner perplexed him and urged him on.

"I suppose I bore you almost beyond endurance," he said to her that evening.

He had hurried across the fields, his setter at his heels, as soon as the Eldridge dinner was over. The dog was sitting leaning up against Judith, and she sometimes stopped sewing on a garment she was making over for one of her sisters and gently stroked the handsome chestnut head of the dog. The action seemed to comfort her. She looked across Random at his master.

"No, you don't bore me at all," she answered, in her truthful, straightforward way.

"And you like to have me come?"

Now the girl hesitated. Her eyes fell beneath those of her companion.

"Oh, Judith," he exclaimed, sorrowfully, "you can't tell a falsehood, and you hate to hurt me!"

"I do like to have you come—in a way," she replied.

"In what way?"

"Because your coming shows how kind you are." She spoke promptly now, as if she were sure that she was saying the right thing.

"Oh yes, I'm awfully kind," he responded, mockingly. "I dislike extremely to come here, but I will do it out of kindness to you. You see what a fine fellow I am, don't you?"

Judith said nothing. She took up her sewing again.

Lucian gazed a moment at her in silence. He was confusedly asking himself how it happened that there could be a girl like this right here in his own town—a girl with a dark, rich face that was full of a bewitching suggestiveness. Now, in this sunset light, she might be— Ah, well, Lucian did not try to tell himself what she might be. He was well aware that, mingled with all that Southern opulence of personal appearance, Judith had that individual power which comes from the mere ability to be able to determine, and to abide by that determination. There was something somewhere in her face—he could not tell where—that showed this power.

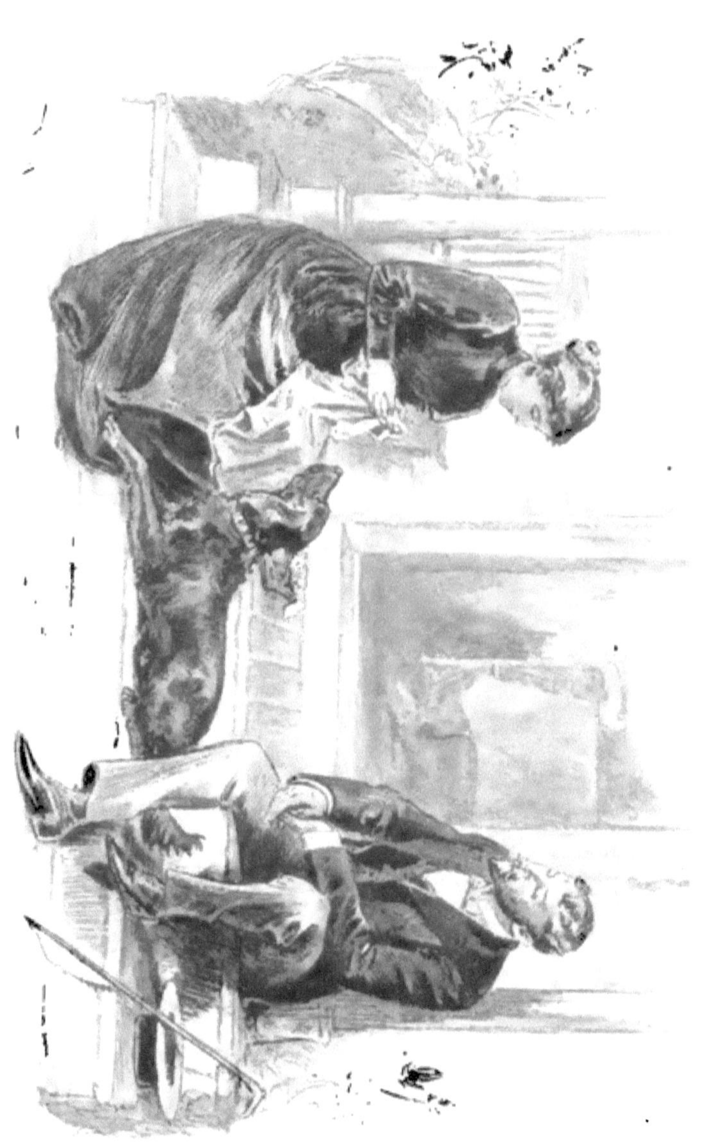

Young Eldridge continued to look at her. Suddenly he leaned forward and put his hand authoritatively on hers that held the half-completed frock. She withdrew her hand with an impatient movement and put it over her eyes. He saw her lips quiver.

"Judith," he whispered—"Judith, you are not angry with me? You must know I can't help loving you."

She hastily placed her other hand up to her face. He bent still nearer her, but he did not touch her. The dog reached forward and rested his head on the girl's lap.

"How weak I am!" he heard her murmur.

"You know I've got to love you," he went on, with that impetus which comes from a previous constrained silence. "And I've got to tell you of it, at last. But you must have known it—oh, surely you knew it!"

Now he bent and kissed her hands, that were still covering her face. He kissed them again and again. She withdrew them and tried to look up at him, but her eyes, full of tears, drooped heavily. But the one glance made him seize those hands and hold them in a masterful way. His face shone with that transfiguration which comes sometimes in a man's life, and makes him for one moment a being to be envied of the gods.

"De.   ! oh, my dearest!" he whispered.

A little later he insisted, as lovers will. He begged her to say she loved him. It was not enough that he believed it; she must tell him.

"Oh yes, I love you," she answered.

Having said this she thrust him from her with a savage movement. She tried to rise. But Lucian held her within his arm. He would not be thrust away in that manner. He immediately assumed that her confession gave him some rights.

"I must go! I tell you, I must go!" she exclaimed, her voice low but imperative.

"No, no! You must give me this moment," he returned, in the same voice. "Do you think you are going to starve me, my love? My love! Oh, you don't know what you are, Judith! You are lovely to me. You are magnificent! And you are mine! Yes, you are mine! I've been tortured for the last few weeks. You don't know how I've suffered. But this makes up for everything. This would make up for a thousand years."

Lucian was smitten with that garrulousness of the suddenly happy lover. He was going on with phrases that would sound extravagant, but that to him seemed contemptibly feeble. Where are the words that are tender enough and passionate enough? Alas! Lucian knew that there are no such words.

Judith placed her hands on his breast, and gently pushed him from her. He stood gazing at her, wondering at the new attractiveness of a face he had thought familiar.

"Let us stop this," she said. "I ought not to have told you that I love you." Her voice suddenly melted to an exquisite cadence. "But I do—I do love you. To-night I will say it. No, don't come nearer." She still held him off. "To-night I will tell you that you are light and joy and happiness—all lovely things in the world to me; that your love is water to thirst, food to hunger." She paused, her eyes fixed on his eyes, and on her face was no maiden shyness, only the majesty of love confessed and unashamed. "I wanted to tell you once. I wanted once to let myself loose from the iron chains that I must wear—only once in all my life. Don't you know, dear Lucian, that I can't be your wife? That would be an injury that I shall never do you. Don't speak yet. I can imagine that I could have been persuaded to marry you if I had been only poor. But it's worse than that. You know how it is. You see, I love you, so I'm not going to harm you. No, no; don't speak. I've thought it all out. Perhaps I'm mistaken. but it's what I believe. And when I believe a thing I must do it. I can't help doing it if it kills me."

She stopped abruptly. She took her hands from his breast and stepped out into the yard.

XXII

WATCHING

LUCIAN remained a moment leaning against the doorframe, watching the girl as she walked aimlessly back and forth. His dog glanced up at him, then gravely went and placed himself behind Judith and paced slowly after her.

Lucian's thoughts were so confused that he could hardly be said to be thinking. His hurrying pulses forbade thought. As yet the sweetness of Judith's words was diffusing itself through his consciousness. The bitterness had hardly made itself felt. Of course he could not believe her when she had said that she would not be his wife. She was sincere, but he could persuade her to change that decision. Her own heart would help him to do that. Still— Here a cold doubt came to him and pressed him away from her, as the girl's hand had just done She paused in front of him. A few yards of space separated them.

The night had come on and the gloom was deepening. It was sultry, and the fire-flies were flitting among the lilac-bushes on the other side of the yard. Lucian particularly noted the fire-flies. The air was filled with the odor of thick clumps of blossoming meadow's-queen and elder-blow that grew in the low land back of the house.

Lucian dimly wished the odor were not so heavy. He almost thought that perfume prevented him from thinking clearly. And there was Judith's face looking very white in the semi-darkness.

"Lucian," said the girl, softly, "you won't think of me in any way that will make you unhappy? You surely won't do that? Oh," with a sudden weakness, "I am wretched enough without having that to remember!"

The young man made a quick movement towards her. But she recoiled.

"No! Don't come near me again! I've been wrong and weak. So wrong and weak! I ought not to have told you. I ought to have let you think I didn't love you."

"Judith!"

"Yes. I ought to have done that. But it was so hard! And I hated to hurt you. Lucian, you don't know how I hate to hurt you."

The pathetic tenderness of her voice, and at the same time the resolution in it, were so disarming to Lucian that he stood there in silence for a space. Then the rebellion, the furious uprising of his whole being against her decision broke forth. His words came so fast that he could hardly speak them. He stood there with his eyes blazing across the distance between them. He begged, he entreated. He tried to tell her how he loved her, and what the world would be to him without her. As he went on she bent her head, but she endeavored to stand erect. All at once she flung out her hands.

"Stop!" she cried. "I can't bear this! And I cannot—no, I cannot, even for you, Lucian—change myself. You shall not marry a woman like me. You would be sorry, and I should be sorry. Now will you go?"

There was that in her manner that made Eldridge know that he must obey her. Without another word he turned and walked towards the road. He had gone a few rods when he faced about and hurried back. The girl was still standing as he had left her. He reached forward and touched her hand, but he did not attempt to take it.

"Judith," hoarsely, "it's because of what they think about you and your father, isn't it?" He could not say the thing more plainly.

"Yes. And I can see that more and more people think it," was the answer. She turned towards him. A strange flash came to her eyes. " Sometimes, when I haven't slept, and I can't sleep much, I have times of asking myself if I could have done that. Yes, I ask myself that. Perhaps, if I were your wife, and you learned that I had a wild temper, you would put that same question to yourself. Then I should die of grief. I couldn't bear that. Now will you go ?"

" Not yet. If I should find out that your father is living, and he should testify—"

" Lucian ! How strangely you talk ! He is dead. I've dreamed and dreamed that I saw him lying dead under the water. Now will you go ?"

" If I should find him alive, will you marry me, Judith ?"

The girl's face at this moment revealed so much love that Lucian thought he was answered. But her words were different. " If I am free," she said.

" Free ! Good God !" He could not say any more. What did she mean ? He would not ask. He turned abruptly and walked away. She looked after him almost as if she would call him back. But she made no movement. The setter-dog gazed up a moment in her face, and she stooped and, in a blind way, patted his head. Then he cantered after his master.

Judith hesitated ; it seemed as if she would go into the house. But she did not immediately do so. She went slowly along the yard and down into the garden. She paused at the patch of ground that she had found time to spade and plant beans in. Following the everyday routine, her mind, as if it were a piece of mechanism, took note of the fact that the patch needed hoeing. Even in the growing darkness she could see that. She dimly saw Em's grave beyond. She stood looking in that direction. She longed to stay out-of-doors in the quiet loveliness of the night. But she knew she could not allow herself that luxury. Her mother might need her. She had already been away from her too long.

Judith went back to the door where she had been sitting.

She gathered up her work and entered the house. She trod
softly, and felt her way in the dark. Her mother was asleep
on the lounge. She heard her breathing. This knowledge
gave the girl a sudden relief from tension. She sank down
in a chair and leaned her head back. The weakness that
came upon her for an instant almost seemed like the weakness of death. And the thought of that possibility had a
strange sweetness in it.

Her mother moved. "Judith! You here?"

"Yes, mother. Do you want anything?"

"Some cold water—real cold. I want it right out of the
well."

So Judith rose and took the pail to the well. When she
gave the glass of water her mother said. "I've been dream-
in'; 'n' I never see anything seem so real 's that dream
did."

"What was it?" for the girl saw that her mother wished
to tell her dream.

"I thought you'd married that rich man, 'n' you was jest
as happy as you could be; and we all was so comfortable.
It did seem so queer 'n' so lovely for us all to be comfortable."

There was no reply to this. The daughter suggested
that her mother go to bed. "And I shall be right here on
the lounge, and shall be sure to hear."

Mrs. Grover obeyed this suggestion. As Judith was turning away from the bed her hand was caught and held fast.

"You know you can't never pay all them debts, 'n' the
moggidge to keep up," the woman said, piteously. "It's jest
beyend you; that's what it is."

"I can keep trying."

"I tell you 'tain't no use. It 'll jest wear you out. 'N'
after you're worn out, you 'n' what there is left of us c'n go
to the poor-house. I don't want to end my days in the poor-
house."

Mrs. Grover was ill enough to find it impossible not to
talk like this. And why was her daughter hesitating in this

way ? Plenty of girls who had money enough of their own would say " Yes," thankfully, to Mr. Gerald.

" I wa'n't a mite in love with your father," began the woman.

" Mother !"

" Well, I wa'n't. It's better for a woman to be married ; and—"

" Has it been better for you, mother ?" suddenly and sharply.

The woman restlessly turned her head on the pillow. " You needn't speak so. Hanford 'd been a good husband if his liver hadn't plagued him so."

There was no answer to this. Judith was turning to leave the room. She was going to the lounge to lie there, awake and thinking, all night. When the dawn began to come she might have an hour's restless sleep.

" Judith !"

" Yes, mother."

" You always did have more will 'n all of us put together. You would give back that money for the seraphine. You made your father awful mad. It's all your doin's. If you hadn't done jest 's you have he wouldn't have gone on the cliffs that night, 'n' then he wouldn't have fallen over, 'n' then he'd be'n here now. You see, you would pay back that money. You see how it's all come about."

This was not accurately stated, but there was reason enough in it to appeal forcibly to the weary mind of the girl. The chain of events seemed to her linked together very much as her mother had said ; and the chain dragged her down.

" I don't feel 's if I should sleep a wink to-night," said Mrs. Grover.

She loved her girl, but it seemed to her unaccountable that Judith should hesitate about accepting Mr. Gerald. In the mother's view it was the luckiest thing that could happen, this offer of marriage. And she had an idea that she was not trying to influence Judith.

"I'll steep you some skull-cap; perhaps that 'll soothe you," said Judith.

"No," with feverish irritability.   "There won't anything soothe me."

"Mother," said Judith, when she brought the drink, "I'll try to make up my mind to-night."   She hesitated before she added, "If you think it's all been my fault—"

"But you're jest as headstrong 'n' wilful 's you can be; you know you are, Judith."

XXIII

DECISION

THE girl went back to the lounge. She arranged the pillow as carefully as if she expected to rest. She wrapped the faded old shawl about her. She remembered the shawl as one which had been put around her when she had been too young to go out-of-doors alone. The article was like a tangible memory to her. Yes, it must be true that she had been young enough once to be free from care. She smoothed the shawl with a wistful, tender motion. She thought lovingly of her mother, who had talked to her so constantly, and yet who seemed to believe that she had not in the least tried to influence her daughter's decision. Of course, her mother had always been like that, only Judith had never known it before. Perhaps all mothers were like that, and perhaps she herself was so. She was continually finding out things about herself.

It seemed that she was very strange to hesitate in the saying " Yes " to Mr. Gerald. And if she was to blame for her father's falling and being drowned—oh, if his death could really be laid to her!—surely she ought to be willing to do what she could; she ought to be willing to accept a splendid position.

It was true that she loved Lucian. Here her hands involuntarily shut themselves upon the old shawl. But it was also true that she was as removed from him as if the world were between them. And it would always be so. Upon that Judith was as sure as if she could see into their whole future lives, and see them forever growing apart.

The girl had so positive a nature that to believe her

own conclusions was habitual with her; and now she was bewildered that she had hesitated so long in making up her mind. But it was made up as regarded Lucian. She could never marry him. She wished that she might pluck out her love and fling it from her, since their ways would be different. She must not, by so much as one thought, consider that love in deciding upon Mr. Gerald's offer.

Here Judith sat suddenly upright on the lounge. She would have liked to walk hurriedly about the house; but no, she might disturb her mother. She went noiselessly to an open window and knelt down by it. It was still sultry. Along the western horizon "heat-lightning" was playing across a bank of cloud. How loud the crickets chirped! Indistinctly the outlines of the familiar scene came to her heart rather than to her vision. She drew the shawl more closely about her and leaned her head on the window-shelf.

This was the first time in her life when she had not made up her mind almost directly upon her course of action. This indecision of itself confused her; she did not recognize herself. There was absolutely no one whom she could consult, and she knew if there were that she could not take advice on such a subject. She felt so strangely alone that for the moment it was as if the world had receded from her; only here still were the seductive odors and sounds of a summer night.

It was not late; the clock had but a short time before struck ten. She heard a rustle among the boughs of the lilacs, then the shadowy shape of a dog appeared. He came directly to her and licked her hands. It was Lucian's setter. Presently a shrill, imperative whistle sounded down the road. Random looked up at his friend, cocked his ears and wagged his tail, but he did not go. He remembered very well how many times within the last few weeks he had come this way when no one but himself and his master knew. So he stood still. The sound of the whistle came nearer. Another shape—this time that of a man—came into view on the road.

Judith was aware that she could not be seen where she was, and she remained quiet. Her strong young eyes were fixed on the man who had now reached the gate; he paused there. The girl's pulses beat heavily. She was telling herself that it was a miserable, desperate love; but, having known it, would she wish never to have felt it? She was morbid to that degree that she was sure that she had been born only for misfortune. How silly it was of her to make such an ado in her mind about her decision! What did it matter, anyway?

Lucian whistled again. Instead of obeying the dog gave a short bark, as if to inform his master where he was. Young Eldridge hesitated an instant. The house was dark; it stood blackly and silently there in the night, and it held the woman he loved. He had strolled restlessly out-of-doors. He had come here, impelled by that power which is forever going to be the strongest of all powers. "I shall disturb no one," he said to himself. He walked in the direction from which Random's bark had sounded.

Now was the time when Judith should have withdrawn into that greater darkness in the house; but she did not. She suddenly whispered the words, "It is the last time. This time I will see him—if he comes."

She blushed as she spoke — that blush of delight and agony which the warm natured can know.

He was sure to come. He had been remembering too keenly her words—"If I am free!" Still, he had not meant to come.

Somehow a lover may arrive in his sweetheart's presence without the least intention of doing so.

"Judith!" he exclaimed.

She leaned forward and held up her hand. "Hush! mother is asleep." He took the hand, but she withdrew it. "I was wrong to stay here after Random came," she said, blushing again.

"It was—it was divine of you," he returned, in a half-voice.

Then he hurriedly tried to speak in a reasonable way. He said that she was going directly against common-sense; she was thinking of making them both miserable just for a whim. They could marry and go the ends of the earth. Really, she ought to be made to see how absurd her position was.

"I can't be made to see it. I tell you I must do what seems right to me. We will not talk about that any more." She shrank back within the room as she spoke.

"When I am away from you I am sure I can make you understand—" he began again.

She interrupted him. A flash of something, she knew not what, decided her terrible question for her.

"Lucian!" She again leaned out of the window, but she motioned him away as he would have pressed eagerly nearer. "I want to tell you that I am going to make it impossible, even in your mind, for us to keep on loving each other."

"You can't do that," hotly. "I shall always love you."

"No; you'll get over it. When you really know how hopeless it all is"—a pause—"then you will begin to say, 'I did think I loved her, but—' "

"What do you mean?" with sharp emphasis.

"I mean that I am going to marry Mr. Richard Gerald."

There was a moment's silence. The words had had a curious sound, spoken into the warm, perfumed air.

Eldridge flung up his head. It is the instinct of some men to stand straight when they are wounded.

"Ah!" he said. Then he continued: "Mr. Richard Gerald has a great deal of money. I can confidently inform you that he has several millions."

"I am going to marry him for his money."

"Indeed! Good-night, Miss Grover. I am sorry that I had not the millions."

He was going.

"Stop!" imperatively. He stood still, his hat in his

hand. "If you had a hundred million I would not marry you as I am. Because I love you, Lucian Eldridge."

She rose from her place by the window and went back into the darkness of the kitchen. She stood there and heard him walk away. After a little she went to the bed-room door and listened. Her mother was sleeping. She stood motionless for a long time.

Then she again sought the lounge and laid herself down upon it. She had said the words. So far as she was con-cerned, it was as if the marriage had already taken place. If her mother should waken she would tell her that she had made her decision. She tried to take comfort from think-ing how glad she would make her mother. But she caught herself saying. "Nothing is of any consequence." She could not find the least consolation in those words. She was conscious of a sudden and terrible loss of self-respect. This was an unexpected sensation, and one she had never known before. She found it impossible to lie still ; so she rose and went to the window again. She leaned far out of it.

Lucian had gone. He had gone forever out of her life. Well, it was of no consequence. And he would not respect her. What of that ? But she would like to respect herself. Yes, she would be glad to be able to do that ; but she never could again.

She threw her hands outside of the window and wrung them. She could not keep perfectly still in this stress of suffering. She moaned under her breath. Then strongly she took command of herself. She sat there with the damp, warm air blowing over her until she heard, muffled in the distance, the town clock striking midnight.

How her mother had slept ! Sleep was a blessing for which she longed, but it would not come. She folded her arms and put her head down on them. In a moment she also was asleep. When her mother called her an hour later she rose, stiff and confused, and wondering what had happened to her.

Mrs. Grover was wide awake, and tossing to and fro on the bed. "I've been calling 'n' calling," she said. "But I s'pose you're all tired out, Judith. I want some more water—right from the well. Be sure you git it right from the well."

When the girl brought the water in one hand and a lighted lamp in the other, Mrs. Grover stared at the face above the lamp and did not notice the tumbler which was extended towards her.

"Merciful sakes!" she exclaimed; "what's happened to you, Judith?"

"Nothing," answered the girl. She did not know how cold she seemed. "I've been asleep."

Her mother took the water, but continued to gaze over the glass. "You look terrible odd," she said, when she had drank. Then she dropped her head on the pillow. "I guess I'm dretful sick," she continued, querulously. "I ought to have the doctor; I know I ought not to let a fever run on so. But we can't have anything. 'Tain't no matter. You go 'n' lay down again." But the girl remained standing by the bed. "Why don't you go? I don't need nothin' more. You go 'n' git a nap. But what does make you look so odd?"

"I wanted to tell you something," said Judith. Having spoken thus far it suddenly seemed impossible for her to continue. It was as if a hand were put upon her mouth. She made another effort and said, "I told you I was going to decide; and I have decided."

Mrs. Grover glanced up eagerly. The face above her was strong and resolute, and already beginning to be hard.

"I shall marry Mr. Gerald," said Judith. "He is coming again in a few days. I shall tell him I will marry him. I suppose he will have money enough to take care of us all."

"Oh, Judith!"

Mrs. Grover's worn face lighted. She put out her hand towards her daughter, who took it and held it tenderly, the touch warming her heart a little.

"You won't be sorry, Judith, I know you won't," said Mrs. Grover, still with the same eagerness. "Why, there ain't a girl nowhere round but would jump at your chance. You've finally been real lucky. He must think an awful lot of you. You ought to remember that. 'N' a woman ought to be married. Somehow women don't seem to have no standin' if they ain't married."

Thus spoke the woman who had been Hanford Grover's wife.

"The Lord won't forgit that you done it for your mother 'n' sisters. Why, when I married Hanford I didn't pretend to be in love with him. 'Tain't necessary. 'Tain't—"

"Don't let's talk any more, mother, please. Try to go to sleep again," soothingly.

"I'm jest as excited 's I c'n be," was the quick reply. "Judith, I always did say there never was no girl like you. 'N' I'm so thankful, now you have decided, that I 'ain't never tried to influence you any."

Part II

XXIV

A RICH MAN'S WIFE

"I s'pose it's longer ago than it seems. Time jest races when one gits to growin' old. It don't seem more 'n six months to me, Nathan. How does it seem to you?"

Mrs. Guild was carefully dusting the rungs of the kitchen rocker. Her husband was sitting by the open window, looking over papers of seeds he had saved for this spring's planting.

"It don't seem no time to me," was the response. "But I know 'twill be two years in the fall comin'."

"That so? Well, I s'pose it must be. But I can't take it in somehow. 'N' I ain't seen her sence the day she was married. Did you say Ellis Macomber met um comin' from the deepo this mornin'?"

"Yes. Course he met um. He sees everybody 'n' hears everything. I wish I could come across them long spine cucumber seed. Where be they, do you think?"

"How'd they look? I d' know nothin' 'bout your garden seeds, Nathan; I never meddle with um. 'D he say how they looked?"

"He said they looked splendid."

"Did Judith know him?"

"Know him?" with a grin. "Do you think she's lost her mind 'cause she's married so rich? Anyway, she had to know him, for Ellis said he jest hailed um; so the horses were stopped, 'n' he shook hands. He says Mr. Gerald's the perlitest feller you ever seen: only he dunno, somehow, what to make of his perliteness. But Ellis don't know much, anyway. He said Judith arst 'bout Mis' Macomber's asthmy. He told me that's if 'twas the queen arskin' after that asthmy."

"I don't s'pose she'll come here," said Mrs. Guild, going to the door to shake her dust-cloth. "But I always did think a lot of Judith Grover, 'n' I always knew she never pushed Hanford off no more 'n she pushed me off. The land!"

This exclamation was uttered after a slight pause. It made Mr. Guild raise his eyes from his box of vegetable seeds and turn them down the road. He saw a woman coming rapidly towards the house. She was not dressed like the village people, though the man could not tell in the least what was the difference. In a moment she had turned in at the gate.

Mr. Guild rose, and his packages dropped to the floor. "If that ain't Judith!" he cried.

The new-comer had put her arm about Mrs. Guild's neck and kissed her. She turned and shook hands with Mr. Guild, who had hurried forward.

"Come right in," said the elder woman, heartily. "My! but I am glad to see you! Se' down. I s'pose you've been to your mother's?"

"Yes, I just came from there. I'm going back; but I wanted to see you."

As Judith spoke Mrs. Guild was gazing at her with a curious intentness. In spite of the fact that she had come so quickly to see her old friend, the woman was aware of some indescribable coldness in Judith's tone, or was it in her face?

Mrs. Gerald's face and figure were strikingly handsome. She was dressed irreproachably, and with that subdued effect which rich material and faultless fitting can produce. She was so aristocratic in appearance that Mrs. Guild, gazing at her, recalled vividly those days when Judith Grover had been the most shabbily clothed girl and the poorest in the town.

"How'd you find um to your mother's?" inquired Mrs.

Guild after a moment, during which the younger woman had been looking about her with the air of one who sees once familiar things after a long absence.

"I found them well," she answered. "I've never seen mother so strong and so prosperous looking. And the farm seems like another place."

"It must seem real good to you to see the old spot so different," remarked Mrs. Guild. As there was no response to this the speaker glanced up in surprise, and repeated, "Don't it seem real good?"

"I'm glad they're prosperous," was the evasive reply.

Mrs. Guild stared in silence for an instant, and as she stared she was aware that the girl's face had changed even more than she had thought. It was handsomer—yes, certainly it was handsomer, but with a sinking of the heart the warm-natured woman decided that it was— Having reached this point in her thoughts Mrs. Guild suddenly found that she could not in the least describe the change in Judith's countenance.

The visitor went on to make inquiries after almost everybody in the village. She listened to the replies, and all the time she knew that her companions were watching her. When she rose she said she was going directly back to her mother's. She was to stay there through the day.

"But where be you stoppin'? To Squire Eldridge's, I s'pose?"

"Yes. But Mr. Gerald is going away in a few days, and then I shall stay with mother for a week or so."

She had risen, and was standing near the door. She looked at Mrs. Guild earnestly, and that woman was aware that her heart began to beat faster.

"I declare," she said, hurriedly, "it's a dretful good to see you back again, Judith."

"Thank you," said Judith. She lingered. "It is curious," she continued, suddenly, "that when I was abroad I seemed to be really here more than there. No matter where I travelled I was always thinking of this village. I was seeing the rocky pastures, the old fences, and this kitchen, Mrs. Guild." Judith's voice had a thrill in it which communicated itself to the consciousness of her hearers. "I remembered how kind you were when little Em died of the diphtheria," went on Judith, in the same tone. "When I was looking at those wonderful pictures in the Louvre, between me and the canvas there kept coming Em's face as it was when I held her that night. Yes, you two were very kind to me always. I didn't want you to think that because I had married a rich man I could forget such things. Even if I should seem to forget, I remember all the same. But I don't think I shall speak like this again."

Judith passed through the open door out into the sunshine of the yard. Mrs. Guild followed her. "I hope you're happy, Judith," she said.

"Thank you," was the answer, in a superficial and yet kind manner, "I'm fully as happy as I deserve to be," with a slight laugh.

Mrs. Guild kept by her side. "I guess the most of us, if we're happy at all, are enough sight happier 'n we deserve to be," she said.

"It does me good to see my mother," said Judith, earnestly. "All my life, till my marriage, she had been suffering from grinding poverty and overwork. She looks like a different woman. You'll come and see us, won't you, Mrs. Guild?"

Judith walked down the road. She went erectly, with an easy swing that was full of grace and strength. The other woman watched her. Then she returned to the room where her husband still sat. "I declare!" she exclaimed.

"Well, what now?"

But his wife did not reply. She took up her dust-cloth and went to work with it. But occasionally she stopped and repeated her words: "I declare!"

Judith went her ways, turning into the field at the same broken place in the fence that she had known—how many years ago? She walked steadily on as if with a well-defined purpose. That purpose was manifest when she began to climb the ascent that led to the path over the cliffs. She had not been there since that night when she had last seen her father.

Now the sunlight was pouring over water and land. There was a brisk east wind; the ocean was a sparkling ultramarine, the waves of the incoming tide rushed along with white crests on them as far as the vision could reach. Every object was sharply defined; the shore line stretching north and south was a bright glitter of white sand.

Judith stood at the topmost part of the path. She unfurled her parasol and held it up towards the sun. The breeze swept her skirts back. Gradually the air brought a glow to her eyes and to her heart. There was life and beauty in that air and in the scene before her. It was a "day of golden glory"—one of those days which come to the New England coast to make you wonder why one should ever spend a summer anywhere else. There were boats scattered on the water; a steamer, far away in the offing, was leaving a long trail of smoke against the bright sky.

Judith watched every object. Finally, without being really aware that she did so, she was watching one sail that was coming nearer and nearer, the craft careening over and cutting the blue water, seeming to make a line right through its surface. There were two men in the boat; one was managing it, the other was sitting in the stern. Having watched it for some moments she was sure that it was coming in at the landing-place where boats had come in on this coast ever since she could remember, a place where the Grover farm ran down to the sea and made a safe, shallow beach. Having decided this in her own mind, Judith straightway forgot the boat, and fell to looking more vaguely at other familiar objects. And how the sight of familiar objects will stab the wanderer who has returned home!

Presently Judith walked slowly down the path towards her home. She was pausing by the gap in the fence that led into the home field, which was no longer unkempt, but now had the look of a prosperous bit of "mowing." She leaned on the wall. She was, perhaps, asking herself where was that girl who had so many times hurried over this farm, always too busy to stop to enjoy anything. Well, that same girl had leisure enough now.

There were steps behind her. She was annoyed, and drew herself up, not raising her eyes, merely waiting for the person to pass. But the steps paused.

"Judith, ain't that you?" asked a familiar voice.

XXV

RETURN

JUDITH turned about sharply, the blood flying into her face, and her pulses trying to throttle her.

"I declare I thought it must be you, though I ain't never seen you dressed up like that before. I guess I sh'll tell um the Grovers have got some luck left," with an accent of pride. "Can't you give your old par a kiss?"

With this question Hanford Grover bent down and put a resounding kiss on his daughter's cheek. Then he repeated that he should "tell um the Grovers had got some luck left," as if this luck had come by his own individual exertions.

Judith had made no reply as yet. She felt her eyes stinging and throbbing in the intensity of her gaze at the man before her.

Mr. Grover had the same expanse of shining artificial teeth, and the same apparent difficulty in drawing his lips about them. In other respects, however, he was much changed. His formerly lean frame was now, to use the country phrase, "quite stocky." Though he was dressed shabbily, he had a physically prosperous look. He did not seem inclined to move on; on the contrary, he showed an inclination to remain where he was as long as possible. His eyes dwelt on the details of his daughter's raiment, and appeared to gloat over them.

"That's a first-rate suit you've got on," he remarked. Then, with a slight laugh, he continued, "You knew better 'n your old par, didn't you? You was fishin' for a bigger fish 'n young Lucian Eldridge. Why didn't you say so?

Them Eldridges are real 'forehanded, but they ain't a primin' to the man you caught, 'n' that's a fact."

Though Mr. Grover spoke familiarly, he yet showed signs of a vulgar deference to the fact that his companion could command money.

Judith listened to him, a conflict rising and becoming stronger and stronger in her mind. She was alarmed at the fury which was taking possession of her. She made a great effort to subdue this feeling. Her eyes dwelt on this man. When she last saw him she was bound down by the galling chains of poverty. But now?—she repressed a shudder. Perhaps it would be best for her not to say anything. If she began to speak she feared that words would utter themselves in spite of her.

She made a movement to go on, but her father put out his hand and stopped her. "You needn't be in such a hurry," he said; "but, then, you never did treat your father right."

Judith resumed her position, leaning again on the fence. "Have you seen mother?" she asked, coldly.

"No; but there's lots of time. She won't be lookin' for me, ye know. I s'pose you have ever so much pocket-money, don't you, Judith?"

Judith thrust her hand into her pocket and drew out her purse. She emptied the contents into the palm of her hand and extended the hand towards the man opposite her.

Mr. Grover made a quick movement and secured the bank-notes before the wind had taken them. He stuffed the money into his waistcoat-pocket.

"You always was a good girl, Judith," he said, unctuously, "but you've got a will of your own. You see, you take after your father." He turned towards the house. He gazed about him a moment before he said, "I s'pose your husband's be'n layin' out money on the place. It looks some better. I 'most wonder he didn't build an addition on to the house when he had it shingled. I s'pose your mar's be'n cultivatin' the farm some. Who's she hired?"

"Mr. Burgess."

"Oh, Ben Burgess? He thinks he knows 'bout farmin', but now I've got home I'll 'tend to that myself. I c'n hire my work done. I guess your husband makes your mar a 'lowance, don't he?"

"Yes."

"That's the best way. How much is it?"

"One thousand dollars a year."

"That so? 'Tain't much, of course." But Mr. Grover's pale eyes sparkled. He swept his tongue over his lips in a way Judith remembered he used to do on those rare occasions when they had a good dinner at home. "No, 'tain't much for a man with millions, but I c'n make it go a good ways. I'll take the burden off your mar's shoulders. Is your mar well?" bethinking himself to ask.

"Very well."

Judith was holding the handle of her parasol closely. She could not take her gaze from her father's face.

"No, 'tain't much," licking his lips again, "but I c'n take the burden off your mar; and mebby now your par's come back your husband 'll see that a larger 'lowance 'll be more 'propriate."

"He would have made it larger at first, only I told him it was ample," said Judith, mechanically.

"Oh, you did!" A disagreeable expression came to the man's face. "But your par's come back now."

Judith took the conversation into her own hands. "We thought you were drowned," she began. "You must have known we should think so." Mr. Grover moved his feet uneasily. He smiled in a somewhat constrained manner. "Where have you been?" As the daughter asked this question her voice rose to a higher key in spite of her efforts to restrain it. She was thinking of many things, and her thoughts were becoming almost intolerable.

As for Mr. Grover, his old, secret dislike for his daughter —that inevitable repugnance of the sneaking, selfish nature towards the being of an opposite kind—was beginning to rise to the surface as he heard her question. He tried to draw himself up with an independent movement. "Oh, wall," he began, "that's kind of a long story, 'n' I guess it 'll keep. You see, I fell off the cliff, 'n' a boat picked me up, 'n'—wall, as I said, it's a long story. I'll tell it when the time comes." Here he tried again to wear a bold front as he added, "I reckon I'm a free moral agent, anyway."

"Since you were not drowned you might have sent word, even though you did not come back."

"I tell you," repeated the man, with some appearance of anger, "I'm a free moral agent. I thought about the matter, 'n' I reasoned on it, 'n' I decided I'd keep still till I come back. 'N' I kep' thinkin' I'd come back any day, you see."

"Did you think that people might believe that I pushed you off into the water? Did you think of that?"

Mr. Grover's face grew a deep red. He made a motion of genuine horror. "No, I didn't. I never thought of such a thing, 'n' I can't b'lieve it now. 'Tain't possible."

"It is true."

The two stood in silence a moment. Then Mr. Grover asked a question in a horrified whisper: "Was you arrested?"

"No. But it was known that we had a disagreement, and that we had unpleasant words on the cliff that night. Do you know what all this has done to me?"

Mr. Grover ignored her question. He rubbed his hands together. He said, hurriedly, that he could make it all right now. But he didn't understand how anybody could suspect a child of his of such a thing. He repeated this phrase twice.

"You cannot make it right." said Judith. She was trying to throw off the dreadful feeling of rebellion—useless and too late rebellion—that was gripping her and shaking her, making her soul writhe.

Mr. Grover was recovering. He smiled broadly and rubbed his hands. "I guess whatever's happened you've feathered your nest first-rate," he remarked. "There ain't a gal round here anywhere 't's done so well. I didn't know but you 'n' young Eldridge 'd make a match, but you was cuter 'n I was, 'n' that's a fact. Was you goin' up to the house?"

"Yes; but you may go on alone now. I will come after a while."

Judith turned away and began to retrace her steps. She went up the cliff and sat down. Her face was turned towards the ocean, but her eyes were blind; they saw nothing. When she came down an hour later and made her way to the house she found her mother walking aimlessly about the rooms. There was a red spot on each cheek and an excited glitter in the woman's eyes.

Mrs. Grover looked a very different person from what she had been at Judith's marriage. She was still bent, she still showed that she had been a hard-worked and worried woman, but her face was more full now, and she carried herself unlike a slave. She ran towards Judith and caught her hands. "You've seen him?" she cried.

"Yes, yes."

"He said he seen you. He said he guessed the Grovers 'd got some luck left. He's gone out to look at the farm. He says I done real well for a woman, but he'll tend to things now. He says a thousand dollars ain't no great—"

"Mother!"

"Mebby he, bein' a man, c'n judge better," went on Mrs. Grover, hurriedly. "But I ain't reflectin' on Mr. Gerald. I think he's done real well. I told Hanford so."

As the woman went on talking thus her daughter watched her, wondering if, in the bottom of her heart, her mother was glad that Hanford Grover had come back.

"'N', you see," she now heard her saying, "folks 'll know you didn't push him in. They'll have that proved to um now. I didn't expect to live to see that proved. Hanford says he'll put a stop to that kind of talk quicker 'n time. Hanford says he's been in a climate 't jest suited his liver. I'll tell you all about it soon 's I can git my wits together. I can't sense much of anything now. I hope, Judith, that your husband 'll understand that a man needs more money 'n a woman with two little girls. A man, you see, 's dif'runt. That's what Hanford was just sayin' to me."

Judith went to her mother's side. She drew her to her, looking down from her superior height with a great pity in her face. The younger woman was very pale. Her lips trembled as she spoke. "Mother, please don't begin to worry now! Please don't! I shall try to have things right for you. You know I shall."

Mrs. Grover dropped her head on her child's shoulder. She began to cry convulsively. "I'm jest as excited 's I c'n be," she sobbed, "'n' I d' know half what I'm sayin'."

XXVI

A LITTLE CONVERSATION

Judith held her mother closely, stooping to rest her cheek on the thin, gray hair.

The two little girls came in and stared hard at the group. They always stared at their sister, and took the gifts she brought them in a petrified kind of silence. They had pale eyes like their father—greedy, selfish eyes, that had no warmth in them. But little Em had been different—little Em, whose grave was green now. The mignonette had sowed itself near the mound and blossomed among the grass.

"He's only jest found out 'bout your marryin' a rich man," said Mrs. Grover, in an indistinct voice, without raising her head. Judith said nothing, but her face darkened. "I mean, he found it out jest 'fore he come home. He said he couldn't wait no longer to see his wife 'n' children. He said I hadn't no idea how he had missed me. I s'pose he's thought more of me 'n I ever knew of." Again Judith kept silence. Her head was raised and her eyes, distended by suffering, were gazing unseeingly on the window.

Presently she said she would go now. To-morrow she would come back and see them all. She spoke so quietly that her mother looked at her with some wonder and disappointment, but she made no reply.

When Judith entered the Eldridge parlor an hour later she found her husband sitting there alone. He had a book in his hand. He rose as she came into the room, looked carelessly at her, then looked again. He placed a chair for her, and remained standing until she was seated. He never failed in any outward act of politeness. He appeared precisely as he did that morning when we first met him. His Prince Albert coat, his mustache, the gleam in his eyes—all were the same.

"You give me the idea of one who has just had an experience of some kind, Mrs. Gerald," he remarked.

"I have." Her eyes were fixed on the gloves she was drawing from her hands.

"Indeed!" Then he waited.

Judith leaned back in her chair. She crossed her hands in her lap, pressing them a little too closely together. She knew that her husband's eyes were on her face. At other times she often had the feeling that he was watching her as if expecting to find out something. "I have just seen my father," she said.

Mr. Gerald sat up straight. He ceased to keep his finger between the leaves of his book. "He has come back?"

"Yes; just now. Mr. Gerald"—she hesitated; she lifted her glance to her companion's face—"I think he will ask you to give more money."

"No matter. I have money enough."

"You are very kind—with money," in a low tone.

"Thank you. I can afford to be. So he wasn't drowned?"

"No; he has preferred to stay away. I don't know yet where he has been. He came back when he heard I was a rich man's wife. It's hard for me to say these things. But you would know I felt them."

"I understand." Mr. Gerald rose as he spoke. He walked to the door and closed it gently. "The family have all gone out to drive," he said, returning and leaning an arm on the mantel, gazing down at his wife, "but I won't run the risk of a servant's hearing us. When a man and wife begin to talk"—here the speaker's face was changed by that smile which his nephew Lucian could never understand, and therefore always distrusted—"one can never predict precisely what they may say."

For several moments after this remark there was silence, so that it began to seem as if this particular man and wife would not utter anything whatever. Mr. Gerald maintained his position where he could look down at Judith. Finally he exclaimed again, "So he wasn't drowned?"

"No."

"And this will clear you in the minds of those who were so blind as to think it possible that you—"

Here the man hesitated, and Judith said, "Yes, it will."

Judith did not look up. She did not see that Mr. Gerald was slightly paler than was usual with him, and that his face was less cynical.

"If this could have been known a year and a half ago you would have persisted in your refusal of me?"

Judith hesitated. Then she glanced bravely up. She flushed as she answered, "Yes."

A faint quiver ran across the man's countenance. But it was resolutely suppressed. "I was sure of it," he answered, quietly. "You would not marry a man who loved you, because of the suspicion against you. Do you think I've been completely ignorant? And I know the man."

Although Mr. Gerald's manner was so quiet there diffused from him a sense of agitation that made Judith's heart beat quickly. She had never seen him in the least like this. Cold, calm, systematically kind, with a curious sneer at human nature in general in his incisive voice, ready to grant any favor to her; that was the way she had found him. To the woman who sat there there seemed something strange in the very air of the familiar room. She glanced at the door as if she would like to escape. He interpreted that glance and smiled.

"We are quite alone now," he said; "please oblige me by remaining a few moments. There are two or three things I want to say. I'm sure we have refrained beautifully from saying things ever since our marriage. In my opinion, a married couple who can refrain from saying things ought to be congratulated. Don't you agree with me?"

" Yes."

Mr. Gerald removed his arm from the mantel and thrust his hands into his pockets. " I haven't been a bad sort of master to you, have I ?" He asked this question in his mildest way, but his eyes were not mild as he spoke the words.

She did not answer. She felt her blood growing hot within her, and she would not speak in reply.

" You know I told you," he went on, " that I should be your master—that I would subdue and control you. Do you remember I told you that ?"

" I remember."

" You would not be likely to forget it, I'm sure. Let us recall a few things. I am in the mood to retrace my steps —in my mind, I mean—and see how my aims have been achieved. Do I weary you, Mrs. Gerald ?"

" Go on," she responded.

" That is like you. You will not politely say I do not weary you, because that would be false. I admire you, Mrs. Gerald. You do not lie — not even in the way of women. You must have discovered that I admire you. Have you not made that discovery ?"

" No."

" No? Is it possible? But I believe you. There is something else of which I am sure you are ignorant. This something else is a very curious fact, indeed."

Mr. Gerald here took a hand from his pocket. but instead of pulling his mustache with his usual gesture he pressed his palm for a moment on his forehead.

" Let us go on to something else," he continued, presently. " I'm going to use very plain words. Euphemisms are not necessary between man and wife, are they, Mrs. Gerald ?"

Here the speaker smiled again. But he evidently did not expect any reply to this question. Judith sat quite still. She was leaning one arm on the chair and her hand was up to her forehead, so that only the lower part of her face was visible. Her husband's eyes dwelt on her for an instant before he spoke again.

"I am going to recall the terms of our bargain," he went on—"our bargain, which the minister who married us referred to as an arrangement made by the Ruler of Heaven and Earth: 'whom God hath joined together.' I suppose you laughed in your sleeve then; I'm sure I chuckled inwardly. I always did like that phrase. Perhaps it is possible that man cannot put asunder what God has joined."

Judith made a slight movement. The man watching her saw her lips press together. Mr. Gerald looked at his watch.

"There's plenty of time," he remarked. "The family have gone over to Lane's Crossing. They cannot possibly be back for an hour. I was recalling our bargain. I did not pretend to love you any more than you made any pretence of love for me. We understood that. I bought you because I thought you were an unusual kind of a woman; I approved of your face and figure and of what I guessed of your character. You sold yourself, not from personal desire for the money and position I could give you, but to benefit your mother and sisters. Do I state the case correctly?"

"Yes."

"I thought so. That's the way I understood it then, and that's the way I understand it now. But what puzzles me is that I should have been so mistaken about you, Mrs. Gerald."

Judith raised her eyes. They were burning and dry, and there was a cutting pain from her eyeballs to the back of her head. Mr. Gerald walked a few steps and came back.

"Yes," he repeated, "mistaken in you—and, I suppose, in myself. I spoke just now as if I had been your master; I told you long ago that I intended to be that. Well, the curious thing, the unaccountable thing, is that never for an instant have I been your master. Did you know that, Mrs. Gerald?"

"No."

The man was pale and quiet, but there were fine beads of moisture on his forehead. He drew out his handkerchief and passed it over his face.

"You did not know it, then? Well, it is true—true as you are, Mrs. Gerald, and I can think of nothing truer. I wanted to make the chains of your bargain gall you as little as possible, but still more I wished to get the control of your nature. I have not done so. It is the greatest surprise of my life that I have failed in this. But I don't give up. I never do give up. I have every advantage. I know that you loved some one when you became my wife. I know that if you had not been under a cloud you might have permitted that love to have its way. Do not grow pale. I know you well. I know your springs of action. You are an honorable woman. You are the first woman I ever knew who even knew what honor meant—just as a man is sometimes able to know it, I mean. Women have a kind of honesty often, but of honor they know pitiably little. I suppose they can't know it. I'm not blaming them. I accept human nature as it is; I long ago learned to do that. Do you care to know something in my mind, Mrs. Gerald? And will you look at me?"

Judith again raised her eyes. Her face had softened. "Tell me," she said.

"You ought to care to know that you have raised my respect for woman."

"Yes, yes, I do greatly care to know that," she said, hastily.

Mr. Gerald bent and took her hand for an instant. He stood gazing down at her. Then he suddenly dropped the hand, turned away, and went to the end of the room. In a moment he returned. He pulled out his mustache and twisted the ends. His voice was still very kind, but it had something of its old tone in it when he spoke again.

"We have come amusingly near to being sentimental, haven't we?" he asked. "And it has been my fault. I suppose the average human being must be more or less sentimental. Now that we are in this mood, pray let me tell you that I am perfectly aware of the exasperating quality in your father's return so late. If he had come back immediately, as he ought, you wouldn't have been my wife. But I am glad he didn't return. You can't get any sympathy from me on that subject."

Judith had risen. She held the parasol she had brought in with her in both hands. The two were looking at each other. In Judith's heart and in her eyes was more softness than she had felt since her marriage. She had opened her lips to speak when a step and voice were heard on the veranda outside. The two recognized the step and voice as belonging to Lucian Eldridge. He had been travelling ever since his uncle's wedding, at which he was dutifully present, and he was not expected home until the fall.

"That is Lucian," said Mr. Gerald. And he removed his eyes from his wife's face.

XXVII

"WHERE'S THE FATTED CALF?"

THE next moment young Eldridge entered the room. He started a little at sight of the two, but he came forward promptly and cordially with extended hand.

"This is an unexpected pleasure, Mrs. Gerald," he said, politely, bending over Judith's hand, "and you, Uncle Dick —I didn't know you had come back from foreign parts."

"Oh yes, we tired of foreign parts," was the response; "we longed for the doughnuts and pies of New England. So we came home. Really, Lucian, if you were only dark you would look quite like an opera villain, with your long hair and beard. Have you turned bandit, or what is the matter with you?"

Lucian laughed and passed his hand over his yellow beard. "You see, I've been with some artist fellows, and we've wandered far and we've wandered near. I took it into my head that I wouldn't have my locks cut until I'd presented myself to my sister Belle. I wanted to hear her shriek. After that I'm going to be barbered."

"I'm sure she will shriek," said Judith.

"Thank you. I wasn't prepared for these compliments. Where are the members of my family? Where's the fatted calf? Where is the rejoicing?"

The young man's tongue ran glibly over these nothings. He had given one comprehensive look at Judith, and now his eyes met hers vaguely, almost unseeingly; but still he glanced at her as fully as good manners required. What he was thinking was, "She is a magnificent woman—magnificent."

As a spring will suddenly fill with water, so the young man's heart filled with bitterness. In spite of himself, when he looked at his uncle his eyes burned. He let his gaze wander over the room. "Things don't seem to have changed," he remarked.

"Nothing really changes," responded Mr. Gerald; "we only grow more and more wicked as the years go on, and the hair and beard of the men get longer and longer in token of this same wickedness. Lucian, you must have been exceeding sinful to expect the fatted calf and rejoicings on your return. It's only the extremely wicked that are greeted in that way, don't you know?"

Mr. Gerald was standing, leaning easily against the mantel again. His voice and enunciation had the same clearness and cynicism which Lucian remembered so well. How had Judith liked this leading trait in her husband? Impossible to tell. She had resumed her seat, but she had an appearance as if she were about to leave the room. She smiled at Mr. Gerald's words, and her face still wore something of that softness which had just come to it. Presently she rose. Her husband moved quickly to open the door for her. She turned and addressed Lucian. She felt that it would seem odd not to speak to him again when he had just returned from a long absence.

"I don't think I ought to stay," she said. "Your mother and sisters will not want any one present when they come home and find you. I can imagine Belle's face when she sees you. We shall meet at dinner."

She went directly into the garden. The Eldridge garden was large and old-fashioned; she had often looked at it with longing as she had hurried by the house in the old times when she had been a working-girl. Now as soon as she could reach a bench which stood under a grape-arbor she sat down. She still had her parasol in her hands, and she held it closely. Then, with an appearance of great care, she laid it on the seat by her side. She folded her gloves and put them beside the parasol. She was deeply intent upon doing these little things. Her whole mind seemed to be in these acts, and she prolonged them to the utmost. At last she clasped her hands and sat quiet. The sunshine came in shifting flecks upon her hat, a soft wind moved the hair upon her forehead. She was thinking of her father. She was thinking of how he had stayed away. And as she thought her face grew paler and paler.

After a while there was a little sound on one of the walks; in a moment a red setter-dog appeared at the entrance to the arbor. He stood there, glossy in the sunlight. He looked inquiringly at Judith, swinging his tail slowly. It was Lucian's dog. Judith extended her hand mechanically. "Come, Random," she said. The dog came and sat down close to her, and she rested her hand on his head.

In the house Mr. Gerald and his nephew were still in the room where Judith had left them. The young man was strolling about the apartment, looking at familiar things and occasionally touching them. The elder man was in a lounging-chair, his feet, in immaculately polished boots, stretched out before him. Sometimes he looked at his boots and sometimes at Lucian—looked through narrowed eyes that saw, but revealed nothing.

"I suppose you've had what we Yankees call a good time, eh?" Mr. Gerald at last asked this question with some show of interest.

"Oh yes," answered Lucian, "if killing ever so many live things called game constitutes a good time, why, then, we've had it. Up there in the Northwest there are creatures endowed with life; we have taken life until I for one felt like a butcher—or, rather, as a butcher ought to feel. I've had enough of it. I will never shoot an animal again save in self-defence."

Mr. Gerald opened his eyes rather more widely as he asked. "Why this sudden resolve? I believe you're an excellent shot?"

"Yes, I am. But one of those creatures gave me a look

when it was dying in defence of its young that I had just killed before its face—well, I won't expatiate on the subject. I threw down my rifle, and I left the other fellows. I came home round by Hudson's Bay. I tell you, Uncle Dick, I've seen Nature absolutely herself. I've hugged myself all alone with her. She smiled on me, and I'm in love with her. If I could get a 'job' with the Hudson's Bay Company I'd jump at it. Have you got any influence in that direction, uncle?"

"Not an atom," was the prompt answer, "and if I had I wouldn't exert it. What you'll do eventually, Lucian, will be to marry some nice girl, settle down here, and help your father run his shoe factory. You are born to shine in domestic life, my boy. Did you know it?"

"If I am, then that's where I shall shine." Lucian laughed and looked at his companion.

"Don't go to Hudson's Bay, whatever you do," went on Mr. Gerald. "You'll throw yourself away. Stay here. When I was as young as you I thought life was a mighty fine thing."

"Don't you think so now?"

Lucian gazed full at his uncle, who shrugged his shoulders as he answered, "Well, after forty the glamour keeps melting. But you won't be forty for this many a long year. Mind you don't go away. Perhaps we can arrange something for you to do. Don't forget that I have an interest in you."

Mr. Gerald spoke with a certain emphasis which rather surprised his listener, though the young man gave no expression to his surprise. Before he could make any reply carriage wheels were heard coming up the drive. Lucian's face lighted.

"There they are!" he exclaimed. "Do you think they'll take me for a bandit if I go to meet them?"

He did not wait for any answer. He ran out of the house and sprang at the horse's head, shouting, "Stand and deliver!"

His mother screamed. He heard Belle cry out, "Gracious, it's Lucian! He's going to be a wild scout of the plains. Oh, let me get out!"

She stood up and held out her arms to her brother, who extended his arms to her, and she jumped over the wheel into his embrace. She was crying with joy and surprise on his shoulder when the rest of the family came up and greeted him with that tender effusiveness which it is so sweet to receive.

Lucian felt his heart melt beneath their welcome. Some cruel stricture seemed to give way at their loving touch. He asked himself how he could have remained away from them so long.

Belle at last drew back a pace, still keeping her brother's hand. "How beautiful these locks!" she exclaimed, but her bantering tone rather failed her.

"I saved them for thee," replied Lucian, in an operatic tone. "Everybody has admired me, from the far Pacific coast to— Oh, but it's jolly to see you again! Let's shake hands once more, all of us. I feel as if I should continue to shake hands indefinitely. Mother, you grow young. Father—"

Lucian paused. He looked with a watery smile at the group pressing about him. He was a soft-hearted fellow, extremely fond of his friends. They all went into the house.

At the first opportunity Mrs. Eldridge took her son one side. Her face showed her anxiety. "Lucian," she said, in a low voice, "I do wish you would do one thing for me."

"You know you have but to mention it," was the reply. The young man bent over and kissed his mother's forehead.

She sank her voice still lower. "Have many people seen you?" she asked.

He looked at her wonderingly as he answered. "I walked from the station, and I did not meet a person."

She gave a long, relieved sigh. "I'm so thankful! Now will you please get up early to-morrow morning and take that six o'clock train to Boston and—and get your hair cut the first thing, and have your beard trimmed, just to oblige me, Lucian?"

The young man burst into a laugh; but there was a curious little feeling at the bottom of his heart even as he laughed. He took out his watch and looked at it.

"I'll do better than that, mother, I'll go up in the eight o'clock train this evening," he said. "I only came in this guise to amuse Belle. I'm sorry you think me lacking in respectability of appearance."

Mrs. Eldridge took her son's hand. She was truly attached to him; he was her son, and necessarily admirable; but there were some things in him that she wished might be different. These things that she wished to have different he of course inherited from the Eldridge side of the house. No member of her family would ever have appeared in public with hair like that. That hair really seemed to make the whole house like a—she did not know precisely what, but something shamefully— Here she was compelled in her thoughts to stop again.

"Perhaps that would be better," she said, in reply to his proposition. "I hope you'll excuse me for mentioning my wish. I should have to ask you anyway, and then I feel quite particular about it, for we are expecting company to-morrow by the noon train, and I should hate to have any one meet you just as you are now. A person would receive a wrong idea."

Lucian's face had fallen as he heard this information. "Who is coming?" he asked. "I did wish we might be alone just for a day or two. Who is coming?"

"Some one we met last summer at the mountains. I asked her here. If I had known you were to be here, and would care—"

"I beg your pardon," said Lucian. "I ought not to be selfish."

"It's Mrs. Jennings," said Mrs. Eldridge.

"I don't know her," was the uninterested reply.

XXVIII

MRS. JENNINGS

"I've changed my mind about our leaving here." It was Mr. Gerald who said this the next morning after Lucian's arrival. He was standing by the window, looking out.

Judith lifted her eyes quickly, but her husband's back was towards her. "You're not going the little journey you had planned?" she asked.

Mr. Gerald, listening, could not detect any difference in her voice. "No. I would rather stay, now Lucian has come. I'm fond of the boy, and I know you won't find it pleasant at your old home with your father in it. I hope you will stay here with me." Mr. Gerald now turned round and looked at his wife.

"Certainly," she said, "if you wish it."

He allowed a decided admiration to come into his eyes, while he was saying to himself, "She has pluck! I knew she had!"

"Yes," he went on, carelessly, "my sister would like to have us stay; but, to tell the truth, I don't stop for that. And you'll be near your mother, and perhaps the company may amuse us. We'll get through the summer somehow. And this Mrs. Jennings, they say, isn't stupid. I wish you would drive over to the station with me to meet her. The rest of them can't go. We must start in half an hour."

Lucian had gone to Boston the evening previous. He came down to the city station that morning looking as differently as a faultless morning-suit and fresh barbering could make him. His naturally fair face was tanned, save for his forehead, which was strikingly white. His beard was trimmed closely to the cheeks and to a point on the chin; his mustache, now grown extremely long, was carefully brushed out at the ends. He had defeated his barber in his intention as to his hair, which was not clipped closely, but hung in a couple of thick, carelessly parted locks on his forehead.

I am, perhaps, too particular in itemizing concerning Lucian's personal appearance; but I am but describing him as he appeared to a woman who had just left a coupé in front of the station, and for whom young Eldridge had the privilege of holding open the heavy swing-door that she might pass into the building. Her eyes flashed comprehensively over the man as she slightly inclined her head in response to his service. He glanced after her as he stood in the large room after entering. She was rather slight in figure, under medium height, with an unmistakable air of style about her, not precisely dashing, but any man would look twice at her. Having thus given his second look, Eldridge turned away and forgot her. But a little later, as he sat in the car which was to take him home, he was rather surprised to see this same lady enter. And she did not leave at any of the large stopping-places, and she was one of the few who remained in the car when the last change had been made.

Eldridge, sitting a few seats behind her, suddenly bethought himself that this woman might be his mother's guest. Having thought of this possibility he immediately became positive that it was she. And he was right. When the train slowed up to the solitary little station there were only two people to alight there, and these were Eldridge and the lady whom he had been lazily watching for the last hour and a half. She allowed a glimmer of remembrance to appear in her face as she saw him step upon the platform beside her.

There was drawn up on the other side of the station an open carriage, which glittered in the sunshine of noon. On the back seat of this carriage Judith sat holding the loop of

the driving-lines, which Mr. Gerald had placed in her hands
when they heard the train coming.

"You can't mistake her, Richard," Mrs. Eldridge had
said to her brother. "There'll be hardly anybody stopping
at our station anyway; and even if there were, you have
only to pick out a woman who is—why, she is stylish, and
something more."

Mr. Gerald had politely protested that that was description enough for even a policeman in search of a criminal.
And two or three times, in driving over, he had laughed a
little, apparently at nothing, and then had explained to his
wife the cause of his hilarity. Now, there he was, hat in
hand, the moment the lady stepped from the train. He
found time to glance sharply at his nephew before he ac-
costed the stranger, and he was saying to himself, "She is
fair. Why did I think she was dark? And she is a woman of the world who knows to the finest fraction how much
her smile is worth. Apparently it has been worth a great
deal."

"I am sure this is Mrs. Jennings?" he said.

Mrs. Jennings acknowledged her identity with a curve
of the lips and a glance that fully justified Mr. Gerald's
thoughts about her smile.

She was conducted to the carriage, and she and Mrs.
Gerald were introduced to each other. Judith made a place
for her beside her on the seat, and she instantly told herself
that here was a woman whom she should not like, and a
woman to whom men would be drawn as naturally and inevitably as steel is drawn to a magnet. Having told herself
this, Judith was puzzled and somewhat confounded, when
Mrs. Jennings turned to her and began to talk with her and
to look at her, to find herself immediately assuming an attitude of mind towards this stranger so different from what
she had, but a moment before, thought possible.

Mrs. Jennings's voice was particularly fitted for the utterance of mocking cadences, and for saying apparently un-
meaning words with a great deal of meaning. Her laugh

also was mocking, but Judith could not understand why she did not dislike it more. Sometimes there would come a sudden feeling into face and tone that appealed strongly, and that overturned some impression that the speaker had made the moment before.

Judith leaned back on the carriage seat beside this stranger, and listened as she talked with the two gentlemen in front. But she did not talk so much with them as with Judith herself, and, to Judith's continual surprise, Mrs. Jennings seemed more interested in her than in the men.

"Do you know," remarked the new-comer, "I am already puzzling my mind about you, Mrs. Gerald. How do you happen to be here in New England?"

"How do I happen to be here?" repeated Judith, in surprise. For an instant the light, green-gray eyes met the dark ones. Then Judith smiled. "I have a particular right to be where I was born."

Mrs. Jennings gave a little exclamation. "Oh, that is impossible!" She leaned forward, "Mr. Gerald, do you know that Mrs. Gerald here is telling me that she was born in this town?"

"Well, so she was. Have you any objection to that?"

Mrs. Jennings laughed. She made no immediate reply. But in a moment she gave Judith a peculiar, quick glance, and murmured, "The isles of Greece! The isles of Greece!"

A slight flush rose to Judith's face. Mr. Gerald's quick ears had caught the words. He turned. "Oh, I know that, Mrs. Jennings," he responded, evidently well pleased to join in this persiflage; "but notwithstanding all appearances, my wife is a true Yankee. She values honor and truth."

"You don't mean to insinuate that the Yankees have a monopoly of honor and truth, Mr. Gerald?"

"Oh no; not by any means. Still, the truth of a Yankee is very thoroughgoing."

Lucian heard in silence. He did not think it in good taste to talk in that personal way, though there was such an

air of lightness in the manner of the speakers. He had
never seen his uncle just like this before, and then he recalled the fact that he had never before seen Mr. Gerald in
such company. He glanced covertly at the man sitting beside him. And as he glanced he was startled at the ferocity
of the rebellion suddenly filling his heart. He shut his lips
tightly under his mustache and turned his head to one side.
He did not try to talk ; he sat with an apparent moroseness
almost in silence during the drive home. But he heard all
that was said. Mrs. Jennings and Mr. Gerald kept up a
lively talk. Judith listened, and smiled vaguely. She did
not care for such talk ; it was to her like something singing
by her ears, but hardly entering her mind. She had, however, learned that "in society" there was much conversation like this, only not usually as bright.

When she and Mr. Gerald were alone before dinner the
gentleman turned to her and asked, "Is that woman a
widow?"

"I don't know."

"What do you think of her?"

"Well—" hesitatingly.

Her husband laughed. "I have a particular reason for
wanting to know what you think of her. And I'm positive
she is a widow. The name Jennings is in a cranny of my
memory somewhere, and I must hunt it up."

"I think," said Judith, slowly, "that she is capable of
being fascinating."

"So do I. Now, the question is, will Lucian agree with
us?" He seemed to expect Judith to make some response
to this remark, but she did not. He walked across the
room. He came back and stood before his wife. "You'll find
out presently," he said, "that my sister is trying her hand at
match-making. That's why Mrs. Jennings is invited here."

"But Lucian was not expected."

"Not now. But you don't know how long-headed my
sister is. She can make a plan that begins here and now,
and that ends fifty years hence in Constantinople."

Judith kept silence again. And her face, though a trifle pale, revealed nothing. She was becoming more and more proficient every day in the art of controlling her features.

When she went down-stairs that afternoon a half-hour before dinner Lucian was standing at the open door of the hall. He had an appearance of waiting for her. He stepped forward, saying, with a slight note of haste, "I hoped you would come down, Mrs. Gerald. I have two or three words to say to you. Let us go outside." He pushed open the wire door and drew back to let her pass. A gentle whiff of warm, fragrant air bent down the flowers of the garden as the two moved along the broad gravel path.

Up-stairs, Mr. Gerald, who had not yet left his room, happened to glance from the window. He saw the man and woman walking slowly away from the house. He gazed at them an instant, and as he gazed a slight, inscrutable smile came to his lips. He drew back; he passed his hand from his forehead down over his face.

"Given honor, truth, a strong will, a passionate nature, against a forbidden love—what will be the answer to that problem?" As if drawn by an irresistible power as his mind pronounced these words, Mr. Gerald went again to the window.

Lucian and Judith were walking back towards the house, and Lucian was talking with apparent earnestness, but he was not looking at his companion.

Mr. Gerald noted also that she was not looking at him, but that her face betokened her interest in what he was saying.

The man at the window now went resolutely away. "It's going to be interesting," he was saying to himself; "not that the play has really begun, by any means."

XXIX

LUCIAN'S SEARCH

"I wanted to speak about your father's return," Lucian had said the moment the two were out of the house.

Judith raised a surprised glance to his face. "Did you know he had come?" she asked, quickly.

Young Eldridge smiled as he replied, "I should rather think I did know it. I brought him over from Jewett's Landing in a sail-boat I borrowed there."

"And it was your boat I saw coming in towards our landing when I was on the cliff-walk?"

"Yes; and I saw you standing there."

"How strange!"

Judith put her handkerchief to her lips; she did not know why they should tremble uncontrollably.

"Not a bit strange," responded Lucian, in a hard, matter-of-fact voice; "only that I believed you to be gazing at the Bay of Naples, and lo! there you were on the Massachusetts coast looking at Massachusetts Bay! I was surprised, I can tell you. But I knew you instantly."

There was no answer to this. Judith was trying to ask where he had found her father; but it was unavoidable that, in this first interview with Lucian, she should be remembering one hour somewhat more than a year and a half ago. After she had become accustomed to seeing him it would be different; of course it would be different. But just now —

"I am very curious," she said at last, and her voice was so dry and so proper that she was justly proud of it. The moment of emotion was now well over. "Father was very reticent to me," she went on; "I don't know what he has told mother. I suppose when he fell off the cliff some one picked him out of the water?"

"Precisely that. It was a friend of mine, though I didn't know about it until a few days ago. I've been trying a great deal to find your father." Here Judith uttered a low exclamation, but Lucian continued in the same business-like way in which he had begun. "Yes, I have followed out a number of what looked like clews, but were not; for, you see, I assumed that he was not drowned, and I wanted to find him. I knew it must be very disagreeable for you to have even one blind fool imagine you could have had anything to do with your father's death."

It was really quite strange the success which Lucian had now attained in making his manner and voice to the utmost degree commonplace. Before he could go on Judith paused in her walk. She put out her hand to detain her companion, though she did not touch him. Her eyes, "daringly warm," were on his face; her own features were not steady. She was not thinking of anything in the past or future, only of what Lucian had been doing for her.

"You wanted to clear my name?" she said, in a whisper. "You thought enough about me to try to do it?"

She had an unerring knowledge that he had done much, though his words did not convey that fact.

"Why, yes," still in that off-hand manner. "Perhaps I have a natural gift at the detective business," with a slight laugh. "Anyway, I've been an amateur detective ever since your father's disappearance. And, after all, it was not skill, but sheer luck, that brought me success. Shall I tell you about it? I shall have time before dinner. I will cut short the details."

"Yes, please tell me."

Judith stooped and gathered up the long folds of her gown. She gave one furtive glance at her hand to see that it was steady. As for Lucian, amid the turmoil in his mind he was trying to be able calmly to see Judith clad in this wonderful, transforming way which lies in the power of wealth. The lace; the diaphanous sweep of the gown; the dressing of the heavy, dark hair; the gleam of jewels; the mysterious glow and sweetness which somehow belong to some women — all this Lucian must be aware of, and he must seem indifferent to it. And in his mind, through every instant of this interview, had been Judith's words that night: "I love you, Lucian Eldridge."

But those words were spoken a hundred years ago, and very soon after their utterance the woman who had used them had sold herself to a rich man. Still, at the moment she had felt them. Lucian was sure of that. Like an imbecile he hugged that belief: at the moment she had felt them. She had strange ideas, and she was wilful. But she was sincere. She did what seemed right to her. What else could any one do?

"It was odd," went on Lucian, "that, after I had travelled hither and yon on this hint and that, I should find what I wanted to find under my own hand.

"One night when we were camping out in the far West, Berwick—that's my friend who used to come here to see me— happened to mention about picking up a man in the cove there by your farm, Mrs. Gerald. I hadn't seen Berwick in a year since the thing happened, which accounts for his not thinking to mention the affair, and it was after he had left me. He's a careless fellow, and only writes to me once in a great while. Anyway, he had never told me this, and he didn't know I had been hunting for a man supposed to be drowned. I caught at his story, but for some reason I didn't let him know why. He said this man was unconscious when he pulled him into the boat—had hit his head on a rock, evidently.

"Berwick was going to join a friend in a yacht which lay off a couple of miles from Jewett's Landing. The yacht was to sail at a particular time, and the wind was just right. It occurred to Berwick that he wouldn't delay to put the man ashore here and hunt up his friends, but would take him along, and when he had recovered—say, by the following

"'YOU WANTED TO CLEAR MY NAME?'"

morning—he would leave him at a town near by on the coast with money enough to take him home, for Berwick, being a medical student with a bran-new diploma, was quite sure that Mr. Grover was only temporarily stunned. And that was the case.

"The yacht sailed, and Mr. Grover recovered consciousness, just as Berwick had expected. But the thing that he did not expect was that the man whom he had rescued declined to be set ashore anywhere. He said he thought it would agree with his liver to take a voyage. He said that if those who had money did as they ought to do they would give more help, in the shape of ocean voyages, for instance, to the people who didn't have money and did have ill-behaved livers.

"Now all this struck Lovering, the young fellow who owned the yacht, and a pile of money besides, as being immensely funny. He said that a man with a liver was the very thing *The Kelpie* needed. So he kept Mr. Grover.

"I suppose you know that your father has a natural knack at cooking, and that he is willing to use this ability upon occasion. Well, he helped the cook, and there were dishes he made himself, and Lovering, though the joke of his presence wore off very soon, let him stay all that season; and he let him go this summer again. I found him up at Calais, Maine, where *The Kelpie* was stopping. You see, I went after him when Berwick told me and said he would bet ten to one that the man with a liver would stick to *The Kelpie*. I don't know whether Mr. Grover was intending ever to come home; perhaps he liked to know he had a refuge. He spent the winter with the cook. But Lovering keeps his yacht in commission five or six months of the year; it's a big boat, and everything fine.

"Well, I found Mr. Grover. He wasn't very glad to see me. He said it seemed that his falling into the water and being saved that way was like the finger of Providence pointing him to a different life. He hinted that he wasn't appreciated in his home, and that he had a very headstrong daughter—pardon me, Mrs. Gerald, but I must explain matters—a daughter who meant to do right, but who was not sufficiently guided by her father. He said he had not heard anything from his family or from this town since that evening. I told him of your marriage. I knew then by the look that came to his face that he would come home. And I was right.

"That is the story. Please, Mrs. Gerald, don't accuse me of meddling in what did not concern me. The cloud on your name concerned your friends. I was an idle fellow, you know, and could afford to occupy myself in the pursuit of the missing man. I couldn't quite give up the idea that it was possible he was not drowned. You forgive me for meddling?"

Lucian tried to look at Judith as she turned impulsively towards him.

" Forgive you? Oh yes, I forgive you," she said.

"Thank you. There's the dinner-bell. I did not think my story would be quite so long."

They walked towards the house. At the lower step of the veranda Judith paused.

" It was very kind "—she hesitated—"very thoughtful—it is a great deal to me, Mr. Eldridge."

She held out her hand. Lucian took it, and immediately released it. He did not look at her.

Mrs. Jennings was at the foot of the stairs on her way to the dining-room as the two came into the hall.

" Delightful old-fashioned garden," she said. " I meant to come down early enough to walk in it before this. Mrs. Gerald, you like those flowers, I'm sure."

"Yes," answered Judith, with a perceptible fervor in her voice, "better than all the conservatory blooms in the world. Will you have some of these pinks, Mrs. Jennings?"

Judith took the bunch of pinks from her belt, separated the flowers, and extended several of them to the woman who was leaning against the stair-post.

" Thank you : but do they become me ?" She held them

up to her face. "Pinks are so trying to most people. But not to you, Mrs. Gerald. Do you think I might venture to wear these?"

"Surely," said a voice from the stairs. Mr. Gerald was descending.

Mrs. Jennings looked smilingly up. She raised her arms, removed from her hair a long silver pin with a large turquoise in the head of it, deftly put the flowers within the braid, and replaced the pin. "If I look like a Dutchwoman it will be your fault, Mrs. Gerald," she said.

"You will never look like a Dutchwoman—as you mean the phrase," remarked Mr. Gerald, with the proper emphasis.

At the table that night Judith's olive face was tinged with more color than usual; her lips glowed more deeply crimson; her eyes, when she raised them, had a humid light in them. She talked very little; she seemed to be listening to the conversation which Mr. Gerald and Mrs. Jennings kept up.

The dinner and the evening were quite different on account of the stranger's presence; there was a brightness and an interest which every one felt.

Belle confided to her brother that "Mrs. Jennings was no end jolly," but that she did not exactly know whether to believe in her or not.

"It isn't necessary to believe in any one," responded Lucian, with something like his uncle's manner and tone.

XXX

"IT WAS WRONG TO DO IT!"

LATER in her life, when Judith looked back upon this summer, she seemed to be gazing through a cloud that obscured her vision and prevented her from judging her own actions. She had an idea that her husband was watching with a cynical questioning and amusement in his eyes. He did not watch her as one who had the slightest wish to control her movements, but as one who was merely interested.

She was tired, strangely tired, all the time. She was fighting, struggling, and never attaining peace. She knew that she did not appear to be engaged in any battle, that apparently she was drifting pleasantly through the summer —driving, riding, yachting; but, in spite of all these amusements, spending many hours of each week with her mother. These hours were the times when Judith came the nearest to knowing repose. She used to sit with folded hands in the old kitchen where she had worked so hard. She had made her mother hire one of the girls of the village who would rather do house-work than be confined in the factory, so there was no more hard work for Mrs. Grover.

Everything was different on the farm now. Two hired men did Hanford Grover's bidding, and Hanford Grover himself seemed a very prosperous man; and he always thought of Mr. Gerald's money, and spoke of it as means which had come to his family by efforts of his own. He used to boast at the store that he guessed there wa'n't any man provided for his family better 'n he provided. He said he wa'n't one to see his folks out of victuals, and he meant to get the very best for um, too. And he did; and he never failed to see to it that the cream of that best went into his own mouth.

Sitting thus in the kitchen Judith would unconsciously release her face from the strict watch she kept over it elsewhere. And her mother fell into the habit of giving long looks at her daughter; after these looks she would breathe a deep breath, turn her eyes away, and presently leave the room.

Suddenly one day Mrs. Grover said, "I s'pose you have all the money you want, don't you, Judith?"

The other woman roused herself. She fixed rather vacant eyes on her companion.

"Oh yes, certainly. Did you want some money?"

Involuntarily Judith's hand began to try to find her pocket.

"No, I don't," rather sharply. "I didn't mean that. I meant—oh, Judith!"

Mrs. Grover rose hurriedly and came to her daughter's side. She seemed to want to touch her, but she did not. Her faded face worked piteously.

"Why, mother! What is it? Have I hurt you in any way?"

Judith's voice was full of concern. She reached forward and took her mother's hands; she gently pulled her down on the lounge beside her. It was the same lounge where Judith had tried to sleep when her mother had been ill.

"Hurt me? Oh no; you ain't one to hurt anybody— but yourself. I've been thinkin.' When I see you settin' here 'n' lookin' as you do—"

Judith smiled reassuringly as her mother paused. Mrs. Grover felt the old sense of strength and comfort coming from her daughter's presence.

"Why, mother, you actually seem to be worrying about me!" exclaimed Judith.

"I can't help it," was the reply. She gazed wistfully up into the young face that was the same, and yet not the same, as it used to be. "You do have everything you want, don't you, Judith?"

"Mr. Gerald is very kind," was the prompt and evasive reply.

Mrs. Grover pushed her hair back as if this would enable her to think more clearly.

"I've been thinkin', 'n' I've been feelin' dreadful 'fraid I didn't do right that time," she said.

Judith did not ask what time. She was silent. It seemed to her that she could not bear anything more. After a while she said, "I don't believe it will do any good for us to talk like this."

"But I've got to talk, or something 'll happen to me." Mrs. Grover spoke hurriedly. "All the while you've been gone I've been thinkin', of course, you was havin' a first-rate time. You'd married rich, 'n' everybody was envyin' you, 'n' me too. But now I see you when you're settin' here with nobody but me, I know I ain't done right. No, I didn't do right."

"Mother, won't you stop?"

"You wouldn't have married him if it hadn't been for me; you know you wouldn't, Judith."

"Oh, do stop!"

"No, I'm goin' to speak now, 'n' you've got to answer me, Judith. You wouldn't have married him, would you?"

"No, mother."

"I was sure of it—I was sure of it. Somehow I've made a dreadful mistake 'bout you. I married 'thout loving Mr. Grover, though I liked him well enough, 'n' you know lots of women are real pleased to be married; somehow a woman ain't thought much of if she don't marry some-body. But you ain't like me; of course I thought you was like me. I can't understand it, I can't. You'd been happier if I'd let you alone, 'n' you'd gone on workin' your fingers to the bone for us all, 'n' tryin' to pay the interest on the moggidge, 'n' everything else, wouldn't you, Judith?"

No answer. The younger face was very white. She was looking at her mother, not as if she saw her, but as if she saw nothing but dreariness and desolation stretching out interminably before her.

"You've got to answer me," went on Mrs. Grover. "I'm your mother, 'n' you can say anything to me, 'n' you can let your face be jest as you feel. I'm your mother, 'n' I love you, though I ain't done right—I see it now—I ain't done right. You'd have been happier, wouldn't you?"

Mrs. Grover's eyes were dropping tears. She drew her daughter's head down to her breast. She softly smoothed the heavy hair.

"Yes," said Judith, in a whisper.

"Oh, I knew it! I knew it!" went on Mrs. Grover. "'N' now I can't never take nothin' back—never. He's kind to you, ain't he, Judith?"

"Yes."

"And you don't love him?"

"No! no! no!"

The two women sat holding each other. The tears continued to fall from Mrs. Grover's eyes, but no tears were in the younger eyes.

Finally the mother said, with piteous repetition, "You ain't like me."

After another silence, Judith, still with her head on her mother's bosom, said, as if she were speaking to herself, "I read somewhere that if a woman marries without love she may thank herself if she gradually becomes a moral leper—if a poison reaches her very soul—that so sacred a relation shall not be polluted without punishment. I don't know about other women, but for me that is true—true."

"Oh, dear!" softly and helplessly cried Mrs. Grover. She stroked the young face.

Judith suddenly raised her head. She drew back a little from her companion.

"I tell you, mother," she exclaimed, "I cannot respect myself! I despise myself! It was wrong to do it! No matter what you or any one suffered, it was wrong to do it! I had no right, no woman has any right, to sacrifice herself like that. We might all have gone to the poor-house together. I wish we had!—oh, I wish we had!"

There was an incredible, a terrible bitterness in the speaker's voice. Mrs. Grover recoiled from it. What did her daughter mean? Surely marriage was respectable. What notions had Judith got into her head? And where did she get them? But as suddenly as she had spoken Judith controlled all extreme manifestation of her emotion.

"Don't mind me, mother," she said, gently; "you know you never did quite understand me. It ought to help me that you are all sure to be comfortable as long as you live. It does comfort me greatly. If it were not for thinking constantly of that I should—oh, well, I should be unhappy. Don't you think it would be better if we talked about something else?"

But Mrs. Grover insisted upon one thing: that Judith ought not to try to conceal her feelings from her mother. She repeated again and again that it would do her daughter good to have one person before whom she need not school her face or her manner.

"You'll jest be ravin' crazy some day if you don't never give way, Judith. When you come here you sh'll set 'n' not speak, 'n' look any way. It don't matter how you be when you are here, you know it don't."

It seemed to be some consolation to the mother that the old home should be a sort of refuge to the daughter, and so Judith came there more and more often. She roamed about the house, or she strolled in the garden and the fields. She always tried to evade a meeting with her father; but when the two did meet Mr. Grover was so pleasant and so deferential that he made Judith sick. He did not attempt to see her, but he never failed to improve the opportunity when he did see her to get from her more or less money. She uniformly gave him whatever she had with her, as she had done that first time when he had just returned.

So a part of the summer passed. Nothing seemed to have happened. Mrs. Jennings had finished her visit and gone, but, at Mrs. Eldridge's earnest invitation, she had promised to return in the early autumn.

Meanwhile, Lucian had made several short journeys, but he always came back sooner than he was expected. He was tormented by an unconquerable restlessness. He grew thin, and there were black hollows under his eyes. Mr. Gerald used to look at him with a curious intentness, and when he withdrew his eyes his face would harden. Then if his wife were in the room he would turn to her and examine her countenance—not openly, but over a book or a paper.

One day Judith had gone to her mother's. She had insisted that she would walk back, and that no one should come for her. Mr. Gerald had been sitting in the garden nearly all the afternoon. The heat was intense. Everything alive was gasping for relief. The sky was cloudless and brassy; the sun, going slowly westward, was red as blood. Mr. Gerald sat with a book in his hand, but he had not read a word. His sister, waving a fan, came down the path towards him. It was one of those times when anything dreadful might happen, it was so relentlessly hot.

"Hasn't Judith come back?" inquired Mrs. Eldridge, not because she cared, but because it occurred to her to ask that question.

"No."

"How warm it is! Lucian is the only sensible one. He has gone out in his boat. He invited me to go with him, but I told him I should die walking to the shore."

Mr. Gerald's face changed in an indescribable way. He very rarely allowed so much interest to show itself in his voice as was audible in it now. He turned towards his sister. "I wish you had gone with Lucian," he said.

"Why?" in surprise.

Mr. Gerald leaned back in his chair. He smiled languidly, and answered in his usual tone, "Oh, I don't know. One isn't responsible for fancies in this cursed heat."

XXXI

"I FORGIVE YOU"

Judith had left her old home in the middle of the afternoon. She was restless from the heat, and she walked slowly down to the bottom of the garden. Coming to little Em's grave, she stood there a long time. The grass was green above it, for she had carefully brought water ever since she had come back, and the drought had not touched the place.

It seemed to Judith as she stood there that her brain was affected by the weather. She looked off over the dry, brown pasture. The heated air shimmered under the red sun. She gazed down at the grave. "I should like to weep—to weep all day and all night," she said, aloud. "Perhaps tears would wash away the dust in my mind." Then she smiled, and added, "I'm getting as morbid as a modern novel."

She strolled along to the cliff-path. She would go back that way. There was not a breath of air from the sea or from anywhere, but the sight of the water might revive her. As she turned towards the cliffs she saw a boat lying in the bit of a cove. The man sitting in it was looking towards the shore. He immediately rose and waved his hat; she recognized Lucian Eldridge.

"Are you going to walk home?" he called out.

"Yes."

"Let me take you by water. It is not quite so insufferable here as on land."

Judith walked down to the beach and waited. Why should she not go? In a few moments she was in the stern seat, and Lucian was rowing away from shore.

"We may stand a chance for a breath of air," he said, "but the land suffocates to day." After a while he pulled in his oars. "Are you in a hurry, Mrs. Gerald?"

"No."

She sat with her open parasol resting on her shoulder. Her hands were clasped over the handle. Those hands were no longer hard from work. They were soft and well shaped, but just now brown from the summer sun. Several rings glittered on the fingers.

Lucian was not looking at her; nevertheless, he saw nothing on ocean or earth but that woman in the stern of the boat. His entire feeling at that moment was one of exultation. Not that he in the least intended to let that exultation be discovered. This was the only time he had seen Judith alone since that evening when she had let him know that she loved him—the only time, save the few moments when he had told her about finding her father.

Well, what harm would it do if he should sit there alone with her for an hour? No harm to anybody, save to him. He wanted to laugh recklessly as he told himself that he was past harming. Perhaps this torrid atmosphere affected his head. He had had a sense of desperation brooding all day over his consciousness. Of course it was the weather.

There came a warm puff of wind from the land. There was in it the odor of elder-blows and the queen of the meadows: the same odor had been in the air that evening. Odd how vividly perfumes brought back scenes and words. What a sumptuous woman that was who sat opposite him! And that was Judith Grover, who had ridden on his sled and worked at stitching in the shoe factory. And she had said that she loved him—only that was a thousand years ago: and perhaps she had not loved him, after all. One never knew much about women, anyway. What was she thinking about now?

The crimson parasol shed a soft glow on Judith's face, relieving the pallor of heat. Lucian now openly looked at her. He had thrust his hands beneath the belt that confined his flannel blouse. His broad hat was drawn over his face to keep the sun from his eyes.

"Do you think in these days, Mrs. Gerald?" he asked, suddenly.

She seemed to withdraw a little from him; then she smiled as if in apology for that involuntary movement.

"I am not guilty of much thinking, I'm afraid," she answered.

"Because you are so occupied in living, I suppose?"

"Perhaps."

"Now it is quite otherwise with me," was the response. "I seem to have plenty of time to think, but I don't amount to anything. I'm an idle fellow. I used to believe I should do something in the world. Now—well—"

The young man paused. He leaned forward, resting his elbows on his knees. A dark flush came to his face; his eyes throbbed and burned. Judith was gazing off over the burnished water. Faintly from the shore sounded the song of a blackbird as he flew down over the Grover meadow.

"Can't you give a poor young man any advice, Mrs. Gerald?" asked Lucian.

Every time he said "Mrs. Gerald" Judith felt like drawing back from a blow, but she resolutely gave no sign of this feeling. Lucian let slip no opportunity to pronounce this name, as one may press viciously upon a wound, strangely longing to bear the pain induced by the touch.

"A man has the world under his feet," said Judith. She still kept her eyes on the distance.

"Oh, does he?"

Lucian burst into a loud laugh. His companion glanced at him anxiously.

"I must laugh at your joke, Mrs. Gerald," he said. Then, after a moment's silence, he leaned forward again, and spoke in quite a different tone. "Do forgive me. I think I must be getting to be more of a brute every day."

"Oh no! You can never be that, Mr. Eldridge."

"You really have faith in me?"

"Why should I not?"

Judith was looking at him now. Her eyes dwelt on his face. It seemed to the young man that his soul clung to that glance, which was only kind—but so kind!

"But why should you?"

He did not know that he had spoken until he seemed to hear the words from somewhere, he hardly knew where.

"I must have faith in you, Lucian—I must!"

Her words and tone had a supplication in them. She could have reached forth her hands to him in pleading. But she sat perfectly still, holding her parasol, her dark face turned to him, and appearing to lift him up from deeps into which he was sinking. He raised his head.

"You have not called me Lucian before since—well, for a long time," he said. There was something boyish and almost piteous in his tone. "Why shouldn't you call me that?" he went on. "We were boy and girl together. I wish you would call me Lucian."

"I will. There is no reason why I should not."

"Thank you—thank you so much."

Lucian lifted his hat that the air might pass over his forehead. He was asking himself why it seemed as if some one were talking through him. Why was the time so unreal? Was it the heat—the relentlessness of that brassy sky? The sun was now down to the tops of the pine-trees on the hills over there in the west.

"I have wanted to see you," began Lucian again, still with that oppressive feeling, as if some one else were speaking. "There was something I wanted to say to you."

He stopped, gazing at her. She did not avoid his glance. Her eyes still had the same kindly look; but her face was now ashen, and a line of still whiter hue was about her lips.

"Perhaps you have decided upon what you will do in the world," said Judith, with an effort.

"No; it wasn't that. Shall I tell you what it is?"

Judith hesitated. She withdrew her eyes, and looked off

to the horizon almost as if she were searching for the answer to his question. She hardly dared to say yes to the inquiry. Her heart was beating so that to speak was nearly impossible. Dominant over everything was the resolution to be true to her idea of duty—to be loyal to her own soul.

"Yes," went on Lucian, "I am going to tell you. It is that I have been trying ever since your marriage to forgive you. I have almost hated you. You know it has been said that there is always some hate in love. I could have killed you. I wanted to kill you. That was odd, wasn't it? You were wrong. Your idea of what you ought to do—that you ought not to marry me—that was all wrong. But to-day, since I've been out in this boat thinking of you—I'm always thinking of you—it came to me that I forgave you. I said aloud, 'Thank God for that!' And then I looked towards the land and saw you going up the cliff. That was providential, wasn't it?—to see you then, and have you come into the boat?"

As he ceased speaking Lucian took up the oars again, and began to row farther out. The sail lay useless, dropped down the little mast.

A keen anxiety was mingling with other feelings in Judith's mind. But she tried not to betray that feeling.

"I'm glad you forgive me," she said, gently.

"I wanted to tell you," he went on. Again he removed his hat and put his hand to his head.

"Have you been out all the afternoon?" she asked.

"Yes; I left the house the moment I had finished lunch. I tried the garden, but it was intolerable. I asked myself how I was going to live until night. I remembered my boat. I invited mother to come with me. I thought of taking Belle, but she said the heat was bound to kill her before night, and she would rather die on land. So I came alone. Now I'm glad of it; I should have been sorry if any one had been with me. Then I couldn't have told you I have forgiven you."

Having spoken thus Lucian took up the oars again and

bent to them, the boat throbbing over the glassy water, the eddies on each side making a pleasant, cool noise.

Judith looked about her. She gazed back at the shore. The village was not in sight, being hidden by the low ridge behind which it lay. But there was the long, decaying wharf, where vessels of small tonnage used to land, the stretch of cliff, the white line of sandy beaches, the tree-covered hills in the background, the flushing sky, the look of quivering, swooning heat over everything — Judith saw it all.

The water was growing darker as the sun withdrew itself, but it did not lose its sultry aspect. The sound of oars in rowlocks and the splash of the blades in the water farther out in the bay made Judith turn her eyes in that direction.

"Awful hot, ain't it?" asked a familiar voice. The speaker was Ellis Macomber. He was sitting in a boat that was rowed by one of his neighbors. He gazed with his usual curiosity at Judith and her companion.

Judith replied to him. She said Mr. Eldridge was taking her home, but it was so warm they were not hurrying; it was more comfortable here than anywhere else.

"Jes' so," responded Mr. Macomber, staring continuously. Judith was always an interesting object to him; he had known her as a very poor girl, and now she was rich— rich. He and two or three other men used often to try to reckon up what Mr. Gerald's income per minute probably was. They would smack their lips over the sum.

"Bob had to go out to his lobster-pawts," now remarked Mr. Macomber, "'n' I was jest about roasted, so I come with him. But, land, there ain't no air out here neither!"

"I guess there'll be a change 'fore long," said the other man. "Gen'rally is; when it's got so hot it can't be no hotter it has to change, you know."

Then the two boats parted company. Judith watched the little craft making its way towards the long wharf. The sun dropped behind those pine-trees on the hill.

Lucian's oars swept out in long strokes, taking hold of

the water with a will. Now that the sun did not beat down upon them the occupants of the boat became conscious that there was a slight refreshment in the air.

"Aren't we getting too far away?" Judith put this question a half-hour later.

She had been sitting in silence, watching the dusk come over the world. Out like this she felt as if she could see the whole universe and watch the beating of its pulses. There came a subtle and strong happiness to her soul. She knew that this happiness would not last, and she felt it all the more acutely for that reason. She repeated her inquiry.

"Don't you think we are getting too far out? It will be dinner-time soon."

Lucian took his watch from his pocket and peered at it. But he could not see the time until he had lighted a match.

"It *is* dinner-time," he answered, with a laugh—"in fact, it is almost an hour past."

He laughed again as he threw the little wax-taper into the water.

"They have waited a few minutes for us, and then they sat down to the table. They will think you have decided to stay with your mother until evening, and that I have forgotten about dinner."

Judith turned her head and gazed back at the shore, now a fast darkening line with not a light upon it. She was anxious, but that curious sense of happiness remained with her.

"I think we ought to go back," she said. "It seems to me that we are a long way out."

"But you are not afraid with me?"

"Oh no."

"Thank God for that!" exclaimed Lucian, fervently. It was the second time that evening that he had thanked God.

"You should have been with me this afternoon when the sun shone on the water," said Lucian. "It gave me visions"—he looked at her for a moment before he went on—

"visions of you—of you and me, Judith—and of the time when we are going to be together. You needn't be shocked. The sun, I found, is a greater giver of dreams than the moon. Did you ever discover that?"

"No."

While he talked Lucian was rowing rapidly. The boat leaped and bounded beneath his strokes.

"Do you know how to use the oars?" he asked.

"No; I never had time to learn. We must go back, Lucian."

"Not yet." He stopped rowing. "Do you think I've suffered what I have, starving, famishing for an hour alone with you, to turn back now?"

His voice suddenly sank to the tone she remembered. She trembled. She grasped the sides of the boat. When she did speak she was able to say, steadily. "It is not like you to talk in that way."

"Oh yes; it must be like me, or I should not do it. Judith, you did a wicked thing when you married Richard Gerald. Even if I had been dead it was wrong. No woman has a right to do such a thing."

The woman's hands gripped the boat still more closely.

"Lucian, please go back!" She spoke with extreme gentleness.

"Do you really want to go?"

"I must."

"Do you not like to be here with me?"

No answer.

"Judith," bending forward, "tell me: do you not like to be here with me?"

Judith sat up straight and aloof. Her eyes burned through the fast-deepening dusk.

"You are not acting like a gentleman," she said.

XXXII

AFLOAT

LUCIAN made no reply, but his face changed. It had been flushed all the time, and this flush seemed to deepen.

"You don't answer me," he said at last, "and the reason is that you dare not tell the truth; and if you speak at all you have to speak truth. I rejoice in your truth, Judith. Always I rest upon that."

"We will talk of something else," said Judith, trying to speak coldly.

"You are not angry with me?" with eager anxiety, reaching forward and placing his hand over one of the hands that was grasping the boat's side.

"Not angry," was the answer, after a moment's hesitation," but disappointed—deeply disappointed." She was unable to keep her voice entirely steady as she said this.

"In me?"

"Yes, in you."

Lucian drew back.

"I want always to respect you," went on Judith, her tone gathering emotion as she spoke. "I cannot, I must not lose my respect for you. That would be—oh, I cannot tell you how dreadful that would be! You and I are to go different ways; and—and—don't you see that we must be able to think well of each other? That is all there is left, and we can keep that—we must keep that. Now, will you take me home?"

She half rose, but sat quickly down. A sudden sense of her helplessness overcame her. The fainting light from the west was on Lucian's face. His eyes were fixed on his companion. And now the wonder as to his manner grew greater and more alarming in Judith's mind.

"Since you are disappointed in me," he began, "it will make little difference if I say all that is in my heart."

Judith bent forward. She took hold of Lucian's hand firmly. She found the fingers cold and the palm burning hot.

"Be silent!" she said, authoritatively. "Don't say what you will be sorry to remember. Something is the matter. Is it the heat? You have been in the glare of the sun for hours. Row home now, immediately."

She spoke as if she had no doubt of his obedience, and, indeed, he took up the oars mechanically and made several long strokes—not towards the shore, however.

"You are going wrong," said Judith; "turn the boat."

"The sun came right down into my brain, but it made thought very clear," he said. "Why do you want me to turn the boat?"

"Because we are not headed towards the shore."

"That makes no difference. We shall get somewhere all the same. And since we are together—"

"Lucian!"

"Judith!"

"Will you listen to me?"

"I always listen when you speak; that is the very worst of it. Whenever you say anything up there at the house where they all are my very heart stands still to hear. That's an old phrase, isn't it? But it's a true one. And I try not to let any one know that it does stand still. So, you see, the whole thing is rather wearing. I've tried to go away, but you may have noticed that I come back. I say to myself, 'She will soon be somewhere where I cannot see her,' so I come back. Yes, you did a very wicked thing when you married and did not marry me."

Judith's courage was rising with the need of it, and she felt that she was never more in need of courage than now.

"Lucian," letting her voice express the tenderness that

she felt, "you must listen to me and do what I say. Will you ?"

" Oh yes — yes !"

" Take the oars, then, and turn about. We must go home. I'm afraid you are going to be ill, and we must be where you can have care."

The young man took up the oars. In the gathering dusk Judith could see that his eyes, always fixed upon her, were shining strangely. As she met his look her face softened even while it took on an expression of still greater resolution. She felt the perspiration starting on her forehead from sheer excitement. She was sure now that their getting home at all, unless they were picked up, depended upon her ability to make Lucian obey her, and he would not obey simply because she commanded.

Lucian skilfully turned the boat towards the shore, which was now only a long black line. The darkness had come down, but the stars were near and softly brilliant in the blue blackness of the heavens. Before he began to row, the young man, holding his oars poised, asked, " If I am ill, will you take care of me ?"

He noted her hesitation. She would not, even now, give her word lightly. He laughed and dropped his oars. She wondered why she had not suspected before that he was already in the first stages of illness. He had been looking wretched of late, and now he had spent this long afternoon between the glare of sun and water, smothered with the heat.

" I don't think that is much to ask from one so kind as you are," he said. " If I could go into the shadow of illness knowing that you were near—"

" I hesitated because I did not know what might be against my keeping the promise," she said.

" Then we will stay here."

She was now fully convinced that it was useless to reason with him in the least.

" If you are ill," she said, after a long pause. " I will help take care of you."

"Dear Judith! Oh, how kind you are! Now we will go home."

He rowed steadily for perhaps five minutes; then the strokes began to be uneven, the boat whirled about.

"I'll rest a minute," he said. "Somehow I don't seem as strong as usual."

Again he drew in the oars, but this time one of them slipped from his hand. Judith sprang to get it; she reached out her arm, the boat tipping as she did so. The ends of her fingers touched the end of the blade; one more effort, and the boat sent a swell that drifted the oar entirely beyond her reach. She drew back and sat down. She did not heed that her arm was dripping. She sat still, her eyes fixed on her hands that were lying in her lap.

Lucian was leaning his head on his hand. He was smiling. "I didn't mean to do it," he said, at last.

"I know you didn't," replied Judith.

"Don't expect me to be sorry," he said, a few moments later.

There was no reply to this.

"I don't want you to be unhappy." He said this anxiously. "Won't you look at me?" he asked.

Judith lifted her eyes. The two could barely discern each other.

"If it were daylight I could soon make some one see us," she said; "but now—why, I couldn't distinguish a boat a quarter of a mile away, and people here rarely go out in the evening. I don't know what to do."

"We can wait," he returned, in a contented tone.

The stillness was emphasized by the distant sound of the rising tide against the rocks on the nearest point of land. The sound carried a long way. Judith found herself listening to it with a strained attention, as if the hearing it could somehow bring help.

"Do you think there is any boat near?" she asked.

"I don't know," indifferently.

"But I care a great deal," she returned, earnestly.

"Lucian, will you shout? Perhaps some one will hear you."

"That is not in the least likely. This is no place for pleasure-boats, and all other kind have gone inshore long ago."

Judith could not fail to detect the satisfaction in the speaker's manner.

"No matter," she answered, authoritatively. "You can try to make some one hear."

"No. Why should a man who is happy make any attempt to be miserable?"

"Very well. I will call out myself. I can do that."

And Judith did call, clearly and shrilly, her voice going over the still water as if some one must surely hear and respond. Lucian uttered an exclamation of remonstrance which his companion appeared not to hear.

"Can you scull?" she asked, presently.

"No; that is, not much. And I haven't any strength to-night. That sun, which gave visions, took my strength away."

"I am so sorry," she said, tenderly. "You see, you are ill, and we ought to get home so that you may have care." She spoke as if he were a sick child.

"Yes, but we can't go. Providence has made it impossible. Some time, I suppose, we shall be picked up—but I hope not."

"Don't talk so, Lucian!"

He came and sat down on the floor of the boat and leaned his arm across her lap. She remained quiet, not showing that his attitude was unusual. In all her life she had never found it so difficult to seem calm. That choking of hurrying pulses in her throat, that suffocating anxiety on account of their position, and that strange, unreasonable happiness — how was she to manage all these emotions?

"Think of the friends who will worry about us," she said.

"Oh, well," easily, "we can't help that, so why should we think of them?"

Another long silence, during which Lucian sat at Judith's feet, looking up at her, while she, her face turned towards the shore, was gazing and listening intently. The world was as still as if there were no living thing in it outside of these two. All that could be heard was that faint, distant swish of the water against those rocks.

"We can't be very far from Rough Rock Point," said Judith.

"Perhaps," was the answer.

A moment later Lucian seemed to rouse himself somewhat. He looked about, and he glanced apprehensively at Judith.

"Are you really suffering," he asked, "just because we are here? We may be kept here for hours. And I can't help it—really, I can't."

"If there should be a breeze we could put up the sail and get to land somewhere. Let us run up the sail now, that we may catch a breath of wind if it comes."

Lucian remonstrated. He urged that a sudden flaw might capsize them; he promised to raise the sail if there was any hope of using it. Very soon after this he seemed to become drowsy.

Judith drew his head to her knee, and he contentedly closed his eyes. A moment later she roused him to ask for what matches he had. She had seen him light one to look at his watch. He gave her a box of wax-tapers from his waistcoat-pocket. Judith poured them into the palm of her hand, and carefully counted them as she slowly returned them, one by one, to the box. There were eighteen. At intervals she would light one. The first one burned straight in the still air, held up at arm's-length. A few moments later she gave another piercing, insistent cry.

Meanwhile Lucian was asleep with his head on her knee—heavily asleep. Judith's hand was on his hair; her eyes, when they were lowered towards him, changed from their strained expression to one of divine gentleness and pity.

14

XXXIII

" NOTHING COULD HAPPEN "

At nine o'clock that evening Mr. Gerald left the garden and strolled out into the road. It was still torrid. The air appeared to hold nothing in it for one to breathe. Hidden among the leaves, the birds held their wings up and their bills open ; they moved restlessly. The noise of the insects was incessant and shrill.

Mr. Eldridge was leaning on the gate in his shirt-sleeves, smoking. But Mr. Gerald was dressed exactly as usual— Prince Albert coat and immaculate linen.

" By Jove, Dick, I should think you'd die in that coat !" exclaimed his brother-in-law.

" I hope and expect to die in it, or one like it, some time," was the answer. " I suppose Judith hasn't come in ?"

" Guess not ; I should have seen her. I've been gasping like a horn-pout on this gate for an hour."

Mr. Gerald walked on along the highway. When he came to the village he found men and women sitting on the door-steps, or on the brown, dewless grass of the yards. They all seemed to be waiting for the weather to change.

Ellis Macomber had a chair tilted back against his yard fence. " Hottest spell for twenty years," he said, as Gerald came near. " I jest as lives be off the coast of South Afriky as to be here. Hotter here, I do believe."

Mr. Gerald paused. " Of course," he said, " this country can get up the most infernal heat this side of hades, we all know."

He was going on, switching his stick on the dusty, roadside weeds.

" Judith's be'n bright enough to stick to the water," said Ellis. " That's where she was right. I wish I hadn't come in myself."

Mr. Gerald paused and half turned his head. He did not speak, but Mr. Macomber went on.

" I seen her 'n' Lucian out in a boat when me 'n' Bob Sisson went to look after his pawts. I jest wish I'd stayed out."

" Yes," responded Mr. Gerald, " this village ought to have a flotilla for these fire-and-brimstone spells."

He spoke lazily, and he went on in his indolent walk, slowly striking at the weeds, his upright figure growing more and more vague as Mr. Macomber watched him. He kept on for more than half an hour. At the end of that time he was entering the yard of Judith's old home. The entire Grover family were out-of-doors. The glimmer of Mr. Grover's shirt was visible at a long distance.

" Ain't Judith with you?" inquired Mrs. Grover. She was never at ease with Judith's husband.

" No," he answered. " Probably she has had walking enough for to-day. But this heat made me restless."

He remained a few moments; then he took the cliff-walk on his return. After he had heard Mr. Macomber's information he had wished to know if Judith had come back to her home. She might have done so. He lounged slowly along the high path. From this height he could sometimes see a faint display of " heat-lightning " in the north, where was a film of cloud. Well, it was eminently proper and natural that Judith should have gone in Lucian's boat if she had the opportunity.

Not the faintest twinge of suspicion was in the man's mind. He knew Judith. A curious change came in the darkness to his face as he stood on the cliff. Then he smiled, and pulled at his mustache. " Odd," he was thinking, " that I never knew such a woman before. Well, I wish she was happier. Tremendously odd, too, that I don't bear her any grudge for not— Ah ! what was that?"

He was looking out into the blackness before him. In the oily stillness of the water was now and then a spark of reflection from a star. But this was not a star. Just a dot of light far out in the bay—a dot that burned a moment and then died.

"Somebody lighting a cigar. I wish I was on the water myself. I wonder if they miss their dinner? I really believe I'm more sorry for Lucian than for Judith. Poor fellow! he looks like a ghost. I wonder what will be the end?"

He thrust one hand into the breast of his waistcoat and sauntered on. After a few moments he found the path so rough that he left it and walked back to the road. As he strolled he was asking himself how long those two would stay out.

At eleven o'clock the whole Eldridge household were asking that question, and some of them were getting angry that Lucian should be so inconsiderate. But Mr. Gerald said, placidly, that he supposed those two were aware of what they were doing. There was no storm and no danger: Lucian knew his boat.

"Dick," said Mrs. Eldridge, "you never did have any feeling."

Her brother did not answer her. He only smiled in his mustache in that quite inscrutable way he had.

Mrs. Eldridge was walking rapidly back and forth along the piazza. The two girls and their father had gone down to the wharf, where they also were walking back and forth. But Mr. Gerald was sitting quietly in an arm-chair just outside the door. He seemed to be watching the fire-flies darting in and out of the big syringa-bushes.

"Richard," again exclaimed Mrs. Eldridge, " I wish you would do something !"

"Really, Caroline, you are quite ridiculous. What do you suggest? There has been no storm—not a breath of wind. Lucian is an experienced boatman. Nothing in the world has happened. They are staying out because they choose to do so. We should cut a fine figure going as a rescuing party and finding them enjoying themselves on the water. I suppose it is comfortable out there, and they dislike to return."

"I'm glad you can be so calm. But it isn't a bit like Judith. She must know we should be anxious."

"No; it isn't like Judith," responded the man.

Then he asked himself if, after all, he knew what was like Judith. Did he know her? It was only a few hours ago—nay, hardly an hour—when he had been thinking that he knew her. After all, perhaps, his lifelong theory concerning women was the correct one: that the best of them were hypocrites; that they did not know the meaning of honor; and that the man was a fool who trusted them.

Nevertheless, he had trusted Judith; he had grown to trust her more and more. He wanted her to understand that she was to act precisely as she liked. He wanted her to follow out what she considered the line of her duty. He watched her month by month. He found that he was by no means her master in that subtle sense in which alone he cared to be her master—that sense in which one personality influences another. And that knowledge brought him no feeling of defeat—rather one of triumph in that such a woman belonged to him. This man, who was cynically sure that he knew men and women, found that here was one kind of human being hitherto unknown to him.

Now, as he sat with such apparent calmness on the piazza and heard the clock in the hall strike twelve, a sudden and horrible doubt sprang upon him. Vaguely he heard his sister exclaim again how very thoughtless it was of Lucian and Judith.

Could it be possible that he had been mistaken in his wife? Possible? Mr. Gerald sat up erect, and he put a steady hand up to his mustache.

"I do almost believe something has happened." That was his sister's voice.

"Don't be silly," he said, in his usual manner. "Probably Lucian rowed out farther than he intended, and you know the sail would be of no account. It's a long task to row back. Ah! who is that?"

Mr. Gerald rose as a white figure appeared running up the walk. He did not advance, however; he stood still, while Mrs. Eldridge hastened forward. The next moment he saw that the figure was Belle. She came up the steps, and her mother caught her arm.

"Well, what is it?" asked the elder woman, shrilly. "Where are they?"

"I don't know. Father sent Maud and me back, but Maud wouldn't run. Father has got Bob Sisson to take him out in his boat. He says he thinks something must have happened."

"Absurd!" said Mr. Gerald. "There's not a breath of wind. Bob'll have to row. Nothing has happened, unless Lucian has deliberately turned his boat over."

"Oh, Richard!"

"You know it is so. It's as safe on the water so far as on your parlor floor."

"I don't care if it is," said Belle, "I'm glad father's gone. I don't know whether Lucian would stay out so, but I'm sure Judith wouldn't. She'd know we should have a thousand fits by midnight. But men don't know anything, even Lucian."

She sat down on the edge of the piazza and began to fan herself with her hat. Mr. Gerald sat looking at her. A glaze seemed to come over his eyes as he looked. The slender figure in white, indefinitely seen in the dusk, changed to another figure—taller, with a magnificent carriage of the whole person, with a dark face and dark eyes that were lustrous and soft and kind and true. Above all, true—true.

It was only by a distinct effort that Mr. Gerald refrained from saying that last word aloud. Still he did not say it; he did not speak. He listened to the question and answer that passed rapidly between mother and daughter. But he

gained no information; there was nothing known. If it had not been for Ellis Macomber and Sisson it would not even now be known that Judith was with Lucian.

"I wish I could feel as easy as you do, Richard," said Mrs. Eldridge, in a whining voice.

"Do you?"

Mr. Gerald rose. He walked down the path towards the gate.

"Sometimes I hate Uncle Dick," remarked Belle.

"Hush!"

"I do. If I were Judith I know I should kill him, and then run away and shoot myself."

"Oh, do be quiet, Belle!"

"Why? Perhaps she has run away. I don't blame her if she has. Lucian has been odd lately. He has either been planning this or he is going to be ill."

"For Heaven's sake, Belle!" Mrs. Eldridge held up her hands in horror.

The girl gave a short laugh. She did not care what she said. "You know Lucian was distractedly in love with Judith," she went on, recklessly; "you guessed it, anyway, or you never would have been resigned to Uncle Dick's marrying her. You would rather he would do it than Lucian, and she suspected of drowning her father! I never shall know why she married Uncle Dick. I—"

"Belle, you're talking like a fool!" sharply from Mrs. Eldridge. "Any girl would have been glad to marry Richard."

"His money, you mean. Very likely. But I can't make out Uncle Dick. He always sneered at women. Why did he want to marry one? But he doesn't sneer quite so much; I'll say that for him. What do you think has happened to Lucian and Judith? Father swore fearfully down there on the wharf. He said if Lucian were not drowned he ought to be horsewhipped. Then he seemed to remember that Maud and I were with him, and he apologized and said that he didn't know but the heat would turn all our heads. There's Maud. Did you see any one as you came back?"

"No; only Uncle Dick, who was as calm as if he were out for a promenade."

Belle gave another excited little laugh. Then she expressed a wish for the most terrible thunder-tempest that ever broke over the earth. She thought that such a tempest might clear her mind, and that nothing less would do it.

Mr. Gerald did not hasten in his walk down to the wharf. He knew very well that it would do no good, and only exhaust him to hurry. The heat was still very great. If one remained perfectly quiet there was a modified kind of comfort, but the moment one moved, save in the most moderate manner, the face became wet with perspiration, the body steamed as if in a vapor-bath. The great vault of heaven was like a hot cover shutting over the reeking world.

Once Mr. Gerald stopped on his way and sat down on a rock by the road-side. He folded his arms closely across his chest; his heart was beating heavily, and he was dismayed to find that he could not help its beating in that way. "A man who has a particle of feeling after forty deserves to suffer," he said, aloud. Then he straightened himself and pulled out his mustache. So an old soldier might do after receiving a bullet which he knew would be fatal sooner or later.

He went on till he came to the wharf.

XXXIV

"I KNEW SHE LOVED HIM"

THE water was lapping against the old rotting planks with a refreshing sound. With the incoming tide there ought to be a breeze from somewhere.

Mr. Gerald stood with his stick under his arm and gazed out over the black water. In the calm he could hear the sound of oars, and he saw what must be Bob Sisson's boat with a lantern fastened forward so that it threw its rays a little distance ahead. And Mr. Gerald could see a figure, grotesque and shadowy, with now and then a glint of light upon it, sitting in the stern. That must be Mr. Eldridge.

Mr. Gerald placed a hand on each side of his mouth and shouted, "Boat ahoy !"

The rower paused, and Mr. Eldridge called in answer, "That you, Gerald ?"

"Yes. You're going on a fool's errand. Let them alone."

The faint sound of an impatient exclamation came across the water from the boat; then Mr. Eldridge's voice, saying, "Something has happened."

The man on the wharf turned away with an oath. The sound of the oars recommenced, and the light of the lantern grew smaller and smaller, going straight across the bay.

After a little hesitation Mr. Gerald sat down on a piece of timber on the wharf. He thought he would stay away from the house for a time, so that he need not hear his sister talk, it was so extremely difficult for him to refrain from breaking forth into oaths as her voice kept rattling

about his ears.   Here everything was still ; no one would
speak to him.   He clasped both hands on his stick and
leaned upon it.   In this attitude he suddenly felt like an
old man.

In the boat Mr. Eldridge had changed his position.   He
now sat forward, behind the lantern, peering all about him,
his hand shading his eyes.   He was continually imagining
he saw the shape of a boat as far off as his eye could
reach.

"Over to the left, Sisson—now row faster."

But it was nothing—nothing but a stretch of dark water
glittering under the light as the boat drew nearer.

"Try towards that cove by Grover's farm."

Sisson obeyed.   The sweat was dropping off his face.
He rowed about, as near the shore as he dared to go, opposite the Grover farm.

"What if we try that water over by Gunner's Point ?"

Sisson rested on his oars that he might draw his arm
across his wet face.   "'Tain't no use," he grunted, "but I'll
go if you say so."

"You can't earn ten dollars any easier than by taking me
round, can you ?" was the sharp retort.

"Gunner's Point it is, then."

Again Mr. Eldridge leaned forward and gazed everywhere about him.   He gazed until his eyes ached, and the
darkness glimmered and danced before him.   And the ra-
dius of that light was so small !   Often he shouted his
son's name at the top of his voice, and then Sisson's
deep, rough bass bellowed across the stillness.   But for a
long time absolutely nothing answered them.

Then, all at once, so close to them that Mr. Eldridge
jumped back, a voice called out, "What in thunder you
doin' ?   You goin' to run into us ?   You'll bust yourselves
if you do !"

Sisson swore ; he veered off so that he did not hit the
craft, save to graze against it.

"Why in the devil don't ye have a light out ?"

"So we did. Can't ye see nothin'?"

It was a small sloop lying with no sails, rocking gently on the water. A man was leaning over her side, looking down at the boat.

"What's up, anyway?" he asked. "Why, it's Bob Sisson! Yer pawts ain't out here, be they?"

"I ain't after lobsters now," answered Sisson, with a grin.

Mr. Eldridge stood up and laid hold of a rope that hung over the sloop's side. "We're looking after a boat that's been out since two o'clock—a man and woman—*The Plover*—we're afraid something has happened."

"There couldn't nothin' happen," was the confident answer, "'thout they wanted it to happen. Stillest time, 'n' hottest time, 'n'—"

"Have you seen *The Plover?*" interrupted Mr. Eldridge.

"Yes, I seen it."

Here the speaker stopped to take some tobacco from his pocket, bite off a piece, and return the remnant.

"Well, where and when?"

"'Long 'bout here. Time, little 'fore sunset. Ain't they got back yet?"

"No. We're anxious. Haven't you seen *The Plover* since?"

"No. We've be'n here—can't stir—no wind. The boat went by us—young feller rowin'—gal in the starn. Seemed to be a good time. There ain't nothin' happened to them only what they wanted to happen, you bet. 'Lopin', mebby. Who be they?"

Here the man winked in the most open and atrocious manner at Sisson, who grinned in response.

"Told ye so, squire," said Sisson. "Don't want to offend, but I told ye there couldn't nothin' happen."

"Hold your tongue!" was the angry response. "I'll knock you out of the boat if you say another word!"

"All right, squire."

"Who be they?" repeated the man in the sloop.

"It's my son," said Mr. Eldridge, with dignity.

"But who's the gal?" persisted the man.

"None o' yer damn business!" was the prompt response from Sisson.

"There's no occasion for concealment," now said Mr. Eldridge, in his most dignified manner. "The lady is Mrs. Richard Gerald."

"That so?"

The man did not know that name, but he chose not to acknowledge his ignorance. He knew Sisson, because he had been to "the Banks" fishing with him.

Mr. Eldridge let go the rope and sat down. Sisson looked at him and waited. Finally he asked, "What's to be done now?"

"Go home — something has happened. But we'll wait until daylight."

Sisson dipped his oars. The man in the sloop leaned over. "Whistle for a nor'wester!" he called out. Sisson nodded. The two crafts parted company.

Again Mr. Eldridge began to look everywhere. His companion gazed at him pityingly. "Tell ye what 'tis, squire," he said, "you'll find everybody 'll tell you nothin' 's happened."

"Hold your tongue!" There was a quivering fierceness in the tone.

Once more Sisson responded, "All right."

After that nothing more was said for a long time. Sisson watched a light just visible down the coast—the Sheep Light-house; he could guess where he was by that, but it was close work after he got too near the coast to see it. Still, he knew the shore almost by instinct, or as one knows an apparently pathless woods which one has threaded from childhood. When the boat grazed the wharf there was a faint light of morning beginning to send long gray lines over the sea.

Mr. Eldridge stepped on the planks. As he did so a figure rose from a little distance, rose rather stifily, and joined him.

"Is it you, Gerald?" again asked his brother-in-law.

"Yes. Any news?"

The two men met and looked at each other in the gray light.

"Have you been here all this time?"

"Yes. Any news?"

"Nothing; only—"

"I knew nothing could have happened," interrupted Mr. Gerald, coldly.

"Only," went on the other, mechanically, "we ran afoul of a sloop. A man on her had seen them."

"When?"

"Oh, before sunset. He said—" Then Mr. Eldridge paused and drew his hand over his face.

"What?"

"Curiously, just what you say. Those two men told me nothing could have happened. If there had only been a storm, or a tempest, or something!"

"A water-spout, for instance, to swallow them," remarked Mr. Gerald, in the same cold, still way. But though he spoke calmly there was a terrible, an indescribable bitterness in his voice. He walked on, swinging his cane, not leaning on it. But his companion seemed bowed.

"I cannot believe it!" Mr. Eldridge made this exclamation after they had gone a few rods. He paused and seized Gerald's arm. "Why do we always believe the worst of people?"

"Because experience justifies that belief," was the prompt reply.

"No! no! How can you say so? I'm not going to give up yet. The world isn't worth living in if it's as bad as you believe."

Mr. Gerald glanced at his brother-in-law with something like contempt. He shrugged his shoulders. "You talk like a child, Eldridge," he said; "I've been a fool for the last time. I did believe in Judith—I had to believe in her. She was absolutely the first woman I ever knew who did not tell

any kind of falsehoods. Perhaps she thought she was living a lie staying with me. Bah! I'm sick of the whole
thing! To be a fool at my age!"

The two men went on quickly. A red color came along
the east, and tinged the ocean and land. The sky was dap-
pled over with "mackerel-scale" clouds. There was not a
breath of wind. The sultriness was so great that even the
sparrows had a languid appearance.

When Eldridge and his companion came in sight of the
house Mrs. Eldridge hurried down from the piazza. She
had on the gown she had worn the night before.

"I can't have that woman speak to me!" muttered Mr.
Gerald. He turned and walked round the house to a side-
door. He went up to his own room and sat down by the
window, looking steadily out. He watched closely the coming of the new day. His mind noted every phenomenon.
Sometimes he pressed his hand on his face.

Finally, when the sun had come up and broken through
the clouds, he rose and went to a desk that stood at the
other end of the room. He opened it. Within it lay a
sheet of note-paper partly written over. The man hesitated, stiffened himself, then carefully adjusted his eye-
glasses. He was sure the note was to him. But no; it
was addressed to a friend in London, and Mr. Gerald scrupulously refrained from reading a word beyond the salutation. He was not a man to read his wife's correspondence.
He compelled himself to glance about him. There was a
shawl lying upon a chair; there was a book turned down
on the table at the place where she had been reading. He
took up the book and read a few lines where it was open.
It was *The Mill on the Floss*, and the page was where Maggie and Stephen Guest were out in the boat which carried
them so far. Mr. Gerald's face became yet more ghastly.
There was a lividness upon it that was frightful to see.

"Can she go after reading *that!*" he said, aloud.

He moved abruptly away. He went again to the desk;
he had not yet found what he sought. From one of the

drawers he took a photograph. It was a portrait of his wife taken a year ago in Vienna. This was what he wanted to find.

He placed the picture upright against a volume and then sat down in front of it, leaning his arms on the table. The beautiful and faithful eyes looked full into his. It was the face of an enthusiastic woman, of one whose nature was full of warmth and intensity. At first one might think only thus of her; then the other characteristics became more and more visible; there was firmness as well as beauty in the mouth, a certain clear-cut decisiveness to the chin.

"Curious that I should wait until my youth was over before I became a blind idiot—blind idiot! Why should I blame her in the least? I knew she loved him. And she can love."

With a quick movement the man turned the picture face down upon the table.

"How long had she been planning this? And all the time her eyes kept that look of utter truth."

He rose, and again went to the desk. This time he opened a compartment and took carefully into his hand a small revolver, which sent out a blinding ray of light from its polished surface as the sunshine struck it. He smiled at this little toy, and passed his fingers caressingly over it.

"What a melodramatic end I could make!" he thought.

He seemed to hesitate. Then he replaced the weapon with a calm hand. He walked to the window and looked out. He was thinking that there were few human beings who had not, some time or other in their lives, had moments when they could contemplate a pistol in that same longing way.

There was a sound of horse's feet galloping along the road. The sound came nearer; it was evidently in the drive.

XXXV

A TELEGRAM

MR. GERALD, at the window, did not move as he saw a boy appear on horseback. The boy flung himself off, and Mr. Eldridge, who was still on the piazza with his wife, hastened down the steps, and took the yellow envelope extended to him. Mr. Gerald remained motionless, staring down.

It was several miles to the station where the telegraph-office was, and it was not open during the night.

Mr. Eldridge turned his face upward to the open window of the room above him. "Gerald, come down!" he cried out. "Here's a message for you!"

Mr. Gerald deliberately descended the stairs and leisurely walked along the hall.

"Do hurry, Richard!" cried his sister.

The man was feeling that if he yielded in the least he might lose that control over himself which he was resolved to maintain at any cost. Did they think he was going to hurry and tremble and exclaim because of a woman who— He reached out and took the envelope. He signed the receipt for it with a steady hand. The boy jumped on his horse and galloped away.

Mr. Gerald tore open the envelope. Then he put on his eye-glasses. It in some way soothed his pride to keep up this manner. Of course this told him they had gone. And he must read it aloud:

"'BOSTON, *Thursday Morning.*

"'At H——— Hospital. Lucian very ill. Will you come?   JUDITH GERALD.'"

"Good God!" cried Mr. Eldridge, "I call this mysterious!"

Mrs. Eldridge was wringing her hands. "There's a train goes at seven thirty!" she cried. "Get the horse round!" She disappeared in the house; she could be heard rustling and panting up the stairs.

Her husband pulled out his watch. "There's time enough," he said. He also turned to go. But he paused and went back.

Mr. Gerald was standing still, his eyes fixed on the bit of paper which now trembled in his hand.

"What do you make of it?" asked the other man, lowering his voice almost to a whisper.

His companion suddenly caught hold of Mr. Eldridge's arm. He held it closely, swaying a little as he did so. His face was gray, his eyes distended.

"You're ill!" cried Mr. Eldridge. "Let me get you something."

"No, no. It will pass. I have these attacks."

The speaker made an effort and held himself erect. Never before in his acquaintance with his brother-in-law had Mr. Eldridge felt any pity for him.

"It means," said the man, proudly, "that I would stake the whole world on my wife's honor."

The two men clasped hands for an instant; then Mr. Eldridge hurried round to the stable.

The tall figure left standing there seemed to make another effort to keep erect. But the reaction was too great. Mr. Gerald almost tottered as he made his way to the nearest chair and sat down. He grasped the arms of the chair and held his head up. In a moment he raised his hand and stroked his mustache. By the time his sister came down she found her brother apparently his ordinary self.

"I'm sure I can't imagine what's happened," she said, in a high voice, "and I don't know how they got to Boston, or whether it's an accident; or maybe it's typhoid. Lucian has looked horrid lately. And how did Judith happen to be with him?"

"What if we should wait?" gravely inquired Mr. Gerald. "Or, if you please, you may continue to put questions. I suppose it amuses you, and I ought to be able to bear it."

But Mrs. Eldridge did not care for the scorn in the man's voice. She bustled round upon the piazza. She drew on a glove and then took it off.

"I don't see but that it is just as mixed up as it ever was," she said. "I don't understand it at all. How did she and Lucian come to be in a hospital in Boston? That telegram doesn't amount to anything."

"It tells where they are," remarked her brother.

"Yes, of course. But it doesn't tell how they got there."

"One doesn't expect a long history by wire," said Gerald's caustic voice.

"That's true. But I really should like to know why Judith dragged Lucian off like that."

"Caroline!"

"Oh, well, you needn't be angry, Richard. But you must own it was odd in Judith to take Lucian off in that way. And it looks so queer, too. I suppose some folks will talk. Some folks will talk if you wear gray gloves when they think you ought to wear brown."

Mr. Gerald pointedly turned and left the piazza. He knew that the telegram explained nothing. But he was none the less grateful for it. He met Mr. Eldridge driving from the stable. As the two came round in front of the house the woman waiting there ran forward. She now had her arms piled with wraps.

"There's the east fog coming up," she explained. "It'll be here before we get to the station."

She climbed in before her husband could alight to help her. As she settled down on the seat she repeated that she was afraid she never could understand why Judith had taken Lucian off in that way.

"Don't be a fool," counselled her husband. Whereupon Mrs. Eldridge fell into a silence which she mercifully preserved during the drive.

Far out at sea was a line of dense mist. It came creeping on towards the land. All at once it caught at the shore and rolled forward. No more sultriness. People shivered and drew deep breaths, and were thankful that they could shiver. But Mr. Gerald did not shiver. He sat in his seat in the car with his coat buttoned about him just as it had been in the heat. He was the only one of the three who seemed unmoved when they were waiting in the reception-room at the H——— Hospital. He would not look towards the door. But he heard the trail of skirts on the stairs, and then Judith appeared in the light, thin gown she had worn the afternoon before. Was it only the afternoon before?

They all rose. Judith walked quickly towards her husband. She put out her hand to him, and he took it firmly.

"I am glad you came," she said, in a low voice.

"Of course I should come," he answered, in the same tone. Their eyes met. They both knew that in their hearts they had never been so near each other before.

Judith was so pale that her face seemed to have sunken. There were black hollows under her eyes. There was a tense line of suffering on each side of her mouth. An attendant was waiting at the door to conduct the father and mother to Lucian.

"I will stay here," said Judith. She moved to Mrs. Eldridge's side. She laid her hand on her arm. "He will not know you," she said. "He is—" Here she paused. She evidently could not go on, though she did not sob, and there were no tears in her eyes.

When the two had gone Judith turned towards Mr. Gerald. "Will you take me out?" she asked. "There's a park near here. Take me there."

The man lifted one of the wraps his sister had brought. He placed it over his wife's shoulders. On the sidewalk he offered his arm, and she took it. They did not speak until they were in the park and sitting on one of the benches there.

"You must have been anxious," she said.

" Yes, very."

Judith wanted to thank her companion fervently for not making any inquiries. She thought that questions then would have been like blows on bruised flesh. Yes, she felt that she could have thanked him with tears and sobs for his bearing towards her now. She looked up at him. But he was not looking at her; he was gazing carefully at a couple of children who were rolling hoops down the walk nearest them.

" I knew it would all seem quite strange," she went on. " Lucian saw me from his boat when I started to come back by the cliffs. He asked me to let him row me home. So I joined him. After a while I thought he was not like himself. Really the heat affected him—so the doctors say—and he was probably coming down with a fever besides. He rowed a good ways out. He would do it, and he wouldn't go back. Then he lost an oar. I couldn't do anything but light matches and hold them up, and shout for help. He was strange. Finally a steam-launch belonging to some Boston people picked us up. They were in a hurry to get back to Boston, and that was the easiest way for us to reach home too. But before we got there it was plain that Lucian couldn't be taken anywhere save to a hospital. The people on the launch were very kind. They found us about eleven. They telephoned to the H——— Hospital for an ambulance when we reached the wharf. It has been—it has been very hard to bear."

Judith's voice sank into silence. But directly she roused herself and continued :

" There's one thing he wanted me to promise, Mr. Gerald. He asked me while we were in the boat, before his mind was really so strange, though he was not himself. I don't know as you will approve of my doing it."

" And if I don't approve ?"

" I shall have to do it all the same. I promised, you know. And Lucian laid such stress upon it, and seemed so relieved when I did give him my word."

Mr. Gerald was now watching an old man coming along the path. He felt his forehead growing moist. He was thinking that the man was very old, and wondering if he had ever had a wife, and if—

"Perhaps you will tell me what you promised?" he said.

"Oh yes. I told him that I would help take care of him if he were ill."

"Then you will stay here at the hospital?"

"Yes. I hope you don't object?"

"But I am helpless if I do."

"Still I should be glad if you had no objections."

"Thank you. I will take rooms at the nearest hotel, for you cannot really stop here—only come when you can. And I will stay with you."

"Oh, Mr. Gerald, you are kind!"

Judith's pale face quivered, but she struggled to steady it.

"Of course I know that you love my nephew."

The man spoke these words as if he had said that he knew his wife liked Glory of Dijon roses. He said them of a set purpose, and he turned and looked full at her as he pronounced the sentence.

The sudden, utterly uncontrollable effulgence that filled the woman's face smote the man full in the eyes. It was a blinding glory straight from her soul. It was for no more than a flash of time, like a flash of lightning from heaven. Then, almost before it had come, Judith was resolutely struggling for self-control. She was worn with the night's experience, weakened by hours of intense emotion and anxiety. Fortunately she was ignorant of what her face had told.

After seeing that face Mr. Gerald felt that any words she could say would hurt little.

"I am convinced it is best for us to have things clear," went on the man. "We are aware of some facts; it will not make them any more facts if we speak of them."

Though he paused, Judith kept silent.

"I knew you loved him when you married me," he went on.

" More than that, I was sure that he loved you. I meant
to break up any plans he had in reference to you. That
was before I saw you. When I did see you, coming across
the pasture there in your shabby gown, I changed my
mind as to the means by which I would prevent Lucian's
marriage to you. I decided to marry you myself if I could.
Before I saw you I supposed you to be a common shop-girl
who, for some reason, had taken Lucian's fancy. When I
did see you I was quite sure you were the kind of woman I
had not before believed existed."

XXXVI

"DO YOU MEAN DIVORCE?"

IT seemed necessary for Mr. Gerald to pause frequently in his talk. But Judith kept silent. She was obliged to be silent, for she could not speak. She had never known before that Mr. Gerald had intended these things. But he might have spared himself everything—everything. It was her own decision that had stood between her and happiness.

She could see now that she had been blind and wrong; nevertheless, she had been obliged to choose as she had chosen, for that way had seemed the right way. And now, having chosen, it remained for her to abide by her own act.

And what did it all matter? A few years, more or less, of happiness, years that would seem brief as days, and then, oh!—her thoughts suddenly broke off—was not God above all? Was it anything to Him that she should do as her conscience told her was right?

She sat rigidly quiet on the bench beside her husband. How kind he had been! And yet how strangely he was talking now! What did he mean? She could not ask. She could only be still and wait.

"I took a fancy that the truth was in you," said Mr. Gerald. "And, besides that, your personal appearance suited me. I knew what you would be in silks and velvets and jewels. And I thought I could—to put it strongly— get the whip-hand of you. Curious what a force there is in simple integrity! Curious, too, that I never had to do with it before. That's why I didn't believe in it. Is Lucian going to die?" This question was put abruptly.

Judith essayed to speak. The first attempt ended in a

mere opening of the lips.   Then she said, " Yes ; I think he
will die."

" Then that simplifies matters, or complicates them—I
really cannot tell which."

Having spoken thus, Mr. Gerald smiled in that stiff way
which makes a face grotesque—like a mask.   Judith had no
idea what was meant by those words, and she could not ask
for their meaning.   Indeed, she cared little.

" Somehow I feel like an old man."   This apparently
irrelevant remark was spoken a moment later.

Mr. Gerald leaned on his stick.   " Some things take hold,
you see," he said.   " I'll tell you what came into my mind.
I don't know how it is, but after an experience like mine a
man looks at things differently.   You see, I have failed miserably.   There's nothing so blind as a human being.   In
spite of the fact that I saw you were not like the women I
had known, I yet acted much as if you were.   I thought I
could mould you, make you attached to me, wean you from
your past, give you wealth and all that it brings—you know
what I mean."

" Mr. Gerald, you have been very kind," in a scarcely
audible voice.

" Pshaw!   Did you expect I was going to beat you?
I've been through a good deal of torture since you did not
come home last night.   Finally, I thought you had gone
away with Lucian."

" Mr. Gerald !"

Judith's whole face flashed out a flame of indignant fire.
She rose to her feet and stood before the man for an in-
stant—stood tall and outraged.   Then she cried out,
" Oh !" and turned away.

The man rose also.   He strode after Judith and put his
hand on her shoulder.   " Come back," he said.   " Let us
have this talk through.   Please sit down again.   The human heart," he went on, with a derisive smile, after Judith
was again seated, " is a very strange organ.   I would not
think, until the very last moment, that you had gone with

Lucian. But Macomber saw you, and the man in the sloop saw you, and there seemed no reason why you should stay away, save for the reason that you and he had gone. And I knew you loved each other. And this is the curious thing about the human heart: notwithstanding all my suffering, there was a spice of triumph in the conviction that I had not been wrong in my old judgment—all women were alike, after all. Even you were not honorable. But I was mistaken. You are honorable."

Again Mr. Gerald took off his hat and pressed his handkerchief to his forehead.

"Now the miserable thing about the arrangement of the universe," he presently went on, "is that to be honorable and to do right does not make one happy."

"It is impossible to be happy if one is not honorable."

Judith spoke hastily, but with great earnestness. Her mind was confused by suffering and excitement; but she could feel what was right to her, if she could not explain it.

"Oh yes, I can conceive that that may be," answered Mr. Gerald. As he spoke he turned towards his wife and looked at her with unmistakable admiration in his eyes. "But I am not merely speculating. Judith," with a sudden, sharp tone in his voice, "if Lucian should live, what shall we do?"

She started: then she clasped her hands and succeeded in being motionless. She did not think of replying. She had nothing to say, and she did not know what her companion meant.

"What should we do?" he insisted.

He evidently meant that she should answer.

"Do?"

She gazed hazily at the man's face. She was asking herself how much more she could bear, and if she were even now in her normal condition of clear-headed capability to think reasonably.

"Yes, what are we going to do? Do you think we might

try the incompatibility dodge? If we agree on the thing, it will all be comparatively easy."

"Do you mean divorce?" Judith's voice was very distinct.

"That's precisely what I mean." Mr. Gerald rose after he had said this. "If you'll excuse me, I'll take a turn along the walk here. It's all a great muddle, isn't it?" He smiled, pulled his mustache, and began to pace up and down the mall not far from where his wife sat.

Judith remained quiet and watched him. She was not at the moment capable of continuous thought. A hundred things jumped and jumbled themselves up in her mind.

Mr. Gerald came back and stood in front of her long enough to say, "Of course, your father and mother would continue to receive just what they do now, and you would have a liberal allowance. And you would be free—free!"

He walked off again, and Judith continued to watch him in the same confused way. She did not even try to think.

Presently she saw her husband coming back for the second time. Would he insist upon her answer now? She put her hand to her head and gazed up at him. She saw something in his face which confused her still more. It was something she had never seen there before. He uncovered his head with what appeared an unconscious movement.

"There's one other item which I think I ought to mention," he said, "though I can hardly expect you to be influenced by it in coming to a decision, and that is—I love you. I did not know I could love in this way, more profoundly, more truly, than I had been able to imagine love. For my love has hitherto been a kind of fleeting animalism —a short-lived something for a few other women. I wasn't ennobled by it. I was degraded. I thought I would tell you, Judith Grover, that I could not live with you and know you without loving you. It was only fair to tell you this. I don't understand these things; but perhaps it is because I love you that I want you to be happy in your own way."

He did not wait for any reply now. He turned and walked away again.

Judith rose also. She could not be quiet any longer. She began to walk in an opposite direction to that taken by her husband. She moved hastily, and she found a difficulty in keeping her body steady. It was as if she were partially intoxicated. Her head seemed to be full of a blinding light which made everything strange to her. She had not gone many rods when a hand drew her own hand within a firm arm.

"It was very unkind of me not to remember that you must be suffering," said Mr. Gerald. "And perhaps you have had no breakfast?"

"No; I forgot about it."

Mr. Gerald took his wife to a restaurant. He made her eat and drink, and he kept silent. Indeed, he had nothing more to say. He had now only to wait for her decision. He considered that he had put the matter plainly before her.

Restored somewhat by food, Judith was able to notice that her companion showed signs of what the night had been to him. She kept back some expressions of concern. She found it very difficult to speak.

It was in silence that the two returned to the hospital. There had been no change in Lucian's condition; there would be no material change at present. He had not known his father and mother. He talked constantly; words without sense or connection flowed from his lips in a turbid stream. The whole party established themselves in the nearest hotel.

Judith, obeying the urgent request of her husband, laid herself on her bed, knowing that it would be impossible to sleep. To her great surprise, she fell immediately into a profound slumber which lasted several hours.

She dreamed vividly, not of anything that had just transpired, but of Mrs. Jennings. That lady was before her, was tracking her everywhere, was talking with her, caressing her, blighting and consuming her in some way. When she wakened, Judith stretched out her arms and clasped her hands above her head.

"Oh," she said, aloud, " I think I hate her !"

Then, without remembering what had happened, she fell asleep again, and at once resumed her dreaming of Mrs. Jennings, who was very lovely to her, but who repelled her, and made her wish to creep away into some place where she could never see her again. But one of the dreadful things of the dream was that she was positive that there was no place in the whole world to which she could escape from that woman. And she did not dislike her, and was pleased to be with her. That was the inconsistency of the dream, and one of the things which made it, she thought, so painful and wearing.

When at last Judith opened her eyes again she saw Mr. Gerald sitting in a large chair by the window. She was now fully awake. She lay for some moments gazing at him. He had a book in his hand, but he was not reading. His head was leaned back, and his profile was clearly defined.

Judith studied that face intently, as, it seemed to her, she had never before studied it. It was the face of a gentleman. She thought she was sure of that much. Then there came into her mind a distinct remembrance of what he had said to her in the park a few hours before. Or was it a few days before ?

The blood rushed up to her head and seemed to make a red film over her eyes. She moved impatiently.

IN THE HOSPITAL.

Mr. Gerald turned his head, but he did not rise. He closed his book, keeping his finger between the leaves.

"So you've wakened?" he said.

"Yes. I've been dreaming so unpleasantly!" was the weary response. Then she added, "I don't know why Mrs. Jennings should be so present with me."

"Mrs. Jennings? That's odd. I've just left her. I didn't know she was in town; in fact, I didn't know anything about her. She has been to the hospital. There's no perceptible difference in Lucian." Mr. Gerald gave this information distinctly.

"I knew Mrs. Jennings was in town." It was some moments before Judith made this remark. She ascribed to her fatigue and anxiety the sudden and curious importance which the presence of Mrs. Jennings had for her.

"Did you?" Mr. Gerald spoke with the air of one who will be very careful not to ask unpleasant questions.

"Yes. I knew by my dream. It was so insistent and so peculiar."

"Oh, there's no accounting for dreams. Mrs. Jennings said she saw you and Lucian when you arrived at the wharf in the early hours of this morning. She had just come in from somewhere by boat. She was in a carriage which had stopped a moment on the wharf. You were standing by while Lucian was being helped into the ambulance. She was about to speak to you—in fact, had left her carriage to do so—when you quickly entered another carriage and were driven off after the ambulance. She learned that Lucian was taken to the H——— Hospital, so she came round this morning. My sister saw her. My sister wept in her arms. Are you going to weep in Mrs. Jennings's arms, Judith?"

Judith shook her head. There was an unreasoning and quite unreasonable terror in her heart. She had never supposed herself fanciful; but she had suffered a great deal of late, and suffering, perhaps, makes one superstitious.

"My sister is making much of Mrs. Jennings," went on Mr. Gerald. "Ever since Lucian has been grown his mother has been arranging matches for him; but the boy has gone unharmed among those pitfalls. Are you going out?"

For Judith had now risen and was standing before the glass, looking at herself and trying to bring her mind to the face reflected there.

"Yes," she answered, without turning towards her questioner. She glanced down at her tumbled and soiled gown of thin stuff which she had worn in the heat the day before. Still, she was not really thinking of her gown, and her gaze was mechanical: but her husband noted it.

"I've been to a place where they have such things," he said, "and ordered a few plain, ready-made frocks to be sent here for you to choose from. It could be done a great deal sooner than we could have anything up from Eldridge's place, you know."

"How thoughtful of you!"

Judith's voice was absent, though she tried to make it grateful, for she really was grateful. Mr. Gerald bowed in silence. He raised his book and appeared to read.

It was a half-hour later that Judith came into the room in a closely fitting black dress, without a bit of color about her.

Mr. Gerald put down his book and looked critically at his wife. His eyes darkened a little as he looked. "Really, Judith," he said, "you can bear any kind of dress." Then, before she could make any reply, he went on: "I must beg your pardon for having bored you by mentioning the fact that I love you. Kindly consider the thing unsaid ; it was an inadvertence on my part. I wish to assure you that you need not dread any return to the topic. It is quite too ridiculous—not that any man should love you," with a polite smile, "but that I should tell you what I did. Please forget that sentence ; and, above all things, don't fear that I shall be guilty of such an error again. I hope you will permit me to accompany you to the hospital."

The two went down the street and crossed the little park together. Midway in the path they met Mrs. Eldridge. She was leaning on Mrs. Jennings's arm, and appeared to be pouring into that lady's ears a flood of words that called tears from her own eyes. Her companion, however, maintained more self-possession, but her air was one of deep sympathy.

Judith paused to greet this woman. As she did so the particulars of her dream came back to her memory and made her manner constrained.

There was Mrs. Jennings before her, as if she had stepped bodily from the dream — that faultlessly gowned figure : the light hair, soft and fluffy, on the forehead ; the gray-green eyes with their thick, light lashes ; the lips so scarlet that in some strange way they seemed the lips of a siren that might smile away the heart of a human being. Judith, as in her dream, was repelled from this woman and drawn to her.

"I have been telling Mrs. Jennings," began Mrs. Eldridge, "how you and Lucian were out in the boat yesterday, and how he could not go so far as you wished without being overcome by that dreadful heat. Of course, you didn't mean it, but it turned out so unfortunately—so unfortunately ! Oh, my poor boy !"

Mr. Gerald's eyes, narrowed and intent, were fixed on the speaker's face. His sister felt them and mentally squirmed under them, but she was not going to retract, although she knew she had perverted the truth.

"There were a great many prostrations from the heat yesterday."

It was Mrs. Jennings who spoke, with the air of one trying to make the conversational atmosphere more endurable; and as she spoke she flashed one look straight into Judith's eyes. That look, so suggestive, so significant, made Judith's heart shrink in absolute terror. In the midst of this emotion she heard her husband's voice saying, with great urbanity:

"My dear Caroline, I wonder where you obtained your information concerning Lucian. You know he spends days on the water, and yesterday was one of those days."

"But," began Mrs. Eldridge, with the maddening persistence of the narrow-minded, "you will, I suppose, permit me to have some knowledge of the actions of my own son."

They all smiled, all save the mother, who looked inquiringly from one to the other, and who finished her examination with a deep sigh.

"I'm sure you can't know what I suffer," she said. "Only a mother could know."

Mrs. Jennings turned solicitously towards the speaker. Mr. Gerald ceremoniously raised his hat, and then drew his wife away.

"I hope you won't think I am very wicked," he said, "if I express to you privately, Judith, my gratitude that I am not compelled to live with my sister. Poor Eldridge!"

He left his wife at the door of the hospital. Twice a day, morning and afternoon, for the next fortnight, Mr. Gerald walked here with Judith and saw her enter the door. Once within the door she went straight to the room where Lucian lay. The nurse in charge admitted her, and she sat down by the bed. She held Lucian's hot hand, she listened to his hurrying words, or sat watching him as he slept that lethargic sleep induced by opiates. She could do nothing; the attendants did everything; but she could keep her word to him.

He did not know her, for he recognized no one; but it soon became evident to the nurses that when this woman who spoke so little, and whose eyes dwelt so upon the pa-

tient's face, was sitting by the bed the tossing and moaning and muttering became less constant, less dreadful to see and hear. Sometimes the young man opened his eyes, and they rested instantly in that dark, gentle gaze that seemed at such moments to envelop him and strengthen him.

Once, lying thus, silently drinking in the soft light from Judith's eyes, Lucian smiled as a child might smile when full of content. He reached out a hot, dry hand towards her, but before she could take it he drew it back, whispering, hoarsely, " No, I will not row. We will stay here. I never see you alone. No, I tell you, I will not row."

A few moments later he said, in a louder voice, " I'm glad the oar is gone. And I am too weak to scull."

And again, starting up suddenly from a sleep, he called out, " Judith, aren't you glad we are a good ways from land ?" Then he laughed as he added, " We may drift out to sea. A man can't do much with one oar."

At such times Judith's face grew yet more white. But she listened, and sat resolutely in her place.

The two nurses who were alternately in charge soon began to watch this woman who came so regularly, and who was not the sick man's wife nor his sister. Unconsciously they grew to like to do little things for her; they allowed her to wait upon their patient, being quick to see that she was grateful for the privilege. They fell to talking and wondering about her; and Judith, without in the least knowing it, drew them to her.

" He does rest better when you are here, Mrs. Gerald," said one of these girls at last. " I don't know why."

Judith, in her chair by the bed, looked up into the pleasant eyes of the girl who had spoken.

" You have such a lovely presence," said the girl, " I don't wonder he feels it. But of course I can't explain it," diffidently.

" That is all a fancy," responded Judith.

" Oh no, it isn't. We've noticed it. We know it's so.

16

Indeed, we must be stupid not to know it. And he's better to-day."

"Is he?"

Judith started. The blood flowed heavily to her heart, leaving her so white that the nurse quickly held a glass of water to her lips.

As she stood there the girl in the white cap and trim uniform was thinking: "Oh, how lovely she is! Of course he loves her. But how mysterious it all is!"

Judith drank the water. She did not need it, she was sure, but the drinking it was a slight occupation for her. She glanced up at the nurse as she returned the glass.

"Thank you," she said. "You see, we had given up all hope, and suddenly to be allowed to hope—"

"Yes, I understand," said the girl, gently.

"And I cannot see as he is any better. Are you sure?"

"Oh yes. I thought so: the temperature, the pulse—and the doctor said this morning that he was better. Perhaps I ought not to have told you, for if he should have a relapse it will be so hard for you to bear it."

The nurse spoke the truth. Lucian was better, and he had no relapse. On those days when the east wind swept through the city, reviving everything, Lucian began to feel life returning to him. But when the salt air gave place to the hot south breeze, he lay panting and sometimes delirious on the narrow iron bedstead in the clean, bare room. But he was gaining. The doctors predicted health for him when the coolness of the fall was established.

Meantime Judith came no more. All the long hours, the interminable hours, when Lucian, too weak to sit up, still too ill to leave the hospital, lay on the bed or sat bolstered up in it, he thought of Judith and longed for her. He could not be assured by his own memory that she had been there. He knew she had, because she had promised. But he desired intensely to remember her presence, and he could not—save indefinitely, as if he had dreamed of her.

His father and mother and sisters visited him every day.

He stubbornly would not ask them anything about Judith.

One evening, after a long, tedious day, during which he had waited and listened until every nerve in his frame was tingling with frustrated hope and weakness, he turned to the nurse who had just entered.

" Has any one else been to see me?" he asked, with abrupt sharpness, feeling a decided self-approbation because he did not begin his speech with an oath.

" Yes."

" Man or woman?"

The nurse gave him some medicine. Lucian held the glass in his hand while he gazed at the girl with a heavy frown on his face.

" Woman," was the reply.

" Name?"

" Mrs. Gerald."

" Ah!"

Lucian drank the contents of the glass. Then he turned his head aside to hide the tears that suddenly filled his eyes and rolled down his cheeks. In his weakness he could have sobbed with gratitude. She had not forgotten him. She had come to him. She had kept her word. Yes, he had been sure she would do that. But it was hard that he could not have known when she was with him.

XXXVIII

"WE WILL BEAR WITH EACH OTHER?"

"WHAT do you say to spending the winter in the south of Europe, Judith?"

It was the first of October when Mr. Gerald asked this question. They were again at his sister's. For some reason which Judith could not understand her husband had quite insisted upon staying there the last few months.

The man was standing by the window. As he spoke he moved so that he could see his wife's face with the light full upon it. He saw a shadow rise and cloud the whole countenance, and he saw, or fancied he saw, the attempt which she made to drive away the shadow.

In these days it was in vain that he tried not to watch his wife. The habit had grown upon him until he could not shake it off. But he fancied that he was generally successful in concealing what he was doing.

In a moment Judith looked up at him and smiled. "Perhaps it would be very pleasant," she said, "and you would like it?" inquiringly.

"Like it?" in a little louder tone than was usual with him. Then instantly getting himself in hand, he continued, "Oh, as to that, I've been everywhere, and most places are all the same—confounded bores."

Judith rose quickly to her feet. There was a faint flush on her face. She put her hands together; then, apparently bethinking herself, she dropped them to her side. She moved slowly to the table, and touched a book here and there upon it.

"What are you thinking?" he asked.

This occupation of watching his wife was one of intense interest to the husband. Sometimes he thought he understood her fully, and the next moment he was quite sure he did not understand her in the least.

Judith turned towards him. She was now resting one hand on the table. Her figure was outlined against the light—a figure full of grace and power.

Mr. Gerald noted the tendrils of hair on the forehead; he saw the perpendicular line coming there. He had learned to associate that line above the brows with some sort of suffering to her; and he began to speculate now, as he always did, as to what particular suffering it was at this moment.

"What are you thinking?" he asked again.

She gazed down at the title of a book. "Of the south of Europe, naturally," she answered, calmly. "Where shall it be—Mentone, or where?"

Her companion was watching her forehead, where the line was deepening; and on the temple nearest him a vein was swelling. In the intensity of his gaze he thought he could almost see the pulse in that blue vein stirring the hair near it.

Mr. Gerald remained standing with apparent ease. "Jove!" he was saying to himself, "but she is made of good stuff!"

He tried to ignore the pang that contracted his heart. Sometimes in this constant watch he feared that he might become a monomaniac. It was not that he suspected Judith of anything but the most high-minded conduct; but with every day increased his feverish longing to read her very soul, to see every mystery of her being.

She was his by law. He was thoroughly conscious that he was quite irreproachable in his conduct towards her. But what were the thoughts and what the sufferings of a noble-hearted woman who had married Richard Gerald and who loved some one else?

Mr. Gerald sometimes found himself painfully impatient for the end of the play. What would the end be? There were moments when he had turned suddenly upon himself

in solitude, and had asked, fiercely, " Great God ! what will
the end be?"   But after such a rare and solitary outburst
he was sure to be more calm, more kind and polite than
usual.

"Can you suggest a place?" he inquired, at last.   He
moved a chair near her.   " Please sit down.   It seems to me
you look tired."

" Thank you."   She placed herself in the chair.   She
glanced up at him.   " Would Algiers bore you?" she asked.

Mr. Gerald's eyes brightened, though his face remained
impassive.   " I should like that," he said.   " Shall we spend
the winter there?   Or perhaps we might go up the Nile?"

" Please make any arrangements you like," she said.   " You
know I shall assent."

Mr. Gerald's eyes grew dull again, but his features and
manner were the same.   " Judith," he said, " I should really
like to do something to please you."

" No one could be more kind," she said.   " Why do you
talk like that?"

" Why, indeed?"

He drew a chair up in front of her.   He sat down in it.
He leaned forward, his hands loosely clasped between his
knees.

" Have you changed your mind about my project of getting a divorce on the ground of imcompatibility?"   He asked
this question slowly, in an absolutely neutral tone.

" No.   Why should I change it?"

" You still refuse?"

" I still refuse if you are proposing it on my account."
The answer was given promptly and decisively.

" Solely on your account," he rejoined, " solely to release
you."

" Then I will not be released."   Her voice rang still more.
Her eyes, distended but full of her resolve, met his.

Mr. Gerald tried to keep the fervent gratitude he felt from
showing in his face.

" Mr. Gerald," she said, " you know I will not draw back

from a contract I made with a full knowledge of what I was doing. We need not discuss the subject again, I hope."

"Certainly not. Still—"

"Still?" she repeated, questioningly.

"Oh, I have nothing to say but the old remark: that I want you to be happy."

"And I—do you not understand that a divorce from you would not make me happy? That we cannot undo anything in that way?"

"Then, for the last time, we will bear with each other?"

"Yes."

Mr. Gerald reached forward and took his wife's hand. He held it a moment; then he raised it, and lightly touched his lips to it. As he put the hand down he looked gravely at her. A pale crimson had risen to her face; in the eyes there were tears. But she did not speak.

It was a week later, and the day before the Geralds were to sail. Judith had been with her mother. She had bidden them all good-bye in the farm-house, and was walking back over the cliffs. She was wondering why she felt the parting from her mother so little, and she was congratulating herself upon the apparent fact that she was growing to have less feeling. "Since to have feeling is to suffer," she said, aloud.

"Judith! Judith!" a shrill voice was calling from below the cliff.

Judith paused. She recognized the voice, and hurried down the declivity. There was her mother, with a shawl drawn close about her head.

"I didn't feel as if I could let you go," the elder woman said, in a trembling voice, when her daughter had joined her.

"Oh, mother!"

Judith put her arm over the bent shoulders. The two stood a moment in silence.

"I jest had to call you back," at length said Mrs. Grover, "and I didn't have the strength to climb up the path. I d' know what is the matter with me, but I feel dretfully 'bout your goin' this time. It was bad 'nough before, but now it does seem as if 'twas too much for me. Can't you persuade your husband not to go? Can't you stay somewhere this side of the ocean?"

Judith hesitated. What if it should come about that she could stay at home? The thought went like wine through her consciousness. Then she put it away from her. She had chosen. And her place was with her husband. And then— As her mind instantaneously followed out some train of thought her eyes changed, and she blushed painfully.

"Mr. Gerald is so kind," she said, "that I don't think I ought to say a word against the journey."

"Then you won't stay? Jest think"—with tremulous eagerness—"if you could only be with me this winter! Oh, dear, I feel exactly as if something was going to happen!"

Mrs. Grover clung to her daughter, who held her tightly, but who did not retreat from the mental position she had taken.

"I s'pose if you jest said the word Mr. Gerald 'd do whatever you wanted," went on the mother. "I never seen a man so thoughtful 's he is; 'n' he so kind of masterful, 'n'— I d' know what; I can't make him out. You'll stay round in this country, won't you, Judith? You won't go that journey?"

Judith felt the tears coming to her eyes. She waited until she could speak steadily; then she repeated, as tenderly as she could, her refusal. It had been Mr. Gerald's proposition that they should go, and she would go.

"Oh, dear," cried Mrs. Grover, "that's jest like you! You won't never give in!"

It was useless to argue or explain. Judith felt that her very longing to assent, to stay in the old home, was the strongest reason why she should refuse to make any attempt to do so. She lingered and lingered, saying everything she could to comfort her mother, her heart sinking lower and lower as she talked.

Finally she said good-bye again, and retraced her steps up the cliff-walk. And the last thing her mother said was, "I can't help it; I do feel just as if something was going to happen."

XXXIX

"LET US GIVE UP THIS JOURNEY"

JUDITH hurried on after she had left her mother. She climbed the path so rapidly that she was panting for breath when she reached the top of the cliff.

The sun was setting, and the water was reddening from the red clouds floating up from the west. It had been one of those days of splendor which come in the fall. A light wind blew from the east. The tide rushed in, almost at the flood. A flock of coots was sailing along towards the shore. Every object was clear and distinct. There seemed to be a vivid, bright light everywhere.

Judith wanted to run, the air was so bracing, but she restrained her pace to a swift walk. Descending the slope that led into the field beyond, and that turned away from the sea, she came suddenly upon Lucian, who was striding along towards the path she had just left. She stopped abruptly. It almost seemed as if she glanced about her to see if she might escape. But immediately she advanced with extended hand.

The two had not met since the last day she had been in the hospital, and then it could hardly be said that they had met, since he had not known her.

"Lucian!" she exclaimed, "I thought you were in the Adirondacks?"

"So I was until two days ago. But, you see, I have come back."

They shook hands.

"So I see," lightly, "and looking what we call here 'tough as a hickory-nut.'"

"Thank you. I suppose I am tough. I thought I ought to come for an hour or two to see the folks before I sailed."

The young man's face was so brilliant that Judith rather wondered. But she accounted for the change by telling herself that he had, doubtless, in recovering his health, recovered from that unhappy idea that he loved her.

"Sailed?" she repeated. "What, are you also going to sail?"

"Well, I should think so," with a laugh. "You are 'making believe' you don't know."

"Am I? When do you sail, and for what port?"

"To-morrow. For the Mediterranean."

"What?" rather sharply.

"You don't mean to say you didn't know it?"

"Certainly I didn't know it."

Their eyes met for an instant. They had both grown white within the last moment. Lucian looked off across the fields.

"Of course," he said, hastily, "I shouldn't have thought of going with Uncle Dick if he had not asked me. He wrote, and urged me to join you and him. He said the trip and the winter in Algiers would be just the thing to restore me to 'fighting-trim.' That was his phrase. He said he should insist upon my going. You know all of our family have always done just as Uncle Dick decided. That's the way mother brought us up. And now father and mother say I would be quite foolish not to go—for I did hold out about it. Judith," pleadingly, and with something of his old manner, "I declare I refused point-blank at first. But I was wild to go. You can't blame me, Judith; you can't. I was deadly afraid that you wouldn't want me along. But I won't annoy you. And Uncle Dick won't take 'No' for an answer."

"Don't apologize," said Judith, coldly. "Of course there can be no reason why you shouldn't accept Mr. Gerald's invitation—not the least reason."

She hastened on across the field. She had not gone

many rods before Lucian ran after her. Without looking at him, she yet knew that his face was much disturbed.

"Judith," he said. "I won't go. I didn't think you'd dislike my going so much. I——"

"Dislike it!" The lips of the woman trembled as she spoke. Then she drew herself up a little. "You will go," she said, in a hard voice of command and decision. "You will certainly go. Why should you not do as Mr. Gerald wishes you to do?"

Lucian stepped back, and Judith walked on quickly. She made no pause until she had reached the house. She was going at the same swift pace up the gravel path when she saw Mr. Gerald in the garden at the south of the building. In a moment she had joined him. His face betrayed some surprise as he glanced at her, and there was a certain tightening of the mouth beneath the mustache.

"So you've said good-bye to your mother," he remarked. "I hope she won't grieve too much."

"Mr. Gerald," began Judith. But her voice did not quite suit her, and she began again, after a slight pause: "Mr. Gerald, I met Lucian on the cliffs. He told me he was going with us—to Algiers."

"Yes; I thought the trip would be just the thing for him. He looks well, but, somehow, he isn't strong enough."

"You didn't tell me."

"No; I thought it would be a pleasant little surprise for you."

"Did you think that?"

Judith was standing in front of her husband. Her head was back, her cheeks and eyes were burning. He gazed at her in undisguised admiration; but there was a lurking spark in his eye that glowed more and more deeply. Judith waited: then she asked her question again.

"Certainly I thought that," he answered. "Can you tell me that you do not find my nephew's presence agreeable?" She did not reply. "You like him?" the speaker changed his form of address.

Judith came a step nearer. She seized her husband's arm. "Yes, I like him," she replied.

"Well, then, am I not doing well in providing him as a travelling companion?"

"You are doing ill."

Judith was trying so hard to keep her hold on at least a degree of composure that her voice sounded strangely to her own ears.

"Ill?" with a smile. "Oh no, I think not. I was afraid that with me only you would be horribly bored, so I provided this surprise for you. And you are fond of Lucian, are you not?"

It seemed malicious, brutal, to Judith that her husband should return to that question. There was a stirring of rebellion and anger in her heart. She looked again straight in the eyes bent down upon her.

"Aren't you fond of Lucian?"

"Yes," she answered, "I am fond of him."

"Yes, of course; I knew that," was the response; "that's why I invited him. As for myself, though I like the boy, I can easily enough spend the winter in Algiers without him."

Judith dropped her hand from the arm she had touched. She walked away a few paces. She came back to where Mr. Gerald stood in exactly the same place. "Let us give up this journey," she said.

Her companion elevated his brows. "Oh no," he answered. "We shall get no end of amusement out of it."

He was watching the vertical line coming and deepening on his wife's forehead. And he was feeling what seemed like a burning knife cut through his brain.

"You insist upon going, then?" she said.

"On the contrary, I don't insist at all," he answered, courteously. "I only ask if you will go with me."

He knew very well that she would assent. He had found out long before this that she always intended to do what he wished, provided it was nothing that went against her conscience. It was really quite a wonderful study for Gerald, the study of his wife's conscience. He found himself continually adjusting his mental vision to a still more minute inspection of this woman's soul.

" If you request it, I shall go," she answered, promptly.

" Thank you, Judith."

Again she turned and walked a short distance, while he still maintained the same attitude, looking after her. He had become by this time nearly as pale as she was. She came back and stopped in front of him.

" Do you know what you are doing?" she asked. " Do you think you ought to do it?"

" I beg your pardon ; I don't quite understand."

"Yes, you do understand."

" But explain."

"Very well. I will. You know I love Lucian."

" Ah !"

Mr. Gerald lifted his head still higher. His face stiffened.

" Yes, you know I love him with all my heart—with all my heart." The low voice thrilled in speaking the sentence. " You know I should have been his wife but for a miserable chance. I was wrong. I suffer for it ; I expect to suffer for it all my life. But I can suffer."

She paused. The eyes of the two met in the silence.

" I knew you loved him," he said.

" Yes, it was no secret from you, but you seemed not to care. You did not love me, but for some reason you asked me to be your wife. Mr. Gerald," suddenly, with an irresistible access of visible emotion, " do you still ask me to go this journey ?"

" Certainly ; why not? Because you happen to love my nephew is no reason why you should not travel with him, since I am to be with you. Really, Judith, you take things too seriously. Nobody takes things seriously in these days. And what if, here and there, a wife doesn't love the right man, or marries the wrong man ?" Mr. Gerald paused to laugh slightly. He went on, "Why, the situation is as common as—well, a hundred times more common than for a woman to marry the right man. That's the unusual thing." He paused again. Judith, gazing at him, saw some peculiar and indescribable expression come into his face. "Haven't I been fairly considerate?" he asked.

"Yes, yes; you have been kind. But you are cruel when you put me—"

Mr. Gerald held up his hand. A ray of intense light streamed from the pupil of each eye straight into his wife's eyes.

"Cruel!" he exclaimed. "God! she calls me cruel!—she, who is squeezing out my heart's blood between her white hands—"

Judith felt her breath leaving her. She tried to step forward and touch the man before her, but she could not move. She stood staring at him. It seemed impossible that he could have spoken such words. They were as utterly unlike him, as she knew him, as words could be: they frightened her. The next instant the spark died out of his eye. His face became dull and flabby. He smiled coldly, and with what Judith thought was self-contempt.

"You didn't know I could perform a bit in melodrama, did you?" he asked. "But a man has a great many odd traits stowed away in his individuality. Now. Judith, I want you to go over to Algiers just as we planned. I'm not a man to harbor any petty jealousy."

"I know you are not," she returned, with some bitterness.

"No; there's not a bit of the tyrant in me, and there is no more ridiculous object on the face of the earth than a jealous husband." He stroked and pulled his mustache, and then he thrust his hands into his pockets. "Whatever happens," he said, "you need never expect me to take that part."

"Nothing will ever happen," she answered. Her face was turned away, and her voice was cold.

"Oh, I'm sure of that. A man really ought to be able to

trust a wife who comes to him and tells him that she loves some one else."

There was something so incredible in the tone in which this was spoken that Judith started, stung by an indignation she would not try to conceal. Had she done right or wrong in thus speaking to him? She had meant to be wholly truthful in trying to make her husband know how vitally averse she was to this journey. She raised her head and looked at him. Then she left him.

She went to the far end of the garden. She must be alone for a time. She leaned against a tree-trunk, her head drooped forward. Did her husband have a mania that led him to try her? Was he putting her in a difficult position to prove her? Yes, it was cruel. Was that a sane light that had flashed out from his eyes—as if a demon had suddenly peeped at her? She moved. She tried to banish the horrible questioning. And she could speak of such things to no one.

THE PASTURES

Judith did not go to her own room ; Mr. Gerald might follow her there. She hesitated after having reached the house. She stood in the hall, in the light of the sun, which poured in through the western window.

Mr. Eldridge came in ; he glanced at her, passed on, then came back and asked, kindly, " Has anything happened ?"

" Nothing," was the dull answer. Then she tried to say, gratefully, " You have always been so kind to me, Mr. Eldridge."

The moment she had spoken thus she knew how strange such words must sound. She saw his look of astonishment.

" Oh, I beg your pardon," she said, trying to smile, " I think I must be getting absent-minded. I have just come from my mother's. She is really superstitious about this journey."

She passed on up the stairs. Then she remembered that she was not going to her room. Nevertheless, she paused there a moment. A book lay on the table. She took it in her hand, gazing down at the title-page without seeing the words. Finally she read "*The Mill on the Floss.*"

She started. Her eyes flashed about her in a frightened way. She had been reading that story on that day before she went out with Lucian in the boat. She remembered that while she was reading she felt sure that Lucian had ceased to love her, and she had been coldly grateful for the belief ; grateful as we poor human beings are when a precious thing that we know we ought not to have is really put beyond our reach. Then she had seen him in the boat —and he did love her.

With the book in her hand, though she was not conscious that she had it, Judith hastened down the stairs. She felt stifled and oppressed, and there was a strange sense of fright upon her. She knew indefinitely that she was afraid of herself. Once more without the house she hesitated.

"Where shall I go?" This question repeated itself over and over in her mind. "The pastures — the pastures," a voice seemed to say in her ear.

She went down the walk. She saw Mr. Gerald still in the garden. The sight of him made the wild tumult in her heart still more tumultuous. She turned her head away lest he should see her face.

As soon as she was in one of the wide stretches of rocky pasture she began to run. She ran full in the teeth of the east wind that was coming from the sea. With the decline of the sun the wind had become chill, and a fog was rolling in towards the land. She could see the bank spreading itself in away out by the white shaft of the light-house. As she ran she watched it coming with a strange interest. She was saying to herself, "When the fog gets to the Point I will stop running."

All at once that fog seemed to have something to do with her destiny. She kept her eyes fixed upon it. She crushed the sweet-fern shrubs under her feet, and she was conscious of inhaling the odor in strong whiffs. With that odor her childhood days trooped up in order in her mind. She stooped and caught up in her hand a bunch of the leaves, pressing them to her face. She recalled how she had run over this very pasture in pursuit of a stray dog who had come to her home, and whom her father had said shouldn't stay there; and he had driven it off. She had longed passionately to find that dog. He had come this way when he had been driven from the house. But she had never found him. "No," she cried now, between her quick breaths, "I never found him."

The fog was at the Point. She stopped still, almost breathless. She was going to clasp her hands. Then she found the book in one hand and the sweet-fern leaves in the other. So she stood still with her hands dropped at her sides. She watched the fog unroll itself from the sea over the land. It was as if some giant were shaking it forward.

Presently Judith's lips were salt with the vapor; her hot cheeks grew damp and cool with it. Heart and soul were as if immersed in that cold, salt fog. The excitement which had controlled her ebbed away as the sun set, and the quick-coming darkness of an October night quenched all the bright color which the fog had not already obscured. In a moment Judith stood shut in by the mist, able to see but a few paces about her. But she knew all the localities of the coast so intimately that she had no fear. She threw back her shoulders and took in long breaths of the sea sweet air. She had a childish hope that this familiar atmosphere would help her drive away the invincible depression which settled down over her soul as the fog had settled down over the land.

What if she should lose herself, and should finally die of hunger and exposure? She knew of marshes where people had wandered in a fog which kept on day after day. At this thought she laughed. There were no marshes here, and she knew her way. She began to descend towards the meadows, stumbling sometimes, going a few rods astray as the fog became thicker, but always, as she thought, getting into the right direction after a few efforts. She was in no hurry. She dreaded the return to the Eldridge house.

And what had her husband meant by saying that she was wringing his heart in her hands—her "white hands" he had said. Oh no; she would not wring any one's heart, save her own. She had been obliged to tell him that she loved Lucian, so that he might change his mind and not make her take that journey. She had been sure he would give up the journey when she had told him that. But no, nothing made any difference. He would not help her; more than that, he assumed that he was helping her.

Ah, here were the bars which led into the lane that wound up from Mr. Eldridge's field into the high pastures. They suddenly confronted her, ghastly in the silver mist. She let down the rails, thinking some one had come through since she had passed that way an hour or so ago, and this person had put up the bars. So she also replaced them and went on. The grass was now damp, and her skirts, trailing over it, were heavy and wet. She threw away the handful of sweet-fern leaves, but she kept the book pressed close to her side.

She began to think of Maggie Tulliver. "To be right in the great moments of life," she said, as if she were talking with some one, "I must keep my word. He trusts me. He knows I will be loyal as far as in me lies—yes, as far as in me lies. It is not the wrong, involuntary thoughts and long-ings which dishonor us; it is the wrong longings which are en-couraged and made much of. And integrity is all there is in the world that is worth while—all—all."

To her surprise, Judith found it a slight relief to speak aloud. The fog was very thick, and now that evening had come it was an opaque wall that opened to let her through and then closed about her, keeping close all the time. She had descended from the uplands; indeed, she was going down a steep incline, and with the salt odor was mingled the scent of wet, fresh meadows. She stopped. This was not the way. There was no steep hill in the lane that led towards Mr. Eldridge's. And those bars through which she had passed could not have been what she had thought them.

She tried to think where she was, and presently she re-called the locality; but though she knew the locality the knowledge did not avail her in the least, for she had lost the power to tell east from west or north from south. She could not even really place the dull sound of the waves against the shore. Sometimes that sound seemed in one direction and sometimes in another. The fog confused her completely. She struck her foot against a rock in her slow progress. She sat down on the rock, sitting perfectly still, not thinking of anything and not caring for anything.

Presently she began to be cold. When she had first started out that afternoon the sun had shone clear and warm, and she had worn only a thin wrap, and this wrap was all the out-of-doors garment she had now. She drew it closely about her, and pulled her hat more firmly on her head. She sat there shivering, and hearing the sounds of the field: the slow, autumn chirp of the crickets, the many mysterious hummings and cracklings and mutterings of the night in the country. Soon she heard the distant, soft step of something drawing nearer and nearer, sometimes stepping on a twig, then coming on over wet gress or thick mud.

Judith drew herself up, waiting breathlessly. At such a moment the wilderness might easily enough be peopled with dragons and goblins. Some shape formed itself in the mist and came closer and closer, until Judith, palpitating and tremulous, sprang from the rock. At the same moment the shape jumped back, seemed to hesitate an instant, then pressed forward inquisitively, while the woman stood still, not knowing where to run, and resolved to brave anything ; for, after all, what did it matter? She inhaled a warm, sweet breath, and a rough, hairy head was rubbed against her arm. She drew her hand along the face, pressing her fingers in the dish-shaped forehead, and smiling to herself that there should be another lost thing abroad this night, for this calf plainly was accustomed to petting, and so was not afield day and night. The animal drew yet closer to her, and Judith placed her arm over its neck, while the calf began to mumble an end of her wrap.

There is no way to judge of time in such places. Judith only knew that it was early in the evening when she had lost her way ; she could not guess how long she had been in this spot. After a while she sat down again on the rock. She heard the calf gently nipping grass now and then near her, and the sound greatly comforted her. She thought it was near midnight when, in the distance, there came the sonorous, deep baying of hounds in full cry. A few moments later there rushed past her something that she did not see at all, and then with a wild dash some dogs after that something, the dogs telling what they were by their insistent baying, in which there already seemed to be a note of triumph.

Judith had been sitting crouched over on her stone, her shoulders raised and her head sunk between them, shivering, and yet dozing now and then in a strange way that did not refresh her, and that confused her greatly. Every time she dozed she began again to beg her husband to give up the journey; then she would start awake to a knowledge that he would not change his plans. Two or three times she caught herself saying aloud, " To be right in the great moments of life—" But she could not think what came next, try as she would.

The calf had evidently laid down quite near her, for she could hear it breathing, and sometimes it chewed its cud. She must have been half asleep. Was that the calf which had risen and— But what was it? Judith rose and stood still, her lips parted, her very pulses listening.

CHAPTER XLI

SOME TALK

CERTAINLY that was a step coming forward in her direction. She moved so as to face towards the sound. Some one was breathing heavily close to her. The next moment the tips of hands belonging to extended arms touched her.

"Good heavens!" cried a woman's voice. "Speak, can't you? What is it? What are you?"

But it was a moment before Judith could speak. The excitement she felt made it impossible for her to command her voice, though she tried to answer.

"Speak, I tell you!" was repeated again.

A gloved hand caught Judith's bare fingers and gripped them painfully. A perfume that was in some way familiar to her exhaled from this person. Judith felt her brain growing dizzy with the suspicion that came to it and with what seemed the impossibility—that the suspicion could be justified by fact.

"Well," she said, as soon as she could speak, "what shall I say? Who are *you*? That is as much the question as who am I."

"Is it Mrs. Gerald?" quickly.

"Yes."

"Thank fortune for that! Oh, how odd this is!"

The speaker broke into an excited laugh. But she caught her breath rather suspiciously as she laughed.

"I made sure I should have to stay all night in this fog."

"And you will now. I can't be quite certain who you are. Your way of speaking— But no—that is impossible —do tell me!"

Judith leaned forward, but she could distinguish nothing.

"Oh, I thought you knew me as I knew you," was the response. "Guess! it will while away one minute if you guess."

Judith unconsciously drew back a little. "I know now," she answered—"Mrs. Jennings. But I don't see how it is possible that you are here—no, it isn't possible. I suppose I am dreaming."

And as she spoke Judith actually thought this apparent arrival might be only a dream. She felt that she was not able to judge just now as to what were realities and what were visions.

The other woman had kept her hold on Judith's hand. She now slowly reached forward and encircled Judith's neck, coming close and putting her face against her companion's. She lightly brushed Judith's lips with her own. She laughed a little. "Now do you know me?" she asked, in a whisper that was even more caressing then her caress had been.

"Yes, I know you," was the answer.

"I can't tell you how glad I am to see you—no, I mean to find you, for I can't see you. And if we are to stay here all night I shall have time to say all I want to."

"I think you'll have time," returned Judith.

"Yes. And I'm thankful to be with you when you haven't your armor on. For it would be quite ridiculous if you wore it when you are lost in a sea fog. Now you unbrace and unhelm, and throw down your sword—eh?"

"My armor?"

"Certainly." Judith thought her companion was going on, but she did not. After a moment's silence, during which the new-comer seemed to be unfolding a shawl, she said, "Since you have found a rock I will share it with you, and this shawl will cover us both."

They sat down. They drew the shawl close, and sat with their arms around each other.

"I'll tell you how I happen to be sitting here beside you,"

began Mrs. Jennings. " I was invited to visit Mrs. Eldridge last week ; I was unexpectedly prevented from coming. This morning I suddenly decided to start. There was no one to meet me at the station, of course ; but I counted on the depot carriage. There wasn't any. I knew I could walk well enough—I'm a good walker—and in this fine October air. But the distance seemed farther than I had expected. I took a short-cut across the pasture, a path I had gone over several times, but the fog came up—now you understand ?"

Judith did not reply. She was recalling her old curiously mixed feelings towards this woman — how she had been drawn to her and repelled from her, all in the same moment. Now, as she sat so near to Mrs. Jennings that she could feel her heart beat, she forgot any repulsion she had ever known : she even had an inclination to draw still nearer, and the mocking voice and deliberate enunciation were pleasant to her ears. She wondered how she could ever have felt any differently from the emotion of this moment.

" I hope you are not sorry I am here," said Mrs. Jennings, softly.

" No ; I am glad."

" And if we die of exposure and the crows eat our bodies, then will you still be glad ?" laughing.

" Perhaps ; who knows ?"

" Ah, yes ! — who knows ?" with a prolonged intonation. "And then when the crows have eaten you, Mrs. Gerald, you will not have to live with that man who has bought and paid for you."

" Mrs. Jennings !"

" Oh, you need not exclaim. Better to be carrion than to live like that !"

Judith tried to shrink away, but could not. " Don't talk so !" she murmured.

" Yes, I must talk so," was the response; " I may even say worse things."

Then she became silent, and in the silence the two could hear the sound of the hounds far away, melancholy and long drawn out, and the faint muffle of the waves. The calf had walked off when this other woman had come, and he could be heard among the bushes near by.

" Are you glad you did it?" abruptly asked Mrs. Jennings.

Judith did not reply. And yet she felt a strong inclination to burst out into a flood of confidences—to empty her heart of all the "perilous stuff" which was poisoning her.

"You needn't answer," said Mrs. Jennings, in a moment; "there isn't the slightest need. I can see into your soul."

"Can you?" in a whisper. And Judith wondered why she did not feel repelled at the thought that any one could do that.

"Oh yes; I can see. Do you remember the first time we met? You and Mr. Gerald came to the station for me, and I sat on the carriage-seat with you; and I looked at you, and felt drawn to you; and I was saying to myself, ' There's another one !' "

" Another one ?"

" Certainly. I suppose Mr. Gerald's money tempted you —not but what some woman might love him for himself— and you married him. But you were not the woman to love him, because—"

" Oh, stop !" cried Judith.

Mrs. Jennings laughed; and then she drew her hand softly down her companion's cheek.

" Don't be afraid," she said. " I'm talking on a subject that is quite familiar to me. I know it well. But you are one of the kind to be silent—to be proud and strong and keep your word, and all that. I'll warrant you never told him you loved him ?"

" Oh no !"

Again the other woman laughed.

" You wouldn't do that. Do you ever want to kill him ?"

Judith shuddered.

Mrs. Jennings went on. " Perhaps not really kill him

with your own hands ; but see him drop dead, and so be done with the whole dreadful business."

Judith tried to rise to her feet, but her companion held her closely, and she soon ceased her efforts and sat still. She replaced her arm about the woman near her ; as she did so she sobbed violently, but without tears. Her eyes were dry and strained open in the darkness. Was this woman going to put into words any more horrible, fleeting fancies? And how did she know? This last question frightened Judith. Did she show in her face, in her very presence, the one thing she tried most to conceal?

" Yes, and so be done with the whole business !"

Mrs. Jennings repeated these words with a kind of diabolical emphasis. There was something in her manner that gave Judith, she knew not why, a wellnigh irresistible wish to make use of the same phrase. But she was not personally repelled in the least. She could not understand that.

" No," said Judith, at last, and in a firm voice, " I do not wish to see him drop dead."

" Oh !"

" I do not wish it!" with increased firmness.

" To wish and to do are two different things," said Mrs. Jennings.

" No, no !" with an approach to violence in her voice; " they are alike. The wish leaves the same stain on the soul —the same ineradicable stain that God himself cannot wash away."

It was only after she had spoken that Judith realized how she was lifting the curtain from her soul, and lifting it for this woman, whom she did not know and whom she had mistrusted. She did not understand why the darkness, the strange position in which these two found themselves, conspired to make her less reticent ; and she experienced a relief, as if some hand which had been constraining her was unclasped for a moment, and for the first time since her marriage she was able to speak and to breathe. But she thoroughly distrusted this relief and fought against it. She thought she was always fighting; she had no moment when she could be her own natural self.

" You are quite wrong," answered Mrs. Jennings. " It is the deed which deepens the stain to ineradicableness. If I were to kill you now—" The speaker paused.

" Perhaps you will," whispered Judith, with a passionate emphasis. Then, realizing what she had let herself say, she began to tremble.

" Is it so bad as that? Is it so bad as that?"

She heard the voice tenderly speaking to her. She felt Mrs. Jennings's gentle touch on her face and hands. There were more words, half spoken, pitying.

" I'm sure I can't imagine why I speak like this," she said, finally, when she could command her voice. " You are the first human being who has ever heard me."

Having said this, Judith felt the tears come burning to her eyes and rush hotly down her face. They came in floods. She would not put her head on her companion's shoulder, but sat with it lowered, letting the drops fall, thankful for them, but at the same time afraid of them. She could never, she was sure, go on with her life if she should become emotional.

" It's because I understand," said Mrs. Jennings. " You had a feeling that I knew. But you don't believe in me all the same. And you need not, for I don't believe in myself.

" Now, there was my husband. I did not love him in the least, and I was afraid of him; and you grow to hate what you fear. I couldn't earn my living, and I liked fine things; and the men whom I loved didn't love me; and my aunt was tired of taking care of me. So I married Dr. Jennings, who didn't love me, but who, for some reason, thought he would have me for his wife.

" I had three years of the life. Every morning I wished that man would die before night, and every night I wished he would die before morning. But I kept on smiling at him, and he actually seemed to like me more and more.

You see, I can't be what is called a refined woman, or I should either have poisoned him or gone mad. No. I'm not a refined woman. I'm grateful for that, though I do give people the impression of refinement. But that's only because my tastes are nice, and tastes have nothing to do with the matter. Are you listening, or are you beginning to be bored?"

" I am listening."

" Dr. Jennings was a great surgeon. Be thankful, at least, that Mr. Gerald is not a surgeon. I was sure that my husband's first thought concerning a person was how that person would look on the operating-table — how he would cut up, you know."

Here Mrs. Jennings paused to give a cruel and yet triumphant little laugh. She went on.

" And I always had a conviction that some time I should have some ailment that would give him the opportunity to put me on that table and plunge his knife into me. You see what fancies can come into the mind of a woman. That idea grew upon me till I imagined the doctor was thinking of his scalpel every time he looked at me. I believe that before the end of the fourth year something would have happened—and he was getting fond of me in his cold-blooded, scientific way. I thought so much about his death that there are times now when it almost seems as if I killed him."

It was Mrs. Jennings now who shuddered. Then she shook herself impatiently.

" He used to ride horseback every day. He was trying a new horse, and it threw him head-first on to the pavement; so he was brought home dead. Actually, Mrs. Gerald, I have had moments of asking myself if, by any occult means, I had introduced my individuality and my feelings into that horse: and I couldn't rest until I had had the horse killed. People thought it was quite natural; they understood why I wanted that horse put out of existence. Had it not been the means of ending my precious husband's life ? But the simple truth was I was afraid of that animal. What if it should some day reveal why it had thrown its rider ?

" It was in the days previous to the doctor's death that I began to carry a little revolver. I had no reason for carrying it, but I liked to have the thing with me ; and I've kept up the habit. I have times of practising shooting ; it takes up your mind. But I don't know why I mention that.

" Did you ever think that a tiny revolver with a shining barrel and beautiful tracery on the handle would be a comfort—just to know it was with you ?" Mrs. Jennings laughed slightly as she asked this question.

" No," said Judith. But she was afraid the idea would have a fascination which would return to her.

" What strange notions will come into a woman's mind," went on Mrs. Jennings. " Now, almost from the first time I saw you I had an impression that I should be somehow instrumental in doing a good deed for you—unintentionally instrumental, perhaps. I don't know what the deed will be, but I can't get rid of the impression."

XLII

RESCUED

WHEN Mrs. Jennings ceased speaking Judith became aware that she had been listening greedily to her words—listening with that creeping of the flesh and rising of the hair which made her, now that her companion was silent, feel as if she were still under the power of some uncanny spell. She moved uneasily. She wondered how she could bear to feel Mrs. Jennings so near her, to be conscious of the warmth of her touch, of the beating of her pulses. She argued that she ought to wish to shake her off in horror. That she did not wish to do so terrified her.

" Are you sorry I told you this?" at length asked Mrs. Jennings.

" No, oh no—at least, I think I'm not sorry."

Hardly knowing that she did so, Judith pressed closely the hand she held. She had a feeling that she was looking into the workings of a human heart and brain, that she saw there sin and resistance to sin in a never-ending battle, just as she might see the circulation of the blood in a prepared subject. She shrank, and yet she was uncontrollably attracted.

" And since your husband died," she began, " have you been happy?"

" Oh no !"

" How terrible! how terrible!" Judith uttered these words in a kind of cry.

" But I have been free. I have been able to respect myself—in the present, when I have not despised myself for the past." Mrs. Jennings spoke exultantly.

Unable to remain quiet, Judith shook herself from her companion's hold and rose to her feet. She took two or three rapid steps forward. Then she stumbled against a shrub; she felt its damp branches dash drops of water in her face. She stood still in the darkness.

"I can at least pray," she said, aloud.

"Yes," said the light, penetrating voice behind her, "we can pray. I suppose there is a God."

"I know there is a God," returned Judith.

She remained where she was, clasping her hands as we involuntarily clasp them in supplication.

"If you are going to pray," said Mrs. Jennings, "let me hear you. I shall believe what you say—while you are saying it." She rose impulsively and groped her way to her companion.

"Please don't touch me now!" said Judith, whereupon Mrs. Jennings drew back.

But though she was left standing alone, Judith found that she could not utter a word of prayer. Her soul was convulsed with a petition that was not able to reach her voice. Her whole being was not demanding release, but only strength to go on with the life she had deliberately chosen—strength, that was all; and surely that was a great deal.

"Why don't you pray?" asked the voice near her.

Judith's hands unclasped and fell to her sides.

"Or perhaps you don't consider me worthy to listen to you?"

Still the other could not speak.

"Do you want me to leave you? There's room enough in this wilderness for us both."

Judith could hear Mrs. Jennings's movements and the rustle of the twigs.

"Shall I go?"

"Stay with me."

Judith's words broke from her in a cry. She turned about, and extended her hands in the direction from which her companion had spoken. The next moment the two women had joined hands again, and stood there as if waiting for something.

"I don't approve of you in the least," murmured Judith.

"Oh, I know that very well."

"Then why have I spoken thus to you?"

"Because you knew I should understand."

"Yes; that must be the reason. But I ought to have died rather than let such words pass my lips."

"That is silly of you—to feel like that. Besides, what have you said? Listen to me now. I have a bit of advice to give you."

Judith fancied there was a peculiar seriousness in the way in which her companion spoke. She waited, and at last Mrs. Jennings said, "Have you ever thought of making a kind of fetich of your husband?"

"A fetich?"

A chill ran over Judith as she heard.

"Yes; possibly that isn't the word, but it will do as well as another. You are bound to be loyal and true, I suppose?"

"Yes, yes."

"Then you are bound to be a fool; but I won't try to dissuade. To every woman her own kind of folly, I say."

"But go on."

Mrs. Jennings laughed.

"Do you know there was once some one who had a husband whom she hated, but he would not die, and she was principled against killing him. So she agonized over the subject until finally light came to her. She succeeded in bringing her mind to the point of believing that upon his life hung all her prospect of happiness, even of life. You see, she reasoned this way and that way until she came to the conclusion that she would do everything in her power to prolong that man's life: she would watch his very breath lest it should stop; she would try to give her heart-beats for his; she would institute a care of him that would lengthen his days, for if she should let him die something dreadful would happen to her, just because, you see, she never could be happy while he lived. You can't find any fault with that reasoning, can you? It is as lucid and logical as a woman can sometimes be. Try that kind of life, Mrs. Gerald."

Judith had been listening intently. She knew the advice was given half mockingly, but in her morbid state of mind she felt herself clutching at it eagerly. And it seemed to her a kind of atonement. Had she been sufficiently attentive and devoted? Had she not failed in many ways?

Oh, how well she seemed to understand that woman who had paid such tribute to her fetich! It was not right to call such a life by the names Mrs. Jennings used. And she would go this journey in a different spirit—she would hereafter show that she could act in any way that she decided to act. Again, what did it matter? What did anything matter?

"I'm glad you told me this," she said.

"Are you?" in surprise.

"Certainly. It's what I've been groping for."

"And can you do it?"

"Yes ; I will do it."

Already Judith was nerving herself for the effort. She was looking forward to a battle which would occupy her entire forces.

"First, however," said the other, in response, "we must be taken alive from this fog."

"But if we are never found—" began Judith, with an exultant tone in her voice. Then she stopped and added, "When the fog lifts we cannot help finding the way home."

"Still," said Mrs. Jennings, "I've heard of fogs that lasted for days—long enough to starve us both."

"They will look for us," returned Judith.

"They may look for you, but no one knows I am here. If I am found it will be by clinging to your skirts. I wish I knew what time it is. If we were men we should probably be smokers, and if smokers we should have matches. It would be a great relief to me to see something, even for the

space of the flame of a match.   I am faint and hungry ; it
must be near midnight."

After two or three attempts they succeeded in finding the
rock again, and they seated themselves upon it, and huddled,
shivering, close together.   They were silent now.   Sometimes Mrs. Jennings's eyes closed for a moment, but Judith's
eyelids were widely open as she stared into the darkness,
thinking, thinking.

She started as her companion moved yet nearer, and exclaimed, " Did you hear that ?"

Judith roused herself.

" I heard nothing."

She did not seem much interested.

" It was a dog barking."

" It is the hounds ; they have been here before."

" No, no.   It is a different bark.   Listen.   Do you recognize it ?"

Judith did listen ; and as she did so the blood rose from
her heart to her face, then set back again in a choking flood,
leaving her white.   But the darkness hid her.   She had recognized the sound.   It was the baying of Lucian's dog
Random.

She opened her lips to say, " I hope they won't find us,"
but she did not speak.

" You know the dog ?" persisted Mrs. Jennings.

" Yes ; it is Random, Mr. Lucian Eldridge's setter."

" Oh, then we shall presently be found and rescued."

The speaker was smiling to herself.   She was thinking that
it was a very interesting drama, and still more interesting
in that it might at any moment become a tragedy.

" We shall shortly hear something more," she said.

And she spoke truth.   Muffled, but still plainly audible,
a man's voice shouted, " Hullo ! Hullo !" drawing out the
sound on the final vowel.

" Answer !" commanded Mrs. Jennings, sharply.

" No."

Judith sat erect, and removed from the woman.

" Idiot !" sharply whispered the other. Then she raised her own voice and shrilly responded: " Hullo ! this way !"

The two waited motionless until, after a few moments, the call was repeated and answered as before. In a few more moments the two heard the sound of an approach through bushes; an animal leaped out and came with the swiftness of vision directly to the two, putting eager front paws on Judith's knees, whining tremulously and joyfully.

Judith leaned over, and the dog licked her face. She suddenly flung her arms round his neck and hugged him. A spark of light was now coming from the same direction; then the spark revealed that it was a lantern carried by a man. The light shone upon a yellow, fog-wet beard and a pale face that at this moment had a brilliance of hope upon it.

Both women were standing now and waiting. The mist glowed about the lantern like a halo. Judith, after the first glance, looked at this halo as if it fascinated her.

Lucian burst through the bushes. " Thank Heaven !" he began; then he stopped suddenly. " What — two of you !"

" Yes," said Mrs. Jennings, finding that she must be the one to speak; " two of us for the brave rescuer. Isn't that glory enough for you for one night ?"

Lucian came forward slowly. He was plainly trying to assume a light manner, and just as plainly he was failing miserably.

" I wasn't thinking of glory," he answered, gravely; " I was thinking of Mrs. Gerald's safety. We didn't know you were also lost, Mrs. Jennings."

" I'm glad the fact wasn't known," began Mrs. Jennings, dryly; " otherwise your anxiety would have been increased."

" Certainly," with still more gravity. He turned aside and drew a revolver from his pocket. " I must give the signal that you are found," he said, before he fired three shots.

" How interesting !" exclaimed Mrs. Jennings, flippantly.

"It is really the first time I was ever rescued. Is it a common experience with you, Mrs. Gerald?"

Judith longed to put her hands over her ears to shut out the light, saucy voice. But she stood quiet, and did not think it worth while to answer.

XLIII

"LET US BE REAL FRIENDS"

BEFORE any one spoke again three answering shots were heard far away at the right, and then, still farther off, three more.

"It is a scene in a theatre," exclaimed Mrs. Jennings, "with all the lights turned down so that the one lantern may be seen; and you are the heroine, Mrs. Gerald. No music by the orchestra; audience thrilled to silence."

"I'm glad you can view the matter so cheerfully, Mrs. Jennings," remarked Lucian, still with that unusual gravity of manner. He had not, after the first moment, appeared to see Judith, by whose side the setter was standing.

"We have had plenty of time to cultivate cheerfulness," was the response, "nights and nights, it seems to us." Mrs. Jennings advanced nearer the lantern and held her watch close to it. "Only a little after twelve!" she said.

She turned to Judith, and the latter now became aware that this woman was making talk that Judith might have an opportunity to recover her self-possession—if she had lost it. An impulse of gratitude stirred in Judith's heart. But Lucian understood nothing of this, and his irritation was so great as to be with difficulty concealed. He had expected to find only Judith if indeed he were fortunate.

"Of course the time has seemed very long," he now said, stiffly. "And it has seemed long to your friends, Mrs. Gerald," turning, with marked reserve, towards Judith.

"I am very sorry," she returned, with the same reserve; "it was so heedless of me to get lost. The fog came up, but I am so much at home on the shore here that I didn't think of the possibility of losing my way."

"There are a dozen men searching in different directions," went on Lucian. "Uncle Dick held out in the opinion that you were not lost, and that you would resent any search being made; but when I got home at half-past ten, and he found I hadn't seen you, we roused some of the neighbors and set out. I think we've been lucky to find you so soon. Shall we start for home now? The firing gave the signal for the people to give up looking."

All the long and tiresome walk homeward Judith was thinking of the few words Lucian had said, which told her that her husband had thought that she was with his nephew. This thought annoyed her so much that she was surprised at the strength of the irritation.

The three reached the Eldridge house a few minutes before Mr. Gerald's arrival, and when that gentleman came his wife met him in the hall. He was so pale that she was betrayed into uttering an exclamation of alarm. She went quickly to his side and took his hand. "I'm so sorry!" she said, in a low voice.

He smiled somewhat satirically as he answered, "Oh, don't grieve about that! You have given us a taste of the pleasures of the chase."

She wanted to shrink back, but she would not. She said something so gently that he gave her a quick, interrogative glance. He was still holding her hand.

"I hope you'll forgive me," she pleaded, "and I hope you haven't been very anxious."

"Oh, a trifle; just enough to give a seasoning to everyday monotony."

Though he spoke thus he did not release the hand. He was looking steadily down at her. The next moment he glanced about him; he saw that no one else was in the hall.

Judith saw a spasm as of physical agony cross his face. His grasp on her fingers unconsciously tightened. "Oh," she cried, in a whisper, pressing nearer, "you are ill!"

" Not in the least," throwing his head back. " I wanted to ask you something, and I know you will answer me truthfully. Really," here he managed to smile, " I find it quite an advantage to have a wife who tells the truth."

Judith now drew back somewhat. " What do you want to ask me ?" she inquired, coldly.

" This : have you been wandering over those cliffs thinking to throw yourself into the water ?"

" No."

In spite of his efforts, Mr. Gerald could not restrain the long sigh that came through his lips as he heard that monosyllable and believed it implicitly. " Thank you," he said, after a moment.

The next day, as they were in Boston, and driving down to the wharf of the Cunarder in which they were to sail, Gerald turned suddenly to his wife and asked, " Why did you shrink so from this voyage ?"

Judith felt that this was almost too much. Her eyes flashed. Then she lowered them. Whatever happened, her foremost effort should be to sacrifice everything to this man. She would treat him as a devotee might treat an idol. Since feeling did not prompt her, she was sure to overdo. But she could not help that, and probably would not know it. And she was already beginning upon the exaggerated plan which Mrs. Jennings had suggested. " If you will excuse me, I won't answer," she said, but speaking with an extreme gentleness.

Mr. Gerald laughed. Then he examined her face with great care. At such times, though she felt as if she were under a microscope, she would not shrink perceptibly. She sat now with her eyes lowered under her husband's gaze, her whole frame thrilling with the intensity of her rebellion. Presently Mr. Gerald laughed again.

" I thought I had arranged everything with the utmost forethought," he said : " A sea voyage, with Lucian along ; a trip to Algeria, with Lucian along ; an indefinite stay somewhere in Africa, with Lucian along. And all the time a useful husband—one who trusts his wife, and who will not be forever present. Upon my word, a woman must be difficult to please who isn't satisfied with such an arrangement."

Judith remained silent. Into her rebellious feeling had now come something like terror. How he returned again and again to this topic! It seemed impossible that any man should make such arrangements, and should talk about them like this. She longed to scan her husband's face closely, but she would not lift her eyes. She sat there motionless. The carriage whirled down on to the dock. In a few moments more they would be on board the steamer.

A fantastic idea that fate awaited them on the boat came into Judith's mind, but she would not harbor the idea. She knew that in these days she could not trust to her impressions.

"Would you like to turn back?" asked Mr. Gerald.

She glanced to her right and saw the shipping. A cold puff of salt water came to her nostrils. She longed to say "Yes—yes—go back!" But she would not say it.

She turned now and looked up at her husband's face. His eyes, with an expression of intensity and questioning, were on her. She had a dreadful wonder as to how plainly her soul was seen under his microscope.

But she had nothing to conceal. So she said, firmly, "I wish to do exactly as you like."

Mr. Gerald threw himself against the cushions. "By Jove!" he exclaimed. What had he wished her to say? No matter; she could not again beg him not to go. And she had made up her mind.

In a moment more they had crossed the gangway-plank, and were standing watching the carriages drive up with their passengers.

Mr. Gerald was politely kind. Judith could have doubted whether he had asked her that question or looked in that way in the carriage. Very soon he conducted her downstairs. She found a magnificent bunch of roses in her

"'YOU SENT THEM?'"

state-room. She bent over them, her face losing its stiff-
ness.

"You sent them?" She looked up, smiling at her husband.

"Yes. I knew you were a real woman about roses."

"Why shouldn't I be?"

Again she came near him. She had taken one of the
roses. She now fastened it to his coat.

"Thank you," he said, formally; and then, immediately,
"I wonder if Lucian has come aboard yet."

He left the room, and Judith sat down alone. But she
turned her back on the roses, and she replaced the one she
had kept in her hand. All at once the odor sickened her.
Then, with that revulsion and curious self-constraint which
so often is characteristic of the nature resolved upon self-
sacrifice, Judith rose and went to the flowers again. She
arranged a cluster and carefully pinned it upon her cor-
sage. While she was doing so she heard the shouting on
the deck, the hurried giving of orders, and she knew that
the boat was about to cast off from its moorings. She
stood still in the middle of the little room listening.

Then, with a sudden passionate movement, she knelt
down by a chair and pressed her face into her hands.
"Oh, God!" she said, in a loud whisper, "keep him away!
Keep him away!" Then a pause; then another whisper,
"But, above all, give me strength!"

She experienced a certain comfort from the very attitude
of supplication. She seemed to be near to the great Giver
of strength, and the nearness soothed her. But she dared
not remain on her knees. The door was not locked, and
her husband might come back at any moment. She rose
and looked out. She now saw that the state-room was on
the side next the land. She could see a portion of the
wharf. As she looked a vivid color came to her face and
a glow to her eyes. A carriage dashed down over the
planks and out of her range of vision. But in the carriage
she had caught a glimpse of a young man with a yellow
beard and a pale, eager face. He was leaning forward, as

if that attitude might hasten his arrival.   It seemed not a moment later when the boat moved and swung away from the wharf.

Judith grew pale. She pressed her hands together. "He was too late!" she whispered.

A sense of desolation, a very keenness of disappointment swept over her before she could rally herself to the attitude of mind it was her duty and her determination to maintain. That natural heart for the instant spoke aloud, but only for an instant.

She had hardly thought he was too late before she said, with strenuous earnestness and utmost sincerity, "Thank God for that! God has heard me."

She had thought of going on deck. But now she sat down, breathless at first; but soon a peace came upon flesh and spirit. Gradually the boat got under some headway. She felt it gliding along beneath her and vibrating to its pulse of steam. It was not many minutes before she heard a step which paused at her door; then a knock. Mr. Gerald came in.

"It's magnificent outside," he said. "A real October glory is in the sunshine. Come on deck and see the shore left behind."

He lifted a warm wrap from a pile of hand luggage, and put it carefully about her.

"Besides, I have a surprise for you; and I've learned that women like surprises. They are always wanting excitement of some kind."

"Are they?"

"Aren't they?"

"No. I'm a woman; and what I want is peace—yes, even the peace of stagnation."

As she spoke Judith looked up in her companion's face.

"Mr. Gerald—Richard," she said, "let us be real friends —close friends; may we not?"

"Why, certainly. Am I lacking in friendship towards you, Judith?"

She turned away with a gesture she could not suppress.

CHAPTER XLIV

EMBARKED

MR. GERALD frowned, but his companion did not see the frown. She was holding her wrap about her, and gazing blindly straight in front of her. The sense that she was confined within the limits of the ship already made itself felt oppressively.

Mr. Gerald leaned his back against the door. His frown was replaced by a smile. "Really," he said, "I shall soon begin to think I am a much misunderstood man. I shall be pitying myself, and if there is anything morbid it is self-pity. Have you a wish ungratified?"

There was something indefinite in the voice which pronounced these words—something which chilled and came near frightening the woman who heard it. It was a perceptible space of time before she could reply, and then she could only use the phrase she had so often repeated.

"You are very kind to me." Then she added, "Shall we go on deck?"

She was expecting to hear her husband say that, after all, Lucian had been too late, and she was schooling herself to receive the news exactly as she ought to receive it.

"Wait a moment."

Mr. Gerald still stood with his back to the door. More than she had ever felt it, Judith now was conscious of some subtle, inexplicable change in her companion. He was different, and she was sure that no one else would notice the difference; yet it was a difference which sent a chill to her very heart.

Mr. Gerald thrust his hands deep into his pockets, and seemed in no hurry at all.

"Now he is going to tell me that Lucian did not come," she was saying to herself, and she might even be obliged to listen to condolences for the young man's absence. She wondered if any woman was ever in such a position before.

"Here I am, a model husband," began Mr. Gerald. "Because my wife has a preference for a certain person, I arrange a journey, I look to it that she has the society she likes; I am ready to efface myself to just the proper degree, but to be in evidence when it is desirable. And yet I have the spirit of a man in me. Yes, by Jove, I have the spirit of a man in me!" He pulled his mustache. His eyes, shining deeply, met his wife's glance. She gazed at him with an appearance of courage that she did not feel. Her heart was sinking, sinking, and she could not have told precisely why. All her misgivings came to life again and clamored for expression; but she would not give them expression.

"I must ask you not to talk like this to me again," she said.

"Not talk like this?"

"There is no need; and you know there is no need. Will you let me pass, Mr. Gerald?"

The man's face changed. He moved and opened the door with ceremonious politeness. Then he followed Judith on deck, his face composed to its usual look. She walked quickly forward, not knowing which way she went, and mechanically moving aside when she met the people who were promenading and watching the shores recede. She went straight to the rail and leaned upon it, staring at the city that seemed at first to be rising upon the horizon, crowned by the gold dome of the State-house.

"I don't care what happens! I don't care what happens!" she was saying, furiously, to herself.

She withdrew her eyes from the land and fixed them on

the dark, blue-black water that was rushing past the ship's side. For the first time the thought of sinking down beneath that water came to her as an almost tangible temptation.

Mr. Gerald had asked if she wished to drown herself. If he asked her that question now she must give him a different reply.

"There is Minot's just coming in sight," said a voice close beside her.

The voice made her pulses stop with a captivating terror. It was an instant before she turned and looked out towards the light-house.

"Do you remember that time we children went out to Minot's in Ellis Macomber's sloop?" asked Lucian.

"I remember."

"And that you were the only girl, after all, who dared to climb up into the light?"

"Of course I don't forget that," Judith said, lightly. "It is not our brave deeds that we forget."

She looked at the young man beside her with eyes that seemed covered by a cloud, so baffling were they. It was her husband who had made this meeting possible; perhaps at that moment she came near to hating Gerald.

Lucian had behaved in the matter of taking this journey quite as you would expect a young man to behave who is drawn strongly and yet who has a conscience. After he had found Judith the night before in the fog he had resolved to throw the whole thing up and go off to the ends of the earth in the opposite direction. He had even arranged to accompany a friend to California. He had gone with that friend to get tickets. His resolution had held out until the moment when he was pushing his money across to the agent. Then it was as if some bodily presence at his elbow seized his arm and drew it away. He thrust the bills back in his pocket.

"What ails you?" asked his friend.

"No, I can't go!" he exclaimed. "I knew all the time

I couldn't do it.   And yet I told myself, with a great show
of resolution, that I would do it.   I tell you, I felt quite fine
and resolved when I shoved my money towards that clerk."

" But what's the matter with you ?" scrutinizing him.

" The matter is that I'm a cursed simpleton."

This was quite strong language, and the other man made
a remark to that effect, adding that he supposed it was true,
and that there was only one reason for idiocy so pronounced,
and that was that Eldridge must be in love.   To this remark Lucian made no immediate reply.

The two young men walked away.   When they were in
Wheaton's room Lucian turned to him and asked, " Have
you ever been in love yourself, Wheaton ?"

" Thank fortune, no !"

" Then hold your tongue on the subject."   Lucian's face
was flushed and his eyes had a fine sparkle.   He looked at
his watch.   " Good-bye," he said.   " I'm going to take that
Cunarder."

" The devil you are !   But you can't do it.   She starts in
exactly thirty-three minutes."

" I will do it."

Lucian tore down the stairs.   He was lucky in getting a
cab, lucky in getting over the ferry, but then he found that
his watch had been a little slow.   Within the last three
minutes he felt that he would die rather than not reach the
wharf in time.   And he took credit to himself, such is the
complexity of human nature, for having held to a resolution
in a way that made him come so near not being able to get
aboard.   It seemed quite a merit that it was barely possible
to scramble on to the boat just as it started.   But the moment he was on deck a beautiful thankfulness and peace
descended upon his spirit, and he wondered how he had
been so silly as to think that he would give up the trip.
He was making mountains out of nothing.   He had sent
his luggage aboard a few hours earlier.   Now he went to
his state-room and sat down for a brief space.   He felt that
he needed a few moments in which to compose himself be-

fore he should go back on deck, for Judith would be sure to be there to see the familiar landmarks of the harbor.

Sitting thus in his room with his feet stretched out and his hands clasped over his head, Lucian smiled at his outrageous folly in taking a fancy to go to California. Why, nothing on earth could have kept him from coming aboard. And why shouldn't he come? He reasoned the whole matter out with the utmost lucidity. He was absolutely sure of himself, and as for Judith, she was very friendly; but that was all.

"Yes, that is all."

Hearing his voice pronounce those words aloud, Lucian suddenly was aware of a pang that was utterly unreasonable in view of the premises laid down by him. He sat silent after this brief soliloquy. He was trying to recall that evening when he and Judith had been in the little boat off shore, and had drifted about until the launch had picked them up. He had often tried to recall the particulars of that time, but everything was indistinct, and a like blur was over all his memory of the days he had spent in the hospital. He was only sure of one thing: that Judith had often been with him. He could remember nothing but the most cordial friendliness on her part since her marriage, and surely that was precisely as it should be.

Then his mind went back still further—to that summer evening when she had said that she would not marry him, but that she loved him. He was not likely to forget that time, but he ought to forget it. The memory of it was disastrous in every way to him; and the worst phase of his mental condition was that he hugged that remembrance to him and made much of it. But he had had no sign from Judith that she had not forgotten what she said then. The sultry scent of the elder-blows came to the young man at this moment as it had come that evening. He started up from his chair.

"I'm a sentimental fool!" he exclaimed.

After a few moments more of lingering in his room Lucian went on deck. Almost the first person he saw was

his uncle Richard pacing calmly back and forth, carefully
dressed, brushed, and barbered — looking exactly to his
nephew as he had always looked.

Lucian advanced towards the tall, notable figure, thread-
ing his way among the people, his eyes glancing eagerly
about him.

Mr. Gerald held out his hand, smiling as he did so. Somehow the young man felt that there was a great deal of glitter
to that smile, but he met it frankly.

" I had almost given you up when I saw you dashing on
board," said Mr. Gerald. " Did you know you came within
a hair's-breadth of not going with us ?"

" Yes, I know it," indifferently. The young man wondered why his uncle looked so keenly at him. " I came
near giving up the trip," remarked Lucian, with the same
careless appearance.

" Did you ?" sharply. " Well," more calmly, " of course
there isn't a great deal to tempt you to go with us. A young
fellow like you can't find much to amuse him with two quiet
people like my wife and me."

Lucian did not contradict this assertion. He stood gazing towards the city they were leaving. He only said quietly
that he had a strong mind to go with Wheaton to California.

Mr. Gerald drew a cigar-case from his pocket, selected a
cigar, and contemplated it as he said, in his most unemo-
tional voice, " Well, my boy, I congratulate you on not going
with Wheaton. You would have decapitated yourself nicely
if you had gone with Wheaton."

Lucian stared hard at his uncle, who now drew a small
box of wax-tapers from his waistcoat-pocket. He put his
cigar between his teeth and took a taper in his fingers.

" I don't know what you mean," said Lucian ; and he
could not tell what it was in the face before him that made
a chill go down his spine.

" Why," said Mr. Gerald, with another smile that glittered,
" I mean this : that you would have decapitated yourself
nicely if you had gone with Wheaton. When I asked you

to come abroad with us I meant that I wanted you to come." The speaker made a pause, and then added, " I often have a special reason for making a request. I have a special reason for wanting you with us."

The words and the manner of the elder man had an extremely bewildering and freezing effect on his listener.

Lucian turned partially away. He was embarrassed without knowing why he felt thus, and that feeling of ice down his spine continued in a very uncomfortable degree.

" It was awfully good of you to invite me, Uncle Dick," he said, awkwardly, " but of course I don't understand what you mean."

"Oh," responded the other man, with sudden cordiality, " I mean that I'm fond of my nephew, and that I'm sure he'll make himself useful. I'm going to ask you to be our courier on this journey."

" All right," said Lucian, relieved, " I'll take the whole thing on my shoulders. Only give me an idea of where you want to go."

Mr. Gerald lighted his cigar. "We are thinking of Algiers," he answered. "And I've thought of Biskra. I want Judith to see something a little different, you know."

" Yes," said Lucian.

"Judith enjoys travelling, you see," remarked Mr. Gerald, " and, odd as it may seem, she enjoys travelling with an old fellow like me."

" Yes," said Lucian again. And added, " But you are not old, uncle Dick."

" Thanks, boy, thanks," with a laugh. " I'm not quite patriarchal yet, but I'm old enough; yes, I'm old enough."

XLV

ACCIDENT?

LUCIAN had an uncomfortable feeling which he could not explain after he left his uncle Richard on the deck. It was quite useless for him to refer the whole thing to his own perturbed state of mind.

The next morning he was pacing the deck and thinking of his uncle's manner when he was presently joined by Mr. Gerald and his wife. They were both well wrapped, for the wind was blowing briskly, and the ship was going ahead with a good deal of motion. Judith took hold of the rail to steady herself as she looked about her. Everything was gray this morning—gray sky, and dark water running fast, as if trying to empty itself somewhere.

"Luckily we are going to a warmer climate," said Mr. Gerald, who did not touch the rail, but stood trying to balance himself. "And there'll be color there—something different from this infernal leaden hue."

As he finished speaking there came a yet sharper lurch. Mr. Gerald was near the rail. He stood with what suddenly seemed to Judith like studied carelessness, and she sprang towards him. At the instant a yet more violent wave tipped the deck still farther. The eyes of husband and wife met in one swift instant. She extended her hands. One more horrible pitch. They all staggered. Mr. Gerald was over the side.

Judith did not scream. Her wild, white face was turned towards Lucian, who was tearing off his ulster.

A cry rang out from below somewhere:

"Man overboard!"

At the same instant Lucian, who had thrown both of his

coats from him, jumped into the water, and somewhere from below a plank was tossed out into the foam. The signal was given, the wheels stopped, backed, churning up the water into a wide froth.

Everybody on deck rushed to the side where Judith stood alone. She stood stiff and still, her face frozen into that look of horror which had come to it a moment ago. A moment? Was it not rather an hour? She was gazing out on that drab-colored water far behind—oh, how far behind it was!—where the plank bobbed about on the waves.

Had either of the men overboard known the plank was thrown out? Surely Lucian had known it.

There! A wet shining head came to the surface—away in the distance.

Oh, would they never lower that boat!

Whose head was it?

Judith's eyes strained forward. No, no, she could not tell whose head it was.

Some one behind her with an opera-glass to his eyes said, "It's the young fellow! No! Yes, it is! By Jove, he's a plucky one!"

Judith heard. That meant Lucian. At this moment nature asserted itself untrammelled. Her heart leaped, but in the next instant it fell again. What right had her pulses to start forward in that thrill of insupportable thankfulness because it was Lucian?

She clung with both hands to the railing. She heard the voice behind her say, "There goes the boat!"

She saw the boat with the two men in it rising and falling—saw it with a film over her eyes that were starting, it seemed, from her head. But she was very quiet. Whatever happened, she would be perfectly quiet.

She turned towards the man behind her. "Allow me to take your glass?" she said.

As she spoke she had a strange feeling that her voice sounded as if she were speaking in a theatre. She took the glass, watching her hand to see to it that it should be perfectly steady as it raised the instrument to her eyes. She was dimly aware that the man to whom she had spoken was gazing at her with a look of wonder. She supposed he knew that it was her husband who had fallen.

Suddenly into the welter of waters that the glass revealed there came the head of a man. That was Lucian. He was alone. He was swimming about. How far away he was! That plank was a short distance from him.

At that instant a loud shout went up from the men on deck. At first Judith could not see what it was that had made them shout. Her hand had become unsteady, and the glass only revealed the stretch of gray, foam-lined water. But now!—ah! there was Lucian, with one arm resting on the plank, the other sustaining some burden which hung limp upon him.

Judith could hold the glass no longer. It dropped with a clash unheeded to the floor of the deck. A man's voice behind her said, "Madam, take my arm."

"No," she answered, and clung again with both hands to the rail.

A dark cloud before her eyes made it impossible for her to see anything for a moment. Then, when another shout went up from the steamer, her sight cleared again, and she saw the boat coming towards them. Lucian was sitting in the stern, and he was supporting Mr. Gerald against his breast.

When the two were helped up the side Lucian's face was as white as that of his uncle, but there was no life in the elder face. The young man turned towards Judith, apparently not knowing that any one else was present.

"Judith," he said, in a faint voice, "I did all I could." Then he staggered off towards the stairs, and somebody sprang towards him as he went.

But Judith had not seemed to hear him or see him. She had knelt down by the still figure which had been laid on the deck. The people pressed respectfully back from her. The ship's doctor was kneeling at the other side, examining the inert body. Judith did not see him. She was looking absorbedly down at the still face.

One of the men in the group who was watching her turned to his wife who stood near him. "There's a woman who loved her husband," he said, in a whisper.

The wife smiled slightly as she answered, "No; I was just thinking that she never loved him. Did you see the look that young man gave her when he staggered up to her?"

"Commend me to a woman for ferreting out something wrong!" was the response.

In a moment the physician raised his head. He looked at Judith, but her eyes were fixed on Gerald.

"There is life here," said the doctor.

The red blood rushed suddenly to Judith's face. She put her hand up to her throat and gasped for breath, but she did not speak.

A woman stepped forward from the group and put a vinaigrette to Judith's nostrils. She eagerly inhaled the pungent odor.

After a little two sailors carried Mr. Gerald to his stateroom. He had breathed heavily, and once opened his eyes upon his wife. Then a spasm had contorted his features, and his eyelids fell.

It was not an hour, however, after the accident before Mr. Gerald was lying on his bed fully conscious, and occasionally speaking. His wife sat by him. As strength came gradually, the man's countenance took on an expression of whimsical surprise and amusement. His first question had been, "How is Lucian?"

Judith hadn't inquired, but she was quite sure he wasn't injured.

"Good boy," said Mr. Gerald. Then he laughed slightly. "Quite a *coup de théâtre*, wasn't it? I hope somebody applauded the rescuer?"

"Yes," said Judith.

"That's right. And you? I'll wager you behaved precisely right?"

"I don't know," replied the woman, wishing to shrink away as she spoke, but not changing her attitude by as much as a hair's-breadth.

"Have Lucian in here," said Gerald, when he spoke again.

So Judith sent for the young man, who came, dressed in dry clothes, with studiously quiet features, though his eyes were glowing like fire.

Mr. Gerald put his hand out towards him. "You're a good fellow, Lucian," he said. Here he smiled, as he added, "But you made a great mistake just now; for, you see, I had as good as died, and now it 'll have to be all done over again some day. But you meant well. Now you may go."

So Lucian walked out of the room without having spoken a word. For twenty-four hours he was a hero on board; then the incident was apparently forgotten.

It was not until the next day that Judith, meeting Lucian on deck, said, "It is so insufficient to thank you, Mr. Eldridge."

"Then don't do it, for it's not like you to do insufficient things," was the flippant rejoinder; and the young man raised his hat and walked on.

Having behaved thus, Lucian was presently seized with a great remorse for his impoliteness. He went on deck at all hours and seasons for the next three days watching for Judith, but she did not appear. She was in close attendance on her husband, who was also invisible.

Here was the voyage half done. Lucian, so bored that he longed for almost anything to interest him, walked miles on the deck, uttered under his breath a great many expletives, called himself a fool innumerable times, and yet knew very well that he would have allowed nothing to prevent him from crossing the ocean on this particular boat at this particular time. But life was a failure, and everything was imbittered. Having come to this conclusion, he jeered at himself for being so weak-minded.

"I ought to cut everything and start anew. I'm handicapped —I'm good for nothing. Wish I could find some nice girl who wanted to marry me and make me all over. I wish—"

" Lucian, would you mind finding our steamer-chairs for us ?"

The young man wheeled round and snatched off his cap. One look in Judith's face, and he was positive that there was no nice girl in the world whom anything could induce him to marry.

" 'Twas better for her despairing," his heart sang.

He pulled the rugs about his uncle, devoting his whole attention to him. He sat down on a camp-stool by his side, and began to discuss guide-books and descriptive catalogues with him, spreading the books open on his knee, not appearing to know that Judith was sitting there on the other side of her husband.

And, in truth, Judith also seemed oblivious. She sat leaning back in her chair, her eyes dreamy, the wind blowing her hair from under her Scotch cap, the color deepening on lips and cheeks.

Mr. Gerald only referred to his accident by saying that it was a very odd thing to be a kind of Lazarus, and that, for his part, when a person seemed to be dead, it was a thousand times better manners to stay dead ; for if he didn't stay dead the surviving relatives were likely to be very confused, not to say disappointed. Here the speaker laughed and stroked his mustache. He glanced at his wife, who smiled and remarked that he didn't give his surviving friends credit for good taste. There was a tone of good comradeship and understanding that Lucian noticed. He congratulated himself that it was so, all the time quite aware of the insincerity of these inward congratulations. So curiously are we able to be hypocrites to an audience of one only, and that one ourselves !

Still, in moments of truthful self-examination, Lucian was always able to say that if driven to the choice he would inevitably choose that his uncle should live and that Judith should be happy with him. Such strange bundles of impossible contradictions are we !

XLVI

GOOD INTENTIONS

THE hours of the voyage now seemed to go more and more rapidly. Nothing whatever happened. The passengers walked and read; and some of them gambled; and some sang, and played the piano of an evening; and they all gossiped more or less; and those who were young enough flirted; and others nearly perished of ennui. The same women asked the captain every day how long it would be before they sighted land, and every day the captain politely answered them.

In the midst of this Lucian strolled, eating and drinking when it was time, and finding the voyage quite a different thing from what he had supposed it would be. He had supposed he would have constant and friendly companionship with his uncle and with his wife. But now he never saw Judith without her husband. They came on deck for a walk every day, but the weather was too cold to sit, save for a few moments.

Judith read to her husband or sat beside him. She was continually seeking to do something for him. Her eyes anxiously sought his face, but if he suddenly looked at her her glance fell.

"You see, you were entirely wrong when you surmised that Mrs. Gerald does not love her husband," said that man who had watched her at the time of the rescue.

"No," returned the wife, with yet more emphasis, "I am right. That is duty, not love."

The man laughed. "Give me duty, then," he said. "But you women are really horrible in your conclusions.

Are you making a French novel out of the man and his wife and the nephew?"

"You men are really blind," was the return, "if you can imagine that Mrs. Gerald would ever lend herself to the making of a French novel. No. I know truth and high-mindedness when I see them in the flesh."

The gentleman took his cigar from his mouth, looking down at it as it smoked between his fingers. He was wishing that he had come to know such a woman as Mrs. Gerald when he had been younger. Then he gave a swift look at his wife's cold face and laughed again.

"What are you laughing at?" she asked.

"I was having a sentimental turn — thinking of Owen Meredith, and that 'whom first we love we seldom wed,' and all that rot," was the reply. And then the man resumed his smoking, while the woman's face grew colder than ever.

Meanwhile below, at one end of the long saloon, Mr. Gerald sat leaning far back in a lounging-chair. Beside him, in a low rocker, sat Judith. She had a book in her hand, but book and hand were lying in her lap. She had been reading aloud, but noticing that her companion's eyes were closed, she had become silent, thinking he might be asleep.

It was useless to pretend not to know that Mr. Gerald had seemed of late almost like an invalid, and now the face against the dark velvet of the chair was pallid and languid. Without moving his head the man opened his eyes, and they rested on his wife.

"I seem to be somehow changed," he said.

Judith's heart began to beat more quickly.

"You see," he went on, "I have never been ill in my life, and I wasn't aware that illness could change one so much. Not that I'm ill now," sitting up erect, his eyes becoming brighter. "Judith," in a very low voice, "you have been really an angel to me."

This remark was so unlike what she had hitherto known of Mr. Gerald that she was almost alarmed.

"Oh," he said, with a smile, as if answering her thought, "I'm perfectly sane. You know I never believed in women till I knew you. Well, I don't believe in them now," with his old manner, "but," bowing, "I have unlimited faith in my wife."

"I am glad of that," she answered, earnestly.

"Oh yes, no doubt. You are one of those who make truth a reality. It is a necessity for you to be loyal. But is that a merit of yours? There are others who must be disloyal. Is that a fault of theirs?"

"But surely—" began Judith, but her companion moved his hand and interrupted her.

"Pardon me. I know you are quite old-fashioned, luckily for me, but I'm going to tell you something."

For an instant his eyes rested in hers. He drew a long breath.

"Take notice," he said, "that I'm well aware that I shouldn't tell you this if I were in my ordinary health. I understand all about that. Are you listening?"

"Yes."

"The other day, you remember—the day I fell overboard?"

"Yes," in a whisper.

He watched her face blanching. He seemed to be drinking in the look of deepening pallor.

"You thought it was an accident?" in the same whisper she had employed.

"I thought so."

"You did?"

"But I had one doubt—one faint doubt—which left me."

"Oh, it left you? I wonder why it left you?"

"I don't know."

Judith was leaning forward yet nearer to him, her face pale as death. A man, passing, turned to look back, hesitated, but finally went on.

"Well," with another long breath, "it wasn't an accident. I went over the boat's side of deliberate decision. You will believe that I have good intentions"—his old manner again.

Judith drew herself up. She clasped her hands tightly, but, mindful of appearances, she kept them on her lap.

"Yes, I was going to drown myself, like a young fool; and you and everybody else would think it was accident, and there'd be no scandal. I've seen a man fall overboard, and I had no idea the ship could be stopped in time. I reckoned without Lucian. He's a good lad. Things are all awry. But I'm to blame for that. However, it's because I'm not quite well that I've told you that I made an effort to set you free. And my will is made."

Here Mr. Gerald gave that slight laugh of his which always grated upon Judith, but she did not notice the laugh now. She was sitting without motion, gazing at her husband.

"You meant to drown yourself?" She asked the question in a low voice, knowing the answer. She was thinking with a dull sense of fear that all her efforts had been worth nothing, and that she would never be at ease again—that a new anxiety would grind her down yet lower.

"But I don't mean it now," was the answer. "That ocean bath has made me bound to cling to life—and to you—at present. Odd what twaddle has been talked about what a man feels and sees when he is drowning! It's all bosh. I didn't think of myself; I was thinking of you. I saw a picture of you and Lucian, happy with each other —vividly, gloriously happy; and I thought you knew that this happiness was my gift to you. Then I had to be brought back to life again. But it's very singular that I seem to be entirely cured of any wish to give you happiness in that way. I'm bound to live now. Are you sorry?"

Mr. Gerald suddenly fixed his eyes penetratingly upon his companion. She met the gaze fully, and for the instant forgot to reply in words.

"Are you sorry?" he repeated.

"Surely not," was the firm answer.

Mr. Gerald sank back in his chair again. His glance roved about the saloon. At the far end of it he saw the slender figure of a young man with a pointed blond beard. Judith, watching her husband, saw a change come swiftly into his gaze, but she would not look to see what had occasioned it.

"Yes," repeated the man, with still more emphasis, "I'm bound to live now."

Judith tried to say something, but her lips would not obey her.

Mr. Gerald's eyes were still fixed on that young man at the end of the saloon who was conversing animatedly with a group of men.

At last, unable to bear the silence any longer, Judith opened her book again. "Shall I go on with my reading?" she asked.

"No. I'm quite in the mood for what some one calls intimate conversation to-day."

She closed the book; but she gazed down at it, spelling out, over and over again, the title-page.

"I suppose I am as fatuous as other men, after all," now said Mr. Gerald; "but for a few days I have actually begun to hope that you might love me—even that you do love me."

He spoke very gently, and with a certain wistfulness in his tone and his face that was piercingly pathetic, particularly as coming from a man like him.

Judith ceased to spell out the words of that title-page; she ceased to see anything, in fact, for her eyes went blind for a moment.

"Perhaps you love me a little?" he went on. "Surely no woman could be quite so kind — quite so tenderly thoughtful—"

Here he stopped, not trying to finish his sentence.

Judith made an effort to think of something to say that should be absolutely the right thing, but her mind was a blank filled only with an indefinite horror.

"Have you nothing to say to me?" he asked.

She trembled. A rebellious feeling that she ought to have been spared this came strongly to her.

"Indeed," she began, in an unsteady voice, "I have an affection for you—I—"

She ceased speaking, utterly unable to go on. She was longing to be able to say "I love you;" but she could not say it, and had a sense of guilt even in trying to say it.

"That will do," he responded, harshly. He tried to draw himself up erect in his chair. His face was gray, his eyes suddenly clouded over.

Judith rose quickly. She leaned over him. An anguish of yearning tenderness was in her heart. "Oh, Richard! Richard!" she whispered.

He roused himself now. He looked up at her with something of his old manner.

"Pardon me," he said, huskily, "I have made a damned idiot of myself. But pray don't think I'm going to keep this thing up. I'll go into my room for a while. Ah! Lucian, lend me your arm for a moment," as that young man now approached. "I'm getting to be rather of an old hulk, it seems to me. But wait until we are settled in that oasis of Biskra, then you'll see a transformation. The air of northern Africa in winter is like wine."

Lucian had hurried forward. He had never seen his uncle look so ghastly, but he said nothing. He did not even glance at Judith, who followed them. And it was in vain that he tried to see Judith later. It was true that she came out to dinner, but she had a look on her face that made it impossible for him to address her. She seemed so absorbed, so far away, and the line between her brows was so plainly marked as to be like a furrow. When she rose from the table she went directly back to the large state-room where Mr. Gerald was sitting reading. As she came in he rose. He said, carelessly, that he had changed his mind; he believed he would go out to dinner, and after

that he would have a walk and a smoke on deck.   Lucian
would bear him company.

Judith wished to remonstrate, but she said nothing.   She
watched her husband as he went out with his usual air.
She thought to herself that Lucian would take care of
him ; at any rate, it was plain that he did not wish for
her company.   She sat down on a high chair by the little
window.   She leaned her head against the wall and looked
out, seeing the illimitable stretch of water, and sometimes
a bird flying across her vision.   She watched for a long
time the curl of foam that ran swiftly away from the
track of the steamer.   She seemed to be absorbed in this
watching.

XLVII

"YOU HERE?"

JUDITH was asking herself why she could not have told her husband that she loved him. She repeated the question until it had lost all sense to her. Then she started up and walked hurriedly across the room, but there was no space in which to walk. She was shut in, imprisoned. She could not breathe. No; why should she say "I love you" when the words would not be true? He ought not to have asked her. It was wrong, ungenerous in him to try her so. But he was changed, indescribably changed. He was not well—but, oh, how cruel to ask her that when she could not answer "I love you."

What would another woman have done? Would another woman have called a friendly affection love, and so tried to deceive him? But he had not meant a friendly affection. Oh no; not that in the least.

She was standing quiet in the small room. The light fell upon her figure in its perfect gown. She was very particular about her dress in these days. Her husband wished her to be so. She glanced down at the glitter of gems on her hands. The sparkle of them struck into her heart. She stretched out her hand and looked at the beautiful things. She was thinking of that time—a thousand years ago—when her dress had been so shabby that even her own mother was half ashamed to see her daughter go about so clad, and her hands had been grimed with the smut of shoe-leather and hardened with unending work. Well—

There was a sharp, imperative knock on the door.

Judith, now always thinking that something might happen to her husband, sprang quickly to open it. She stepped back with a movement of uncontrollable astonishment.

"What! You?" she exclaimed.

"Yes, I," replied Mrs. Jennings. "Ask me in, please, for I can't stand."

Judith put her arm about this unexpected guest, and led her to the lounging-chair. Mrs. Jennings sank into it and held a vinaigrette to her nostrils. She was as white, almost, as the handkerchief she held in her hand, and her face was so thin that her eyes were unnaturally large, and were faded to a dull green-gray. There was no hint in them now of what might be there upon occasion.

"You didn't know I was on board?" she asked, as soon as she could speak.

"No. How should I?"

"Mr. Gerald knows. He didn't tell you?"

"No. But now I remember that he mentioned when we came aboard that there was a surprise for me. Still, I had forgotten."

"Perhaps I am the surprise, then," with a wan smile.

Judith hastened to pour something from a decanter into a glass, which she brought to Mrs. Jennings.

"Is it wine?" whispered that lady.

"Yes; drink it."

"No; give me brandy."

When a few drops of brandy had been sipped, Mrs. Jennings said: "I have almost died of sea-sickness. I have been in my berth nearly every moment. It is always so when I cross. My maid has been sick too. I have been in purgatory from the time we started. Give me your hand for a minute. It's a good hand, my dear Judith Gerald." She smiled at her companion. "Do you know, when I am with you I wish I were a Quaker, so that I might be permitted to call you by your real name? By your real name I mean Judith." She paused, but Judith did not think these remarks needed any reply. She stood closely holding the woman's hand, while the two looked steadily at each other.

Mrs. Jennings had the appearance of a ghost. There was not a vestige of color in her face; even her lips, generally so scarlet, were now like ashes. Her head was tipped back against the chair so that she could gaze absorbedly at her companion.

"It's so curious about me," she said, at length. Her voice was very weak, but still possessed that peculiar quality of—I cannot call it anything but the quality of seduction; for it seemed to draw a person to her, if she so wished, at the same time that it gave no guaranty of good faith. It was sometimes as if it were mocking at her own self.

Judith, standing there, felt strongly and, at the same time, unreasonably glad that Mrs. Jennings was on board. A woman, even a happy woman, often longs for the companionship of another woman. There is continually something which calls for a glance or a word from one of her own sex; and Judith, during this voyage, had dully felt this want, hardly knowing what it was. Now, holding Mrs. Jennings's hand and feeling how weak it was, though it had even now its personal touch of power, Judith recalled the dream and the impression it had left upon her.

"What is it that is curious about you?" she asked, at last.

"Why, this: that I'm a poor sort of person myself, given to evil, I suppose, and not having high ideals, and all that; but I never fail to recognize one who does have ideals, and I'm always drawn to that sort—if they are like you," with a slight laugh.

"Oh, you are so mistaken!" exclaimed Judith, with a pang at her heart. "I could almost say that I try not to have any ideals. I want to live only in each prosaic moment as it comes."

"Do you?"

As Mrs. Jennings asked that question her face suffused with feeling, and, for the instant, she was utterly charming. She bent her head and just touched her lips to the hand she held. Then she reached forth and took the glass of brandy again, drinking a little of it.

"Sit down by me," she said. And when Judith had drawn a chair near, she went on : "You must know that I often act on the impulse of the moment. I find I'm just as sure to be right as if I studied days on a question. That's how I came to be going to England now. I suddenly asked myself, 'Why not go in this steamer?' and so I started. But I didn't suppose it necessary to tell Mrs. Eldridge. I did tell Mr. Gerald, though. My aunt is in London. It occurred to me that I would go over and spend the winter with her. If she is writing a novel, for she just what you might call welters in the writing of novels, I would not interrupt her, and if she were not writing I might amuse her. She doesn't dislike me, and now that I have married she doesn't feel responsible for my unmarried condition. To be a widow is a fine thing ; you have the glory and respectability of having been married, and you also have the greater glory and freedom of not being married now." Here Mrs. Jennings took a few more drops of brandy, and then laughed. "Yes, there are many fine things pertaining to widowhood."

"So you go to London ?" remarked Judith, ignoring the last phrase.

"Yes. But you—what is it about Algeria ?"

"I don't know that anything is settled," was the answer. Then Judith's face flushed. She spoke impulsively. "I wish you would come with us to Africa."

Mrs. Jennings's eyes shone. A faint pink colored her cheeks. "That would be lovely," she answered. "But are you sure you want me ?"

Judith never knew why she did not seem to hesitate, for deep in her heart there sprang up something which pulled her back. Still she responded, instantly and truthfully, "Yes, I am sure. Will you join us ?"

"Yes ; and be thankful to do so."

Judith turned away. She took up a trifle, she knew not what, from the small table. She looked at this object for some time before knowing that she held a penknife in her hand. And she wondered why she should feel as if she had done a thing which she might wish undone. Why should she wish it undone? She was grateful to have this woman's society. She glanced at her companion now.

Mrs. Jennings had leaned back and closed her eyes, but her cheeks were still pink. "Shall you go through France to Marseilles?" she asked, without opening her eyes.

"I think so. Really, I haven't cared to ask. Mr. Eldridge takes charge of the details."

The eyes flashed open, but they did not dwell on Judith's face. Some things she might say in the darkness of a foggy night on the coast, when they were both lost; but she was not likely to return to the subject. She felt truly that Mrs. Gerald would not forgive any resumption of that topic.

After a few moments more Mrs. Jennings rose. She grasped quickly the back of a chair. "I always pay a great price for an ocean trip," she said, growing ghastly as she spoke. "Now I'll go back to my bed, where I shall lie on my back until we arrive."

Judith hurriedly placed her arm about her friend, then walked with her to the door of her state-room. When she had returned to her own room she sat down with an air of resolution. She was thinking of the invitation she had given, and reproving herself for considering it of mysterious importance. What could there be mysterious about it? Then she found her mind drifting away again to that dream which had not been definite—when is a dream definite?— but which had stamped itself on her mind. So powerful was the memory of it, now that she was alone, that she started up and walked as far as Mrs. Jennings's door, thinking she would recall the words she had spoken.

She stood by the door, hesitating, telling herself she was weak-minded, when Mr. Gerald appeared. "What is it?" he asked, without a sign of what he would scoffingly have called his "sentimental manner." "You are standing like a Peri at the gate. And whose door is that?"

"It is Mrs. Jennings's door.   Is she your surprise?"

By this time Judith's face was under her control.

"Yes, she is.   But I had forgotten her."

"I've done something you may not like."

"Ah! I'm glad to hear it."   Mr. Gerald seemed in high spirits.   "Confess."

"I've asked Mrs. Jennings to go to Africa with us."

She watched her husband's face.   But she could learn nothing from it.

"Ah!" he said again.   And that was the only remark he made on the subject.

So at last the end of the voyage came, and the end of the journey across France, and the arriving at Marseilles. And nothing whatever had happened; and Mrs. Jennings was wholly recovered from her sea-sickness; and Mr. Gerald kept up his good spirits; and Lucian made the best of couriers—was always ready to assist any one of his party, was gay as possible, and continually trying to find some way of making the tour more delightful.

The people on the route envied "those Americans" their fine spirits, and those Americans themselves felt that they were doing their very best.

XLVIII

"IT CAN BE DONE"

"Now here one might believe he had left his old self behind and had taken on a new body, at least; and the body modifies the spirit, you know."

It was Judith who spoke. She and her husband were standing in the steep, narrow street which is called the Casbah. They had come down from the old fortress of the Deys, and were going into the Moorish town. Sauntering slowly on ahead of them were Lucian and Mrs. Jennings, but Mr. Gerald had lingered here and there until they were practically by themselves.

"You would like to leave your old self behind?"

Mr. Gerald stopped as he asked this question. His wife returned his gaze with more freedom and lightness of spirit than she had felt for a long time; she could almost have said than she had ever felt, for life had had very little freedom for her. Perhaps it was the clear brilliance of the heavens, the indescribable sweetness of the air, the utter strangeness of everything. She wished that no one would ask her a serious question now. Her mind partook of the buoyancy of the atmosphere, and she desired to flit here and there without really thinking of anything.

"You would like to leave your old self behind?"

He repeated the question, evidently insisting upon having an answer. He continued to look at her. He was noting the loveliness of the dusky pallor of her face, the veiled, dreamy splendor of her eyes. She was standing under a white umbrella which was tipped back on her shoulder. She wore a light gray travelling-gown, with white gloves,

long and wrinkled on the wrists. A languid, drooping red
rose was fastened on the lapel of her close coat. Some tendrils of darkest hair were creeping from under her white
sailor hat, and they lay damp upon her temples.

Yes, Judith Grover's suggestive promise of physical attraction had come to fruition. Still, hardly a man or woman of any penetration who looked at her would have thought
of her beauty first. Rather they would have said, "Ah,
there are truth and honor," and a woman would have added,
in astonishment, "and she doesn't know that she is attrac-
tive!" Perhaps this latter fact went far towards explaining
why Mrs. Jennings liked to be with her.

Judith now tried to laugh as she replied, "If I had the
choice, I don't suppose I would really leave my old self behind me. After all, don't you think we cling to our individuality, even though we haven't been particularly happy in it?"

As she finished speaking something suddenly sent the
lightness out of Judith's consciousness. A peculiar expression flashed into Mr. Gerald's face. His companion could
not explain it, and she tried not to think of it. It seemed
as if a spark of deep cunning (no, it could not be that, Judith said to herself; but what was it?) came to the man's
eyes—came and faded instantly.

"I don't feel that way," he responded. "I'd be thankful
to anything that would free me from my old self and give
me something different. To tell the truth, I'm cursedly tired
of my old self." He turned now quickly and significantly
towards her as he said, "What man wouldn't be deadly
weary of a personality that had failed to win your regard?"

Judith moved hurriedly nearer to him. "Oh," she cried,
remonstrantly, "you haven't failed to win my regard!"

"You know what I mean," he answered, with some fierceness. "What's regard? Who cares for regard from a
woman with a face like yours? I didn't mean to use that
word. I meant love—love!" He struck his stick against
the wall of the house near which they stood. But before
Judith could speak again he continued, "Pray pardon me,

Mrs. Gerald." He took off his hat and passed a hand over his forehead. He began to walk on again, and Judith kept by his side. She was wondering if the same benign resplendence was in the sky and sunlight that had been there a few moments before.

The two ahead of them had stopped in front of a mosque. There is nothing more bewitching to the ordinary American than his first acquaintance with a mosque, unless it is his first hearing of the muezzin's call.

"Wait a moment," said Mr. Gerald, laying his hand on his wife's arm. "I was going to say," he went on, "that when you spoke of changing one's individuality you mentioned the very subject that I've been thinking of lately. Now I want to tell you something. Are you listening?"

"Certainly."

She wondered at the look of triumph that came to the face before her.

"Well, then, I tell you it can be done."

"What can be done?"

Judith felt herself growing cold, even beneath that sun.

"Why, what we are talking about—the changing of one's individuality."

"Of course," said Judith, calmly, "we may greatly modify our characteristics—"

"Oh, I don't mean any rot of that kind. You see, the case is just here: if I were a different person there is the possibility that you might love me. Therefore, I've nearly made up my mind that I'll make the change. Do you follow me?"

Judith, though she was looking straight up in her husband's face, yet saw, far ahead of them, Mrs. Jennings turn and gaze towards them, making some movement with her umbrella as she did so; and she saw an Arab cross the narrow street, his dingy white burnoose and swarthy face outlined as if in a camera before her. It seemed to her that she never saw objects so distinctly as at that moment when her heart was throbbing to her very finger-ends with an anxiety that she would not name.

"Do you follow me?" The question pursued her sharply.

"I think I follow you," she replied.

She was feeling thankful that she had her umbrella handle to grasp tightly.

"I knew your mind would take in the idea," was the response, "and that you would approve. Being an honorable woman, you would much prefer to love your husband rather than to have a lover. Now you are aware that you have tried to love me; but no human being ever yet succeeded in loving because of trying. You see plainly that the only remaining thing to be done, on the chance of gaining your love, is for me to become somebody else; and it can be done. To tell you the simple truth, Judith, all mysterious changes can be accomplished in a land like this. Think of the centuries of marvellous history behind us. It was here that many of the old miracles were performed, and the same conditions remain."

Again Mr. Gerald took off his hat, a pith helmet that appeared extremely out of place in conjunction with the Prince Albert coat.

Judith saw a bony, mangy cur trotting along the middle of the street, stopping to nose in the dirt. She tried to speak. A second time she tried, but before she could pronounce a word Mr. Gerald touched her arm lightly, and smiled in his old whimsical way as he said: "Come now, Judith, confess that I have given you a real fright. I wanted to see how you would take such a theory; and your own remark suggested the whole thing. You remember? It was a huge joke of mine."

"Was it a joke?"

Judith was conscious that the tension upon her whole frame was relaxing so suddenly that it was all she could do to keep from trembling.

"Of course it was," with a laugh, "but I didn't know I could deceive you so easily."

Judith put her umbrella down to the ground and leaned heavily upon it. A rising sense of anger was beginning to make her blood tingle. She averted her face lest her husband should see how irritated she was. One resents being frightened just for the amusement of another. The silence which followed was so expressive that Mr. Gerald presently said: "I know you must think me unkind, but really I didn't suppose you would care. And you started the talk."

It seemed odd to Judith that he should recur again to the fact that she had made the first remark upon the subject. It was trivial that he should do so. She tried to answer good-naturedly: "Since we have been only talking 'for fun,' let's forget the whole thing."

She began to hasten on, stumbling as she did so, for a sudden dizziness came to her. Her husband drew her hand within his arm, and as they walked along he began to talk glibly and instructively concerning Algiers—its capture by the French and subsequent modernization.

Judith listened, or she thought she was listening. She heard the words and she knew what they meant, but afterwards when she tried to recall them they refused to come.

Lucian and Mrs. Jennings had disappeared. When Judith discovered that they had gone she suggested that they also hurry back to the hotel. What if they should miss the train to Biskra? But Mr. Gerald evidently did not wish to return to the hotel. He looked at his watch. He proposed that they climb to the top of the Casbah. So they went on up the wretched, picturesque street until they stood at the top of that angle where the old city stops in its ascent of the hill, and pauses as if to look off over the sea and down upon itself.

Judith's eyes kindled as she gazed. The Mediterranean glittered below, stretching out in one long expanse of pulsating, ravishing beauty—calm under the blinding sun. But to the New England woman, longing for warmth and sunshine, no glow could be too bright. This was the sea of which she had read, which had seemed to her as far away as heaven. But here she was, standing above Algiers, and with the water below her. All at once, between her and this scene, there came the picture of the old cliff-walk at home, and the foamy reach of Massachusetts Bay, with the sails of the fishing-boats upon it. She seemed to see Ellis Macomber sitting on the rotten old wharf watching the lobster men go out in their dories. And her mother. But she resolutely thrust away from her the thought of her mother. Was the wind east at home to-day? This wind that came like a caress upon her face was both soothing and life-giving.

"Why not stay in Algiers?" she suddenly asked.

"Don't propose that," said Mr. Gerald. "We must go on—we must go to the edge of the desert."

"Must? Do you care so much to go to Biskra?" There was astonishment in her voice as she put the question.

"Yes," he answered, "I care greatly. I am to meet some one there."

She said no more; but the curiosity in her mind was flavored with dread of she knew not what — that vague, formless dread which is worst of all to bear. She looked down at the wharves. She saw the steamer *Ville d'Alger*, in which they had just come from Marseilles, lying at her moorings. She yielded expression to the wish that was as strong as it was sudden. She seized her husband's hand in both her own, her parasol falling to the ground.

"Let us take the steamer back!" she exclaimed, her tone thrilling with her earnestness.

"Take the steamer back?" Mr. Gerald's tone was raised in his surprise. "What do you mean?"

"It is not often that I ask a favor of you—a personal favor," she said.

"No, you do not."

Mr. Gerald's eyes, narrowed to mere lines in his face, were fixed on his wife's countenance, but she saw very well that there was no relenting in his expression; rather there was something hard, something she had never seen before.

"Why do you pitch upon this one thing to ask?" he inquired, with a rasp in his intonation.

"I pitch upon it because it is the thing I want."

"Well, you can't go back in the *Ville d'Alger*. You are going to Biskra with me. The doctors say Biskra has a perfect climate in the winter. Besides, I am to meet some one in the desert. It is quite necessary for my happiness that this meeting take place. And you can see that if we return to Marseilles that— But you women never understand explanations. Shall we go back to the hotel now? I really hope, Judith, that you are not going to do like other women —take up notions."

Judith answered nothing. She walked down through the strange, narrow streets of the old Moorish town till they came to the new town, where their hotel was situated. And all the time she was retracing her steps she was thinking two things: one was that Mr. Gerald had never spoken in that way before; and the other was that her mother had begged her not to cross the ocean this time, for "something was going to happen."

XLIX

BISKRA

A HOT sky and a hotter desert. Behind, the roofs of Biskra, that strange little settlement on the oasis. Ahead, the hard and stony wilderness that seems limitless, as if it occupied the whole world.

Judith and Mrs. Jennings are mounted on two Arab horses. They have found that Arab horses can be very sorry beasts, with well-defined ribs and hard mouths. These animals will amble if they are continually urged to do so, and they will also sometimes surprise one by running away, dashing wildly over the rough ground, their long, thin heads stretched out as they fly on into the unknown lands of Africa. It seems that they are going into some dreadful *terra incognita*, and that nothing can ever stop them; that they are going on forever—at least, such tales had been told concerning these Arab steeds by people who had ridden them. But it was a peculiar fact that no one who had not actually been run away with by one of these animals would ever believe it could run.

"I suppose," remarked Mrs. Jennings, "that we are in Africa."

"Yes," answered Judith, "I think there's no doubt of it."

"And I never was in such a cold place in my life," shivering. "The wind that blows over the snow on the Aures Mountains is the coldest wind that ever blew, and it never stops blowing. I am surprised at Africa. For sand I was prepared—yes, even for the amount I have in my bedroom, and on my bread and meat, but for— But, Mrs. Gerald, you are not listening."

"No; pardon me, I didn't catch what you were saying."

"I was saying sand and cold." Mrs. Jennings urged her horse yet nearer her friend. "What is the matter with you?" she asked. "You look like a person who lives in constant fear of something. This look has grown on you ever since we landed in Algiers."

"Nothing is the matter with me," was the reply. Then immediately, "I think I shall have to tell you. I must tell some one."

Mrs. Jennings leaned forward from her saddle. "You certainly will have to tell," she said. "You can't go on looking like this and not tell. And why am I here if I can't be of any use to you? There must be some reason for my being in Biskra instead of in some part of the world where they have fewer canned meats than they have at the Victoria here."

"I hadn't noticed that the meats were canned."

"Hadn't you? Have you noticed that there is a gale blowing most of the time—a gritty gale that sets your teeth on edge and makes you know the very taste of the desert?"

"No; I hadn't thought of these things."

Judith bent over and absently stroked the ragged mane of her horse. She was conscious that all the time her companion was talking in this way she was thinking of the something that worried her; and the presence of Mrs. Jennings was a comfort to her. If it were not for this presence there would be no one to whom she could speak of things that never left her mind, and that grew harder and harder to bear.

"We won't have any attendant this morning," suddenly said Mrs. Jennings. "Surely it is safe for us to ride out a little way towards Chetma. We will keep the roof of the Victoria in sight."

So they told the servant whom Mr. Gerald had ordered to go with them to remain at the hotel. They rode out into the desert, the horses going at that distressing creep which tends towards desperation in the mind of the equestrian.

The day previous Mr. Gerald and his nephew had started on a hunting expedition, taking two men, a tent, and some canned food. They hoped to get a gazelle, but they would not despise even a hare.

The two women thus left immediately experienced that sense of freedom which comes from the absence of the supervising, masculine element in a party. When half a mile had been traversed Mrs. Jennings's horse suddenly stopped, then tried to turn round towards Biskra. Then Judith's horse did the same. After a short struggle with the animals they consented to walk on side by side.

"Well?" said Mrs. Jennings. She looked at Judith, who suddenly cried out, sharply:

"I cannot endure it!"

"My dear!"

Judith had held herself in hand night and day until the relief of even this cry was very great.

"I cannot understand," she went on, hurriedly. "There is a shadow over me—the shadow of a blow; and when it will fall I cannot tell. But perhaps I ought not to speak. Don't you think we ought always to bear in silence?"

Judith turned excitedly towards her companion. Her face was unlike itself, the eyes full of wildness.

"Go on," said Mrs. Jennings, imperatively. "If you do not you will be insane."

"To be insane!" repeated Judith, in a tone of horror. Then she evidently placed a great restraint upon herself. "Well, I've got to tell, that's all; I have got to tell," she said. "You know we have been here a week," she went on—"a week yesterday. Seven days—seven times I've had that hour to live through. Does that hour show in my face? I look in the glass every morning to see if my hair is gray."

"Mrs. Gerald!"

There was keen alarm in this exclamation. Mrs. Jennings tried to catch the bridle of the horse near her, but the horse gave a jerk away from her.

Judith took the bridle more closely. She placed herself more firmly in the saddle. " Don't worry about me," she said. " There is never need to worry about me. Have you noticed Mr. Gerald of late?" She put the question abruptly.

" I have thought he seemed in unusual good spirits," was the answer—" as if," with a smile, " he had been drinking champagne."

" But he eats nothing !"

" That is true; still, there is nothing to eat in Biskra. We are expected to live on air and sand, and the sand of the African desert is not edible."

Mrs. Jennings spoke thus that she might not speak in a far different manner. Indeed, she was greatly alarmed, and feared to show that feeling.

" Mr. Gerald expects to meet some one in Biskra," said Judith, not apparently hearing her friend's words.

" Some old friend, perhaps ?"

" No, Mrs. Jennings, it is not an old friend. That is the remark I made to him. He turned and looked at me ; he told me that I was a fool—a stupid fool—to think he should want to see an old friend. Mr. Gerald is very polite ; it made me jump to hear him call me a fool. He said that he did not know the person whom he was to meet, but that it was of the last importance that the meeting should take place."

" Not know the person ?" Mrs. Jennings stared at the face near her. A terrible suspicion that Judith's mind was unbalanced by the strain under which she lived came to her, and made it impossible for her to say any more.

Judith's face flushed as she spoke. " Are you going to doubt what I tell you ?" she asked, sharply.

" No—no."

" Very well. But I would not blame you if you did doubt ; for I am bewildered, and can hardly believe my own senses. Now listen to me. Every night since we have been in Biskra, between one and two o'clock, Mr. Gerald leaves his bed. He dresses quickly. Then I rise and dress quickly. I am shivering with excitement, but he seems perfectly calm, and he dresses accurately, even to his necktie; and he brushes his hair, and files and cleans his nails; and he does all this with incredible celerity. The first time he did this I asked him why he rose at such an hour.

"'Because I am afraid I shall miss the meeting,' he answered.

"'What meeting?'

"'With that person—that person who comes to me at Biskra.'

"'Do you expect a man or woman?' I put this inquiry calmly, for I somehow knew I must speak calmly, though my heart was hammering in my throat, and I was huddling on my clothes, my fingers so stiff that I could hardly use them. He answered, impatiently:

"'How can I tell? It may be a man or it may be a woman. It doesn't matter. What matters is that I mustn't miss the meeting.'

"'I will go with you,' I said; but I was surprised that he made no objection to my going.

"He took his cane and his hat before I was ready.

"'I can't wait,' he said, 'for I shall not be waited for.'

"I would rather have died than let him go alone. In my haste I could find nothing. I seized a blanket from the bed and wrapped it around me. Mr. Gerald did not seem to notice that I had done so."

In a momentary pause Mrs. Jennings said, eagerly, "He was asleep. He is a somnambulist."

"No; he was not asleep. He was perfectly awake. Don't you think I would be glad to believe that he was asleep? I've tried to believe it, but I know better.

"We went out at the door of the hotel as noiselessly as if we were thieves. Can you imagine my sensations as I followed him through the grounds and along the street that we have just traversed? I kept close to him. My blanket trailed on the ground with a soft noise. The wind

"'I KEPT CLOSE TO HIM'"

blew cold from the mountains, my teeth chattered; but he did not seem cold. He walked on ahead of me in his tightly buttoned coat, swinging his stick, but looking sharply to the right and left all the time. Though he did not notice me, I felt sure that he was aware of my presence.

"That first night there was a moon—a fading moon, not very long risen, and it made everything ghastly. It made the mountains distant monsters that would presently spring upon Biskra and devour it, and I longed for their spring. I wanted to be crushed in their jaws and to be done with everything."

Judith stopped. Though she was very pale, her face was composed. She was gazing straight ahead of her.

When Mrs. Jennings spoke she started as if she had forgotten that she was not alone. "Where did you go?" was the question.

"We left the town, but only for a short distance. It was piteous, the eagerness with which Mr. Gerald looked about him. Two or three times he stopped and bent his head as if listening. All at once he turned to me, and asked:

"'Do you hear anything? You are younger. You may hear where I cannot.'

"I listened; I felt myself listening with every nerve in me—more, my blood seemed to stop that it too might help me to hear the approach of some one. I even lay down on the ground here in the desert and put my ear to the earth, holding my breath in my anxiety. Mr. Gerald stood close beside me, his features rigid in the great tension that was upon him.

"'Judith,' he said, 'you must be able to hear something.'

"But I could not. The wind did not blow then, and all the world was silent. I rose and stood beside him. I longed to see his face more plainly. He would have resented the fact that I pitied him had he known it, but my heart was breaking with pity for him. After a few moments more he pulled out his watch, but it was not light

enough for either of us to see the time, so he lighted a
match. It was twenty minutes after two.

"'It's too late,' he said, and then we turned back towards Biskra.

"'How do you know it is too late?' I asked.

"'How do I know?' He looked at me in astonishment.
Then it seemed to me that he tried to think of some words
that would appear reasonable, but he could not.

"'A man knows some things simply because he does
know them,' he said, at last, 'and that's the way I know
that after a quarter-past two in the morning it is too late to
look for that person.'

"I did not speak again as we hurried back. I held my
blanket very closely about me. All at once Mr. Gerald
glanced at me and smiled in amusement. How could he be
amused at such a moment? I was exasperated by his smile.

"'Why did you choose that wrap?' he asked.

"'Because I had no time to find another.'

"Then he laughed, not quite like himself; but when he
begged my pardon a moment later he was quite as usual.
When he reached his room and went to bed he was asleep
immediately. But as for me, it seems to me I have not
really slept since that night—the night we arrived—until
last night. Am I boring you? It is a great relief for me
to speak."

Judith pressed her lips together. She stroked her horse's
mane again.

"You are not boring me. You must speak." Mrs. Jennings's face was nearly as white as that of her companion.

"Yes," resumed Judith, hurriedly. "I must speak. I am
getting to have strange thoughts—thoughts that frighten
me."

She paused. She was still stroking the horse's neck.
Both horses were standing quietly side by side. Mrs. Jennings reached forward and took the gauntleted hand, holding it closely. But Judith did not look at her. She was
gazing out over the desert—gazing blindly, despairingly.

" And every night you have gone out thus ?"

" Every night.   Mr. Gerald goes to sleep and sleeps until about one.   He is sure to wake then and to rise directly. As for me, I am awake.   I cannot sleep.   My head is very light."

She took off her hat and pressed her hand on the top of her head.

"I TELL YOU YOU ARE WRONG!"

"Mr. Gerald goes out eagerly each night. Each night he is sure that the meeting will take place. Once we met one of the gentlemen at the Victoria. He stared hard at us, but Mr. Gerald explained, with great suavity, that he was troubled with insomnia, and I had been good enough to walk out with him. How long do you suppose this will last?"

Mrs. Jennings did not answer. She pressed the hand she held.

"If Mr. Eldridge had not taken him away yesterday I do not believe I could have behaved like a sane woman to-day, for the time had come when I must sleep or be frantic, and I could not sleep when I was watching and waiting for it to be one o'clock, and for us to start on our expedition. Last night I slept. I was like a log. I went to my room directly after dinner. Did you ever feel like that? As if you had drunk laudanum? as if the world might come to an end, but that you would sleep? It is almost as dreadful as when you lie awake hour after hour."

"Have you told Mr. Eldridge?"

"No—no."

"But why not?"

Judith's eyes and face had a coldly surprised expression as she turned towards Mrs. Jennings.

"Why not?" she said. "Indeed, I see no reason why I should tell him."

"Perhaps he suspects that something is wrong, and that is why he took his uncle out hunting."

"It is not probable," indifferently.

"Oh, how proud you are, Mrs. Gerald!" exclaimed the other woman.

"Proud?"

"Certainly."

"But you need not explain why you think so."

Mrs. Jennings nodded her head and smiled. Then she asked, "Have you told me all?"

"No."

Judith gazed about her like a prisoner who is seeking for some way of escape.

"The last night," she presently began, "that we came out thus I ventured to ask Mr. Gerald why it was that it was necessary that we meet this person."

Here the speaker stopped, and was silent so long that Mrs. Jennings at last said:

"Did he tell you?"

She spoke under her breath, as if some one would hear her in that wilderness, and Judith answered her in the same way. She even glanced about to see if any one were near.

"Yes, he told me. He said that this person for whom he is waiting is one who has wonderful power. He has power to change Mr. Gerald into another individuality. He says that he is bound to be changed, because then—because then it may be that I shall love him."

Having said this in an almost inaudible voice, Judith suddenly bent forward on her horse's neck, dropping the bridle and covering her face with her hands. The strange, eerie pathos of the situation so appealed to Mrs. Jennings that her own face blanched still more and her eyes dimmed. She sat still, staring at the figure before her, unable at first to say anything. At last Judith lifted her head. Her eyes were dry and burning.

"What a wretch I am! What a hard-hearted wretch I am!" she cried, in a low voice. "And what shall I do to make myself over?"

"Why do you call yourself hard-hearted?" asked Mrs. Jennings, with some sharpness. "You are not hard-hearted enough."

"Don't mock at me."

"Mock at you? I must be sharp with you, or I shall set to at crying myself. Why don't you make him think you love him?"

"But I don't. He has always known from the very first that I didn't love him, and he didn't love me when he married me. He only thought I was the kind of woman he wanted for a wife. You know what notions some men have. And I married him for his money, not for myself—oh, I can't tell you about it, and it would do no good if I could. I was wrong. I did a wicked thing, and I ought to be punished—yes, I ought to be punished."

"Now don't talk like one of those weak-minded people who assert that God punishes us for doing just what creatures with the attributes he has given us must do. You are a strong woman. Just now you are worn out for lack of sleep."

Mrs. Jennings's imperative voice penetrated like some keen knife into Judith's consciousness and stimulated her. She drew herself up and turned to her companion.

"You counsel me to deceive him," she said, reprovingly.

"Certainly," coolly, "why not?"

"I don't know. Only it isn't natural for me to deceive."

"Was it natural for you to marry a man you knew you did not love?"

The question was hard and cutting. Judith drew herself up still more. She looked in amazement at the woman beside her. Mrs. Jennings's greenish eyes had not now a particle of softness in them. The pupils were contracted to pin points, and were fixed on Judith's face.

Judith wanted to writhe as she sat there in the saddle, but she did not move. She remained silent. She was asking herself if it could be possible that this woman was right.

"As for me," said Mrs. Jennings, after a silence, "I am not so finical about the truth as you pretend to be."

"Pretend to be!"

Judith's eyes flashed. In her indignation the strain upon her relaxed somewhat.

"Yes. I know you don't think it's pretence; you think it's natural. But I should like to ask you what act of deception can be more decided than your marriage?"

"But I explained my position to Mr. Gerald. I did not deceive him."

Mrs. Jennings shrugged her shoulders, but she said nothing. Her companion felt that she was very exasperating.

At last Mrs. Jennings spoke again: "What are you going to do?"

"Nothing, save that I will take care of Mr. Gerald."

"Do you know the danger you may incur?"

"I do not care for the peril." Judith spoke as one who should say, "I am glad of the danger."

"You have no business not to care."

This time it was Judith who shrugged her shoulders.

"He is not responsible," went on Mrs. Jennings. "What if, some time, out here in the desert, he should take it into his mind to kill you?"

"'It is not so difficult to die.'"

As Judith made this quotation she turned towards the woman beside her and smiled. As she saw that smile Mrs. Jennings uttered an exclamation, she knew not what. She trembled, and for months afterwards the memory of Judith's face at that moment would come to her with a vividness that made her weak and faint.

Judith apparently tried to rouse herself. "The difficult thing is to live," she said—"to live, and to do the thing you ought."

"Perhaps you have no doubt as to what is the thing you ought to do?"

"Not the least doubt," firmly.

"And that is?"

"To sacrifice myself in every way for Mr. Gerald's happiness," still more firmly.

"I tell you you are wrong!" with violence. "You will give him the best of care; but have you any more right to sacrifice yourself than you have to sacrifice—me, for instance, or Mr. Gerald himself? Are we called upon to immolate ourselves?"

"Under the circumstances, I am called upon," said Judith, with an air of finality so decided that the other said no more on that subject.

"Do you fully recognize that an insane person may at any moment become violent, dangerous, to himself or to others?"

"Yes, fully."

There was no dejection now in Judith's manner or voice. She was like a soldier girding himself for a conflict.

Mrs. Jennings gazed at her admiringly. A whole-hearted sacrifice has a power in it which stirs and exalts the witness of it as if it were something transcending human nature, even though the sacrifice is a wrongful waste.

"You need not fear," said Judith. "I am certain that I can safely take care of Mr. Gerald, and it may be that this is only a passing hallucination."

"Oh, I am not afraid," was the hasty response. "I am not afraid for myself. But you ought to let me tell Mr. Eldridge—"

"No, no. I will bear my burden alone. It has been a relief to me to tell you. You must forgive me for doing that. It will be a comfort to know that you know. But perhaps I was weak. Do you think I was weak?"

Judith's softened, anxious eyes were fixed on her companion's face, and Mrs. Jennings, in spite of all her efforts, could not at first command her voice. "It is not that you are too weak," she said, at last; "it is that you are not weak enough, and you are wrong."

The two now, as by common consent, rode on together towards Chetma. But they did not go far. Presently they turned their horses about, and as they did so Mrs. Jennings said, "However, Mr. Eldridge will soon find it out. Thank fortune for that."

To this there was no reply. When Judith reached the hotel she went to her own room, and, taking off her hat, but not her riding-dress, not even her gloves, she laid herself down on the bed. She lay quite still. After a while she moved and found that she was holding her whip tightly in her right hand. She flung the whip from her.

"That woman is wrong," she said, aloud. "All there is left for me is to sacrifice myself; and sometimes sacrifice is blessedness—but not happiness. He trusts me—he believes in me."

She sat up on the bed and began to pull off her gloves hurriedly.

"But I cannot—no, I cannot even try to make him think I love him. He was never to expect that—never—never."

A knock at the door made her rise to her feet. She hesitated before she answered the summons, though she believed it was Mrs. Jennings who was there. When she did open the door one of the hotel servants handed her a card and walked away.

Judith saw the name, "Mr. Lucian Eldridge," on one side of the pasteboard, and her fingers began to grow cold. But they were steady as she turned the card and read:

"Please see me immediately in the small reception-room."

She instantly walked down the stairs.

"ANOTHER INCARNATION"

THESE two, though they had met every day, never saw each other alone, and met only as casual acquaintances. The most suspicious observer would have said that Judith was hardly aware of the existence of Lucian Eldridge. When she looked at him as she addressed him it was as if she looked at a chair or a table—a glance of sheer indifference. Mrs. Jennings, watching her, sometimes caught herself saying, "That woman is a block of wood—only her face is not wooden."

Lucian was standing in the middle of the room, impatiently watching the hallway, which was visible from the open door. His face was grimed with dust, and he was in corduroys and leather leggings, just as he had jumped from his horse.

Judith walked down the hall and up to him. She was so white that Lucian expected to see her fall. But she did not fall. She caught hold of his sleeve.

"Where is he?" she asked, and her voice, though it was hardly above a whisper, seemed to echo in the room.

"I have ridden like mad—I have almost killed my horse —to find out if he were here," was the reply.

"No." She looked vaguely about the room.

The young man took her hand and tried to lead her to a chair. But she resisted his movement. "Do you think I will sit down?" she asked, harshly. "Let us go. Why do we lose time?"

Lucian held her hand firmly. "Wait," he said: and there was a command in his voice that penetrated to Judith's sense of reason. "Let us know what to do first," went on the young man. "You are sure he hasn't come back? I wouldn't ask any one here, save you. I knew how sensitive he would be about—about—"

"Yes, yes," whispered Judith. "And if he came back he would surely, surely come to me."

Lucian winced even then, but he replied, "I was certain of that. I shall never forgive myself for sleeping last night—but I suspected nothing. How could I?" He was speaking so rapidly that his words tripped against each other. "I slept soundly, for we had ridden far and had had good sport. Uncle Dick was in fine spirits, and he went to sleep in our tent last night even before I fell asleep. Who could have suspected anything?" repeating his own words. "I knew that he hadn't been well of late, but— Judith, you should have told me—you—"

"Oh, don't! don't!"

Her piercing voice of entreaty made Lucian exclaim, quickly, "You see, if I had only had any warning—"

"I did as I thought he would like to have me do," said Judith. "Always I have done that."

"Yes, yes; I know you have. I will tell you as soon as I can. Perhaps it is not so bad."

Lucian could not any longer look at her face. He walked away a pace and he bent his head. With his eyes on the floor he went on. "Once in the night, before twelve, I wakened and looked at my watch. The match I lighted showed me that Mr. Gerald seemed to be fast asleep, rolled in his blanket, at the other side of the bit of a tent. I was restless, and finally I walked outside. Our man whom we had taken with us was lying asleep on the sand there. I did not stay long, and when I went back Mr. Gerald spoke to me. He said I had no business to be a poor sleeper, and then he immediately began to breathe heavily again. I don't know when I fell asleep, but I wakened just before daylight, and I wakened with a sense that something dreadful had happened. I turned and looked towards where

Uncle Dick had been lying. The place was so near that I
could touch it by reaching out my hand. The blanket
was flung aside and the place empty. Judith, I am telling
you so particularly, for perhaps the smallest item may
suggest something to you. I sprang towards the opening of the tent; then I asked myself why I should be
alarmed if uncle had happened to rise before me. I stood
still, looking about me. On the tumbled blanket I saw
this."

He pulled from his waistcoat-pocket a bit of paper that
had evidently been torn from a small note-book.

" In two minutes it will be one o'clock. I go to meet the
person whom I expect to meet. If I don't come back now
I shall come back in another incarnation, and then who
knows but that she may love me? I hope, Lucian, that
you won't be a fool and try to find me. But a young man
is never a wise man. I wish I had more time. I feel like
writing freely. What I mostly fear is that you, Lucian, will
be a fool. If you are wise, you will say to Mrs. Gerald
that I was called away, and that I am perfectly safe. Another incarnation! Ah, ha! Why don't more people think
of that? It is such a simple way out of a set of circumstances. If I only had time to write more, I could make
things perfectly clear."

There was no name signed; but there was no need of
any name. The words were written in the small, legible
hand which both knew so well; and there was no appearance of haste in the writing.

Judith held the paper closely. Having read it once, she
immediately began to read it again.

Lucian stood and looked at her, thinking that he had
never felt so powerless; and feeling a sort of despairing responsibility that sat on him like an incubus.

" Judith, is there any one?" he asked.

" Any one?"

She tried to think clearly. The terrible necessity that
she should think clearly and rapidly made her brain reel.

She involuntarily put forth her hands, with the paper held fast in one of them.

Lucian did not touch the hands; he continued to gaze at her. He felt that he could have killed himself out of sheer despair that he had no help to offer. He was groping in darkness. He made a step towards her, saying, hurriedly:

" You must tell me if you know if there is any one whom he would be likely to meet. You must keep back nothing, for I am going to find him. Help me what you can—help me—and speak quickly. Every moment—"

" I will speak quickly," interrupted Judith. She glanced round as if for something to lean against.

" Will you not sit down ?" Lucian brought a chair.

" Oh no. We are going to find him—certainly we shall find him in a few hours. Shall we not, Lucian, in a few hours ?"

" We will try. But you must tell me—"

" Certainly—yes. But there is nothing that will be of any help—absolutely nothing."

Then Judith related in a few words how Mr. Gerald had been in the habit of going out at precisely the same time each night since their arrival in Biskra. Lucian almost groaned as he heard her.

" Why didn't you let me know this before?" he exclaimed.

" Was I wrong?" she asked, piteously. " But I wanted to be right, and I know how annoyed he would be if I told even you. Yes, I wanted to do exactly what he would like. Oh, was I wrong ?"

Lucian did not reply. It was hard for him to stand there as insensate, apparently, as a stone. And he was human enough and weak enough to ask himself in that moment if, after all, she loved her husband. Then he grappled with his own soul, and said to himself, " Then all the more must we find him."

" I have ordered fresh horses saddled," he said. " I waited only to see you."

He turned towards the door. She was beside him in an
instant.

"But I am going with you."

"Yes ; I knew you would go. There is a horse for you."
He spoke coldly, but she seemed not to notice.

She hurried forward, and sprang from the step into the
saddle. Then she saw that Lucian had gone on into the
hotel. She was angry that he lost so much time. It seemed
to her that she could not breathe until they had started.

A thousand memories came like ghosts to her mind. She
shut her eyes as if to shut out those memories. How her
husband had tried to throw her more and more into companionship with Lucian. There had seemed something
strange and diabolical in this attempt to her, but now she
was sure that he had not been quite himself. She had resolutely, until this moment, refused to acknowledge this ;
she had clung to the thought that if she did not acknowledge it then the thing would be some way less a fact.
Have we not all done this? And have we not all found
how fruitless was the endeavor? Mr. Gerald had been a
little strange, perhaps, but— Oh, it would all surely pass!

Would Lucian never appear? A servant came out. She
sent him back to find Mr. Eldridge. The man presently
returned to say that the gentleman was coming directly. A
step and a trailing dress sounded on the veranda behind
her. Mrs. Jennings spoke. "What! out again, Mrs. Gerald ?"

Judith sat rigidly on her horse. She did not turn her
head as she answered, "Yes."

The other woman came round in front of her friend. She
was herself very pale, and her eyes were quite green in their
brilliance. She hesitated : then she walked close up to the
horse and leaned upon it.

"Where are you going?" she asked.

"I don't know. Anywhere--everywhere. Mr. Gerald is
missing."

"Has Mr. Eldridge come back?"

"Yes. I am waiting for him."

"But you can do no good."

"Will you stop talking?" fiercely. "I cannot bear your talk. Do you think I can stay here and let others look for my husband?"

"He might return, and then you should be here to receive him."

"I must go. Thank God, there is Lucian!"

Lucian ran out and mounted. He did not seem to see Mrs. Jennings. She stood watching them as they galloped away. "I say he may come back," she repeated, in a whisper. Then she walked slowly into the house. But in a moment she came out. She could not be quiet. She stood there when several men rode away from the other side of the hotel. She saw that they went in different directions.

"I have arranged that others start in the search," said Lucian. "I could not find the least clew as to which way Mr. Gerald rode from our tent, though I tried. I know of no reason why we should go this way or that."

"We will go to Chetma," said Judith, decidedly.

"Very well."

They galloped on. Two or three dusky men in the flowing white burnoose of the East stepped out of the narrow street to make way for the horses. Two donkeys driven by one boy scrambled aside lest they should be run down. The sky, like a concave of clear, hot, blue metal, arched above, and the sun climbed up the arch.

Lucian did not speak. Sometimes he glanced at his companion. She was always looking eagerly about her, searching the great stretch of desert, and the desert revealed nothing.

Back at the hotel Mrs. Jennings was trying to kill time. She was excited, and she rather resented the fact. She tried to read a novel. She went to her room and took up a dainty box of cigarettes; but she did not really care for cigarettes, and had only tried them because men seemed to like them so well. She was much given to making experiments in different kinds of sensations. The cigarette sensation was not interesting to her. She wondered when some of the searching-parties would return, and she wondered where Mr. Gerald had gone. Perhaps they would find him dead. How much better that would be than to think that he was somewhere in the world, and might appear at any moment. That would give Judith the kind of freedom which drags continually a ball and chain.

Mrs. Jennings finally took her revolver, and went out to practise at the target she had caused to be set up. This was a pastime which always amused her. A group of dirty, dusky children gathered at a little distance to watch her. Some lank dogs came up and whined, standing ready to dart away at the first hostile movement. Beyond was a moving picture of donkeys and horsemen, and sometimes a camel walked solemnly across the line of the woman's sight.

The day had passed somehow. Mrs. Jennings had been so excited that she had been unable to have her afternoon siesta. Now the sun was near its setting. Its vivid red rays fell from behind her full upon the target. She had fired one round. She had just filled the chambers again when a voice asked, politely, "Will you allow me to try what I can do?"

Mrs. Jennings wheeled quickly. She smiled. There was Mr. Gerald standing there. He also was smiling slightly. He was as immaculate in appearance as ever; his Prince Albert coat was buttoned closely; there was a pink rose in the lapel. He wore his pith helmet, which he lifted as the lady turned. In each of his eyes burned a warning fire, but Mrs. Jennings would not be warned. She used to say afterwards that she felt as if she were in the hands of fate and must obey its dictates—that she was obliged to do as this man requested, and was as much an instrument in his hands as was the revolver in her own grasp.

"I told them you would return here!" she exclaimed.

"Certainly. Why shouldn't I return here?" with a slight

elevation of eyebrow. The next moment he added, in a hesitating, explanatory manner, and as if he were trying to remember something, "But I believe I really did not intend to come back. There was an excellent reason—what was it?" He impatiently shrugged his shoulders. He extended his hand. "Pray allow me to try and see what I can do," he repeated.

Mrs. Jennings gave him the pistol. He took it steadily; he examined the ornamented little thing.

"I have mislaid my pistol," he remarked. "Sometimes I suspect Mrs. Gerald of secreting it. Mrs. Gerald watches me lately. I can't imagine why."

He looked intently and suspiciously at Mrs. Jennings. And now she began to tremble. She made a movement as if to take the weapon from him. He stepped back. He smiled in a brilliant, tantalizing way.

"Yes, I have mislaid my revolver," he repeated.

He gazed down at the toy he held, and drew the point of his finger along the chasing on the handle. Without raising his eyes he went on, in a conversational way, "I am afraid that person who has promised to meet me is deceiving me."

And in the same tone he added:

"For another incarnation I fancy this is decidedly the quickest and best way, since that person who holds the power will not meet me."

With a gentle and yet rapid motion Mr. Gerald turned the muzzle of the weapon to his temple and fired. He flung up his hands and fell dead at the woman's feet.

Straight as the homing pigeon goes back to its nest, so Judith went back to the old farm-house in Massachusetts. There she could press the knife into the wound and feel the pulsating pain. There she could know in all its power the dreadful truth that she had made a mistake—a vital— nay, a deadly mistake. She had had no right to marry as she had done. She who loved truth had deliberately put herself in a false position where her life from hour to hour was a lie, and where her self-respect could not live.

Remorse, unavailing repentance, filled her consciousness. Had she been hard, unsympathetic? Could she have been kinder, more tender to her husband? But she had tried—yes, she had tried!

One day she took up a book. Listlessly turning the leaves, her eye caught this paragraph :

"Why is it that in the very upright character there is often too much granite—too little of the tender pardon which poor human nature must forever crave? But the answer is plain."

She shut the book and covered her face.

"Oh, how he must have suffered!" she whispered.

Even now, however, Judith did not make the mistake of thinking that if Mr. Gerald were alive she should give him that love he craved. Everything within her volition should be his, more he could not have. It had all been wrong—all wrong.

She did not tell her mother these thoughts ; but once her mother said to her, after a long, wistful gaze into the worn young face, "Judith, you are young. and the young can get over anything. But the old—no, the old can't do that."

Still the daughter had not believed what her mother said about the young. And still, here, if anywhere, her bruised life could heal itself.

One day Mrs. Grover came in from a long walk. She sought Judith and made her sit down beside her.

" I've been to see Mrs. Eldridge," said the elder woman, abruptly. " I've been thinking I'd go. and I'm glad I went. I knew you were laying everything to yourself. I couldn't stan' it. I wanted to find out something, and I've found it out. I asked Mrs. Eldridge if any of her family beside her brother Richard had ever been insane. She set out she wouldn't tell, but I made her."

Judith had taken both her mother's hands, and she was

holding them tightly. Her burning eyes were trying to plunge into the eyes before her.

"She tried to get out of it by saying 'twas usually mild; that her children belonged to the generation that had always been skipped; that they didn't know anything about it, 'n' I mustn't tell them. I told her I didn't want to tell anybody but you. Now you c'n stop layin' every possible thing to yourself. Will you?"

Judith put her head down on her mother's shoulder, and her mother's arm drew her close.

Judith liked to stand on the cliff-walk and look over the bay. Often when she turned she could see her father with his hired men in the field below her. Her father was very deferential and considerate in his manner to her, for Mr. Gerald had willed all his fortune to his wife—willed it when there could be no doubt about his sanity.

It was the second summer after her return from Biskra. Lucian Eldridge was still abroad. No one knew when he would come home. Ellis Macomber, down in the village, freely told every one that if "he was young Eldridge he should make a try for a nice young woman like Judith, who had thousands of dollars jest a-rottin'."

He thought Mrs. Guild a silly woman when she remarked, in response to his words, that "mebby Lucian was so proud it galled him to ask such a rich woman to marry him."

Whereupon Mr. Macomber spat with emphasis, and replied, that "he guessed Lucian wa'n't a dumb fool."

THE END